Frank Coates was born in Melbourne and, after graduating as a professional engineer, worked for many years as a telecommunications specialist in Australia and overseas. In 1989 he was appointed as a UN technical specialist in Nairobi, Kenya, and travelled extensively throughout the eastern and southern parts of Africa over the next four years. During this time Frank developed a passion for the history and culture of East Africa, which inspired his first novel, *Tears of the Maasai*. He followed with *Beyond Mombasa* and *In Search of Africa* and his next African story, *Roar of the Lion*, is to be published in early 2007.

Also by Frank Coates

Tears of the Maasai
Beyond Mombasa

IN SEARCH OF AFRICA

FRANK COATES

■ HarperCollins*Publishers*

HarperCollins*Publishers*

First published in Australia in 2006
This edition published in 2007
by HarperCollins*Publishers* Australia Pty Limited
ABN 36 009 913 517
www.harpercollins.com.au

HarperCollins*Publishers*
25 Ryde Road, Pymble, Sydney, NSW 2073, Australia
31 View Road, Glenfield, Auckland 10, New Zealand
77–85 Fulham Palace Road, London, W6 8JB, United Kingdom
2 Bloor Street East, 20th floor, Toronto, Ontario M4W 1A8, Canada
10 East 53rd Street, New York NY 10022, USA

National Library of Australia Cataloguing-in-Publication data:

Coates, Frank.
    In search of Africa.
    ISBN 13: 9780 7322 8271 4.
    ISBN 10: 0 7322 8271 3.
    I. Title.
A823.4

Cover design by Darren Holt, HarperCollins Design Studio
and Anthony Vandenberg, Mayfly Graphics
Cover image (landscape) courtesy of Photolibrary
Cover image (elephants) courtesy of Rosalind Williams
Cover image (couple) courtesy of Getty
Author photograph by Stephen Oxenbury
Map by Laurie Whiddon, Map Illustrations
Typeset in Sabon by Kirby Jones
Printed and bound in Australia by Griffin Press on 50gsm Bulky News

5 4 3 2 1   07 08 09 10

To my dear friends in Africa

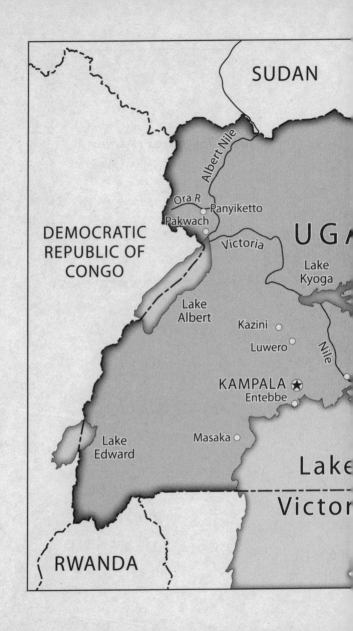

1944

'Five minutes to target, Ernie.'

The voice over the intercom was flat, unemotional, but Flight Lieutenant Ernie Sullivan knew the navigator had a knot of tension in his belly just as he had. It never got easier, even after this, his twelfth mission over Germany: the butterflies in the tummy, the sweaty palms — his body's response to the possibility of imminent death.

He hooked a finger under the back collar of his flight jacket and felt the sweat trickle down his spine. The cockpit was stuffy; his jacket too tight across his chest. He knew the flak would start at any moment. He pulled his lucky charm from his shirt pocket and fingered the smooth black wood in the semi-darkness. He felt the small paint ridges under his fingertips — the dots and waving lines of red, yellow and white.

The Stirling's four engines droned on, every now and then slipping into a thrumming beat as their frequencies converged, met, and moved apart. The noise resonated in Ernie's head. The Stirling's cockpit seemed to close around him.

Other Stirling bombers stretched off to left and right as far as he could see into the night, each at their maximum altitude of a little over three miles. The remainder of the seven-hundred-strong mission, the Halifaxes and Lancasters, were stacked nearly a mile higher. Up there in the darkness, Ernie knew, they would be converging into a tight lethal formation to confuse the enemy's radar. Soon they would rain their incendiary devices onto the Hamburg railway marshalling yards. Ernie also knew he had as much chance of being hit by a friendly bomb as by enemy flak. He really didn't like the old Stirling on those occasions.

'Two minutes.' The navigator's tone held a touch more urgency.

The beam of a searchlight illuminated the plane. Other white daggers swept in on large arcs to join it, pinning the bomber like a moth in a display cabinet.

'Shit!' Ernie said. Flak explosions popped around them as he dived and climbed and swerved to lose the lights.

'Ernie, we've got a pool of petrol down here.' It was the wireless operator.

'Shit! Shit!' Ernie said as the fumes rose to his cockpit. A piece of flak had probably broken a fuel line. Before he could begin to think about how the fuel loss might reduce their range, the Stirling came under fire from a pair of Me109 night fighters. His gunners had lost their night vision in the glare of the searchlights and took some time to respond.

'Sweet Jesus,' Ernie muttered. 'How much more?'

The Messerschmitts were despatched but not before the bomber took a few hits.

The starboard inner engine burst into flames. With the cabin reeking of petrol fumes, Ernie feathered the engine and plunged the aeroplane into a steep dive. But the fire did not extinguish. He levelled out and called for the crew to abandon the aircraft.

Pandemonium erupted via the intercom. Ernie trimmed the controls to keep the Stirling in the air as long as possible so the crew could bail out.

The navigator was in the cabin behind him, shouting above the roar of the engines.

'What?' yelled Ernie.

'Your 'shute. Where's your 'shute?'

'My 'shute? Right. Stowed behind you, I think. Thanks, mate.'

The navigator passed the parachute to Ernie and pointed to the bomb aimer's compartment below him. It was ringed with flames. 'I'm going out the hatch,' he yelled.

Ernie gave him a thumbs-up. 'See you in the Ploughman's Arms,' he said with a reassuring grin.

The navigator waved and jumped into the compartment, but the hatch wasn't open. As the flames engulfed him he panicked, falling back into the bay.

Ernie tried to get out of the cockpit, but his parachute bag jammed him in the opening.

The navigator scrambled out of the compartment with flames leaping from his petrol-soaked boots and dashed back into the cabin in fright.

'No!' Ernie screamed, but the navigator was lost in a whoosh of heat and flame as the cabin ignited. The explosion flung Ernie back into the cockpit, slamming his head into the instrument panel.

When Ernie became aware of his surroundings again, the cabin was an inferno. Flames blocked his path to any of the lower escape hatches. He climbed onto the pilot's seat and tried to open the top escape hatch. It was stuck. He thumped it with his balled fist and it flew off, sucking the flames in from the cabin. He leaped into the opening and the slipstream flung him into the cold night air.

The plane's tail section hit him squarely in the back.

As he slid into unconsciousness, one hand automatically went for the parachute's ripcord.

PART 1

KIP

CHAPTER 1

1952

Kip darted down the jungle track, his too-big shorts flapping around his skinny legs. The moss on the banks of the Nanyuki River glistened and slanting rays of afternoon sun forced their way through heavy shadows to form green islands on the forest floor.

The boy vaulted a fallen log, sending a bolt of pain from his toe to his groin. He fell, rolling into a ball on a mat of succulents, until he came to a halt at the foot of an old fig.

He took a moment to examine his foot again. The nail on his biggest toe was red, very red. When he gingerly touched it, he was repaid by a stab of pain. The jigger flea was burrowing in. Mother said it served him right because he wouldn't keep his shoes on. He imagined the worm was eating at him like a maggot might burrow into a corpse. The thought of it made him sick.

The man he had found in the forest was like that — a corpse, with maggots burrowing in. There wasn't much left by the time Kip came upon him, while following a hyena's spoor. The hyena, the jackals and the vultures had done their work. And the maggots. That was a week ago and Kip's nights hadn't been the same since.

But he couldn't tell his mother, or Aunt Kathleen.

At the thought of his mother he leaped up, brushing the crushed moss from his school shirt. There was no damage done, not even mud.

He touched his toe to the ground, testing it before he ran on, then favouring it as he splashed through the shallow crossing of the river. A bushbuck sprang into alarmed flight from its shadowy hide.

Kip was worried more about being late than the jigger now, and he burst through the clawing vines at the water's edge, scrambled to the top of the bank and broke from the forest into Raymond Hook's back paddock. Slipping through the fence like an eel, he hit the murram road at full speed, running *hippity-skip* to protect his sore toe.

A hundred yards ahead was the slab-timber pub his mother owned. 'Equatorial Hotel', the sign said, and in smaller letters: 'Enjoy a Pint in Both Hemispheres'. It was said that the equator passed through that exact point and the pub's previous owner had painted a bold line on the bar with 'The Equator', written over it in white paint. Patrons were encouraged to try beer poured from taps either side of the line, to see which best suited their palate.

Kip wasn't allowed in the bar during trading hours unless it was to empty the drip trays — one of his many chores. His mother beat him if he spoke to any of the clientele, so he went about his business with head down and eyes averted. After a time, the regulars assumed he was a bit weak in the head and ignored him. But Kip heard everything that was said, including arguments about whether northern beer tasted better than the beer pulled from the same tap and drunk in the southern hemisphere, and discussions about water going down the plughole in opposite directions on different sides of the equator.

Kip ran around the side of the hotel and plopped himself on the step at the back door. He gently pressed the flesh around the quick of his toe and, predictably, the pain returned. He pulled his sandals from his pockets and carefully slipped them on, annoyed at himself for making the toe throb again. *Don't pick at it — you'll only make it worse* was a phrase all too familiar to him. *Stupid boy! You'll never learn* was another, and it was demonstrably true — he was always getting into trouble.

Inside the back door he took a moment to collect his thoughts. How could he explain himself? He could say he was late because … because Mrs Philgrove had made him clean the schoolyard. No, that would bring on an inquisition about what crime he had committed to deserve the punishment. He was late because … because, *I have a sore toe*. No, that would trigger the lecture about always wearing his sandals. In desperation he wondered if the truth might work. *I was stalking guinea fowl and all of a sudden the time was gone.* No, the truth never worked. Nothing worked when his mother had the *kiboko* whip in her hand. And nothing stung more than a hippo-hide whip.

He crept into the kitchen, which was soaked in late afternoon sun. He listened. Silence hummed in the heat.

He peeked through into the bar. The windows were shuttered, stools were upended on the bar and the front door was locked. The pub was closed.

But the pub was never closed!

A handwritten sign was stuck on the inside of the front window. Kip read it back to front.

A wave of relief swept over him. He felt he'd been reprieved from a death sentence.

His throbbing toe reminded him of his other predicament. He had to remove the revolting creature. He couldn't bear the thought of it digging into his flesh for a moment longer. Kip knew there was a hooked pin, the 'jigger pin', in his mother's first-aid kit. He searched the cupboards — even the ones high up, with rows of boring jars containing flour and the small spheres of sago that his mother served as a 'treat' with tepid milk and not enough sugar — but the kit was nowhere to be found.

He looked around him. The door to the big bedroom was ajar. His mother and Aunt Kathleen had obviously departed in a hurry — they never left that door unlocked. It was the most logical place for keeping the first-aid kit and, with great trepidation, Kip pushed the door open.

Something clunked behind it. A hangman's noose, swinging from a hook. He jumped backwards and fell into the kitchen's fearless sunlight. He lay on the cool linoleum until his heart stopped thumping. He knew it wasn't a hangman's noose, had known immediately he saw it, but the *kiboko* whip scared him, made him act weird.

He looked towards the bedroom again, the door now obscenely open, allowing the pure kitchen light to invade.

Kip climbed slowly to his feet and crept forward until his shadow fell into the darkened room. Above the bed was a statue of the Virgin Mary. Her upturned hands beckoned. Kip moistened his lips, and took another step. In the dark warmth of the room the smell of his mother's powder wafted around him like an avenging angel.

His toe throbbed. He moved further into the room. The high double bed that Mother and Auntie shared dominated the darkened space. On the wall opposite the curtained window was a framed picture of a dark, wood-panelled office with dogs wearing men's clothing. There was a bulldog in a three-piece suit and a bloodhound, also well dressed, holding a cane. Various other canines sat around a table, smoking, laughing and having a good time.

On each of two bedside tables were matching paraffin lamps. Their shining brass bases supported shaped cover glasses with handpainted flowers that curled up to the narrow, fluted openings.

There was a dressing table with two drawers against the wall near the window, a chair in front of it, and, at the end of the bed, a large, plain wooden box covered with a zebra skin. Kip had sometimes caught a glimpse of the skin on the rare occasions the door was opened in his presence and had always felt an almost irresistible urge to dash into the forbidden room and stroke it. Now he reached a tentative hand towards it. The carpet of black and white hairs let his hand run smoothly in one direction but resisted its return. He ran his cheek along it and again felt the mat welcome him in one direction and rebuff him in the other.

His mother's scent came to his notice again, this time from the zebra skin. He backed away. The skin had lost its appeal. The Virgin Mary scowled.

The only other item of furniture in the room was a slim two-doored cupboard with a couple of shelves containing a dozen or so books. Kip rummaged among the shelves for the distinctive metal box with 'Capstan Ready Rubbed' written in gold letters on a metallic green background that contained the first-aid kit. There were spools of cotton and sewing things, but the kit wasn't in the cupboard. His eyes went again to the large box at the end of the bed.

He folded the heavy zebra skin back with a kind of reverence. A waft of musty air rose from the mildew-mottled timber. When the box opened, the hinges gave a *crack* like a rifle. Kip's heart thumped and he dropped the lid. He waited a moment for his courage to return, before trying again. The second time the chest opened with a murmur, releasing the pungent odour of naphthalene.

Inside were a number of folded quilts, pillows and an old purple chocolate box that was tucked down one side. Kip knew the box could not conceal the first-aid kit — it was too small — but some demon made him peep into it. It was perhaps the same demon that had once prompted him to creep up to a lion kill and hide behind an aloe bush while the pride snarled over their grisly feast. He often wondered why he did stupid things like that.

The snug cardboard lid came off with a puff, but the box was undamaged, except for the edges, where the colour and some of the cardboard had flaked off. It held two tattered envelopes bearing strange stamps. One had a picture of the king on a green background with 'Australia' printed beneath. The other was of the king facing the other way with the words 'Great Britain' underneath. There was also half a newspaper page with an advertisement for Dr Thar's Ointment, and a small piece of smooth black wood with odd patterns painted on it in red, yellow and white. Kip ran his finger over it, feeling the pattern of lines and dots. The paint must have been thick when it was applied. The other half of the curved wooden thing had been snapped off, leaving a jagged end.

He tilted the chocolate box to tip the wooden piece into his hand and a small gold band fell to the floor with a clatter, rolled in a wide circle around the timber floor and disappeared under the bed.

In a panic, Kip scuttled after it. He slid onto the floor on his stomach and swept his hand under the bed through dust and fluff until he hit something metallic. It was the first-aid tin. The ring had come to rest beside it.

Kip quickly returned the ring and other contents to the purple chocolate box and slid it back beside the quilts. He carefully closed the lid of the chest and rolled the beautiful black and white zebra skin back into place. With the first-aid tin under his arm, he ran from the bedroom to the comforting warmth of the back step, where he slowly and painfully extracted the jigger from beneath his toenail.

There were more than fifty people in the crowd outside the Nanyuki Pioneers' Hall. Kathleen nodded at some of the neighbours, but Marie avoided eye contact as she fanned herself with a copy of the flyer advising of the meeting. It was certainly a good turnout. It looked as if the whole district was in attendance — proof of the concern everyone felt. It wasn't every day that the District Commissioner came up from Nyeri, but the Mau Mau was on everyone's lips. Bad enough that raiding parties had been picking off the outlying homesteads for whatever they could eat or use, but just a week ago a body, horribly mutilated and as yet unidentified, had been found in the mountain foothills, not five miles from the outskirts of the town.

Marie stole glances at the Miles girls, who were always the first to wear the new fashions. As usual they were ridiculously overdressed, particularly for Kenya. The younger wore a yellow waisted dress with a straight skirt, which was belted and had cuffed cap sleeves. Fake pockets echoed the shape of the sleeve cuffs. The older girl wore a red and white striped dress, also with capped sleeves, a fitted waistline, and contrasting belt and full skirt. The outfits appeared to be made from the new nylon and cotton material. Both women wore silly brimless hats, more like berets. Quite impractical, Marie decided, considering Nanyuki's position plumb on the equator.

The younger Miles girl caught her staring and Marie quickly turned away, nervously patting at the material of her shirtwaister floral dress that tended to bunch at her belt, making her look quite a lot dumpier than she was.

Kathleen bent to whisper in Marie's ear and her wide-brimmed felt hat caught the brim of Marie's straw bonnet. She wore practical grey slacks and a buttoned and double-pocketed shirt. 'Take a peep at old Dudley Bastard, will you, Marie?' She rolled her eyes. 'Have you ever seen the likes of him?'

Dudley was famous for two things: his considerable girth and the number of his children, which at last count was nine by his present wife and seven from his first. The saying in Nanyuki was that you couldn't walk down the street without seeing one Bastard or another.

'Do you suppose he's put on more weight?'

The two women watched as Dudley seemed to roll rather than walk from his car to the hall. In the back seat were his four *totos* — the small black children he employed to get his car started.

'He couldn't have, surely,' Marie said, shaking her head.

Dudley was so fat that his gut overflowed the gearshift of his old Austin, making it impossible for him to change gear. The *totos* would push the Austin until it had gained enough speed for Dudley to engage top gear, then had to make a mad dash to jump on board before the Austin outran them. This process had to be repeated at each stop, making a nuisance of any enforced pause in his journey. Everybody in town knew it was dangerous not to give right of way to Dudley Bastard.

Marie tapped Kathleen on the arm, nodding in the direction of the door where the crowd was filing into the stifling heat of the hall. They found two seats together in the middle rows.

After he was introduced, the District Commissioner made some preliminary comments before coming to the point. 'I am here today to reassure you good folk that there is no need for panic in the light of these new attacks.'

'Very well for you to say, Mr Boverie. You've got the army at your beck and call.'

The voice came from the end of Marie and Kathleen's row. Marie peered past her neighbour to find the speaker was Cliff Randall from Cedarville farm. She turned back to Kathleen and whispered, 'If old Cliff is worried with his troop of grown-up sons, what hope is there for the likes of us?'

Kathleen nodded. 'His girls are the ones I'd be afraid of,' she whispered.

Marie smiled.

'Sir,' the District Commissioner responded, 'the army is at the ready. We have a battalion of the

King's African Rifles garrisoned not five miles from here.'

'What good are they if they can't find the Mau Mau?' called another voice.

'I lost five cows and more'n a dozen sheep last week,' a third voice added to a growing chorus.

'Order!' the chairman thundered, giving the table a mighty rap with his gavel. 'Order, I say. Let the District Commissioner speak his piece.' He glared at the gathering until there was silence. 'Carry on, Mr Boverie.'

'Thank you, Mr Chairman.' Boverie used a thumb and forefinger to prise his khaki shirt from the sweaty patch on his chest. 'Some of you may not be aware that two days ago, on the twentieth of October, the British Government declared a state of emergency in Kenya.' He paused to let the news sink in. The gathering was hushed. 'Yesterday, the Second Battalion of the Lancashire Fusiliers arrived by aeroplane from the Middle East. And over the coming weeks we shall see a significant escalation of our response capabilities. A significant escalation,' he repeated. 'I am talking about army, navy and air forces.'

The District Commissioner continued in this vein for several minutes, quoting statistics of men and materials. He finished with a rousing tone — 'We shall not be defeated by a ragtag rabble of ignorant natives!' — and took his seat to a ripple of polite applause.

The chairman thanked him and looked around the room. 'Are there any questions for the District Commissioner?'

Cliff Randall stood.

'The DC has given us some interesting numbers to think about,' he said, 'but my question is, will these conventional forces be suitable? I was with Brigadier General Wapshore in the last war. We chased von Lettow all over Tanganyika. Had a devil of a time cornering him. Jungles and swamps, just like here.' He looked around the meeting; he had their complete attention. 'These blasted Kikuyu are raiders, just like von Lettow's lot. Strength of numbers don't matter in that terrain. You can't engage them in battle. They go around you; attack small targets. Like our farms.'

A buzz of concern ran around the room as Randall sat down.

The District Commissioner smiled condescendingly. 'Our local King's African Rifles boys can handle any skirmishes around these parts, I'm sure.'

'What about the soldier found dead in the forest last week?' said someone from the back rows.

Members of the audience exchanged glances.

'An isolated incident,' Boverie said.

Cliff Randall was on his feet again. 'And I'm going to make sure it remains so.' He looked around the assembly. 'Me and my boys are armed and we intend to patrol our farm and those of our neighbours. Who'll join us?'

A chorus of shouts and cheers arose. The meeting broke up in disarray.

CHAPTER 2

At first, Ernie thought he had died and gone to heaven. He was briefly aware of bright lights and a floating sensation before he was rudely dumped onto a solid surface and the lights went out again.

Some time later he awoke in hell. His leg ached terribly, but it was nothing to the pain in his hands. And there was something smothering him. He couldn't breathe. He tried to feel his face, but his hands were enormous blobs filled with feathers.

He opened his eyes and strained to focus.

A black face loomed above him.

Ernie fainted.

The black face was still there when he awoke. He studied it for some time. It was younger and less intimidating than his first impression. 'Who are you?' he asked, when he was sure it wasn't a dream.

The face broke into a smile. 'I am Nasonga.' The voice was resonant with a rich timbre. It was a voice older than its owner.

The answer didn't seem enough. Ernie slowly shifted his gaze. The room was stark. A single fly-specked bulb hung from an off-white ceiling. 'Nasonga what?' he asked, not sure why. He had far more important questions for the black man to answer, including *Where am I?* and *How the fuck did I get here?*

'I am Zakayo Nasonga.' The smile broadened. 'Don't you want to know where you are?'

'Matter of fact, I do.' Ernie's throat was raw, his voice little more than a croak.

'Well, you are in the hospital of prisoner-of-war camp Stalag Luft 7 at Bankau.'

The black man was sitting on a chair at Ernie's bedside. He had a broad friendly face with a short mat of extremely black hair. Ernie knew he wasn't an Aborigine. His features were different, and so was the accent, which might have been slightly pommy.

'Why?' Ernie asked.

The man's brow creased into a frown. 'Why what?'

'Why am I here?'

'In hospital? Because you have a fractured skull, second-degree burns to your hands and a broken leg, like me.'

Ernie looked down at his right leg. A tin splint reached from his ankle to his crotch. The black man lifted his left leg to rest on the edge of the bed. His splint reached his knee.

'See? We are a good pair.' His teeth were large and white. 'They brought you in yesterday. Maurice says you are going to be all right.'

'Maurice?'

'He's a Belgian POW, and a doctor, thank God. Otherwise, I don't know what would happen to us all.'

'And what about you, um . . .'

'Nasonga. But you can call me Zakayo if you wish. Me? I am a sergeant in 10th Division, British army. Our platoon was cut off at Monte Cassino. I foolishly fell into a hole. I have been here for nearly one month.'

A chunk of Ernie's memory came back with a rush. He lifted himself on his elbows and looked wildly about the room. 'Where's my clothes? Where's my stuff?'

'Don't worry, I washed your clothes. They're outside trying to dry in this terrible weather.'

'And my other stuff?' He looked at the side table and scanned the room.

'The guards probably took your wallet and anything else valuable. Did you have a watch?'

'Yes, but what about my boomerang?'

'I beg your pardon?'

'My boomerang. Half a boomerang. It's a piece of black wood, with yellow, red and white —'

'Oh, that.' Nasonga reached into a shirt pocket and handed it to him. 'Here it is.'

Ernie took it and let his head drop back onto the pillow. 'Whew,' he said as a memory of Marie, and the time he'd broken the toy boomerang in two, returned. He had given her half with the promise to come home safely when the war was over. 'Thanks. Thanks a lot.' He gave a dismissive shrug. 'It's, you know, kinda sentimental.'

The black man nodded. 'I understand. I think you call it a lucky charm?'

'That's it.' Ernie laughed. 'Not really lucky this time, though.'

'It could have been worse. But we look after each other here. Well, some do. But you must not worry, I will look after you, Ernie.'

'Appreciate that, mate. You've done real beaut so far, I reckon.'

'It is nothing.' Zakayo studied Ernie with a frown. 'But you look tired. Can I get you something? I have a little food hidden.'

Ernie looked down at the pair of broken legs,

one white, one black. 'You look like you'll have as much trouble as me getting around the place.'

'I can manage.'

Ernie liked the man. 'Zako, you and me are gonna get on just great, I reckon.' He indicated their broken legs. 'For a start, we only need one pair of shoes between us.'

Zakayo Nasonga had been a young man of impending importance in his home village of Panyiketto before he left Uganda for the war. His village was on the mighty Albert Nile, not far from the Belgian Congo. As a result he could speak passable French, which was one of the reasons the British Army had accepted him as a volunteer. But they wouldn't have been interested at all if he had, in 1941, told them he was only sixteen. He was big for his age, the benefit of long hours hauling on the nets, and he passed for eighteen without a question.

Panyiketto was often in his mind. He imagined wandering down the river path to Doreen's village. She would be there, at the river, washing her clothes; a bright smile would light her face at his approach. Or she would be at her parents' hut, squeezing milk from coconut meat. Their hut stood on the rise above the river, crowned by a mass of purple bougainvillea. Palm trees nodded over the wide grey-blue expanse of the Nile where children speared fish in the shallows and threw stones at crocodiles for fun. In the gardens were maize, cassava and leafy vegetables of many kinds. And everywhere were bananas: the small, sweet ones whose cluster looked like the hand of a fat child; the noble *kabaka* bananas, big and firm; and the uncultivated green ones, inedible off the tree, but delicious when cooked and added to maize meal porridge. Zakayo hadn't had a banana in years.

Unlike at home, since his discharge from hospital to the POW camp seven months ago, he had been almost friendless. The black Americans kept to themselves. The Belgians seemed uncomfortable about his status, as if a special class of prisoner of war should have been created for him, the only black African in camp. The British pretended tolerance, but were slow to include him within their circle. The Germans treated him like a ghost. What place did a primitive from Uganda — a country virtually unknown outside Africa — have in the global conflict? He wasn't even supposed to be in Stalag Luft 7 — it was an air force camp, not a camp for British Army types like him. It didn't seem to matter to the Germans. He might as well have been invisible.

His only real friend was the nuggetty Australian, Ernie Sullivan. The friendship grew slowly at first, but soon Ernie began to share his irreverent humour with Zakayo. It was a turning point. The pair went into business together.

Being ignored by the Germans had its advantages, Zakayo thought, as he made his way towards his hut. It lessened the risk of being stopped when he was making his rounds to collect bets in the Sermon Time contest.

Sermon Time involved guessing the length of the Catholic priest's sermon each Sunday. The men could buy time slots of ten seconds for a small fee. The man holding the time slot closest to the actual length of the sermon won the kitty, less ten per cent, which Zakayo and Ernie shared. Boredom was a constant menace in the camp. Even the prisoners' senior officers didn't make an issue of the men's once-a-week flutter if it helped to break the numbing routine.

If the men had no cash they could barter with Red Cross chocolate or tobacco, or whatever other commodity was available. Ernie set the price of the various commodities depending upon supply and demand. He and Zakayo would move around the camp, buying, trading and selling to retrieve cash. Sunday started the whole process again.

Ernie was sitting on the step of their hut in Sector F, nicknamed the 'foreign legion' because it housed men from countries with too few members to constitute a community such as was enjoyed by the British, the Belgians and the Americans. He was wearing his usual lopsided grin, and a jacket that fitted his body but was at least a size too long in the arms.

'G'day, Zako,' he said as the African joined him on the step. 'Everything sweet with the Yanks?'

'No worries, mate,' the African replied, mimicking Ernie's broad Australian accent. In the seven months since Ernie had arrived, Zakayo had accumulated quite a considerable vocabulary of Australian slang. In return Ernie had picked up a few Swahili words, including swear words that he used at every available opportunity.

Ernie cast a quick look around the compound and plunged a hand deep into his pocket. 'Here, add this to our kitty.' He put a handful of cash into Zakayo's hand. 'Cigarette?'

'No, thanks. We are getting quite a nest egg these days.'

'Too right.' Since the liberation of Paris, which the camp had heard about from the Belgian Resistance network, speculation about the imminent end of the war was growing. 'What do you reckon you'll do with yours, Zako?'

Zakayo leaned back on the step and stretched his legs. 'Ah, now you are asking me something.' His share of their profits was enough to buy several cows — enough for a dowry, and a good start to his herd. An image of Doreen came to mind.

'So, I'm askin'.'

'What would an Australian kangaroo understand about Africa?'

'I might surprise you. Try me.'

Zakayo actually wanted to talk about Doreen; somehow it would make her feel closer. But he didn't want to seem too eager. If Ernie was African, Zakayo would know exactly how to handle the conversation, but white men had problems dealing with sensitive issues. Not that he and Ernie had not touched on many delicate subjects, including their respective sexual exploits, but Ernie had rarely mentioned his wife and their life together. Zakayo had taken this as his lead and kept Doreen to himself.

'I'm going to ask my girlfriend to marry me,' he said.

'Beauty, mate. That's the stuff. Who's the lucky girl?'

'Her name's Doreen.'

'*'Er name's Doreen ... Well, spare me bloomin' days!*' Ernie's normally coarse accent had become a nasally twang. '*You could er knocked me down wiv 'arf a brick!*' he added.

Zakayo stared at him. 'What the hell are you talking about?'

Ernie continued:

'*I just lines up an' tips the saucy wink.*

'*But strike! The way she piled on dawg! Yer'd think*

'*A bloke was givin' backchat to the queen ...*

'*'Er name's Doreen.*'

He finished with a broad grin, obviously pleased at some private joke. Zakayo muttered under his breath.

'What's that? I heard that!' Ernie forced a frown to cover his smile. 'Did you say *mbolo*? Uh? You did, you bugger. I know *mbolo* — it means "prick".'

Ernie was teasing him but Zakayo was wounded. There were some things that should not be the subject of amusement.

'Hey, I was just chiacking you.' Ernie gave him a nudge.

The young black man eyed him; he seemed genuine enough. 'Then what's all this *takataka* about Doreen? And that means "bullshit", if you don't already know.'

'I know *takataka*. And it's not bullshit, it's poetry.'

Zakayo sensed Ernie knew he had gone too far and was trying to appease him with his humour. 'What kind of poetry is that? I cannot understand a word of it,' he said.

'C.J. Dennis. The best. He's talking about his new sheila called Doreen.' Ernie made a theatrical gesture with his raised hand.

''*E allus wus a bloke fer showin' off.*

'"*This 'ere's Doreen," 'e sez.*

'"*This 'ere's the Kid.*"

'*I dips me lid.*'

Zakayo shook his head. '*Takataka*. You cannot call it poetry. Poetry is words, of beautiful things, and of love . . .'

'"The Sentimental Bloke" *is* about love. You've just got to look a bit harder to find it.' When the Ugandan didn't reply he went on. 'Okay, let's skip the poetry.'

'Good.'

'Now tell me about your Doreen. Where's she from? Where'd you meet her?'

'And you won't go on with any more *takataka*?'

'No *takataka*,' Ernie said with a frown that was meant to indicate sincerity.

Zakayo was pleased to have the subject back on track. He could see his Doreen again, smiling at him, with flowers in her hair, on the day they first met at the Friday market. He was just fifteen, she thirteen. 'She's from another village. Remember I was telling you about our village in Uganda?'

Ernie nodded.

'Well, she's from a few miles upriver. The village is small, about the same size as ours. I had never been there to visit because we don't have any relatives there, which will make it a bit difficult for my father to negotiate the marriage, but I can't think about that yet.' His mind was racing ahead. 'It's a problem for another day, isn't it?' He felt he needed reassurance from the older man.

Ernie nodded again.

The African was warming to his topic. Sharing the memories felt good and Ernie had stopped his teasing. 'We met at the weekly market,' Zakayo added, smiling as he recalled the day.

Ernie sat straighter on the step, trying to suppress a grin. '*I seen 'er in the markit first uv all.*' He raised the theatrical hand again. '*Inspectin' brums at Steeny Isaacs' stall.*'

Zakayo rested his elbows on his knees, slowly lowered his face into his hands and groaned.

'*I backs me barrer in — the same ole way —*
'*An' sez, "Wot O! It's been a bonzer day ..."*'

CHAPTER 3

Kip sat on the step staring into the distance, where the wooded hills climbed above the savannah grasses, becoming grey-green as they continued into the impossible heights of jagged Mt Kenya. But he wasn't thinking about the snowcapped mountain; instead, he imagined himself on horseback, galloping after a bongo as it twisted this way and that, trying to avoid Kip's twirling lasso. The big red antelope balked, tossed its spiralled horns and snorted in defiance. Kip wheeled his stallion around and dashed back before the bongo had a chance to bound away. The lasso twirled and Kip released it in a perfect arc, to capture the noble horns in a secure loop. He jumped from the horse and wrestled the animal to the ground — another thirty pounds in his pocket.

Kip knew the going rate for all the animals in the Mt Kenya region: thirty pounds for a bongo, twenty for a leopard, fifteen for a cheetah. He'd learned them from being around Mr Hook, who had a farm down the road from the hotel.

Raymond Hook was a hunter first and farmer a distant second. He made his money — thirty pounds a time in the case of the bongo — by capturing animals for one of several zoos overseas. It seemed the ideal life to Kip, combining his existing love of the outdoors and his overwhelming desire for wealth. He suspected that, compared to the big pastoralists, Mr Hook was not really wealthy, but in Kip's eyes, thirty pounds was more money than he could imagine. Bagging a bongo, or a cheetah, or whatever else the zoo required, would be a great way to acquire the wealth he needed to escape.

It wasn't Nanyuki that he wanted to get away from, but his miserable childhood. And, staring into that peerless blue sky with only the mountain and a few puffy white clouds to break its spell, he had to admit it was also his mother.

He felt bad about that. All the other eight year olds at school seemed to like their parents, their mothers in particular. Maybe they were lying, but he'd never know because he seldom had the opportunity to witness how life was in their homes; and his friends could never witness what Kip experienced because he was forbidden to invite them to the house.

He left the back step and wandered towards the furrow that channelled their water from a feed in the Nanyuki River. The flow was little more than a trickle. Something had blocked it upstream. It would be another chore he'd have to do before dark. He looked into the west: it was less than an hour before dusk. He kicked a stone into the furrow and shoved his fists into his pockets. He felt something there.

The crunching sound of hooves on gravel came from the front of the pub. Women's voices drifted from the veranda to where he stood, staring at the black wooden object in his hand. He had forgotten to replace it in the big box at the end of his mother's bed, and now she was home again.

Kip dashed to the back door, scooped up the first-aid kit — further evidence of his invasion of the bedroom — and scrambled up the steps. He ran through the kitchen into the darkened bedroom, sliding the last few feet until he came to rest near the bed.

The first-aid kit was quickly in its place, but the piece of painted wood lay like a smoking gun in his hands. He shot a glance at the zebra skin, calculating the time it would take to get the accursed wooden thing back in the chocolate box. The zebra skin looked as heavy as a tombstone on the chest.

His mother's voice came from the bar. Kip was frozen with fear and indecision. He would be caught replacing it, or later be discovered as the thief. Either way he'd be punished. His eyes flew to the *kiboko* whip. He wrung his hands and hopped from one foot to the other.

He reached a hand for the zebra skin and recoiled in horror. He couldn't do it. He would be caught red-handed. He could hear his mother in the corridor now, coming from the bar. A wave of dread swept over him and his heart thumped in his chest. He was rooted to the spot.

Finally, as he heard the knob rattle at the access door to the bar, he leaped to the bedroom door, carefully pulling it closed behind him. The hallway door was opening. He fled into the kitchen, through the back door, vaulted all four steps and hit the dirt running. In moments he was in his tree hide, shaking and weeping in terror.

The offending wooden thing was still in his hand. He ran a finger over the blobs of paint. He had made good his escape, except for it. How could such an odd piece of wood cause him such agony? Perhaps it was cursed? The dots and squiggled lines reminded him a little of Kikuyu markings.

'Rupert!' His mother's voice brought him back to his present predicament. 'Rupert!'

Kip hated his name: Rupert Laikipia Balmain. Not one of them was worth painting on a dog's kennel. He had chosen Kip as the least worst of them, but his mother and aunt knew nothing of his nickname. He knew they wouldn't approve.

Marie screeched his name again.

Kip closed his eyes and tried to close his ears too. With each shriek he curled into a tighter ball. Eventually he felt he had become invisible.

CHAPTER 4

The floppy brim of the felt hat slipped over Kip's eyes again. He pushed it to the back of his head, but then it threatened to fall off backwards. Taking it in both hands, he grabbed the brim and put a sharp bend in it. He could see much better now, and he hurried along the forest trail after his friend Maina Githinji, who continued to press confidently through the dense scrub.

Maina had told him before they started that he must wear a hat. Kip knew the oversized hat with the floppy brim would be a big mistake, so he'd denied owning one. But in the end he had to wear it, ill fitting though it was, because it was Maina's rule and, like all Maina's rules, it had to be followed to the letter.

Maina said the hat was to conceal his 'mzungu white hair'. And the ash on his body was to hide his 'mzungu white skin', the latter said with a curl of disgust on his lips. Kip accepted this criticism with equanimity. Maina was his friend and his hero. At twelve, the Kikuyu boy was a head taller than Kip and his sleek black body had begun to ripple with the muscles Kip had seen on Maina's father and the other black men who worked the Grearsons' vegetable gardens.

These men's torsos were the only ones Kip had ever seen, and he covertly studied them to learn their secret. For hours he lifted stones and threw logs into the river, then, on the point of exhaustion, would hurry to the mirror in the bathroom to examine his biceps. They remained small, rounded bumps on his thin arms. He began to think that white flesh might be congenitally weak, and may never develop the knots of strength he noted on the Kikuyu. He secretly wished he were as black as Maina.

Kip hitched up his baggy shorts and trotted after Maina, ten paces in his wake. Any closer and he would be whipped by the undergrowth rebounding from Maina's passing; any further behind and he risked losing him to the jungle.

Kip loved hunting with Maina. For the first few outings he'd believed Maina's intense concentration was to add realism to the game. Later he realised that Maina was a serious hunter; his family actually ate what he brought home. Kip was always hungry but he had never considered eating mongoose, or the noisy rat-like hyrax, or a porcupine. It was only after returning one evening to retrieve his hat, which he had left in the Githinjis' *boma*, that he realised the fate of their trophies. Mama Maina, as Mrs Githinji preferred to be called in the Kikuyu fashion, was turning skewers of meat over the open cooking fire. Kip stood goggle-eyed as he recognised portions of a vervet monkey Maina had speared, having first knocked it from a tree with a well-aimed stone.

Kip realised now that he'd lost sight of Maina and hurried through the bush in the direction he assumed he'd taken. He was grabbed by the arm and yanked off the trail. He had no time to yelp as Maina clapped a hand over his mouth and glared at him to be quiet. Ahead was a reedbuck, a small antelope that Kip recognised from *Mammals of East Africa*, one of several books he'd found under the bar when they first moved into the hotel. It was frozen for an instant in dappled sunlight, then leaped out of sight without a sound. Maina pointed at Kip's feet and made a sign for silence, then he picked up Kip's too-big hat and plonked it back on his head to cover his *mzungu* hair before he scuttled after the reedbuck in a crouch.

Kip followed as silently as he knew how, taking care not to step on a twig, but every time he looked down at his feet his hat dropped over his eyes. He changed his technique, hurrying ahead with a hand on his hat and his eyes on the ground. This didn't work either. He needed a hand in front to avoid the flailing branches left in Maina's wake.

He felt he was losing ground and made a determined effort to catch up. He thrust through a particularly dense piece of scrub, head down, hat low, and bumped into Maina as he was about to release his spear at the reedbuck.

By the time the two boys had disentangled themselves the quarry had fled.

Victor Grearson stepped from the shade of the veranda into the blazing sun. He squinted into the cloudless sky as he headed towards the barn. 'C'mon, Jessie!' he called to the kelpie who had watched him with expectant eyes from the moment he had opened the screen door. The call was superfluous as the bitch seldom let Grearson out of her sight. She leaped to her feet and trotted beside him, tongue lolling.

Vic had been given the black and gold Australian cattle dog as a pup. Since then, there had been few occasions when Jessie was not at his side, either working the cattle — a task at which she excelled — or at home, with her chin on her paws at his feet. As a working dog she had no time for others. Even Grearson's son, John, who early on had spent countless hours trying to win Jessie's affection, had failed. Jessie was a one-man dog.

Grearson swung his leg over the saddle and nudged the roan into a steady walk. No need to rush the pace this afternoon. He would make a call on Githinji to check on the farm work, then check the stock on his way to the meeting at Cliff Randall's.

As he neared the thorn *boma* surrounding the collection of small thatched and sheet-iron-roofed huts, he noticed Githinji's boy and the kid from Hook's hotel come out of the bush to the east. He never thought of the Equatorial by any other name than that of its first owner. Old Logan Hook knew how to run a pub, and no doubt made a good living while the army camp was in full swing. He had the good sense to sell it to the two women soon after the war ended. Balmain's Equatorial Hotel didn't seem right. Balmain: was it French? He imagined the women were finding it hard to reconcile the book profits with their present level of business. Perhaps the extra men the District Commissioner said were being posted to the old army camp would help business pick up. He shook his head, wondering why two women would take on a hotel in a place like Nanyuki. Odd birds. He'd heard they were originally from Australia.

The Balmain kid was a strange one too, trotting behind the Kikuyu boy like a lost puppy. Grearson and Maude had just one of their own, and he knew she'd never let young John run wild in the jungle like that, nor outdoors without a hat and a decent pair of boots. At least the Balmain boy was wearing a hat today. *But, God, what a hat!* Grearson thought.

'You there, *ntoto*,' he said to the older of the two.

The Githinji boy stopped abruptly and the smaller one, whose vision was obscured by the brim of his hat, collided with him. There was a moment of confused shoving during which the Balmain boy lost his headwear.

Grearson stifled a smile. 'Where have you been, boy?' he demanded of the Kikuyu.

Maina dropped his eyes to where his big toe made lines in the dirt.

'*Wapi?*' Grearson repeated.

The black boy raised a finger to the bush. 'Hunting, *bwana*,' he said, daring to look into Grearson's eyes.

'Humph, can't be much good at it,' he said, noting they were empty-handed. 'And you, boy ... What's your name, son?'

The white boy was staring open-mouthed at the mounted white man.

'Well? Do you have a name or not?'

The boy glanced at the Kikuyu, who dropped his eyes, indicating it was up to him if he answered or not.

'Kip, mister.'

'Kip, is it?' Grearson studied the boy. While he'd seen him often around the *boma* and farm, he hadn't taken time to quiz him, believing he would eventually go off and find more suitable friends. There wasn't much of him, but even though he deferred to the older boy, there was a line of determination on his thin lips. 'What the hell is that on your face?'

Kip's hand went to his cheek. He examined the ash on his fingertips before replying, 'Black stuff.'

'Well now, young Kip Balmain, you are not to wear black stuff on your face around my farm. Savvy?'

Kip squinted up at the man in the saddle and nodded.

'Now you, young Githinji, follow me.'

Grearson rode to the vegetable garden, where six of the Kikuyu women were working, backs bent among the rows of greenery. The older Githinji was sharpening a *panga*, and stood as he approached.

'*Habari*, Githinji,' Grearson said in greeting.

'*Mzuri, bwana*,' the black man replied. '*Habari yako?*'

'*Mzuri*. How are the beans?'

'They are not well, *bwana*. We need the rain soon.' Only the string lines kept the stunted plants upright.

'And the maize?' Grearson stretched in the stirrups to peer into the far paddock, but he knew the corn was brown and almost lost to the drought.

'Also, not very fine.'

'We do what we can,' he said philosophically, then turned to find the two boys standing in silence some paces away. 'Now what about this young colt of yours?'

'*Bwana?*'

'Why is he not at school?'

Githinji could not match Grearson's gaze. 'He is a poor student, *bwana*. And our garden is in need of his attention.'

'What you do with your patch is your concern. But if this boy has the time to spend galloping through the bush for sport, he could bloody well put some time into schooling too.'

'Yes, *bwana*.'

'See to it.'

Grearson pulled on the reins to leave, then noticed the Balmain boy staring at him. 'And what about you, young man, does your mother know where you are all these days? Hanging around with this young layabout?'

'No, sir, I mean, yes, sir.'

Grearson felt inclined to threaten to have a word with the mother, but thought the better of it. He wouldn't be comfortable telling a white woman how to raise her child.

'Jessie,' he said to the dog staring up at him with adoration written all over her face. 'C'mon, girl.'

He pulled on the reins and trotted the horse towards the south fence.

The men gathered around Cliff Randall's veranda were all familiar to Vic Grearson. Most had been in the area for as long as he had; some even longer, like the Hooks, the Bastards and, indeed, the Randalls.

They looked grim, the Randalls. Standing beside Cliff were his four big, red-bearded boys, arms like mottled posts folded in a no-nonsense way. Even Randall's five daughters, three of whom were present, standing like freckled pillars at the edge of the family line-up, carried an air of belligerence. Grearson suspected that three generations in the colony, fighting every inch of the way, would breed them that way. The two absent Randall girls had found husbands in Nairobi. Maude said it must have been a relief to poor Edith Randall, who might expect the remainder of the brood to take some time to fly the coop.

Grearson nodded to Cliff as he joined the crowd, and shook hands with George Johnson beside him under the umbrella acacia. They struck up the kind of desultory conversation men of the land shared; men who rarely met socially but had no difficulty in finding a topic of mutual interest when they did.

On the veranda, Cliff Randall rubbed his hands together and craned his neck to see over the heads of those nearest him. The gesture seemed to signal his preparedness to speak, and a hush fell over the gathering.

'Men,' he began, 'I'm not going to waste your time today, so I'll get on with it.' He ran his eyes briefly over the group. 'Most of you were at the meeting in town the other day. You heard the DC speak on these Mau Mau uprisings and how our armed forces are going to straighten them out. Well, I think that's a load of bosh, and you might remember I told the DC as much last Wednesday.' He paused to let it sink in. 'Absolute bosh. And I'll tell you why. You know as well as me that the KAR men up there on the mountain road, with their formation marching and set-piece military nonsense, are next to useless against these savages. They've been sneaking around, stealing a sheep here, a cow there. It's got to stop! Why, my grandfather chased off better men than the Kikuyu when he settled here. Real fighting men — the Maasai. And did it with a rifle and the old *kiboko*. No Marquis of bloody Queensberry rules for him. Eye for an eye — that's the only rule the black man understands. Been drummed into them for generations.'

Randall paused. His sons were nodding. Others followed suit.

'That poor bugger they found out near the Equatorial,' he went on, and flung an arm in the direction of the pub, 'had his ... had a terrible thing done to him. You men know what I mean. Are we going to stand around hoping the King's bloody African Rifles will be on our farms when we need them?' He glared at them. 'No!' he spluttered, the colour rising up his cheeks.

A voice came from the crowd. 'But what are we to do about it, Cliffy?'

'Right you are, Ben, what are we to do about it? I know you are with me on this. So let me get to the point for the rest of you. There's not a native in this district who doesn't respect the *kiboko*. Give me a troublemaker — and there're always a few — and I'll straighten him out with just a touch of the hippo hide. There's not a one of them that don't deserve it one way or another, and if we were to give each and every one of them a tickle with the *kiboko* once in a while, none of these so-called insurgents would poke their heads over the furrows on our farms. All this shilly-shallying is playing into their hands.'

He scanned the crowd for any dissension. Grearson's eyes roamed the group too. All attention was on the speaker.

Randall continued: 'We take up arms and we go after the bastards.' He threw an apologetic glance at his wife. 'We dish out what they would do to us, and let's see how many of them are brave enough to bushwhack a lone traveller then.'

'But we've got farms to run. Families,' said one voice.

'How can we go charging off into the bush after every nigger who takes a poke at a cow?' said another.

'We form a Home Guard, Bill. A Home Guard just like they have down in Nairobi. But we'll run it ourselves. Everyone has a rostered night. We fan out. We patrol all our farms and,' Randall punched a fist into his open palm, 'we make them pay.'

Grearson shifted from one foot to the other. Around him heads were nodding in agreement. Others held their tongues and, like Grearson, seemed unsure of what Randall was proposing. The whole thing had started after they'd found the white body in the bush near Grearson's farm. As far as he was concerned it was a leopard attack. Popular imagination had made it a Mau Mau mutilation before the body had even been taken to Nairobi for examination.

'Cliff Randall,' Grearson called over the crowd.

'Yes, Vic?'

'Are you saying we make wholesale attacks on all the natives around these parts?'

'No, Vic, not all of them. I'm talking about the Kikuyu. Others too, if they've a mind to start anything, but it's the Kikuyu we're after. They're the troublemakers.'

'But surely not all of them are —'

'Now you're sounding like the District bloody Commissioner, Vic. A touch of the *kiboko* never did a black fella a bad turn. Teaches them to behave.'

A general chorus of agreement arose.

'You men might know about that fancy-talking leader of theirs — Kenyatta. You know as well as I do that he's egging them on. He's spruikin' Kikuyu culture and land, but we all know he wants us lot out.'

The crowd were becoming noisy in their anger.

'Well, I say to hell with Kenyatta. I'm not gonna give up my place for the likes of his kind. And I'll kill any black man who tries it.' Randall raised his arms over his head. 'Enough talk. It's time to act!

All in favour of forming a body of armed men to defend ourselves and our farms and families, raise your hand and say aye.'

'Aye!' rang across the fields.

'I therefore declare recruitment for the Nanyuki Home Guard open. All volunteers should now step up here and register.'

CHAPTER 5

Ernie gave up trying to avoid the puddles. Water squelched in his thin socks and his toes were numb with cold. Zakayo trudged in silence beside him. The camp commandant believed that incarcerated men needed the rigour of the parade ground, preferably during bad weather, to maintain discipline.

That miserable morning's parade had a note of comic relief to help pass the boring half-hour or so that they'd spent trudging in circles. One of the guards, an older man with large bloodshot eyes and a nervous tic in his cheek, had gone on a screaming, cursing, shooting spree before his comrades had disarmed him. By then he was stark, raving mad. He'd been carried out of his cabin on a stretcher that morning, foaming at the mouth and trussed like a Christmas chicken. The orderlies had loaded him into a covered military vehicle, which, inexplicably, remained at the edge of the parade ground while the prisoners did their circuits.

The men could hear the madman's ramblings every time they passed. Ernie began to needle him, using the few German words he knew, and, when they became repetitious, resorting to English. By then the insane guard had become apoplectic with rage.

'Carn the Tigers,' Ernie said on one pass.

'Ahhh!' the man in the truck screamed.

On the next pass he said, 'German dogs stink like frogs.'

'Ahhh!' came from the truck again.

And on the next circuit: 'Yankee Doodle went to town, riding on a pony.'

By the time the men were finally called into assembly, the tormented man had been driven into a screaming fury. The commandant — a short man with a high peaked military cap — looked very annoyed as he climbed the podium he used to elevate him above the height of his prisoners.

Four of the senior warders were seated each side of the speaker's podium. One of them signalled to a guard to attend to the disturbance coming from the truck, but before the guard reached it, the madman threw back the canvas. There was foam at his mouth, blood-speckled from where he had bitten his lip. His hair was dishevelled and wet with perspiration and rain, and droplets flew from his head when he spun it wildly from side to side in search of his tormentor. In his hand was a grenade. His eyes bulged as he slowly unscrewed the safety and grasped the firing cord.

The commandant took a step back on his podium.

Nobody else moved.

Ernie swallowed hard.

For an older man, the throw was excellent — long, looping and with a vengeful accuracy. It came straight at Ernie.

For a moment Ernie was paralysed. Then, with the grenade only yards away, he bolted after the rest of the men who were already well on their way to safety. In his panic he collided with Zakayo, who went down in the mud with him.

Zakayo saw the grenade coming, but could do nothing to defend himself. It thudded into the mud and landed on his chest. Ernie scrambled to his feet, and dashed to a safe distance, where he stood, white-faced, among the four hundred others, before he realised Zakayo was still on his back in the mud, still clutching the grenade.

No one moved. After long moments it became obvious that something had prevented the grenade from exploding. Perhaps it was a faulty device that could explode at the slightest nudge.

Ernie crept from the crowd towards his friend. 'Good catch, Zako,' he said, leaning over him.

'W-w-what should I do with it?' Zakayo's eyes were large white orbs in his black face.

'We learned about these Kraut grenades in training. Just in case.'

'What ... where's the pin on it?'

'Dunno. Must have missed that bit.'

'*Mungu angu.*'

'He won't help. Look, ah, let's see ... Just keep doin' whatever you're doin'.' He leaned over to study the grenade. 'Can't make anything out on it. Mud everywhere.'

'So what do you think?'

'Hmm ... Dunno.'

'*Ernie!*'

'Okay, okay, Zako, keep your shirt on.'

A fleeting moment of regret for his impetuosity passed through Ernie's mind. He dismissed it. After all, what were friends for? It was unlikely that Zakayo could throw the grenade beyond danger from his starting position, flat on his back.

'Tell you what — why don't I just grab it and throw it?'

Zakayo thought for a moment, 'You'll have to be quick, no?'

'Yes, I'll be bloody quick all right. Wasn't I the best wicketkeeper in the comp?' Ernie moved around Zakayo's prone body. 'What if I came in from this side and kinda ...' He made a trial lift-and-toss motion. 'Nah, need to pivot on me wrong foot.'

'Ernie? Can you be quick, please?'

'Take it easy, Zako, gotta plan this kind of thing. Now if I came in from here ...' He moved to the other side. 'I could lift, cock and toss. Like so.'

'Yes, that's better,' Zakayo said encouragingly. 'Let's do it that way.'

Ernie made another couple of trial motions until he was confident with his moves. 'Right-oh, mate. I'm ready.' He looked down at Zakayo. 'You ready?'

'I'm ready.' The African grimaced, as if preparing himself for an explosion.

'Right-oh ...' Ernie reached tentatively for the grenade, then paused. 'What if it's got, say, just a fraction of a second on the timer?'

Zakayo looked like he might weep. He controlled himself by biting his lip. 'Then I won't have to worry about the ten pounds I owe you, Ernie,' he said through gritted teeth.

Ernie grinned, then began to chuckle. His chuckle could not be contained and soon he was laughing uncontrollably. 'Mad bastard!' he said, tears rolling down his face. 'You're a real mad bastard, Zako, you know that?'

'Ernie!'

'Right-oh, right-oh ... just don't make me laugh. This is serious.'

He began to chuckle again, then forced himself to concentrate before he carefully planted his feet in his tested position. 'Here we go. One ... two ... *three*!'

He grabbed the grenade and spun into his throwing stance in a single movement. As he was about to hurl the bomb into the distance he saw his fellow prisoners in his throwing line stagger back in horror. Ernie stopped himself mid-action. He spun further around. More men. The circle was complete.

'*Ernie!*' Zakayo screeched. 'For the love of God! *Throw it!*'

Ernie spun again and launched it with all his might. The grenade hurtled high in the air. It landed with a thud, skidded through the slush, and came to a stop under the commandant's podium.

There was a moment of suspended silence, then timber floorboards, chairs and a ton of mud flew into the air with a mighty *whoosh*.

'You awake, Zako?'

'Yes.' A shuffling sound came from Zakayo's cell. His voice was closer when he spoke again. 'What is it?'

'Oh, I dunno. Just bored, I reckon.'

'Me also. How long has it been?'

Ernie looked at the slot of light high on the wall where the shift between grey and black indicated the passing of time. 'Not sure, three, four days.'

'Halfway,' Zakayo said.

There was silence for a few moments. Then Ernie heard Zakayo's throaty chuckle coming from the next cell. He smiled at the sound. 'What's so funny?' he asked.

'Look at this.' Zakayo reached his hand around the wall between their cells.

Ernie took the short length of muddy cord and began to laugh as he realised what it was. 'It's the rip fuse from the kraut grenade.'

'Now we know how those — what did you call them? *potato mashers* — work, ah?'

'We do. Unscrew pin, pull cord.'

The deranged German guard had unscrewed the pin but forgot to pull the cord to trigger the ignition sequence. It wasn't until Ernie grabbed the grenade from Zakayo, who had unwittingly held a firm grip on the cord, that it was pulled from the mechanism.

'*Aiya*, the way those German officers ran ...' Zakayo tried to contain his laughter, but it rumbled in his chest. 'Can you see them still, Ernie?'

'I can, me old mate. Heads down, bums up. Goin' like buggery.'

'And then the mud. All over them. Oh my God, I thought I would die.'

'Nearly did, Zako my boy. Nearly did.'

The laughter from the next cell continued for a few moments then dwindled into silence. 'Thank you, Ernie,' Zakayo said into the darkness.

Ernie recalled his unworthy thoughts as he'd stood over his prone friend. The split second it took him to realise that to leave him there to die alone was more than he could have lived with. 'My pleasure.'

'I mean it, Ernie. You saved my life.'

'Bullshit. You would have done something African with that potato masher.'

'Something ... African?'

'Yeah, like that *jui-jui* you talk about.'

'*Juju*. Not me. I have no such magic.'

'Yeah, well ...'

Silence descended again. Ernie made himself as comfortable as he could on the hard stone floor. He'd kill for a cigarette.

'I've got a kid somewhere in Sydney,' he said eventually. 'A boy.'

Silence in the next cell.

'You hear me, Zako?'

'I did. I didn't know that, Ernie.'

'He's nearly two now,' Ernie added.

'Do you miss him?'

'I've never seen him.'

'Do you have to see him before you can miss him?'

'No. You're right. I probably love him more because of it.'

'So you have no way of knowing how the boy is, or where he is?'

'No.'

'Oh.'

'Yeah, I know. Shithouse.'

Ernie walked unsteadily back from the latrine, hoisting his trousers higher and tying the cord he used as a belt around his shrunken abdomen. 'Eight friggin' stone wringing wet, I reckon,' he muttered to himself. 'A man's dropped two flamin' weight divisions in a week and a half.'

He dragged himself to the top of the steps of the Sector F hut and lowered his head into his trembling hands. He had just reached the latrine in time and, being as weak as he felt, he wondered whether the next time might be the one when he actually shit his pants. As if in warning, a pain spasm gripped his gut, and he clutched at it, waiting for the explosive feeling in his bowel, but it subsided. He sighed with relief.

Fortunately, the commandant of Stalag Luft 7 was not a vindictive man and let unwell prisoners like Ernie be absent from the enforced physical exercises that were a proud hallmark of his administration. But for Ernie, being alone was worse than the despised marching and callisthenics. It gave him too much time to think. And when rendered miserable by something like this attack of dysentery, he was prone to fits of uncharacteristic depression.

He would reminisce about his life before leaving home for the war, but his mind wasn't filled with the happy memories of his young wife, their wedding, or the good times they'd shared. Instead, he'd dwell upon his many failures as a husband, and a man.

Ernie had always been successful with the ladies. Not that he was good-looking or charming — far from it: he had a small round tatie for a nose and ears like the map of Ireland — but he could make women laugh, and they couldn't resist him. Ernie never thought much about it. It was just how he was. As a single man, the gift was a blessing. His problems began when he married. Old habits die hard, and he never could resist the soft squishiness of a round belly or thigh.

He was just thankful that his most recent indiscretions had occurred far from his home town. He couldn't expect to be so lucky on home soil.

His abdomen rumbled with the arrival of another compelling stab of the cramps. 'Ahhh,' he moaned, climbing gingerly to his feet. 'Bloody hell! Not again!' He took the stairs cautiously, one at a time.

In repayment for his good fortune in escaping his recent indiscretion without his wife finding out, Ernie decided to make a new start when he returned to Sydney. There would be no more philandering. He would settle down and make a happy home for his family.

'*Jesus!*' he yelled, unlashing his belt and sprinting for the latrine.

CHAPTER 6

The treehouse hide hummed in the afternoon heat. The paradise flycatcher that occasionally shared the tree with Kip flitted among its branches, its too-long chestnut tail twitching in agitation and its *twit-twit* call saying it had seen Kip and did not approve of his presence. At other times, when Kip was concealed behind the bark slabs lining his hide-out, the flycatcher would warble its love song, fluff up its black velvet skullcap and look about as gorgeous as any bird could. At those times Kip could watch for hours as it preened itself, then darted through the surrounding shrubbery, its long tail flapping like a chestnut ribbon in its wake.

Kip knew about birds. He knew about animals too, but birds were his favourites. He didn't have to go searching for birds. All he had to do was sit, and the birds would come.

He did a lot of just sitting. Mostly in his treehouse. It was safe there. Neither his mother nor Aunt Kathleen could climb his tree. When in the treehouse he could disappear. People on the ground didn't know if he was inside or not because of the slab of packing-case timber he'd found outside the Nanyuki Post Office and installed as the treehouse floor. Sometimes his mother made him come down because she didn't approve of idleness. She said idleness was the devil's helper. He wasn't sure what the devil could do with idleness, but had never had the courage to ask his mother what she meant.

Kip liked this time of day best. As the equatorial sun slid towards the Laikipia Hills, he could be reasonably sure of being able to sit quietly for an hour or more. His mother would be busy in the bar serving drinks, and Aunt Kathleen would be fussing around people's feet, sweeping, or whisking ashtrays from under the smokers' tapping fingers.

The paradise flycatcher gave a few more scolding remarks then abandoned its attempts to shame the intruder into leaving the neighbourhood. Kip lifted the lid of the biscuit tin and rummaged among his treasures. There was a hippo's tooth, a desiccated gecko trapped by death in a wide-mouthed grimace, half a ball of almost new string, several small bones and horns, and the painted wooden thing, which he reverently removed before closing the tin's lid.

The painted wooden thing hadn't been discovered missing from the chest at the end of his mother's bed. It still amazed him how he had escaped with it that afternoon two months ago. But, with the increasing passage of time, he felt more and more confident that his theft had gone undetected, and the painted wooden thing became a rare trophy. He had committed a crime, probably a mortal sin, right under his mother's nose and escaped her wrath — an almost unheard-of accomplishment.

He idly traced the lines of paint on the piece of wood. He instinctively knew the patterns were from another time. They spoke to him of the land and the sky. Although he'd initially thought it African, he could find nothing in it in common with the Kikuyus' art, or that of any other tribe that he'd seen. It was not only a relic of a distant time, it was an alien in Africa. It was out of place.

Being out of place made Kip's thoughts fly to the dust-dry classroom he attended at the Nanyuki Primary School. There were four rooms: two old ironclad ones and two newer ones, of timber cladding. Kip was in one of the older ones, in the middle grade.

He hated school. He had always hated school. His earliest recollections were of being gawked at in one playground or another. His problems with school had begun in a Catholic kindergarten in Sydney. He'd started midway through the year — he couldn't remember why. Probably because of another of his mother's many changes to their accommodation — they always seemed to be on the move. At this particular kindergarten, all the children had to kneel on the hard floorboards until they could recite the whole prayer starting with *Now I lay me down to sleep*. Until they did, they weren't allowed to take their afternoon nap. Kip's classmates had the benefit of weeks of practice, but he found it very difficult to remember all the words; the more so with a nun standing over him with a ruler, which she used on his bare legs for every mistake.

One day he completely forgot what came after *I pray the Lord my soul to keep*. He knew if Sister Mary Sarina would just leave him be it would come to him, but the more he stammered and tried to remember the words, the more impatient and threatening she became. As she hovered over him, ruler at the ready, red-faced and hostile, he wet his pants. The warm flood ran down his bare legs and headed in a determined stream towards a little girl with red plaits and freckles who had already bedded down on the floor.

Sister Mary Sarina squawked and rushed to evacuate the red-haired girl and others in the immediate area. Kip bolted.

In panic, he headed for home, where his mother went into an absolute fury because Kip had disgraced himself, and her. She dragged him back to the kindergarten and waited while Sister Mary Sarina gave him a thorough beating. After that, the other children avoided him.

Since arriving at Nanyuki Primary School halfway through last year, he'd again had trouble making friends. Only Mohan Singh occasionally sought him out at lunchtime and recess, but sometimes even Mohan found the ostracism more than he could bear and found an excuse to be somewhere else.

The screen door of the house slammed. A moment later Kip heard his mother calling him. 'Rupert, Rupert, are you in that tree again? Come down here, boy. Do you hear me?'

Kip peeped between the slats. His mother had her hands on her hips and was tapping a foot. Not a good sign.

'Rupert! You'd better get down here right away. You've got some explaining to do.'

Kip ran through all the possible reasons he might have some explaining to do. As usual, he thought he was innocent of any wrongdoing.

'Rupert!'

Now she'd lost her temper. He couldn't appear now without an immediate beating for his tardiness, to be possibly followed up by further punishment for whatever misdemeanour he had committed. He was frozen into inactivity.

Aunt Kathleen joined his mother. She had the *kiboko* in her hand. There were words exchanged and they both started towards his tree. Kip's teeth began to chatter. It was inconceivable that his mother and aunt wouldn't hear the noise. He clamped his hands over his mouth but now his breath came in strangled gasps, again so loud as to be heard halfway to Nanyuki. Tears welled in his eyes. He squeezed them shut.

The women were directly below him. He heard his aunt say, 'Will I get the stepladder?'

Kip grabbed his crotch and held on tight as his terror threatened to overflow. His bladder was about to gush; his knees felt like jelly. He frantically searched for a thought to fill his head, to blot out the terror that grew like a great black storm cloud about to burst. Nothing came. His every waking moment was usually filled with wild imaginings, but now, when he so desperately needed to cling to something of beauty or strength or peace to prevent him from crying out and disclosing his whereabouts, nothing. Suddenly words flooded his mind. He mouthed them frantically, silently, repeating them over and over until they consumed his consciousness.

'No,' he heard his mother say after a moment. 'We're not going to break a neck for the likes of him. He'll be home when he gets hungry.'

The boy scarcely dared breathe until he heard the screen door slam again. Even then, he continued to chant the words in his head. It was minutes before he could summon the courage to peep through the slats. The yard was empty.

He began to cry. Not for the relief of his escape, but in utter self-pity. It had been an age since he had last been called upon to recite these words, but the verse he'd been chanting inside his head, while his mother and aunt stalked below like hungry lions, would never be forgotten.

If I should die before I wake, I pray the Lord my soul to take.

'Not in the house, please, Victor.' Maude Grearson was at the kitchen bench, her hands deep in a mound of flour. Karanja, their cook — some would say their resident master-of-all-trades — hovered at her side.

'Sorry, love.' Grearson turned to the kelpie who had followed him into the house. 'Outside, Jessie.' The dog pleaded with her eyes, but Grearson smiled and pointed a finger to the door. The dog dropped her tail and turned, pausing for a moment before nosing the screen door opened. 'Good girl,' he said as her black and tan tail disappeared.

Grearson removed the beaded doily covering the water pitcher on the table and filled a glass. 'Karanja, bring more water, *tafadali*.'

The Kikuyu cook, who had been with the Grearsons since Maude's pregnancy, nodded and took the pitcher outside. Grearson watched as the black man paused on the veranda to give Jessie's ears a playful ruffle.

'What do you make of that kid from over there at Hook's old pub?' Grearson asked before taking a long swig from his glass.

'You mean the one who comes over to play with Githinji's boy?' Maude had flour up to her elbows as she vigorously kneaded the bread mix.

'Yes, that's the one.' Vic picked up the day-old newspaper and scanned it as he spoke.

'He's a bit of a strange one, that. Takes after his mother and aunt, I suppose.'

'What do you mean?'

'Well, just after they arrived, I went over there to say hello and you'd think I'd come to repossess the hotel.' She straightened and brushed a wisp of hair from her face with the back of her hand. 'Didn't I tell you about that?'

'I think you did,' he nodded, flipping a page. 'They keep to themselves, all right.'

'They certainly do. Anyway, why do you ask?'

'Ma ...' Their son, John, had appeared at the kitchen door. 'When'll dinner be ready?'

'As soon as I finish this bread. Why? Are you hungry?'

'Starving.' John sidled up to his father, who had taken a seat at the table, and slouched against him, looking over his shoulder at the open newspaper.

'Didn't you eat all your lunch then?' his father asked, pulling him onto his lap.

The boy wriggled free. 'Nah. Wasn't hungry.'

'Tell me, son, are you in the same class as the lad over there at the Hook's pub? I think his name's Kip.'

'You mean that stupid Balmain kid? Yeah.'

'John, that's no way to talk about your school friends,' Maude said.

'What do you mean, stupid?' Grearson asked.

'Stupid. Never joins in. Mummy's Boy, we call him. Runs home after school.'

'Why don't you be his friend? He comes over here a lot, you know.'

His son shrugged. 'He only wants to play with Maina. Let him. Who cares? He's just stupid.'

The boy ran off. 'Don't go far, Johnnie,' Maude called after him.

'Why are you worried about the Balmain boy, Vic?' she asked as she slid the bread mix into the oven.

Grearson stood and kissed the flour on his wife's forehead. 'Oh, I don't know. He's a strange little bugger.' He put his arms around her. 'With all this talk about the Kikuyu, about not trusting them because they're all Mau Mau terrorists, it's strange to see a lonely white kid preferring a black child as his friend.'

Later that night, Grearson and five other neighbours formed a column of riders behind Cliff Randall and his four boys. It was the second muster since the formation of the Nanyuki Home Guards. The Randalls carried lanterns, and only the *swish-swish* of the horses passing through the tinder-dry grass of the drought-stricken land, and the soft thud of their hooves, troubled the silence.

Grearson had been disturbed by Randall's briefing before they left Nanyuki town. He'd told them that Tom McDougall had lost a thousand bales of barley to a fire said to have been started by the Mau Mau, and down in Nyeri, someone had been slashed to death. According to Cliff, it was time for the white settlers to balance the ledger.

Grearson understood the need to defend home and farm, but Randall had told them they were going to make a 'punitive visit' to a nearby Kikuyu village — a village, so far as Grearson knew, that had no record of troublemakers.

The pace quickened as they neared their target. Some of the villagers came out from their cooking fires to see what the commotion was about.

The Home Guards swept in like a storm, slashing at everyone in their path. Men, women and children were cut down with batons or *kiboko*-hide whip handles. Grearson, holding back from the violence, saw one woman dragged by the hair by one of the Randall boys, almost lifted off the ground and dashed into a tree. In moments, there was not one Kikuyu not bloodied or moaning on the ground.

Grearson knew these men, his neighbours. They were decent, law-abiding citizens. Family men. But this was a cold-blooded, callous and totally unjustified assault on a peaceful community. He was sickened by what he saw, but kept his thoughts to himself, watching in silence as the guardsmen ran amuck.

As he rode home later that night, he decided he would take no further part in Randall's Home Guards.

CHAPTER 7

All morning, government buses had been bringing Kikuyu people into town. Vic Grearson had come into Nyeri for business, but now his curiosity was aroused. He stood near the front of the crowd, keen to see what the Administration was doing. The Nairobi press were out in force. Something big was planned, and he decided to stay to find out what it was.

In the preliminary speeches it became clear that this was a demonstration of Kikuyu solidarity against the Mau Mau. Speaker after speaker reiterated the same message: Mau Mau is evil, Mau Mau is bad for the Kikuyu and for Kenya. Grearson didn't know all the names, but the line-up included Harry Thuku and Eliud Mathu, men who had been labelled as Mau Mau sympathisers. After an hour, he had heard enough and was about to leave when the District Commissioner introduced Jomo Kenyatta as the next speaker. Grearson had seen newspaper articles about this British-educated economist, and decided to hear what he had to say.

The crowd parted and Kenyatta appeared. He was not a tall man, but he commanded attention. He climbed the stage holding his lion-like head high. His eyes, almost predatory in intensity, swept the applauding audience. He was a consummate performer — costumed and poised. A beaded Maasai *kinyata* circled his ample midriff, a coloured cap sat on his massive head. He acknowledged the crowd, milking the applause, but silencing them before it offended the egos of his fellow speakers.

Kenyatta denounced the Mau Mau with theatrical swipes of his white colobus monkey-hair fly whisk. He said the Mau Mau had spoiled the country and that its members should be hunted out and killed. Grearson thought Kenyatta's words lacked conviction and decided to leave before he finished his speech.

By the time he had reached the edge of the crowd, the next speaker, introduced as Chief Koinange, was on the stage. He was a frail old man with an incredible face; his skin had been wizened by age into a mask of leather. Only his eyes, which seemed to reach out and grab Grearson, held any life.

'I can remember when the first European came to Kenya,' the chief began almost wistfully, holding Grearson in his gaze as if addressing him directly. 'I worked alongside your father, and you are my son. In the First World War you asked our young men to go to fight with the British against the Germans and many were killed. In the Second World War you came again and asked us to fight against the Germans and the Italians and our young people were again ready to go. Now there are Italians and Germans in Kenya and they can live and own land in the highlands from which we are banned, because they are white and we are black. What are we to think? I have known this country for eighty-four years. I have worked on it. I have never been able to find a piece of white land.'

Grearson felt compelled to protest. Yes, there had been mistakes made, but he was not of that breed. He tolerated his Kikuyu squatters. He paid a fair wage for a fair day's work. He let them sharecrop his land. He didn't brand them all as conspirators and potential murderers.

If Koinange had been a young hot-head or someone like Kenyatta, a professional politician, Grearson might have dismissed the charges as mere posturing. But this old man, with his passion and his sense of betrayal, had stung him with his words. He wanted to protest his innocence, but couldn't. He drove home feeling saddened. The country of his birth was galloping towards an abyss.

Cliff Randall was a barrel of a man. His chest and hips were broad and of about the same width. His heavy belly tugged at his trousers and threatened to snap his belt. He looked much more athletic on a horse than on his feet. When he walked, he rolled from side to side as if he was poling a bathtub across a pond.

Grearson met him at the home paddock's gatepost, and led him up the stairs to the veranda where he asked if he would like tea. Randall politely declined.

'Take a seat, Cliff,' Grearson said, nodding to a chair beside the table he and Maude used for afternoon tea. 'Are you sure you don't want tea?'

'No thanks, Vic.'

Grearson sat and drummed his fingers on his knee. He knew why Randall had come. 'Rain's late.'

'Yeah. Bit dry, all right.'

'Certainly could use a drop or two.'

'Yeah.'

Grearson endured the silence, which seemed to stretch for minutes. He was determined not to be first to raise the issue. He had made his decision. It was final.

'Did you hear about the massacre at Lari, Vic?'

'Yes. Dreadful.'

'Men, women and children burned alive in their huts. Hacked to death with *pangas*.'

'There's a lot of trouble among the Kikuyus down there. The Mau Mau play one side off against the other.'

'Newspaper said a woman saw one of the Mau Mau cut her son's throat and drink his blood.' Randall shook his head in disgust. 'Animals. Nearly a hundred murdered in their beds. Poor buggers.'

Vic had heard the rumours that the Home Guards, late on the scene and gung-ho, had fired indiscriminately at any Kikuyu who lifted his head. To most of the Home Guard, the Kikuyu, not the Mau Mau, were the enemy. Instead, he said, 'Seems like it was co-ordinated with the attack at Naivasha earlier on.'

'The Naivasha Police Station? Not bloody likely. That wasn't the Mau Mau.'

Grearson couldn't believe Randall wasn't making mileage out of that attack too. The police had been caught napping, literally. One had been shot and the eighty or so raiders had made off with sub-machine-guns, rifles and a truckload of ammunition. Then they'd freed nearly two hundred prisoners, many of them suspected terrorists.

'But the Mau Mau commander — what's his name? Kaniu, Major General Kaniu — claimed his men did it.'

'Major General Kaniu!' Randall scoffed. 'They give themselves fancy titles, don't they? Bunch of savages. No, that was a military operation, that one. There were no nappy-haired kaffirs in charge of that raid. Mark my words. Communists. Out here to destabilise the infrastructure.'

'Destabilise the infrastructure' was not part of Cliff Randall's usual vocabulary. Grearson thought he must have read it in one of the more inflammatory newspapers.

'My word. They're just using the Mau Mau as foot soldiers, those commies,' Randall went on. 'It's about time we declared war.'

'A war seems to be what we have. I read we have nine Lincoln bombers, each able to carry half-ton bombs. It's enough to flatten the Aberdares.'

'Bomb them to smithereens as far as I care,' Randall said with a snort.

'But bomb who, Cliff?'

'Look, Vic, you know as well as me those shiny-arses in Nairobi don't have a clue what we settlers are going through. Never did have. Droughts, blight. They wouldn't have a clue. That's why we should take over.'

'Take over? Take over what?'

'The bloody government, of course.'

Grearson stared open-mouthed at him. 'Are you saying ... are you saying you are seriously considering a coup?'

'Never mind that, that's not why I came here. It's about you going AWOL.'

'You mean my resignation from your Home Guard, Cliff?'

'We need every available man, Victor. You see what happened to the fusiliers? By the time they got to the Naivasha Police Station — just down the road, for God's sake — the Mau Mau'd done a bunk. Traditional military people can't stop these animals.'

'And you believe that indiscriminate thuggery will?'

'Don't you understand, Grearson? They're after our land. *Your* land! And there's only one way to stop them. We have to be strong. We have to be tough. All they understand is the *kiboko* and the bullet.'

'There are as many Kikuyu against the Mau Mau as for them. Surely we're just forcing them into the other camp?'

Randall stood, his chair clattering to the veranda floorboards. 'I just can't understand your type, Vic. It's as plain as the nose on your face. We're at war. We have to wipe them out or they'll massacre the lot of us.'

He stormed down the steps and swung onto his horse. He began to ride off but swung his mount around. 'God forbid, Vic,' he flung back at him, 'but when they come at you with *pangas*, I hope you remember this.'

CHAPTER 8

'What have you heard?' Ernie Sullivan handed a rolled cigarette to his friend, Zakayo Nasonga.

The black man accepted the cigarette and pulled a book of matches from his shirt pocket. 'They say Hitler is on the run.'

'My little Red Cross lady tells me we've taken Cologne.' Ernie held the roll-your-own in the flame and puffed. 'I'd say this tobacco is another good sign. Finally gettin' through after all this time.'

Zakayo leaned back on the step of their hut and looked out over the compound. The Germans had lost their enthusiasm for structured activities. Men stood or sat around in groups. 'The Germans know it is over,' he said.

'Yeah. Be gettin' out of here soon, I reckon.'

'Hmm ... yes ... What is the first thing you are going to do, Ernie?'

It was a regular topic in their conversations. The responses varied depending on their mood, but were mostly frivolous, the answers ranging from finding a posh hotel in Piccadilly and drinking it dry, to hiring the entire chorus line of the Moulin Rouge for a weekend of debauchery in Paris. In the twelve months they had been incarcerated together, they had not repeated a story, nor tired of the game.

Ernie sucked on the fag and blew a line of smoke at its burning tip. 'Gotta check if my wife knows I'm alive, I reckon.'

'Wouldn't the Australian Air Force let her know?'

'Dunno. Maybe they can't, in case the people who reported me okay get clobbered. As far as she knows, I'm still missing in action.'

'And then you'll see your son.'

'Yeah.'

'It must be wonderful to have a son.'

'Reckon.'

Zakayo thought of Doreen, and dreamed of the time when they would have children, many children, of their own. His sons would work beside him in the long rows of bananas. His daughters would be beautiful beyond belief. He and Doreen would thank the gods for their blessings.

The insipid sunshine of a German spring made it difficult for him to imagine his home in Africa. He missed the Ugandan sun, which at noon hit the back of the neck like a well-aimed club. He missed the swift brown waters of the Albert Nile, where long sleek crocodiles lurked and boisterous bull hippos did battle for mating territory. Everyone in Stalag Luft 7 knew he was an infantryman out of place in an air force POW camp. But no one, not even Ernie, understood how much his heart ached for home.

For four years, he had not joined with his friends in the village, drum in hand, to dance the *bwola*. He had missed four dry seasons in the northwest — the land of his Nilotic ancestors — and the seasonal *dwar arum,* when the men would band together for the hunt. He had not tasted sorghum, or simsim, or pigeon peas, in the same four years. He'd had not a sniff of a banana since leaving Uganda. He had not spoken to a brother African for well over a year.

With the end of the war so near, he felt a superstitious dread that he, Zakayo Nasonga of the Acholi tribe, from the headwaters of the Nile, and just twenty years of age, might yet die in this cold and foreign land without ever seeing his beloved country again.

The initial excitement that had swept through the POW camp on a wind carrying the sweet tang of imminent freedom, had, over recent weeks, slowly abated until it lay like a lazy dog in the sun.

The camp guards, crushed by the realisation that the good life the Führer had promised would not eventuate, allowed the men to spend many leisurely hours anticipating reunions with loved ones, friends and family. Even those pleasures had waned, until a purgatory of boredom became everyone's daily burden.

Ernie lounged on the steps of the Foreign Legion hut, smoking. Zakayo joined him, and stood leaning against the veranda post in silence. There was nothing to say that had not been said a dozen times before.

Ernie groaned.

'What is it?' Zakayo asked.

'Don't look now, but the good Father is on the prowl.'

Father Michael Kissane was making a determined beeline towards them — head down, arms swinging. The chaplain seemed to be the only one imbued with any sense of purpose. Ernie had heard the priest was making a frenetic dash to visit all his parishioners before the POWs were evacuated from camp.

'Good morning, Mr Zakario,' he said, beaming at Zakayo.

'Zakayo. Good morning, Father.'

The priest inclined his head in apology for his mispronunciation. 'Sorry, good morning, Mr Zakayo.'

'Nasonga.'

'Pardon?'

'It's Mr Nasonga. Or just Zakayo.'

'I see. I do beg your pardon.'

'But you may call me just Nasonga — it's the African custom to use family names. Or Zakayo. Whatever you wish.'

Father Kissane's smile faded a little, but undaunted, he turned to Ernie. 'And Ernest! Good morning to you.'

Ernie forced a smile. 'Good morning, Father. How are you today?'

'Very well. Very well indeed. I'd like to —'

'Getting ready to pack up and move out, are you?'

'Presently. But I have been trying to catch up with some of my ... what shall I call you? My lost sheep! Yes, my lost sheep.'

'Sheep?' Zakayo appeared confused.

It was a quiet day. Ernie decided to let the chaplain explain himself.

'It's a manner of speaking, Mr Zakayo ... anyway, how are you today?'

'Very fine. How are you, Father?'

'I'm fine too.' The priest smiled, but quickly put on a serious face. 'This morning I would like to talk to you, both of you, about Jesus, if I may.'

Zakayo nodded. 'Okay.' He settled himself on the step with Ernie, leaning back against the opposite veranda post.

'But before I do, we should spend a moment to reflect upon the Creator.'

'Okay.' Zakayo nodded. 'You mean Jok.'

'Jok? No, I mean God the Father.'

'That's right. His wife was Earth and his son was Luo.'

Father Michael looked at Ernie for support, but Ernie, straight-faced, said nothing.

'I'm afraid you're thinking of Adam,' the priest smiled condescendingly. 'Let me begin again. In God there are three entities. There's God the Father, his only begotten son, Jesus, and there's the Holy Ghost.'

'A ghost? We have ghosts too in Africa. Although ours are not holy, but they *are* magic. There's one called Labongo. He was born with bells on his wrists and ankles, and had feathers in his hair.'

'No, no. Let's not get off the track talking about —'

'He liked to dance. We Acholi like to dance too.' Turning to Ernie, he said, 'You remember me telling you about our dances, Ernie?'

'Yes, I do,' Ernie responded. Turning back to the priest he said, 'You should hear about these dances, Father. They're *really* interesting.' He hoped he wasn't applying the irony too thickly.

'Lovely ... but what I am trying to —'

'When he danced, the bells jingled.'

'Yes, I suppose they would.' The chaplain held a finger up to stop further distractions. 'As I was saying, there's Jesus, God the Father, and ... the other one. Now, God sent his only son, Jesus, down to earth — *our* earth not —'

'Not Luo's mother.'

'Exactly. And —'

'That's strange,' Zakayo said, rubbing his jaw in contemplation. 'Luo had only one son too.'

'Hmm ... what a coincidence. And when Jesus arrived —'

'His name was Jipiti.'

'— he appointed a man, as I mentioned before — St Peter — who would be his representative on —'

'And Jipiti had a daughter called Kilak.'

Father Michael smiled patiently, 'Zakayo, my son, what I am trying to say is that, in the Catholic Church, we have an unbroken line of succession reaching back to St Peter, the first Pope, whereas the simple tales you are reciting lead nowhere.'

Zakayo sucked his lip as he weighed up the priest's proposal. 'No ... that is not so, Father Michael, because after Jipiti and Kilak came the line of *rwots* — the chiefs. Their line comes down from hundreds of years, even down to this day. Just like you were saying about the Catholic Church.'

'Hundreds of years? Surely not, Mr Zakayo.'

'Yes, Father. Would you like to hear about them?'

The priest began to make an excuse, but Zakayo said, 'It won't take long. I talked about Kilak, well, she had no children, until she wandered off into the bush where she was tempted by the devil — his name was Lubanga, who became the father of Labongo, the one I said had magical powers. Anyway ...'

Ernie took pity on the priest. 'Zako, old mate, I think Father Michael might be a bit busy for that at the moment. Got plenty of other folk to see, I suppose, Reverend?'

The chaplain blinked, dragging his mind back from Zakayo's litany. 'What's that? Oh, yes indeed. Thanks for reminding me.'

Ernie smiled, pleased with his strategy to deflect the priest from focusing on him — one of the few in camp who admitted to being a Catholic. It was not that he was against the religion, but he had practised it in his own way for many years, and didn't need a priest to remind him of his duties to regularly partake of the sacraments. It was a personal matter between Ernie and his God.

'But before I do,' Father Michael said, 'I would have a quick word with you, Ernest.'

Ernie stifled a groan. 'Me?' He didn't want to hurt Father Michael's feelings. As a matter of fact, Ernie felt obliged to him — he and Zakayo had made a lot of money thanks to the priest's unpredictable sermon times — not that Father Kissane was aware of it.

'Last time we spoke, Ernest, you told me it had been years since you had taken Holy Communion.'

'You know, Father, I believe in horses for courses.'

'Now, Ernest, you've just got out of the habit. You will be surprised how welcoming the good Lord is when you open your heart to him.'

'Yeah ... well, I don't know about that, Father ...'

'Do you know, Ernest, I myself had a crisis of faith and Our Lord took pity on me.'

'Really?'

'Indeed. I was at my wit's end and my prayers were answered,' the priest smiled. 'It might be hard to believe these days, my services being as popular as they are, but I once thought I had no skills at all in the pulpit. Can you imagine? I had very low self-belief, and felt that people were simply not interested in hearing my sermons.'

Ernie opened his mouth to speak, but thought better of it.

'Nowadays, look at me! Why, the men simply flock through the chapel doors just to hear my sermons. My prayers have been answered.'

'I know what you mean, Father.' Ernie cast a glance at Zakayo, 'Our prayers have been answered by your sermons too.'

The convoy of Russian trucks began to rumble out the camp gate. Zakayo stood with Ernie alongside the truck that was to take the Australian to one of the Russian camps a few miles north of Berlin. From there he would be repatriated back to London. Zakayo was still awaiting his movement orders.

'I'm sure we'll end up in the same place,' Ernie said. 'It doesn't make sense that the whole foreign legion would go to one camp, and you to another.'

'No, you are right,' Zakayo said. 'It is very strange.'

'I mean, okay, you weren't supposed to be in here with us in the first place, but you were, so . . .' Ernie knew he wasn't sounding convincing.

'Somebody will see the error and fix it. Do not worry.' Zakayo patted Ernie on the shoulder.

'I'll bet you a fiver you're there within a couple of days.'

'Too right, mate.' It was one of Zakayo's better impersonations of the Australian's twang, but Ernie's mind was elsewhere.

After months of false reports and optimistic predictions, in the end the news of victory had come unexpectedly. Suddenly the Germans were very efficient, reorganising huts and preparing paperwork for the Russian troops who were sent to take custody of the prisoners. Zakayo had been whisked out of the foreign legion hut and into another on the far side of camp.

One of the Russians banged on the side of the truck, then jerked a thumb, indicating the group should climb aboard.

'Tell you what,' Ernie said in the whisper he used whenever he was hatching a scheme, 'jump in with us. These buggers aren't to know who you are.'

Zakayo looked at the Russian soldier who was checking the men's papers. He had a sub-machine-gun draped from his shoulder. 'I don't think that fellow will let me,' he said.

'Oh, bugger him. Look, I'll create a little diversionary move and you hop over the side.'

'What about those ones?'

Ernie hadn't noticed the other Russians forming up along the road. *Oh shit*, he thought. He was annoyed with himself for not having planned something sooner.

Zakayo sensed his concern. 'Look, Ernie, don't worry about me. It will be fixed in a short while. They cannot leave me here, *si ndio*?'

'Tell you what, let's meet at the Ploughman's when we get back.' Ernie smiled. 'Your shout.'

'Shout?' Zakayo shrugged.

'Your shout, your turn to buy the beer. Jeez, don't tell me I've forgotten the most important part of your Aussie education.'

Zakayo smiled, but Ernie knew he was forcing the humour, trying to lighten a moment that threatened to become too emotional for him to handle.

The Russian was beckoning to Ernie and becoming irate. 'Okay, okay, Ivan. Don't get your knackers in a knot.' He turned back to Zakayo and grabbed his hand. 'Look after yerself, ya woolly-head,' he said, attempting to ruffle Zakayo's tightly curled hair.

The African slapped him on the back. 'I will. You too.'

Ernie had a foot on the first rung of the ladder, but stepped back quickly and thrust something into Zakayo's hand. The Russian roared.

'Take it for luck,' Ernie said.

'But . . .'

'Give it back to me at the Ploughman's, or I'll have your nuts for a necklace.'

Zakayo waved until the truck had rolled out the gate and out of sight. Then he looked at the little half-boomerang and smiled.

CHAPTER 9

Kip could sense the magic drifting around him. It looked like a mist, but there was more to it. The fine white hairs stood up on his arm and his skin took on the texture of a plucked chicken's. His fingers were numb. There was definitely something more than mist in the silent foothills of Mt Kenya that morning.

Sitting in the deep shadows beside the Nanyuki River, Kip felt like every breath threatened to break the spell. On their brisk march out past Block's Mawingo guesthouse both boys had begun to gasp, the steam clouds of their breath igniting in the dawn light. They'd had to sit on the rocks beside the river until the blood stopped pounding in their ears. Maina's eyes shone. Kip sniffed and wiped his arm under his nose. Above them the jungle was ribboned with mist and mystery. When Maina nodded and they moved across the river, Kip felt they were entering a place of worship.

Even Maina was affected by the magic that morning, and had not yet found cause to berate Kip for any of his usual offences, like his white skin, or his noisy tramping. It crossed Kip's mind that it might have something to do with his hat. He had padded the band with wads of paper and, although it sat on his head like a pitched tent, it stayed put.

In the shaded uplands, the hunters moved forward on careful feet, Maina pausing from time to time to check the spoor and to listen, an ear cocked to one side. Kip listened too. What he had thought was silence was actually an abundance of small sounds. Insects — crickets and beetles, the *wot-wot* song of a hornbill, a soft mewing call indicative of a browsing antelope, and, faintly, the rumble of an elephant's belly coming from somewhere in the dense understorey.

Kip hefted his spear, seeking reassurance in its weight. It was a straight length of olive, shaved, then scorched to give it a hard point. It had appeared more significant in the half-light back at the Grearsons' farm. Maina's spear was similar, but had a roughly forged iron point.

A flutter of wings overhead made Kip's scalp tingle.

He had crept from his bed in darkness, and found Maina waiting near the Githinjis' *boma* as planned. The Kikuyu boy had given him a rare smile in the pre-dawn light. Kip had beamed and forgotten the fear he'd felt creeping alone to the Grearsons' farm with the dark bush and the sounds of the night surrounding him.

Magic had a chill to it. Now that the heat of their march had left him, Kip's bare feet grew numb in the soft wet soil of the slopes above the river valley. Each time Maina stopped, Kip wiggled his toes to encourage the circulation. Just when he was thinking he might dare to suggest there was nothing suitable in the big jungle to spear for a meal, Maina froze and reached behind to touch Kip in a warning. Kip's heart leaped into his mouth and he strained to see what Maina had seen, or sensed, in the jungle. A faint rustling sound came from dead ahead. Maina crept forward, Kip now very close on his heels.

A brown streak flew from cover ten paces away. Maina's spear arm flashed and there was a thud as the iron point pierced hide and flesh. A shrill scream came from the animal but Maina was upon it, his *panga* glinting. There was a sound like a knife slicing canvas as he made a quick sawing motion across the animal's neck. Blood gurgled in its throat and it kicked twice before slumping dead in a circle of delicate ferns.

Maina took a step back, staring at it for a moment, then turned to Kip with a grin and an expression of wild excitement on his face. '*Eeee-yow!*' he howled and danced around the carcass, shouting and singing something in Kigikuyu.

Kip was struck dumb. The antelope was by far the biggest and best meat they had ever killed. After the disbelief had subsided, Kip joined Maina in his little jig. They chanted and danced, circling the antelope with spears raised in triumph. After some time they fell to the ground laughing. Maina rolled from side to side in an ecstasy of joy. Finally he spun to his knees beside the animal and studied it more closely.

'It is *kipoke*,' he said, reaching a hand towards the blood to dip a finger in it. 'What is it in English?' he asked Kip.

'Duiker,' Kip replied, kneeling beside him. 'A white-bellied duiker, I think. It's an antelope — like a reedbuck.' Kip immediately regretted bringing the incident with the reedbuck back to mind. 'Or a wildebeest, or a topi.'

'Hmm,' Maina said, 'not so big like a topi.'

'No, but it's good eating.'

'The *wazungu* eat this ... this ...'

'Duiker.'

'Duiker. The *wazungu* eat this duiker?'

'Yes. Mother has it sometimes at home.'

Maina looked guardedly at his hunting companion.

'Oh, but I don't want any of this one.'

Maina's smile returned. He slapped Kip on the back. 'Good. This be my duiker. Next time we find a duiker, there will be some for you.'

Kip couldn't take any part of their catch home anyway, as it would disclose that he had been hunting — a forbidden pastime. He was just happy that his career as Maina's hunting companion had been saved in the nick of time. Maina's smile was all the reward Kip needed.

Tears rolled down Kip's cheeks. Try as he might, he couldn't stop them. But he would not beg. He was a hunter now, a big boy. Nearly eight and a half years old.

Kip often received beatings without knowing what he had done wrong. This time he knew what it was, but didn't know why it was so bad. And it must have been very bad, because both his mother *and* Aunt Kathleen were furious. His mother had screamed at him and said, 'Rupert Balmain! You are a wicked, wicked boy.' That meant he would get a thrashing, which was when he'd started to cry. Not great howling sobs, but quiet tears that rolled softly down his cheeks, like a big boy who wasn't quite old enough to not cry at all. But he would not beg for forgiveness like he usually did. He hoped he was big enough to manage that much. In the light of Aunt Kathleen's lantern, though, when he glimpsed the evil *kiboko* whip in his mother's hands, he knew it was going to be difficult. He stumbled through the darkness towards the chopping block, fighting a strong urge to hold his crotch so he wouldn't wet himself, and tried to understand the nature of his sin.

He had awoken during the night with a full bladder. On his way to the outhouse he heard a long, low moan coming from his mother's bedroom. It sounded like she had a bad stomach ache. Maybe he thought he could help in some way, because he crept to the door, which was slightly ajar. In the flicker of candlelight beneath the Virgin Mary he could see his mother lying on her back in bed, with what at first appeared to be a large mound between her legs. She was puffing like she'd run a mile. And her moaning scared him.

It was a relief when the mound turned out to be Aunt Kathleen, but his mother was furious when she saw him at her door. That was when she started screaming at him and telling him how wicked he was.

Now his mother swished the *kiboko* with menace. Kip stole a glance at Aunt Kathleen, who had often been the voice of reason during his punishments, calming his mother as she released her fury upon him. But there was no solace to be found there. Aunt Kathleen stormed through the darkness muttering angry words, and scything the night with the kerosene lantern.

Kip's pyjama legs were wet from the grass when he reached the chopping block. He looked over his shoulder at his mother, hoping for a last moment's reprieve, but found no compassion in her thin-lipped countenance. In the lantern light his aunt's face was red with anger. He kneeled and grasped the chopping block.

This was his last chance to beg for pity, but he would not. To take his mind from the temptation and to prepare for the *kiboko*, he tried Maina's trick. The Kikuyu boy had taught him how to block his mind in times of unbearable pain. Kip hadn't tried it under real circumstances and thought this was as good a time as any. Maina had told him to conjure up a special vision; something beautiful he could hold fast in his mind while the pain was on him. Kip thought about the bicycle in Patel's General Store, but it didn't seem right for this occasion, and, if the truth be known, not exactly beautiful either.

Behind him his mother was rolling up the sleeve of her dressing gown. Kip gritted his teeth. *Beautiful ... beautiful ...* He realised he didn't really have a concept of beautiful.

'Now, Rupert,' his mother said, taking a deep breath. 'This is for your sins.'

Thwack!

The first blow struck him on the seat of his pyjamas. He yelped and gripped the block tighter. The pain burned into his buttocks. New tears welled in his eyes. *Beautiful ...*

Thwack!

The second caught him a little higher — on the small of his back. He gripped the chopping block with all his might and recalled his most treasured memory.

Thwack!

At the time, he hadn't thought of it as beautiful, but he'd known he would always remember it as a perfect moment. Perhaps that was enough. He decided to give it a try.

He was alone in the glade, sitting beside the pool at the foot of the Nanyuki River waterfalls. The spray swirled up and caught in the ferns before forming small sunlit diamonds at the ends of the fronds. One by one the drops returned to the pool, forming flawless circles where they fell, completing the cycle.

Thwack!

On the other side of the pool a bongo appeared through the greenery. Being so close, it looked enormous — as big as a bull. But its eyes were large, round and soft.

The bongo shook its huge spiralling antlers. A shiver ran down its russet flanks, making its white stripes ripple. It gave a soft mewing sound, as if in acknowledgment of Kip's presence, and turned its gaze on Kip and held him with its black eyes, as placid as a kitten's. Kip couldn't decide if he wanted to leap for joy or simply weep. His animal book said these shy forest creatures were rarely seen.

Moments passed as antelope and boy maintained their unique peace. The bongo was the first to move, taking a bold step to the pool and lowering its velvet muzzle to the water. It made slurping sounds before lifting its head again and coughing. Again it looked at Kip and again gave its gentle mewing call. As silently as it had arrived, it was gone.

'Rupert!' His mother's strident voice intruded. She was standing over him, the *kiboko* at her side. 'Get up now, and go back to bed.'

Vic Grearson patted his wife on the shoulder. 'There, there,' he said between her sobs. 'There, there.'

It was all he could think to say. He could barely control his own emotions. This, the latest in a run of bad luck in a bad year, seemed the most pointless. It was hard to make any sense of it.

'It's just one thing after another,' Maude moaned. 'When will it end?'

His thoughts exactly. It had been a terrible year. There had been plenty of them during his life on the land — so many, in fact, that at times he doubted there were sufficient good years to make it balance.

Balance was a key factor in Victor Grearson's life. Balance and moderation. And fairness. Which was why he felt aggrieved that his maize, weakened by the drought, was lost to a dry storm, just two years after the Nanyuki River had swept away the crop of 1951 in a sea of red mud. The flattened maize now looked like a sheet of spiky brown parchment spread across his ninety acres.

That wind, two months ago, had brought nothing but red dust and bad luck to the Laikipia. It was the real beginning to the troubles. One of Dudley Bastard's older sons had been shot outside Nanyuki in a battle with over a hundred Mau Mau bandits, shortly after old Eric Bowker was murdered at Njoro. The old man was known to be fair to his natives, and was so confident he had nothing to fear from his servants that he didn't even own a gun. He was slashed to death in his bath. The police arrested his cook and servant the next day.

A very bad year.

And now someone had poisoned the Grearsons' two best milkers. This senseless killing of their stock emphasised the immediacy of the threat. The cows had staggered around the home paddock for two days before Vic humanely ended their agony with two bullets.

'Why?' Maude demanded, wiping the tears from her eyes. 'Why would someone poison our cows? What did they do to deserve that?' She looked up at her husband. 'For that matter, what did *we* do to deserve this, Victor?'

It was a statement more than a question, but he answered anyway. 'Nothing, Maude. Nothing at all.'

He had no doubt that the poisoner knew the farm intimately, and therefore was one of their Kikuyu. From a herd of forty milkers, the bastard had chosen the only two eight-galloners they owned. He had to face the possibility that it was a warning. But a warning for what? He had played no further part in Randall's thuggery and, as everyone knew, he treated his Kikuyu well.

Victor went to the stove and poured them both a cup of tea. He patted Maude on the shoulder and handed her the brew. 'Here, love, a cuppa will make you feel better.'

Maude had a sniff and took a sip. 'It's war, isn't it, Vic?'

'Well ... perhaps a guerrilla war.'

'You mean like in Ireland in the '20s?'

Grearson just shrugged. In the 1920s, the British had fought a few thousand Irish guerrillas with nearly a hundred thousand regulars. In Kenya Colony they had only six hundred Lancashire Fusiliers, and around two hundred of the Black Watch sent straight from Korea. Of the local forces, there were two or three regiments of the King's African Rifles. Against them stood possibly a million Kikuyu. What the Royal Marines down in Mombasa might accomplish was anyone's guess. To Grearson, the Air Force's bombing of the mountain vastness was a complete waste of time.

He didn't want to admit his fears to Maude, and searched his mind for something positive to add. As the silence between them lengthened, the pall of gloom deepened.

'They say the number of Kikuyu taking the Loyalty Oath is growing all the time,' he said to fill the void. 'And then there's the Home Guard, of course.'

His wife shook her head. 'I'm not sure if the Home Guard are helping matters at all. You certainly weren't happy with Cliff Randall's mob. The likes of them could turn the good ones bad.'

She took a sip of tea, reflecting for a moment before she raised the issue they had both been avoiding until the poisoning issue. 'What's your thoughts now about our squatters?'

She referred to the Kikuyus living on their land, who farmed a portion of it in return for their labour. Many of the Grearsons' neighbours had had workers taken away for interrogation, and many had never returned, being instead interred in one of the confinement camps.

'I've been thinking about that — particularly the house help. They say we should lock them out after dark.'

'Lock them out! Well . . . I never! What about the things that have to be done after dark? The cooking and serving. And seeing to the cleaning up?'

'And arming ourselves while we're inside.'

Maude stared at him. 'Arming ourselves? Guns? In our own home? That's ridiculous.'

'It's what old Boverie says we should do.' The District Commissioner had set up local advisory boards following the declaration of the Emergency. Grearson was on the Nanyuki board, which held regular meetings to discuss and disseminate recommendations. 'He says the domestics are the most dangerous.'

'I can't see old Karanja being a danger to anyone. He's too fat and lazy to get out of his own way at times.'

'It's what they all say.'

'Did I tell you I took him, Kariuki and Mbugwa to the pictures the other day for their annual outing?' Maude said. 'We went to see the film showing Elizabeth returning home.' She smiled, recalling it. 'They sat enthralled, mouths open, and not moving a muscle for the whole time. After the film I asked Karanja what he thought of it. He said the Princess had the finest and best-trained mules he had ever seen. He was talking about the Windsor Greys, for goodness' sake.'

Grearson smiled too, but he grew serious again. 'All the same, love, I think I should get you a handgun.'

Maude looked at him. 'Is it really that bad, Vic?'

Grearson loved his wife dearly. He would do almost anything for her, but he couldn't lie to her, even if it gave her comfort. 'I'm afraid it is, love.' He nodded his head gravely. 'I'm afraid it is.'

CHAPTER 10

The smoke stung his eyes and the stench of seared hair and hide invaded his mouth. Maina focused on the incessant, shrill chanting of the old men, no longer noticing the words — *Kill the whites. Reclaim our land* — but filling his mind with the drone of their voices, the clatter of seedpod rattles and the hissing accompaniment from those on the outside of the fires, trying to lift his mind from his body as his father had taught him.

Maina stood within the fiery circle with his six fellow initiates. He recognised Karanja — the cook from the Grearsons' house; he was trying to cover his private parts by the careful placement of his large fat hands. Like Maina, the six grown men were naked. He knew they shared his fear. All seven — a mystical number among the Kikuyu — stood in silence. Waiting. Waiting for the pain, the humiliation and, ultimately, the oath that would bind them to the Movement — the organisation that the *wazungu* called Mau Mau.

His father, now standing somewhere in the crowd beyond the flames, had shown Maina how to take his mind to another place in preparation for the pain of his circumcision. If he'd even flinched during that important event, he would have brought disgrace upon himself and his family.

Tonight, he needed the trance for his initiation, but it was not the thought of the pain that continually dragged him back to consciousness. It was the horror of the ceremony.

He had watched a man copulate with a dead goat before the beast was butchered and its sex parts and internal organs removed. The sex parts were used for disgusting acts and the blood was used to coat the initiates' faces and bodies. The seven also wore its hide, cut into a long ribbon and forming a loose garland linking them together.

The oath-giver called the seven forward. Maina tried again to escape into his spell but the words intruded.

'If you ever disagree with your nation or sell it, may you die of this oath.

'If a member of this Society ever calls on you in the night and you refuse to open your hut to him, may you die of this oath.'

A gourd filled with goat's blood was passed from one initiate to the next. Maina nearly gagged — an unforgivable crime — but he held it back and only a little blood escaped to trickle down his chest.

'If you ever sell a Kikuyu woman to a foreigner, may you die of this oath.'

Before the ceremony began, one of the old men had taken him aside and, gripping him tightly by the arm, had whispered stories of white atrocities, of how the early settlers had hunted, killed and eaten Kikuyu babies. He said the Kikuyu gods still awaited retribution.

'If you ever leave a member of this Society in trouble, may you die of this oath.'

He'd said that every member of the Movement must kill a foreigner to assuage the gods. If Maina did not do this, he and his family would die a terrible death.

'If you ever report a member of this Society to the Government, may you die of this oath.'

Maina thought that the only white he would ever have a chance to murder was the white boy who came often to his hut to play.

He wondered if the death of a single white child would be sufficient to appease the gods.

It had been many weeks since Maina and Kip had been hunting together. Kip had sensed a change in his friend, as if he'd suddenly tired of the companionship of an eight-year-old white boy and gone on to matters more appropriate to a Kikuyu on the verge of manhood.

On the few occasions Kip had found Maina at home, he'd been withdrawn and more than usually irritated by Kip's suggestions for games. And when he could be encouraged to join him in play, he was aggressive and made no allowance for Kip's smaller size and strength. Consequently, the games ended in a one-sided rout, which Kip thought Maina surely couldn't find enjoyable, and in which Kip was hurt more than once. The Kikuyu boy also laughed and made cruel references to his puny *mzungu* body. Kip was used to Maina's chiding remarks, but these days they held a savage intensity. At such times, Kip was lost. He felt he didn't know his friend at all.

So when Maina suggested another trip into the foothills, he was delighted. 'You mean near Mt Kenya? Where we got our duiker?'

'Yes, but this time we go for big meat. Not animals for children. We go for *nguruwe*.'

'Yes, let's go for *nguruwe*,' Kip replied, putting

as much enthusiasm into his voice as he could muster. He had never seen a bush pig. His animal books advised caution, but he wasn't about to jeopardise the return of their friendship because of an ill-chosen remark. Then he recalled that the Swahili name, *nguruwe*, could describe two types of animal: the bush pig, and the much larger forest hog.

'*Nguruwe ndogo?*' he asked hopefully, referring to the bush pig.

Maina shook his head, '*Nguruwe kubwa,*' he replied with a cruel grin.

At home, Kip climbed into his treehouse and referred to his animal books. *Adult forest hogs*, said one, *weigh over three hundred pounds. They can be very aggressive if provoked.* He looked at the illustration. The brute had a thin covering of coarse black bristles that ran along its spine to the ruff at its neck, where they hung like a pauper's cloak. It had shifty piggy eyes and seemed to have hunched its shoulders, reminding him of the half-man, half-beast on the poster advertising a horror film coming to the community hall in Nanyuki. The poster creature had blood dripping from its lips. The forest hog's outwardly curving tusks seemed to give the animal a nasty sneer. It wasn't hard to imagine them dripping with blood. Kip chewed on a fingernail and read on.

They wallow in mud, live in well-concealed earth hollows and feed on nearly anything including roots, fruits, insects and carrion. Kip wished he didn't know about the meat part of their diet. *A wound from the forest hog's tusk is likely to become severely infected.* He looked again at the illustration and started on another fingernail. *Forest hogs are seldom found alone, the usual family being around six to ten individuals, which may attack as a group if startled.*

Over the following days, the forest hog was never far from Kip's thoughts.

The chatter of a Sten gun jolted the silence of another hot afternoon. Kip ran towards the sound, knowing it was a Sten gun without knowing how he knew it.

Playground talk over recent weeks had been of nothing but the raging war between the Mau Mau and the white settlers. Kip had listened from the sidelines and hung on every word as the older children embellished tales they'd heard in whispers between adults. Stories of cows with their eyes gouged out and left standing blinded and bleeding in the paddock, and an account of a macabre murder of a loyalist Kikuyu, where the man had been tied to a stake out over a siafu ants' nest with honey over his testicles — the boy had called them his 'goolies' — and had eventually been eaten alive.

The Sten gunfire, now mixed with the *crack-crack* of an Enfield, grew closer. Kip knew the sound of a .303 — Mr Hook had used his Enfield to shoot a leopard that had been taking his goats. The shots came from where the leopard had been found — on the slopes leading to the snows of Mt Kenya. When Kip reached the place, puffed and sweating, he found an army lorry parked at the side of the track. The soldiers had fanned out into the bush, leaving behind the radio operator, who was too busy shouting into his mouthpiece to notice Kip climbing onto the vehicle's canvas covering.

From his vantage point, Kip heard, rather than saw, the progress of the battle. A flurry of gunfire beyond the fringe of jungle was answered by shots from higher in the densely covered hills. There would be long intervals when nothing seemed to be happening, and then the shots would again rise to a crescendo before another interlude.

After a period of extended silence, another lorry rumbled down the road and a posse of Dorobos — the fierce fighting men of the forests — tumbled out. They charged into the bush, led by a white man with stripes on his arm, to join their white comrades, but they obviously found nothing as the guns remained silent.

'Hey, you!'

The angry voice almost made Kip fall from his canvas lookout. An officer was standing below him, hands on his hips, beside a jeep.

'Get down from there!' he ordered. 'Do you want to get shot? Did you hear me? Stupid boy. Get down, I say!'

Kip scrambled down and, not waiting for further instructions, bolted towards home. Before he reached the hotel, the convoy of two trucks and a jeep roared past him. The officer glared from his jeep as they rumbled by. Kip made ready to run for cover, but the convoy continued to Nanyuki.

When Kip was at the back door of the house, a distant but heavy explosion made him rush back for a view of the mountain. A cloud of smoke rose from its slopes. As he watched, a volley of ten or twelve more explosions rolled across the plain, rattling the glass in the hotel's wooden windows.

He saw two Lancaster bombers bank for a second run over the mountain.

Another roll of explosions peppered the hills a few minutes later. The sky filled with squadrons of squawking and screeching birds. In Kip's imagination he could see a drama developing deep in the jungle at that very moment. The forest hogs were gathering in numbers, gnashing their teeth in anger at the attack on their home and plotting fearful revenge upon the first humans foolish enough to venture into their jungle.

CHAPTER 11

'You! Maina! Ssst! Come here.'

Karanja was outside the *boma*, kneeling behind a narrow bush. Maina almost laughed at the big man's futile effort to conceal himself, but the Grearsons' cook held an important position in the Movement and was not to be insulted. Maina hurried through the thorn bush and squatted on his haunches beside the older man. He greeted him in the respectful way and politely waited for Karanja to speak, as was the custom.

'You will come to the river tonight. The Movement will meet at the place where the fallen acacia makes a bridge. Bring no light, the moon will be enough.'

In answer to Maina's expression, he added, 'The Society wants more from us. They say that we have merely been playing games. They want more from me, from all of us.' He looked deeply into Maina's eyes. 'It is your time. You have been chosen to fight for the Movement.'

Vic Grearson drew his horse to a pause before spurring it towards the gate at a gallop. The black and tan markings were unmistakable, but he leaped from his horse and ran to the gatepost in the hope that he was wrong.

The body hung, nose-down, from the post. He lifted the dog's face to him and looked into Jessie's lifeless brown eyes. The strangler's rope was still around her throat. With a sob he pulled the limp body from the shaft that pinned her to the post, and laid her gently on the dry red dirt. A fat blowfly worried her sightless eyes. Grearson shooed it away.

He looked back to where his horse stood nibbling at the grass stubble at its feet. He could think of nothing in his pack to wrap the kelpie in, so he removed his shirt and used it as a shroud, carrying the old dog's body to the saddle, where he lashed it across the pommel.

Returning to the gatepost, his eyes clouded with rage. He grabbed the spike caked with Jessie's blood and gave it a mighty yank. Holding the broken Kikuyu spear in his hands, he turned his head in the direction of the homestead. Here was an indisputable second warning.

Fear closed around his throat. Maude and his boy were at home alone.

Maina stormed down the mountain road with Kip trotting behind, barely able to keep up. He dared not protest. Maina hadn't said a word since his grunt of recognition when Kip arrived at his *boma* before dawn. If Kip had been hoping for a return to the camaraderie they'd shared on their last expedition, Maina's black mood soon put an end to it. Kip began to wonder why he had been asked.

By the time they passed the Mawingo guesthouse Kip was gasping, but Maina ploughed on. It wasn't until they reached the river, still in deep shadow, that he stopped.

Kip fell to his knees among the rounded stones on the river bank and sloshed handfuls of water into his mouth. When he had satisfied his thirst he continued to splash the chill of the river over his face until his shirt was dripping wet.

Maina was staring at him when he stood. Kip expected to be teased for his excesses and waited for the snort of derision before Maina launched into his taunts. But Maina had a strange look in his eyes. He was peering at Kip, but not seeing him.

'Why are you here, *mzungu* boy?' Maina said. They were the first words he had spoken all morning.

Kip blinked at him. 'To hunt bush pig or ...' But he realised that wasn't what Maina meant. He fell silent again.

'Why are all you *wazungu* here?'

Kip took off his hat and ran a hand through his hair. He quickly replaced it, realising his blond hair increased his *mzungu*-ness. He wasn't sure why he felt guilty about being a *mzungu* and being there, but Maina made it sound like a crime. He had no answer and shifted his weight from one foot to the other. This wasn't Maina's usual form of teasing. He had no smile in his eyes. Not even a sneering one.

Maina snatched up his spear after a few moments of Kip's silence. 'Come,' he said, and was across the stream and into the forest before Kip could retrieve his own spear from the bank.

The wallows they'd seen on previous trips were in a narrow strip of marshland below the rapids. The hogs and pigs — the *kubwa* and the *ndogo* — would be there if they were anywhere. Maina's insistence on hunting the larger hogs had been for his amusement at Kip's fear — Kip understood that; it was Maina's way. What he didn't understand was why, after all that, Maina had changed direction and was heading away from the wallows. But he had little chance to ponder the matter further as Maina was charging ahead through the bush, releasing branches that thwacked Kip's face and chest in a barrage. Kip became annoyed. This wasn't stalking. Hunting required stealth and care. This was a gallop through the jungle. A waste of time. Kip wasn't having any fun at all. Even the excitement of the hunt had paled.

They climbed up a hillside broken with shale. Kip slipped and skinned his knees more than once. On the ridge, which was not much more than a ledge of about twenty yards before a rock face reared to the next level, Maina paused. He ran his eyes along the cleared ledge above, found what he was looking for, and strode off before Kip had a chance to catch his breath.

The place where they finally stopped had an opening into a shallow cave.

Kip was aching with exhaustion, but by now was so angry he jabbed his spear haft into the ground and demanded to know what the hell was going on.

He was expecting a huge argument, *wanted* an argument, but, to his surprise, Maina ignored his outburst. Instead he placed his spear carefully against the cliff face and removed his shirt and shorts. He was naked except for a short loincloth of soft hide. His chest was painted with white stripes and he ran a wet finger along one to remove enough paint to make a white line down each cheek. Then he repeated the motion, adding lines to his forehead. Finally he circled each eye with paint. He was transformed into a human owl.

Kip felt cheated. He had prepared himself for a hunt and here they were playing a completely different game.

'What are we doing here, Maina? You said we were hunting pigs! We should be down on the river flat. In the marsh. This is no place for bush pigs.'

'No.'

'Then why are we here?'

Maina's large, unblinking owl's gaze held Kip transfixed.

'Well?'

Still Maina said nothing.

'Maina? Are you all right? You look ... kinda sick.'

'You should not have come here, white boy.'

CHAPTER 12

Cliff Randall removed his glasses and placed them on yesterday's copy of the *Nanyuki Chronicle*. He rubbed his eyes hard and lifted himself from his chair with a heavy sigh.

At the edge of the veranda he leaned against a post and tried to ease the tension from his shoulders. The day was typical of the season: a brilliant sky, and air so clear he felt he could grab Mt Kenya in both hands and shake it. On the other side, to the west, stretched the Laikipia Plateau, and his land. In 1912, his grandfather had helped to herd the Maasai off the Laikipia and now his cattle dotted the yellow pastures as far as the eye could see. The Laikipia Plateau was part of the White Highlands — an area the Mother Country had declared to be for the exclusive use of Europeans. For his efforts in clearing off the Maasai, Cliff's grandfather was granted this tranche of twenty thousand acres. It had been Randall land for three generations. His own sons would inherit it some day.

Above the road to the south, a line of red dust rose, floating above the still air of the savannah like an angry god. Randall watched it approach and soon recognised his Land Rover. His sons were returning, having taken their mother down to Nyeri where she would lodge with her brother and his family until the danger eased. The youngest boy would stay with her until she calmed down. Agnes hadn't wanted to leave, particularly as their daughters had already gone to Nairobi to stay with one of their married sisters. She said she felt bad about leaving the men to fend for themselves, but Cliff had insisted. He made light of it, saying she could do with a good holiday, but he was worried that the recent atrocity was the beginning of a general uprising.

The Land Rover pulled up and the three young men climbed out and lumbered towards him.

'Your mother all right?' he asked.

They nodded.

'Bob and his family?'

'They're all good,' the eldest, Tom, said. 'Uncle Bob gave us the *East African Standard* for you. It's got more stuff in it about the Grearsons.'

Randall read the headline: 'Family Hacked to Pieces'. The subheading said: 'Mau Mau Strike Again'. He went inside and sat at the table. The boys followed him in. He began to read, then looked up at his sons. 'Have you three read this?'

'Tom has,' said Bryan.

'Well, you should all hear it. Sit down.'

They dragged the chairs out from the table and Randall began to read aloud.

'Nanyuki. Tuesday, 18 August 1953. The horribly mutilated bodies of a farmer, his wife and young son were today found in their farmhouse eight miles from Nanyuki town.

'Local police chief, Sergeant Maxwell Corning, said the deceased are Victor Michael Grearson, about forty-two years of age, his wife, Maude, of about the same age, and their nine-year-old son, John. The bodies were found around eight o'clock Sunday morning by one of the family's Kikuyu servants.

'Members of the Home Guard rounded up the Grearsons' domestic servants and *shamba* workers and handed them over to the police in Nanyuki for questioning.

'Neighbours reported that Mr Grearson had no problems with his Kikuyu staff. "He was very good to his natives," one neighbour told this reporter. "He never beat them, even when they deserved it."

'A member of the Home Guard, who would not identify himself, said the whole area was infected with Mau Mau and Mau Mau sympathisers. He promised the Home Guard would take vengeance if the government continued to do nothing.'

Randall ran his gaze around his three sons before he continued.

'This latest Mau Mau atrocity outside the Kikuyu Reserve brings to ten the number of whites killed by Mau Mau terrorists. It comes as a reminder of the murder of Mr Ian "Jock" Meiklejohn at Thompson's Falls on 22 November last year. He and his wife, a retired medical practitioner, were viciously attacked with *pangas* and left to die. Most fortunately, Dr Meiklejohn, who was well known for her kindness in treating any native man, woman or child who knocked at her door, survived.'

Randall slammed the paper onto the table. 'Doesn't this just go to prove what I've been saying? Look what happens if you trust them — any of them. If you show one sign of kindness, they'll take it for weakness — which it is — and they attack. The Grearsons were the same as the Meiklejohns — too soft for their own good. And look what it got them.'

'There's more talk in Nyeri,' Charlie said.

'What kind of talk?' Randall asked.

'About the killing. They say Vic Grearson's balls were cut off and stuffed in his mouth.'

Randall looked at his hands. They were shaking. He made them into tight fists.

'And the kid was cut open from arsehole to breakfast and ... What?' Charlie said as his older brother gave him an elbow in the ribs.

'Tom's right, Charlie,' Randall said. 'A bit of respect for the dead, son.' He frowned, then nodded for him to continue.

Charlie rubbed his side and gave his brother a glance before continuing. 'He was cut open. His heart was missing.'

Randall stood and walked to the open doorway. His sons watched him in silence, then Tom said, 'Wish I'd been on duty on Monday. Damned if those black bastards would have made it to the Nanyuki lockup.'

'We should string 'em up,' Charlie mumbled.

His father gave him a baleful look.

'String 'em up in the town,' Bryan added. 'So every Kikuyu from Nanyuki to Nairobi will know what happens to animals like that.'

Randall glared at each of them in turn. 'I've told you all before,' he said. 'There'll be nothing done that can be witnessed and reported. We'll settle with them all right. But it'll be on our terms and in our own time.'

The sound of galloping hooves shook Maina from his dreams. Within moments, screams came from surrounding huts. Then his father was at the door and someone with a very harsh *mzungu* voice ordered him out.

Maina followed his father to the door and peeped after him when he went out to speak to the *mzungu*. His mother and four younger siblings joined him.

A neighbour's hut burst into flames and the family ran screaming into the compound. A white man galloped his horse at Papa Githau, who fell to the ground. The *mzungu* reined in his horse and turned it onto the fallen man, stomping him until he scrambled to his feet. The horse reared and the white man struck Githau on the head with a sword. He fell again, and did not move.

Maina's mother screamed. It brought Maina back to the scene outside his own hut, where his father cowered under a man on a black horse who rained blows on his head and upraised arms with a solid wooden club.

His mother dashed from the hut and tried to pull his father away, but the *mzungu* turned on her and, with a mighty swipe, sent her reeling to the ground.

Now it was Maina who screamed and screamed.

His father flung himself on Maina's mother, now senseless, and tried to push the horse away, but the terrible beating continued.

Maina pushed his younger brothers and sisters into the hut and locked the door tight behind them. He ran at the black horse, now as much a villain as the mounted white man. He punched the horse's nose, and dodged around it and between its legs.

The horseman cursed and swung his club, but Maina was too nimble.

He heard the screams, but they were lost in the chaotic sounds of the night: men shouting, women crying, the occasional report of a weapon. Then he realised his father was inert on the ground beside his mother, and the terrible screams were coming from his hut. It was ablaze and his siblings were still inside. He stared, momentarily rendered immobile by the obscenity of the flames leaping from the thatched roof. He ran towards the locked door, but the rider and his club found its mark. Later, he would remember fighting to remain conscious before he fell into a black hole of nothingness.

When he awoke, he found the charred and still smoking bodies of his four siblings in the corner of what was once their home. Their mouths were locked open in an endless scream of agony.

His parents lay where they had fallen, in a blackening pool of mingled blood.

He couldn't cry. Tears would not come. Horror, rather than sadness, filled his heart. He turned towards the jagged mountain, Kere-Nyaga, and ran as hard and as fast as he could from the nightmare.

Maina ran and ran.

He ran from the sight of burning huts and of the mounted *wazungu* storming through his village, beating his neighbours. He ran from the memory of his parents cut down by savage blows, then trampled beneath the hooves of the Home Guard's rearing horses.

Sounds, terrifying sounds, hounded him into the jungle. His ears still rang from the horseman's blow, but that couldn't block the screams of his four brothers and sisters, trapped inside their burning hut.

Through this cacophony came the roar of water — of the raging river near the rapids. He ran towards it, and fell into the waters where they leaped and thundered from the lofty heights of sacred Kere-Nyaga. But even underwater the sounds endured.

He dragged himself from the Nanyuki River's icy grip, coughing and choking. The ringing in his ears became a high-pitched keening call — the sound of a fish eagle calling its mate.

When he could run no more, he gave in to the pain somewhere in the forest. He curled into a ball like a baby to await the peace that sleep would bring.

He awoke under an old army greatcoat, shivering so hard his teeth chattered. The Mau Mau's rough care had somehow saved him from a frozen death.

He gradually regained his strength, and forced memories of lost loved ones, and of a white boy who had dared to befriend him, from his mind.

But he could not forget the night of horror — a night of violent men; of terrifying flames.

And the keening cry of the eagle.

PART 2

ZAKAYO

CHAPTER 13

1962

Zakayo strolled through the market with his new baby boy cradled snugly in the crook of his arm. Stallholders saluted him from behind towers of bananas, sweet potato and maize, or from among mounds of pigeon peas, cassava and beans. Friends stopped him to admire the child, to sigh, and to spit for good luck, to enquire about Doreen and whether she had a long labour, and to promise a visit to pay their respects.

Palm fronds and flowers adorned almost every market stall and the bold red, black and yellow of the new Ugandan flag fluttered from a makeshift mast lashed to the fly-pole above the Administration's hut. The decorations were not intended to celebrate the arrival of his child, but Zakayo was pleased with the confluence of the two important occasions. Today, 9 October 1962, was both the birth of independent Uganda and of his seventh child.

The baby mewed and screwed his soft brown hands into fists that he waved ineffectually until one caught him on the nose, bringing forth a cry of indignation.

'So you are a greedy one, my friend, uh?' Zakayo whispered to him. 'Your first taste of mother's milk is gone already. I'll remember this when it's time to name you.'

He had one name in mind, but dared not voice it, even to himself. Like many in Africa, the Acholi believed it was tempting fate to name a child at birth. Better for it to survive nameless for the first weeks than to be buried with a name.

'Come then,' he said. 'I'll take you home to your mother.'

All their other children had been sent off to relatives when Doreen was in the final stages of her pregnancy, except for two-year-old Rose. When the time came, Rose got under the feet of the midwife and was unceremoniously dumped into the large woven basket they used to dry the sorghum heads. From there she watched round-eyed before falling asleep on the bed of orange and red seeds. By the time she awoke, her mother had given birth and was feeding her new brother.

The muddy red murram road from Panyiketto wound among Zakayo's neighbours' *shambas*, with occasional visits to the banks of the Ora, before it arrived at his own farm with its rows of green vegetables and the naked stands of harvested maize. The long-rains maize crop had been good to him — had been good to all of them. It had reimbursed the Panyiketto farmers handsomely after two years of poor yields. In Zakayo's case, it was one of the rare years when he had been able to pocket some cash after settling his debts.

A burst of sunshine forced its way through the lingering wet-season clouds. He made a cowl with the ends of the blanket to give his son some shade. The child was asleep. Zakayo smiled into the sheltered space, breathing in the warm smell of the baby.

Home was in sight — a piece of land given him by his father and on which Zakayo had built a large thatched hut, followed by several others as the number of his cattle and children grew. As he swung open the stock gate at the entrance to their *shamba*, he could not wipe the smile from his face. He had all a man could want: a caring wife, seven fine children, and now cash to invest in their future. October 9, 1962 was a grand day for Uganda and a grand day for the Nasonga family.

Zakayo recognised the faltering gait of the *rwot* as soon as he rounded the bend from the river. He walked down the road to greet the old chief, who had been a friend and comrade-in-arms with his grandfather when the Acholi fought the British and their allies from the south, the Baganda of Lake Victoria. Zakayo had not seen him since before the birth of his son, now six weeks old.

Despite his age, and the traditions he was duty-bound to encourage, the chief had never stood on protocol with Zakayo, treating him like a son. He seemed to enjoy their robust discourses on politics and life.

Zakayo met him smiling. 'Thomas, old friend. I thought you were dead.'

'Oh-ho! Did you now. And you might be right, but I won't lie down until I've put these useless eyes on your new child.' They embraced. 'Is it true? You have a new son?'

Zakayo took his arm and led him towards the house. 'It is true, my friend.'

'Then praise Jok,' Thomas cackled. 'Or is it the white man's god you foreigners follow?' The *rwot* loved to tease him with references to his years in Europe.

'Praise them all as far as I'm concerned, old one.' Zakayo was smiling with the chief. The chiding had started already.

'And you have named this boy of yours, I suppose?'

'I have.' He glanced at the old man before saying, 'Akello Ernest Nasonga.'

'Ah, now you have said something. Here,' Thomas indicated a log in the shade of a tree beside the road, 'let me rest before I see this Akello Ernest. I don't want to spit my dusty breath over one so young.' They sat. 'And now, tell me about those names.'

Zakayo nodded. 'I thought they would interest you.'

'First, what have you bought?' The *rwot* referred to '*akello*', meaning 'I have bought'.

'Nothing. Yet.'

The old head nodded. 'But ... ?'

'But I am looking for something in Kampala. A place where I can sell some of the surplus — mine, and that of any other Acholi who needs a fair dealer.'

'Oh-ho, a story within a story.' The best Acholi tales always contained riddles. 'But let me return to that in a moment. First let's talk about Ernest. Is this your *mzungu* side coming out after all these years?'

'Perhaps it's not only your breath that is dusty, but also your brain. Don't you recall my story about my *mzungu* friend in the German prison? The one who saved my life?'

The ancient brow furrowed. '*Mzungu* friend ... Of course, the Canadian pilot.'

'Australian. Ernie Sullivan.'

'Yes ... yes, I do remember that story. *Aiya*, this brain of mine. So that's the Ernest.'

'It is.'

The old man's eyes glistened. 'Akello Ernest Nasonga.' He nodded. 'Your father and your grandfather would be pleased with that name. It has the past in it with the name of your old friend, and the promise of the future. It is a good name, my son.' He patted Zakayo on the knee.

'Thank you, my father.'

'And now, coming back to the *akello* . . . ?'

'We are sick of the price we get from Kampala. Those Asians are squeezing us. I'm going to set up a storeroom in the city and act as broker.'

'Didn't someone try that many years ago? It was just after the governor removed price control and opened up cotton ginning to us. But it didn't work.'

'That was under the British. Now we are independent. Our government has said it will encourage African enterprises.'

'Yes, I've heard that too. This new prime minister, what's his name?'

'Milton Obote.'

'Yes, Milton Obote, he has promised much. I wonder what kind of man he is.'

'He's one of our Lango cousins, of course. Didn't you teach me the proverb: *Wat osiko*?'

The old man chuckled. 'It is good that something stuck in that wooden head of yours. Family is for ever, it's true. But Milton Obote is now chief of all Uganda. How many mouths will be whispering in his ear these days?'

'I don't know, old father, but he has promised.'

'Hmm . . . Do you also remember: *Wacho ok e timo*?'

'To say is not the same as to do — yes, I know that one too. Action speaks louder than words.'

'Exactly. The Acholi have been promised many things. Promises by the British at the making of the peace, promises by so many governors down the years. And now from this Lango, Milton Obote. We are near the end of our patience, we Acholi. Many of the *rwot* speak of secession, but it will mean another fight, so we will again wait, and wait. I hope I live to see the day when our people have full bellies and happy children in the huts.'

'As we all do. We've never had a better opportunity than now. That's why I want to organise this co-operative. Getting a fair price for our crops is a good start.'

The old head nodded, and continued to nod as the *rwot* stared into Zakayo's eyes. He seemed to have drifted off in some reverie of his own. 'You are a good man, Zakayo Nasonga,' he said after some time. 'A good man. I hope your dreams come to fruit.' Then he took a deep breath and seemed to brighten again. He patted Zakayo on the hand. 'Now, help me up. I want to see this son of yours.'

Thomas let the lumbering bullock wagon rock him into a half-sleep. Zakayo had offered to have his oldest son, Adam, drive him home. He was grateful. His visit to Zakayo had taken a toll on his strength, but he'd had to come. It was true he wanted to see the new child, but that was his excuse. He had been compelled to visit Zakayo ever since his dream.

Zakayo was more like a son than any of his own. He had promised Zakayo's grandfather, as he lay dying on the field of battle, that he would take care of the Nasonga family. He had done so in the case of Zakayo's father, who had died young in a hunting accident, and he would do so for Zakayo and all his children.

When Zakayo had left home in 1941, a boy of sixteen who had to lie about his age to be admitted into the British Army, Thomas thought he would not see him again. He was right. The Zakayo who departed never returned. Most in Panyiketto thought he had, but Thomas knew he had profoundly changed. What many could not see, but Thomas could, was that the fire in Zakayo's eyes had died. Gone was the Acholi warrior who had marched away to put the Germans in their place. The new Zakayo had no more fight in him. As a warrior himself, Thomas knew the toll that endless killing could take. It appeared that Zakayo had seen enough.

It worried the old chief, who also knew that a man had to fight to survive in this harsh land. And to succeed in his new venture, Zakayo would have many battles to wage. Thomas had seen administrations come and go. From his years of experience dealing with them, he knew the machinery of government ground slowly. He could not see the Obote government, or any other, changing the lifetime habits of the petty bureaucrats who made the system work. Zakayo was an innocent in the workings of government departments.

The Asian businessmen — Indian nationals in the main, although many carried British passports — would be his competitors. This was a problem of a different kind. They were not likely to open their doors to any competitor, particularly one of a different colour. The Asians ran Uganda's commerce. It had been so since Thomas was a young man. In the early days, the British gave the Asians a monopoly over cotton ginning and some other positions, arguing that Africans could not manage them. In 1949, rioters burned down the houses of pro-government chiefs. Eventually the British relented, and the brokering in cash crops was opened to all. But by then it was too late. The Asians held a vicelike grip on all sectors of the market, from grower to customer. In many cases, particularly in sugar cane, they also owned the farms. The *rwot* hoped the experience would not break Zakayo's heart. He was a good man and his intentions were worthy.

Thomas sighed. If he had merely gone to Zakayo to caution him about his business venture and failed to do so, he would not be so annoyed with himself. But he had gone to see him on a matter far more important, and in the end could not speak of it.

In the past he would not have been so reticent, when his reputation as a seer was matched by the courage to disclose his visions and to fearlessly act upon them. Nowadays he was more circumspect. The modern generation did not follow the old ways. People like Zakayo, who had been over the great seas, were rare in their community, but many had travelled. All had been influenced in some way by the modern world. So he had hesitated about disclosing his dream. Zakayo had been so optimistic about the new Uganda, so happy with the birth of his son, and so enthusiastic about his plans for the co-operative. Ultimately, the old man had lost his nerve.

The bullock cart jolted into a hole and stirred him from his drowsiness. The sun had broken through the clouds on its way to the west. They had passed through the town and would soon be at his hut. The boy knew where to take him, so he closed his eyes again. The day was too bright and his thoughts too morose.

He wished he had been strong out there at Zakayo's *shamba*, but it was not a day for the foretelling of doom. His dream and what it meant would have to wait for another day. Seeing Zakayo with the babe in his arms, and his wife, Doreen, smiling proudly next to him, Thomas could not say that he had seen Zakayo and his family scattered over the land — a land red with blood.

CHAPTER 14

1965

Doreen straightened up among the rows of sorghum and, placing her hands on her lower spine, painfully stretched her back. She pulled her kerchief from around her throat and wiped her neck and chest. Over the bobbing seed heads she could see her four older children scattered around the plot.

Grace was hoeing the row nearest her mother. Her buttocks were now well rounded for a girl of eighteen and her full breasts filled her cotton blouse. It would soon be time to talk marriage with the family of the young man who had been seeing her on every possible occasion. Fortunately, Grace seemed to enjoy his attentions.

Adam was loafing again. He was leaning against his hoe that was tucked under his arm. Doreen thought the posture probably required more effort than the hoeing. He was only two years younger than Grace, but at least five in maturity. He must have felt her gaze on him because he glanced up and immediately began to hack vigorously at the soil at his feet. She sighed. Zakayo hoped that Adam would soon be able to run the farm while he was in Kampala, but she doubted it. He had no interest in farming, preferring to run wild with his friends, and he had missed school on several occasions that she knew of.

Dembe was on the other side of the plot. Her father must have known her character when he named her. She was studying some small creature she had found in the furrow. A dreamy fourteen year old, she was completely at peace with the world, as her name implied.

Eleven-year-old Macmillan worked with a fury. Unlike his older brother, he was keen to be the farmer of the family. He idolised Zakayo, and hounded him for knowledge on crops and harvesting, and how best to crutch sheep, and how long a calf should be allowed to suckle at its mother's teat. Doreen had no doubt that Macmillan would one day be a very good farmer.

The younger ones, Rose, six, and four-year-old Akello, were in the care of George, a serious eight year old who, Doreen believed, would, like Macmillan, be successful at whatever he chose to do. Even today, Saturday, he had arisen before the others so he could work on his school assignment. She had no doubt he would be still working on it whenever the younger ones gave him the time. Farming was not for him, although he didn't shirk his share of the work when it was required; but a bank or an office would call him one day, and he would do well at it.

Zakayo had been gone four weeks this time. Each visit seemed to demand more and more of his time. Even when he came home, he was darting around the district, arranging future consignments or having meetings with other co-op members. It was always co-op business these days. Doreen and the children ran the *shamba*.

'Mama! Mama!' It was George, dashing through the rows of sorghum in her direction.

'What, George? What is it?'

'Mama, Rose has run away again.'

'George, stand still and tell me. You're trampling the sorghum.' It was not unusual for Rose to wander off. She had been doing so ever since she could walk. 'And why weren't you watching her? You know what she's like.' Doreen picked her way through the crop towards him.

'I *was* watching her, I promise, but she sneaked on me.'

'She sneaked. And you can't watch for *sneaked*?' She took him roughly by the arm and dragged him from the garden. 'Come now, show me where she was when last you saw her.' She had left Rose some cotton material offcuts to play dress-ups with. It usually kept her amused for hours.

'She was ... I don't know. I was just there, cutting my papers for class.' George pointed to the bare patch of ground outside the main hut, where Akello was sitting spooning water from a bowl into a growing pool of mud surrounding him. 'And she was ... she was gone.'

Doreen scanned the compound. The gate was open. She hurried to it and searched the murram road in both directions. To the west, the road ran straight for a mile and their goats had closely cropped the dry-season grass on both sides of it. There was nowhere Rose could conceal herself in that direction. To the east, the roadside was similarly bare, but the road curved behind trees about half a mile away. Rose was nowhere in sight. Doreen's heart leaped. Beyond the bend, the Ora River ran quiet and deep to the Nile.

'Grace! Adam! Come quickly. Dembe, Macmillan!'

The children stared, unable to grasp her meaning, then Grace bolted after her mother, who was already well down the road in the direction of the river. In quick succession, the others followed, uncertain why.

George watched them dash by, one after the other. He chewed on his bottom lip. Something terrible was happening — his family was in a panic and it was all his fault. He started to run after them, then looked back at Akello, who had begun to cry. George was stricken. He hopped from one foot to the other, not knowing what to do. Tears welled in his eyes as the whole family disappeared down the road.

Grace, on her long legs, passed Doreen before they had got halfway to the river. Then Adam raced by. Doreen's breath came in strangled gasps as she battled terrible mental images.

She arrived at the river bank with Macmillan. The two older ones were searching the bank and the muddy waters. Doreen followed their eyes. 'What? What do you see?' She could find no sign of Rose.

'She's not here,' said Grace. 'Maybe she went further.'

Doreen didn't think so. 'Grace, you and Macmillan go upstream.' She pointed towards the village. 'Adam, Dembe. Come with me.' She ran back along the road to the first of the narrow paths that disappeared through scrub towards the river. 'You two find the next path. Go!'

Doreen was sobbing with exhaustion as she dashed through the thick undergrowth. She could see no more than a few paces ahead of her and the clawing bush tore at her face and clothes.

Suddenly the undergrowth opened to reveal the river bank made bare by last wet-season's floods. Rose was sitting on her heels at the water's edge.

'Rose,' she gasped with relief. Her baby was safe, swathed in the cotton material of her play. She slowed to a walk, her legs heavy after the exertion.

At that instant Doreen saw the pair of nostrils and eyes approaching Rose at speed. For a moment she was fascinated by the clean lines of the bow wave, unable to believe it was a crocodile bearing down on her daughter. Then, 'Rose!' she screamed.

The child stood with fright, turning towards her mother.

The crocodile lunged.

Doreen was in the water as the crocodile snatched Rose by the leg. She grabbed the beast's head and tried to prise open its massive jaws. They were steel traps. Its tail lashing viciously, the crocodile began to drag them both towards the deep water. In an act of pure desperation, Doreen hauled back her fist and punched the brute in the eye. Abruptly, Rose was in her arms, screaming in terror. Doreen dragged her through the mud back to the bank, where she held her and rocked her and cried hysterically until Grace arrived, cool elegant Grace, and lifted her to her feet, her bleeding child still clutched to her breast in a vicelike grip.

Zakayo passed the tobacco pouch to Thomas, who teased loose a wad and tamped it into the bowl of his pipe. The old chief lit it and took a few contented puffs, before he continued their conversation. 'I went to see them on the following day. Little Rose was still shivering with fright, poor child, but the doctor had given both of them something that brings sleep.'

'Sedatives.'

'Yes, sedatives,' Thomas agreed. The two men were sitting in the thatched awning beside the *rwot*'s hut. His third wife, who was much younger than the old chief, had served tea and departed.

'By the time I got here from Kampala, the infection was better,' Zakayo said. 'Rose's leg is healing well, but Doreen's hands might never be the same. The doctor said that when she tried to open the crocodile's jaws, the teeth cut something in her fingers. We won't know how bad it is until the wounds properly heal.'

'That is not good. But they survived by Jok's love. Not many have returned from the river when the crocodile pays a visit.' Thomas blew a satisfying puff of smoke into the breeze. 'Does this mean we will see you around Panyiketto for a time?'

'No, I can't. When I got the telegram I had to rush away and leave my application in the government office.'

'Application?'

'For an export licence. I believe we can get better prices in Kisumu.'

'Kisumu? So far. How will you manage it?'

'It's not so bad. We put the goods on a truck to Port Bell, about a half-hour from Kampala, and the Lake Victoria Line takes it to Kenya.'

'And you need an application for that?' The old man shook his head.

'There's paper for everything. And if you are not there, checking, checking, it never gets done. Even tea money doesn't help these days. The Baganda are still angry about losing their king.'

'Ah, the *kabaka*, our ex-president.'

'Yes. So every Bagandan clerk in Kampala is making life difficult for us. Especially if you are one of what they call Obote's lot.'

'So we Acholi are one of President Obote's tribe these days, ah?'

'Acholi, Lango. Near enough for them.'

'And what else is happening in the big city?'

'The army colonel that Obote appointed, Idi Amin, is in the news again.'

'What now?'

'He marched into Barclays Bank with a Congolese gold bar in his bag. Demanded it be cashed on the spot.'

'I don't understand this one. A bar of gold, from the Congo?'

'The rumour has it that he got it from Patrice Lumumba for some arms delivery.'

'Is he stupid?'

'Stupid. Mad. Who knows? But he has too much power. Obote has let the army get out of hand ever since the mutiny of '64.'

'But didn't you tell me last time that he was loading the ranks with Acholi and Lango soldiers?'

'He has. Why he chose Amin, an ignorant Kakwa, nobody knows.'

'*Aiya*. It's too much for this old head. Politics, the army, gold bars. Let's talk of better things. How is the family?'

'The family?' Zakayo reached for his papers and tobacco to roll another cigarette. 'That Adam,' he sighed. 'Doreen says he skips school. Thank God for young Macmillan — he does twice the work Adam does. And with a ready smile. There's a farmer in that one.'

'And Grace?'

'Grace has her eye on a boy in Panyiketto. Doreen has arranged a meeting between the families.'

'So I've heard. A young Luo fellow. The family are from Kisumu.'

Zakayo, nodding, knew where his friend's line of thought was heading. 'I know. She may move away after she marries.' He had not allowed himself to consider that possibility until that very moment. He felt heavy at heart.

'They all eventually fly the nest, my boy. You have to be prepared.'

Zakayo nodded again. It seemed only yesterday that Grace, their first, was suckling at her mother's breast.

'And Dembe grows every day,' the old chief said. 'Another fine young woman you have there.'

At this Zakayo smiled. 'And a blessing for her mother. Doesn't seem interested in the things in the town.' He shrugged. 'But that will probably change.'

'I hear young Macmillan is a champion student.'

Zakayo realised his old friend was trying to prevent him from dwelling upon Grace's imminent departure. But the mood brought his thoughts back to his oldest boy. 'He mixes with some bad types from somewhere up the Nile, you know.'

'Macmillan?'

'No, I'm back on Adam again. He worries me.'

The *rwot* nodded. 'I've seen them. They come down from Pakwach on fast motor boats. Go downriver into the forests, so I've heard.'

Zakayo raised his eyebrows. 'Poachers?'

'I am not sure. He's a good boy, your Adam, but it would be wise for you to watch him.'

Zakayo knew his oldest son needed closer discipline. Doreen had been telling him as much for months, but he had no idea it had got to this stage. 'It is difficult for Doreen. The boy takes no responsibility in the *shamba*. Has no time for his family.'

'He needs you, my friend.'

Zakayo looked into his eyes. He knew Thomas was right, but with the co-op at a tentative stage, he needed to be in Kampala. He said nothing.

CHAPTER 15

1971

'What does it mean, Zakayo?' Doreen said in a whisper. 'Will the trouble spread to Panyiketto?'

'No, of course not, Doreen. It's far away in Kampala. Not even Kampala. It happened down in Mbarara. At the army barracks there.' He was regretting telling his wife the news. He didn't think she would be so worried by it.

'But they were Acholi soldiers, you said.'

'Yes, Acholi and Lango.' It still shocked him. It shocked every civilised person in Uganda. But not one would dare accuse Colonel Idi Amin, or his fellow Kakwa tribesmen, of the slaughter of scores of their own.

'But why only Acholi and Lango?'

'Amin is afraid of them. Obote recruited them after the attempt on his life. Amin doesn't trust them.'

'Why? Are they not Ugandan soldiers too?'

'Of course they are, Doreen, but —'

'And I hear that people just disappear. How can that happen in our country, Zakayo?'

'Doreen ...' he began, but her questions were unsettling him. Some things were better left unsaid.

'I'm frightened,' Doreen whispered.

Zakayo was also afraid. The attack on their

fellow Acholi tribesmen had sent a rush of alarm through the north. In Panyiketto, as in all other Acholi and Lango villages, the air was electric with fear.

But Zakayo's fear came from a different place. It came screaming from the battlefields of Europe, where his young mind had been nearly broken by the terror and barbarism of war — a war made more horrible by the fact that it was conducted between what he had been taught to believe were the most civilised nations on earth. These civilised white men used diabolical machines to kill with brutal efficiency. There was no passion in their conduct — not like his people's tribal wars of long ago, when men fought and died for the land needed to feed their children. The white man's war was fought over vague notions, over politics and imaginary lines on a map. But the dismemberment, the maiming, the eyeless torn faces, the gangrenous open wounds, were starkly real. So too were the bodies stacked in a trench on a bloody, muddy field. He had never recovered from the gut-wrenching terror that his sixteen-year-old life would come to a violent end so far from his peaceful land. Ever since then, the sight of an army uniform so intimidated him, he became almost dysfunctional.

'What is it, Rose?' Zakayo asked his daughter, who had come into the space they used for a sitting room. He hadn't realised she was in her bedroom behind the curtain. Again he was taken by how she had changed since his last visit home, three months ago. She had grown, with legs like a young gazelle and two small breasts that could not be hidden under a school blouse.

'Why is this happening, Papa?'

Zakayo took a deep breath. Even if he knew the answer, how could he explain the complexities of power politics to a girl of eleven. Or was it twelve? It was like Germany and the Second World War — everyone wanted a simple answer but there was none available. He could share some of his theories with her. Firstly, that the British plan for a democratic Uganda was flawed at the outset because the Baganda people were given a privileged position by Britain, one to which the other districts strongly objected. And how Obote, although clearly a winner at the elections, by 1966 could not accept his impending impeachment, and used the army, and Idi Amin, to retain control. An attempted assassination two years ago had hardened Obote's resolve and he had again added to the powers of the military. How could Rose, a child living far away within this rural backwater, understand all this, when the population of Kampala, who saw things first-hand, could not?

He called his daughter to him and, taking her hand, said, 'There's no need to worry, Rose. These things only happen in the big towns and cities. There are no army people in Panyiketto. Why would they bother with us?'

'Papa, can you come home and live with us again?'

Zakayo looked at Doreen, but she dropped her eyes to the floor. 'But I do live here. When I can. You know I have the business to run in Kampala. Everybody in Panyiketto needs me there to sell their crops.'

'Yes, but ...'

'But what? Look, I am here until after Christmas. Now, don't argue with your father. Run outside — I need to speak with your mother.'

Rose dropped her head and stole a glance at him from under her furrowed brow. It was a pose that normally never failed to sway him, but Zakayo frowned and pointed. She scuffed her feet to the door.

'You should have supported me there, Doreen,' he said after Rose had gone.

'How can I support you when you well know I have the same question in my mind?'

'Don't be so childish, woman.'

'Childish, is it? That I want my husband home with his family more than two or three times a year.'

'You exaggerate.'

'No. I do not exaggerate. Is it exaggerating when I tell you that Adam is a wild thing, and Rose is unhappy at school, and Akello is a poor student. And ...' She stopped herself as the tears began to fall down her cheeks. 'Zakayo, we need you here too.'

Zakayo stood and went to where his wife had hidden her face in her hands. 'Doreen, my love, I miss you, and the children. Of course I do. But it's three days' journey from Kampala, if I'm lucky. By the time I get here, it is time to return.'

'Then take us to Kampala with you.'

'What about the *shamba*? Who will look after the stock? The gardens?'

'Then let us come for a short while. Just me and the young ones next term break.'

'Doreen, didn't I just tell you how it is in Kampala these days? There's so much violence. Nobody is safe.'

'Then come home ... please.' She looked into his eyes and he could see the girl she once was; her eyes had the same wistful pleading that she used when they were young and she wanted to get her way. He almost forgot all that Kampala demanded of him and agreed. But he couldn't. He had made a web for himself. He was caught between two lives.

'Soon,' he said, but he could see that Doreen knew he was lying.

Zakayo climbed down from the Gulu–Kampala bus in the pre-dawn light and stretched his aching body. The so-called express service, scheduled to take eighteen hours, had taken a day and a half. The usual mechanical problems had caused most of the delay, but there were also the occasions when the driver simply went missing for an hour or two, to have a meal, a beer, or a nap — nobody knew. Most likely it was to visit one of his 'wives'. Even married long-distance drivers had girlfriends in towns along their route.

The first part of the journey from Pakwach had been no better, causing him to miss his connection to Kampala and forcing an overnight stay in Gulu. Overall, he had been on the road for four days — two days longer than planned.

The turn-boy was on top of the bus, hurling passengers' baggage to the street. Zakayo managed to catch his single piece then fought his way through the mêlée to the pavement. The bus station was usually pulsating with activity at any hour, but tonight there was only one other bus in the terminal. It looked like it had broken down earlier in the night and had been abandoned until dawn.

He stepped over the concrete ridges between terminal bays and looked across Kiwanuka Street to where three floodlights threw a golden glow over the mist that shrouded the vacant taxi parking area. A lone figure stood bathed in the misty light, patiently waiting for one of the few taxis prepared to work the dead-man's shift.

Zakayo sighed. The drivers could demand outrageous fares before the cross-city buses started to run, but he was tired and anxious to get home. He jiggled the carry strap into a more comfortable position and started towards the taxi stand, hoping that the man ahead of him might be prepared to share the ride.

As he drew nearer, it surprised him that the person at the rank was a woman. She was unusually petite, seeming almost fragile as she huddled under the shelter, hidden from the glare of the floodlights. She watched him approach, then stepped into the harsh golden light.

His heart thumped in his chest.

'Amelia?'

'Yes.'

She was in his arms. He held her to him, feeling her small body fill him with warmth.

'My love,' he stammered. 'What are you doing here?'

'I missed you.'

'But ... at this time of night!'

'It is nearly morning.'

He held her chin gently between thumb and forefinger. At twenty-six, she had the sophisticated beauty of a young city woman, but in her heart was the shyness and the childlike innocence of the Banyoro village girl. It was this part of her nature that, three years ago when she appeared in his office, had first attracted him.

'Come, it is a good time to walk,' he said, suddenly remembering her inviting body, always ready for him when he arrived home in Kampala. 'And the taxis ...' He swallowed, his mouth now dry.

They walked in silence along Kampala Road, where a nightwatchman on a squeaky bicycle wobbled towards them through the golden circle of a single street lamp. He turned down a side street a hundred yards before reaching them.

The sun was rising behind one of Kampala's seven hills, its thin light giving form to the blanket of humidity. Zakayo ran his eyes along the sweep of stores and office buildings on this, the city's main thoroughfare. Only Amelia made Kampala seem like home. The city was like a defiled princess, the few proud remnants of her colonial days now overshadowed by the developments of the post-independence rush to riches.

Zakayo adjusted the bag on his shoulder. A rumble came from behind them. He thought it strange that a train would arrive at that time of day, but he said nothing to Amelia, preferring the silence and the serenity of the view down Kampala Road towards the station.

Nana's restaurant was still battened down tight against the night. Zakayo and Amelia occasionally dined at Nana's, and they paused to study the menu framed behind the steel grille.

The rumbling sound came again, this time accompanied by a metallic rattle. It grew louder until the street was filled with an unremitting clatter.

A tank emerged from Entebbe Road and made a series of lurching shifts towards them. In the shadow of the awning, Zakayo drew Amelia in behind him and pressed back against the shop's metal grille. The tank jerked again and straightened, before rumbling left up Parliament Avenue.

Zakayo watched until it stopped, almost at the corner of Said Barre, where it made a rickety ninety-degree turn on its iron tracks and raised its cannon to the parliament building.

It had begun. War was upon them.

Zakayo felt the icy grip of foreboding close around his heart. It was more than his fear of conflict. He knew, by some form of instinct, that this war between fellow Ugandans, between the tribes, between cousins, would be truly horrifying.

CHAPTER 16

1973

Panyiketto never changes, Zakayo thought as his bus lumbered through the potholes on the outskirts of the village: goats on the road, a few dusty children bowling bald tyres along the paths, chickens scratching in the dirt. It was always the same.

He felt an affinity with Panyiketto because his children were there. Well, five of them were — Grace was in Kisumu with a child of her own now, and Adam was God knows where. Zakayo was home because his second-eldest daughter, Dembe, was to be married. And about time too. She was not an unattractive girl, but had always been content to stay around the farm. The boy she was to marry was a relation of some family friends, so Doreen was pleased that Dembe would stay in Panyiketto after the wedding, due in three weeks.

As simple as Panyiketto remained, Kampala had changed.

When he first went to Kampala, he was delighted by its easygoing society. There were many diversions and many women who seemed to enjoy the escape from the confines of their traditional village life that the city offered.

Amelia was different, and he became very fond of her quiet ways. When she fell pregnant, he made a commitment to help her raise the child.

As time went on, his life in Kampala with Amelia became more relevant to him than the narrow life that he left behind in Panyiketto. Back there, his children had grown and were finding lives of their own, and Doreen had become increasingly distant, whether by her own inclination or in response to his own sense of alienation, he was never sure.

Life in Kampala was no longer carefree, however. There were many changes; nobody was sure what was going to happen next.

President Amin had recently signed an expulsion order for large sections of the Asian community. Zakayo had dealt with many Asians in attempting to secure his co-op business, and found them difficult; without exception, they were tough negotiators. It was true that many were also quite reasonable and honest people, but in common with most of his black countrymen, Zakayo felt no pity for their plight. Like him, most Ugandans believed they had been exploited by the Asians all their lives, and no one was particularly concerned to see them go.

The exodus of the Asians meant he had to quickly establish new contacts for his business. The company he used to transport his goods, his bank manager, his landlord and many of his customers had changed almost overnight.

Zakayo had already been absent from Panyiketto for many weeks, but had to remain in Kampala until the boy was named. In Amelia's Banyoro tradition, it was Zakayo's responsibilty to hear the suggestions of her extended family and, after no less than three months, make his decision. The Banyoro named their children after the major anxiety affecting them at the time of the birth. This meant Zakayo had the depressing choice between names dealing with death, sorrow or poverty — the three main fears in Banyoro life. He chose Itema, being the best of a bad lot. It was Amelia's request. 'Itema' meant distrust between neighbours.

He was quite proud that he could be so pragmatic about the naming. Most African men would insist upon following their own traditions in the important matter of children. He imagined it was because he had now been part of three cultural groups. He sometimes wondered how people like Ernie Sullivan would view his behaviour. What would he make of his double life? He shrugged. This was Africa, and a man had his needs.

The bus jerked to a halt opposite the dirt road leading to the village. Zakayo caught his bag thrown to him by the turn-boy and waited for the bus to move on before crossing the road through a cloud of dust and diesel fumes.

Ahead, a crowd had gathered at one of the small shops on the main road. There were raised voices and people were throwing jibes at someone in the shop. As Zakayo approached, he saw old Thomas standing in the doorway. It was Patel's haberdashery, with Patel himself standing erect behind the old *rwot*, staring defiantly at the crowd.

Zakayo eased through them to the front. 'I see you, old Father,' he said.

'Zakayo! Welcome,' the chief answered, taking his hand and shaking it enthusiastically, before returning to the confrontation.

The exchange was quite heated, and Zakayo looked from Thomas to Patel to get an explanation. Patel was grim-faced. Zakayo noticed he held a short length of timber, which he slapped threateningly into the palm of his hand.

'What's going on, Thomas?'

'Ah! These stupid people. Wait.' He turned to Patel. 'Patel, go into your shop. Shut the door.' Patel hesitated. 'Go on, man. You're only making it worse.'

The door closed and there were loud jeers from the crowd.

'Go on! Home with you. All of you.' The old man's voice broke into a screech, but the crowd had lost their bait. A few made some parting insults directed at Patel, then they all drifted away.

Thomas took a corner of his headscarf and wiped his brow. '*Aiya*, these people ...'

'What is happening here, Thomas?' Zakayo asked.

'Oh, my boy ... what is happening in this country these days? Come.' He led Zakayo to the tree in the centre of the road that served as a meeting place for the village. He sank to the bench and patted the place beside him. 'Let us sit here, my friend.'

Zakayo waited while the old man caught his breath.

'This Idi Amin Dada,' he began. 'This Kakwa lunatic —'

'*Shhh*, old one,' Zakayo said. Language like that was never spoken in Kampala. He glanced nervously around them. 'You are never safe to speak like that. What if the soldiers were here?'

'The soldiers *are* here, my boy,' the *rwot* said. 'That's the whole problem. They've been here to Patel's and ordered him out of this business. Patel! He's a Ugandan. Been here all his life, and his father before him.'

'The soldiers are here? In Panyiketto?'

'Yes. Yesterday they came. With their big lorries and fancy uniforms.'

'In Panyiketto?' Zakayo could not believe it. As he was leaving Kampala, there was chaos at the bus terminal as thousands of Asians fought to catch transport to the airport, to Kenya — anywhere out of Uganda. But why would Kampala want to interfere with this sleepy town so far from the centre of things? Surely Amin had enough on his hands with Milton Obote's attempt to force his way back into the country from Tanzania? 'How many lorries, Thomas?'

'Ten, maybe fifteen. Only two stayed, the rest continued north.'

As if summoned by the *rwot*'s words, an army truck, with about a dozen uniformed men, in the back lumbered down the main road. The khaki-painted truck looked like World War II vintage. It came to a shuddering stop outside Patel's shop. The soldiers leaped from the truck and stormed the door. Without hesitation, they kicked it open. Moments later, two soldiers dragged Patel out. His wife and three children followed in tears.

Thomas leaped to his feet before Zakayo could restrain him. 'Oh-ho! You men! What do you think you're doing, ah?'

The uniformed men ignored him and roughly pushed Patel and his family onto the truck. A sergeant strolled up to Thomas, giving Zakayo a withering look before addressing the chief. 'What business is this of yours, old man?'

'What business?' Thomas spluttered. 'I am the chief of this village. That's what business it is.'

'This is a military matter, old man. Be gone.' He turned his back on Thomas to see to matters in the army truck.

Zakayo took the *rwot* by the arm to lead him away, but Thomas shrugged him off, rounding on the sergeant. 'I demand you release that family,' he said, dragging the sergeant by the arm to show he should not treat an elected chief with such rudeness.

The sergeant smashed the back of his hand into Thomas's nose and the old man fell against Zakayo, now frozen in fear.

The soldiers seized the chief and threw him onto the truck.

The sergeant stared at Zakayo, waiting, perhaps hoping, for a response. Zakayo backed away. The army man smirked and barked his orders.

A pair of shoes — Thomas's old, brown half-sandals — was thrown to the roadside before the truck moved off. It rumbled down the main street. Patel was standing in the truck between his guards, eyeing the crowd, some of whom jeered him as he passed. Zakayo could not see Thomas.

He stared at the shoes. The symbolism was well known in Kampala. It began with the disappearance of High Court Judge Ben Kiwanuka. Before being bundled into the boot of a car, the judge was forced to remove his shoes, which were left on the street outside his office. He was never seen alive again, and an abandoned pair of shoes beside the road had become a bizarre yet effective form of state terrorism.

The army truck dissolved into a cloud of dust.

Zakayo picked up the shoes and turned for home.

The road from Panyiketto to his house seemed further that day. Thomas's shoes weighed heavily in the crook of his arm. Suddenly Panyiketto was no different from Kampala, or any other place in Uganda for all he knew.

He couldn't understand why the soldiers would descend on Panyiketto as they had. Unless it was Amin's plan to punish the Acholi and Lango troops for supporting Obote's disastrous foray from Tanzania.

In Kampala, the violence was everywhere, but never personal. The atrocities could be discussed discreetly over tea. In Panyiketto — his home — everything was personal. Even Patel's eviction was an obscenity. He couldn't bear to think of Thomas.

He was approaching the last bend where the road touched the Ora before straightening towards his *shamba*. He would have to explain to Doreen again why it had been so long since his last visit. In truth, he may not have come even now except for his daughter's marriage. He had responsibilities in Kampala. There was Amelia and the baby to protect.

Eighteen-year-old Macmillan was more than capable of running the *shamba* in his absence. Even with George down in Pakwach, studying accountancy, Macmillan could manage with the help of Rose and Akello. Rose was — he had to think about it — Rose was now thirteen. Akello, eleven. They were old enough to do a reasonable day's work. Macmillan only needed help at harvest time, when he might hire a few from the village to assist.

On his left, the Ora ran swift and deep towards the Nile. The *shamba* and the house came into view. He looked at his watch — it was just after two o'clock. Strange that Macmillan was not working the crops or tending the stock.

When he opened the gate he sensed something was wrong. He couldn't quite place it, but he braced himself for bad news. Halfway to the door he heard the sobbing.

It took him a moment to adjust his eyes to the darkened room. Macmillan was standing; dried blood coated his hair and the shoulder of his shirt. Akello was squatting in a corner, hugging his knees. Doreen's headscarf was undone and her hair was wild about her face. She nursed Dembe in her lap as she would a baby. Rose dabbed her sister's face with a wet cloth.

Dembe's clothes were torn; her eye was swollen closed. She had cuts to her shoulders and face.

Rose looked up at him, tears streaming down her cheeks. 'Papa,' she said through her sobs. 'The soldiers came.'

CHAPTER 17

Zakayo was again trudging down the road towards Panyiketto. It seemed as if he'd done nothing else since arriving home four days ago. All the journeys were difficult, but this one was dangerous.

The first journey had been to find the doctor for Dembe. He hadn't wanted to make that trip. He'd wanted to tear his house apart in his rage, to smash and destroy everything within his reach. He wanted to scream against the injustice. He wanted to demand the army find the men who had raped his daughter and have them severely punished. He wanted to be the firing squad. Most of all, he wanted his daughter as she had been, an hour before he arrived home. Just an hour.

But he should have been home weeks ago. If he had been, he might have averted the disaster. Instead, he choked on the bitter taste of powerlessness.

It was Doreen who made him shake himself out of his black mood to go for the doctor. But the doctor was not home, and he'd searched Panyiketto for him.

When he finally found him, the doctor was attending a man who'd had both legs broken by rifle butts. The doctor told Zakayo he had too many serious patients to see, and what was wrong with his daughter that was so urgent. Zakayo tried to put words to his daughter's physical injuries, but they were nothing in comparison to the pain he could see in her eyes. The doctor listened patiently as Zakayo made a stumbling attempt to describe this to the doctor, but the words would not come. In desperation he said, 'She's been raped by the soldiers.' And he wept again at the crime of it.

The doctor was sympathetic, but couldn't spare the time. He sent him away with sedatives.

Dembe had said nothing of her fiancé. Zakayo thought she probably realised what he already knew — there would be no marriage. That became clear on another of his journeys, this time to her fiancé's village. He'd hoped the boy would want to hurry to comfort Dembe, but that was not the case. His family was shocked and, like the doctor, sympathetic, but they felt it was better for Dembe to be alone for a time. They said they would visit when she was rested, but they could not meet Zakayo's eyes.

On this, his latest journey, he was again on his way to see if Thomas had returned from wherever the soldiers had taken him. There was no sign of Thomas's wife, who had obviously fled to one of the children's houses. The neighbours' house was at some distance and they had seen nothing.

The township was strangely quiet. The reason was apparent when he saw an army truck parked outside Patel's shop.

Zakayo crossed the road and watched from a distance. The soldiers laughed as they emptied Patel's stock into the truck. Bolts of cloth, even display cabinets, tables and furniture items, were loaded under the canvas tarpaulin. He watched until they had finished and driven out of sight.

Zakayo hurried on to the chief's house, but he knew as soon as he saw it that Thomas was not there.

He called a greeting before pushing the open door ajar. The room had not been touched. Thomas's shoes were where he had put them on his first visit. They looked out of place in the middle of the bare floor.

Zakayo was stricken. He had promised himself he would do something about Thomas if he were not at home this time. The twin tragedies of Dembe's rape and Thomas's abduction were somehow linked. Resolving one, he felt, would mitigate the circumstances of the other. He had already done all he could for Dembe, which was little more than showing support and sympathy for his daughter, so negotiating Thomas's release was his best chance for peace of mind.

He already felt bad about waiting so long, but the soldiers were Kakwa, the traditional enemy. More than that, they were the military.

The war had left him physically unharmed, but there were nights when he would awaken in the cold sweat of fear as something, some half-forgotten scene from the hell of battle, invaded his mind. He would often have to dash to the latrine as his bowel and stomach voided.

He couldn't remember having such intense feelings when it was all happening. Perhaps it was a trick of the mind to disable emotions during times of unimaginable horror.

At home again in Uganda, he had decided to have nothing more to do with the military. Peace was what mattered. It was his hope that after the war there would be peace for his country, for his village, and for his family. One by one his hopes had fallen — casualties of war.

He grabbed the shoes and retraced his path to Patel's, then turned into the side road in the direction that the army truck had taken.

As he'd expected, the soldiers had made camp beside the river. A truck came rumbling towards him. Another followed. Zakayo dived into the bush at the edge of the road. As they passed he heard the soldiers' voices from the canvassed enclosure. They were joking together, as soldiers do.

The camp was in a clearing where a number of tents made an irregular circle around a large tree. He could see no sign of life. The silence sent a chill up his spine. Somehow he felt it would be easier if the camp was active, with soldiers going about their duties, too busy to care about one of the villagers coming to visit their commander.

He headed towards the clearing, but lost his nerve, deciding to take an indirect route along the river to take advantage of the cover provided by the bushes on its banks.

Zakayo could hear his own breathing above the soft buzz of crickets. He moved cautiously along the bank, keeping an eye on what he thought might be the officers' quarters — a larger tent with a Ugandan flag hanging limply from a rough flagpole.

He was now uncertain about his strategy. What if the commander emerged to find a man creeping along the boundary of his unguarded camp? What would he do? Zakayo could see into some of the tents. Beyond the big tree only the officer's tent with the flagpole had its flap closed.

Now that he had moved some way to the edge of the circle of tents, he realised there was a man tied to the tree. He was slumped against his bonds, his head drooping sideways and down.

Zakayo was drawn towards the tree, knowing the bedraggled figure was Thomas, but hoping he was mistaken. He lifted the old head but the face was unrecognisable, beaten so badly his eyes were swollen shut. Dried blood made a line from his lips to his bare chest, and there were signs he had bled from his ears. Only the slight wheezing breath gave the sign that he still clung to a thread of life.

Zakayo opened his mouth to speak, but the words wouldn't come. 'Thomas ...?' he said at last, with a voice too dry to be heard. 'Thomas,' he repeated.

The old man's head jerked slightly, but it was a reflex motion from within his unconsciousness. Zakayo lowered his head to rest again.

'You!' A man was at the flagpole, pointing an accusing finger at him.

Zakayo froze, staring at the man who was dressed only in his underwear.

'Who are you?' The soldier's voice was heavy with threat. 'Stay where you are,' he ordered, and dived back into his tent.

For a moment Zakayo did as he was told; years in prison camp had conditioned him to obey authority without equivocation. The tent flap flew open and the officer re-emerged carrying a rifle.

Zakayo bolted for the river.

The .303s pinged past his ears. He dodged and weaved as the river drew nearer. Fifty yards. Forty. He felt a blow to his shoulder, which spun him sideways. He got tangled up in his own legs and crashed to the dirt, rolling and scrambling to regain his feet. He caught sight of the officer who was gaining ground and reloading. He cradled his arm as best he could and ran on, the burning pain in his shoulder making it difficult to continue his evasion.

Another bullet struck him, this time in his side, but it was a grazing blow and he ran on. Twenty yards. Weaving again, he was becoming exhausted. Ten yards. Another bullet missed his ear by inches.

He reached the bank and dived as far as he could into the river. His lungs were burning, but he stayed beneath the muddy waters of the Ora until he thought he would burst. He came up with a whoosh, gasping for air.

The soldier had given up the chase, content to let the crocodiles find his blood scent and finish the job.

Doreen's demeanour had changed little since the soldiers had invaded their home. She bathed Zakayo's wound in silence, responding only briefly to his attempts at conversation. When he said he had to return again to Panyiketto, she brooded.

It had been two days since his escape in the river; eight since Dembe's attackers had destroyed his daughter's prospects for a happy married life.

He thought it a wonder that the family had not suffered more damage. Luckily, Rose and Akello were at the far edge of the farm and had hidden in the sorghum until the soldiers had gone.

Doreen went about her work as usual, organising the children in their tasks in the hut and around the farm, but she had lost the smile behind her eyes. When the children indulged in their usual playful banter, she snapped at them to have respect for Dembe. If a fleeting moment of happiness arose unbidden between them, Zakayo watched her battle her guilt at the brief lapse in her mourning, as if it were a sin to smile.

Zakayo's shoulder had not broken when the bullet passed through it, but something had been damaged deep in the tissues because the slightest touch released a bolt of pain. The wound itself was clean, thanks to the Ora's rushing waters and Doreen's attention. The gash on his side was only troublesome when he tried to lie on it in bed.

'Why must you go back into Panyiketto?' Doreen said after a long silence.

'Doreen, I must. I can't sleep not knowing about Thomas.'

'But you can do nothing for him. You tried, and they almost killed you.'

He couldn't argue. From what he had seen and read in Kampala, it seemed nothing the new regime did could prompt an outburst of public outrage. Amin's State Research Unit spread fear and insecurity across the city. Scores mysteriously went missing daily. People learned from radio broadcasts that they were about to disappear. Here in Panyiketto — an Acholi outpost too far north for anyone to care — the army had even less regard for discretion.

'I will go anyway. I must know.'

She said no more, which in itself told of her altered state of mind. Normally she would not have conceded so easily.

Zakayo started out with determination, but at the outskirts of Panyiketto he hesitated. The village was unusually busy for that time of day. An army truck was parked in the centre and it brought the hollowness of fear to his gut. But the crowd gave him reassurance, convincing him it was safe to continue.

It wasn't until he noticed the soldiers mingling among the crowd and questioning people that he realised his folly, but by then it was too late to change his mind: a soldier was eyeing him as he approached.

Zakayo avoided eye contact, but the soldier, a man shorter than himself but with the cocky air of the oppressor, stepped into his path. He tried to appear calm, casually gazing around him as the army man sized him up from all sides.

Ahead were another pair, soldier and local, engaged in a similar situation. Without warning, the soldier punched the local in the right shoulder. The realisation came to Zakayo the instant before his own interrogator struck. The blow to his shoulder was not powerful but the pain exploded in his brain. The soldier stood under his nose, observing his reaction. The pain burned like a red-hot poker, but Zakayo remained rigid. He moved his head away as if to observe others around him, blinked away the tears that welled in his eyes, and returned his gaze to the soldier.

The army man looked disappointed. He sneered, and grunted his dismissal. Zakayo moved on, trying not to favour the shoulder that tortured him with each movement.

Now he wanted simply to find a way to get out of the village. The wound on his shoulder was bound to start bleeding, and the confrontation with the soldier had robbed him of his courage. He pressed through the crowd assembled around the gathering tree.

The crowd's silence curbed his urge for immediate escape. He tried to find an explanation in their faces and finally followed their eyes to the middle of the encirclement where, after pressing on a little further, he saw a naked, headless body in the dirt. It was Thomas. The head, lying a few feet away, was battered beyond recognition, but the grey hair and beard could belong to no one else.

Zakayo almost gagged. His hands flew to his mouth to stay it, and the stab of pain brought forth a sharp cry. Blood seeped through his shirt.

Silent faces in the crowd, some of them familiar, turned towards him, but there was no acknowledgment. Nothing passed between him and them except fear; they did not want to know this man. Those nearest him shuffled away, as if by proximity they could be implicated in whatever he had done.

He put his hand over the blood patch and crept away as fast as he dared without drawing further attention to himself. Free from the press of bodies, he made his way towards the other end of the village. Behind Patel's haberdashery, he vomited.

PART 3

DIANA

CHAPTER 18

1964

'Get on up to Milimani Road, young fella,' the chief game warden said, tossing Kip the keys to the Land Rover. 'Someone's spotted a lion near the T-junction.'

Kip caught the keys, but stood staring at his boss.

Willie Hale frowned at him. 'Look, son, this kind of thing happens. You'll have to tackle them on your own sooner or later. You're a game warden now.'

'I understand that, Willie, but ... where's Milimani Road?'

'Oh, for God's sake! It's off Delamere, on the right going up the hill.' He looked at his new man. 'You do know where Delamere is, don't you?'

'Yes, sir,' Kip said.

'Well, get going. I'll have somebody up there to help as soon as I can.'

Ten minutes later, Kip was caught in traffic at the roundabout at Delamere Avenue, drumming his sweaty palms on the steering wheel and itching to give a blast on the horn to speed matters along. He had only been in his new job for a month and had yet to become accustomed to peak hour in Nairobi city.

He craned his neck to see if he could steal a run along the footpath, but a line of parked cars blocked the way.

When his chance came, he threw the Land Rover into the left-hand turn at Delamere Avenue and accelerated hard. The heavy diesel responded under protest.

Milimani Road ran up a shallow valley between a string of old colonial houses, a small hotel and the Milimani Primary School. In less than half a mile he came to the junction Willie had described. There were a number of houses dotted amongst dense gardens on the Milimani Road side, but beyond it was a steep slope extending a few hundred yards into a lightly wooded valley.

Kip had found that Nairobi had quite a few roads like Milimani. They started off with conviction, ran a mile or so, then gave up when the going got tough. When the suburbs filled, Milimani Road would go down this slope and continue, as was intended, but for the present it remained a no-man's-land, thick with lush wet-seasonal grass and more than a sprinkling of scrubby vegetation. Kip knew a lion could be sitting in full view under any bush and be completely camouflaged by it.

He slipped the shotgun out of its jacket, checked the cartridges and snapped the barrels closed. He was about to descend into the valley when he remembered the binoculars.

A woman pulled up in a sedan, climbed out and hurried up to him with two small children in tow. 'Have you seen it?' she asked.

'Seen what, madam?' he answered guardedly.

'Why, the lion of course. I was just over the other side with some of the neighbours, but you can't see anything from there.' Kip followed her pointing finger to the sound of distant muffled voices from the far side of the valley. 'I just heard about it on the radio,' she added.

Kip groaned inwardly. 'Look, lady, this is no place for you, or your kids. Just get back in your car, go home and tune in to your radio.'

The woman seemed to be sizing up the twenty year old. Kip was tall for his age and still growing, but his boyish good looks and mop of fair hair gave a lie to his air of authority. She hesitated.

'Now!' he said, trying to look threatening.

She frowned before turning on her heels in a huff, dragging her children behind her.

Kip tucked the shotgun under his arm and decided he would make a brief sortie then await the reinforcements. He pressed carefully through the tall grass. Occasional clumps of bush were dotted about the valley. If the lion was there, it had the advantage. His palms began to sweat again; they always did in these situations. As a boy in Nanyuki, he had seen Raymond Hook bag plenty of lions, but Hook would never go into this kind of scrub unless on a horse, and with a few good dogs. Kip began to feel he had embarked upon a foolhardy mission, and wondered if he should turn back and await the assistance Willie had promised.

A lone bush fly made persistent buzzing darts around his face. Kip brushed at it while keeping an eye on the bush surrounding him. In a stand of tall grass, the uppermost seedheads shimmered. Kip checked the top of a tall shrub nearby. There was no sign of wind. The wavering grass moved towards him.

Kip released the safety on the double-barrelled shotgun. A trickle of sweat itched at the corner of his eye. The bush fly returned, its buzz now deafening in the intense silence. A dun-coloured form passed through thinning grass on the other side of a bush, but was gone in an instant. Kip raised the gun to chest height. He had nothing to aim at, but he knew that when the charge came he would have only an instant to react.

A body came crashing through a frenzied flurry of grass and fell a few yards from him.

'Shit!' it said.

'Jesus!' Kip spluttered, having almost pulled off a barrel at him.

'Oh my God!' the man said in a loud whisper from his prone position. 'I thought you were the fucking lion. You scared the devil out of me, you did.'

'Who the hell are you?' Kip whispered back, lowering his shotgun. 'And what are you doing creeping about like that? I nearly blew your fucking head off.'

The man climbed to his feet, checking a large, complicated-looking camera hanging from his neck. He was short and thickset, and the dark stubble of his unshaved cheeks ran into a tangle of uncombed dark hair. 'Phew,' he said, brushing the dirt from the camera. 'It's okay.' His beige safari jacket bristled with pockets. He retrieved a roll of film from the ground and jammed it into a pocket already stuffed full.

'Don't you know there might be a lion in here somewhere?' Kip whispered, his heart still thumping in his chest.

'I bloody well hope so!' The man extended his hand. 'Harry Forsythe. *East African Standard*. Spotted him yet?'

Kip shook his hand in spite of his annoyance. 'Kip Balmain. No.'

'Bit young for this, aren't you?' Harry looked him

up and down. 'Christ, you couldn't be more than my age. What are you — twenty-two? Twenty-three?'

'Old enough,' Kip replied. He tucked the shotgun under his arm again.

'I hope you know what you're doing.' He nodded at Kip's gun. 'You'll need a solid slug in that. So they tell me.'

Kip decided to treat the comment with contempt. 'Come with me,' he said, heading towards the voices on the other side of the valley. He would lead the cameraman out of trouble and take control of the neighbours while he was at it.

Harry made no protest, keeping close on Kip's heels. 'What I mean is — about the solid slug — they say you can bring a lion down with a shotgun but —'

Kip put a finger to his lips. 'Shhh,' he said.

'Sorry, matey, you're right,' the photographer continued in a lower voice. 'Harry can be a bit noisy at times.' After a moment he whispered, 'You'll need to be quick too, you know. That is, if he comes at us. I've heard that —'

'Harry . . .'

'What is it, old darlin'?'

'Shut up.'

'Right you are. No, you're quite right. Point taken. Need stealth for this one. Not totally ignorant about this stuff, you know, but —' Kip's withering glare stopped him mid-sentence.

Kip parted the grass before placing each foot carefully and silently in front of him. To his credit, Harry followed suit. They crept into a gully between the folds of two inclines.

The ping of a rifle sent them diving to the dirt. The bullet split a boulder and whined across the valley. Harry whimpered an oath.

Kip cupped his hand around his mouth and, using his most authoritative voice, yelled towards the top of the valley. 'Hold your fire! I am a Kenya game warden, here to take control of the situation.'

Silence from the ridge.

'Bloody amateurs,' he muttered, and signalled Harry to follow again.

At the top of the ridge, they found a small crowd gathered. A number of the men carried weapons of one kind or another. Kip glared at them. No one spoke or admitted to the irresponsible pot shot.

Back on the Milimani Road side of the valley, cars were now packed bumper to bumper. A few reckless souls were creeping along the edge of the valley, peering over tall grass for a sighting. Kip decided the situation was quickly getting out of hand and someone was likely to be hurt if Willie's support didn't arrive soon.

He scoured the valley with his binoculars. There was no sign of the lion, but a cluster of shrubs in a wide drainage ditch caught his eye. It was an ideal hiding place. He focused on it for some time. Finally the twitch of an ear confirmed it was the lion's lair. He warned the men to unload their rifles and stay put.

Kip headed back into the valley and Harry followed him over the edge of the ridge.

'Where do you think *you're* going, Harry?' Kip asked.

'With you, me ol' diamond.'

'Oh no, you're not. Stick to studio work, Harry, this is not a photo opportunity.'

'Look, mate, my editor will kick my arse out of the country if I don't come up with something soon. I really need this shot. Have a heart.' He inclined his head to one side like a cocker spaniel begging for a biscuit.

Kip thought a moment. He knew what it was like to be a new boy trying to make good. 'Oh shit. Come on, then. But keep out of my line of sight.'

'I will. Definitely. I really appreciate this, really I do. If you could just see my editor you would completely understand what —'

'Harry ...'

'You're right. Quite right.' He put a finger to his lips. 'I'll, you know, shut up.'

Kip and Harry edged down the slope and again entered the long grass. The wind was in the right quarter, and Kip had noticed a clump of cactus near the lion that would give a good cover for the shot.

A few yards from the cactus stand, Kip motioned for Harry to sit, then continued alone until he stood directly behind the cactus, twenty paces from the lion. After a pause, he eased himself sideways. The lion's hindquarters came into view. He merely had to take a step out and his target would be exposed. The sightline was perfect. He would be firing down into the ditch so, should he miss, the slug would not fly off into the surrounding houses.

He moved back behind his cover and took a few slow breaths to steady his nerves, then peered around the cactus again. He slowly raised his shotgun into position then froze. The lion's flank had tensed. It was about to flee, or charge. Kip saw why: a big yellow Labrador dog was trotting straight towards the lion, tongue lolling, drool dripping, completely unaware of the lion in its path.

Kip decided to act before the dog interfered with his shot. He stepped sideways to bring the lion's flank into his sights and fell over Harry, who had crept up beneath him. At the same instant the Labrador caught the scent of the lion and gave a loud *woof*.

The lion leaped from its hide, bounding straight towards Kip, who had just found his feet. The big, black-maned male balked for a moment, then, feeling trapped, began its charge at the man blocking its escape route.

Kip fired.

Harry's camera clicked.

'What I want to do, what I *really* want to do, is take pictures of naked women.'

Kip took a sip of beer. He smiled at Harry. 'At least you're honest.'

'If not naked, then scanty stuff. Lingerie. Bikinis. Did you see Brigitte Bardot in *And God Created Woman*? Jesus, what a body. Want another?'

Kip had a drop left. 'I should be going,' he said, looking at the electric clock mounted on the wood panelling over the Sportsman Bar. They had been there for over an hour while Harry rocked back and forth on the bar stool, relating his many plans for the future.

'It's not every day you shoot a lion, mate. Have another, then we'll go. Can't wait to see what I've got on that roll. Reckon it'll be perfect.'

'Well ... okay. Another quick one, then I've definitely got to go.'

'That's the shot. Your buy.'

Kip signalled to the big black man behind the bar. 'Two more, *tafadali*,' he said, then turned back to Harry. 'But if you want to shoot pictures of naked women, why come to Africa? It's not the sort of thing Kenya is known for.'

'I know that, mate. But Harry tried everything back in England. Nothing but hack work. So I thought, if I have to do hack work, why not do it somewhere interesting? So here I am.'

Kip nodded, putting a ten on the bar for the drinks.

'Cheers!' Harry said, draining a third of the contents in a single mouthful. 'And what about yourself? Where'd you say you were from again?'

'Australia, originally.'

'Yeah, but what's the town you're from, up near Mt Kenya?'

'Nanyuki.'

'That's it. Nanyuki. Family still there?'

Kip hesitated. 'Yeah.'

'Wouldn't mind seeing Mt Kenya one day. Let me know when you're going home for a visit.'

'I wouldn't hold my breath if I were you, Harry.'

'No? Don't go home much?'

'No.' He didn't add that he hadn't been to Nanyuki since he'd left home at age fourteen.

'How did you get into the wildlife business?'

'The only job I ever wanted. Started out cleaning the office part-time at the National Park headquarters building.' He didn't mention sleeping rough in the deep scrub beside Langata Road until the pay packets became regular. 'Then I graduated to mucking out the pens at the animal orphanage.'

Harry smiled, took another mouthful of beer. 'A noble beginning.'

'Then I got lucky. One of the wardens got me a start as a trainee.'

'We all need a kick-start in this world. Harry was lucky to get the job with the *Standard*.'

'How long have you been with them?'

'Six months. Another?'

'No thanks, Harry, I really have to go.'

'Back to the grindstone, eh?'

'Got to get ready for a trip to the Aberdares. There's a few Kikuyu farmers outside Mweiga who've reported losing some cattle. But after they moved the cattle, three people disappeared.'

'Wow. A man-eater. How does that happen exactly? I mean, why do some turn man-eater and others don't?'

'The boss reckons those Hollywood people up there a few months ago let their lion go loose. He said it was an old fleabag of an animal, and that they left him here to save on transport.'

'Wouldn't a lion they used in the pictures be, you know, tame?'

'Probably was, and that's the problem. He'd have trouble hunting for himself and, with no fear of humans, a Kikuyu farmer would be easy meat.'

'Mweiga. That's near the Country Club, isn't it?'

'It is. And Treetops. Another reason why the boss is anxious to get me there quick. We can't have any rich and famous tourists being eaten.'

'No, indeed. Are you staying at the Country Club?'

'Are you kidding? Have you any idea how much that place costs?'

'No.'

'Neither do I, but it's more than National Parks will pay, that's for sure.'

'Where'd you learn all about animals, and the bush and stuff?'

'I lived in it every chance I got when I was a kid. When I wasn't, you know, working around the house.' Kip avoided dwelling on his drudgery — the endless hours cleaning the house and hotel, preparing the vegetables and cooking the dinner — while his mother and aunt ran the pub. 'And then there was the traineeship as a warden.'

'Must have taken months and months. Harry would get bored.'

'When all you ever wanted to do is run away from home, you do whatever it takes.'

'Run away from home? Now why would a nice young fella like you want to do that?'

Kip pushed his seat towards the bar and stood. 'A long story, Harry. Some other time. *Kwaheri, bwana.*'

CHAPTER 19

Diana Hartigan climbed out of the car, slammed the door and marched to the front of the Bentley. 'Shit!' she said as she fiddled unsuccessfully with the catch to the bonnet. She had seen it done a dozen times, but there was obviously a trick to it. It wouldn't budge. She banged on the silver-grey duco and tried again. It came free and, with barely any effort on her part, floated upward to hover open above the engine. She examined her nails for damage, then peered at the simmering black metal.

She'd seen men staring at engines many times. Why they looked, and what they expected to find, was a mystery. As far as she could see, the engine was all in one piece. It smelled of hot metal and the slightly sweet odour of scorched felt. Why it would suddenly stop in the middle of nowhere she had no idea.

She looked back towards Nakuru, then over to where the Aberdare Ranges fell like a purple–green curtain from a stark blue sky. The range ran roughly north–south, the sun forming deeper shading in the parts where it folded back on itself.

She couldn't remember the last vehicle she had seen. She unwound the silk scarf she wore in case the air conditioning gave her a chill, and loosened the top button of her silk blouse. She wasn't exactly dressed for a bush road — open white sandals weren't good on a long hike. Then again, when she'd left the property that morning, she hadn't planned on getting out of the car until someone poured her a gin and tonic at the Aberdares Country Club.

Apart from the sough of the warm wind sweeping up from the Great Rift Valley, the only sound that broke the silence was the ticking of cooling steel. Then a blowfly buzzed by her ear and she shooed it away impatiently. 'Shit,' she said again, and grabbed her sunbonnet from the back seat, gathered her long red hair into a pile and plonked the hat over it. Then she closed the door, opened it again, threw in the car keys and slammed it shut.

She had hardly started on the walk back to Nakuru when the faint sound of a car labouring up the incline floated on the wind. It wasn't long before an old National Parks Land Rover pulled up beside her. 'You all right, lady?'

He was young and fair and absolutely delicious. In his green uniform with epaulettes and button-down pockets he looked like a boy scout.

'Actually, no. I'm afraid I'm in a spot of bother. That's my Bentley up there. It just stopped.'

He nodded. 'Want me to take a look at it for you?'

'Would you? That would be so kind.'

He swung the door open and she slid in.

'No problem,' he said with a smile.

Nice teeth too, she thought. The Land Rover shuddered as he let his foot off the clutch. A waft of dust rose from the floor.

The Bentley made the same clicking sound when he tried the starter. Then he put his head under the bonnet. 'Everything seems to be okay,' he said, tugging at a number of wires.

The fine hairs on his forearms were blond against his deeply tanned skin. Diana undid another button on her blouse.

'What exactly happened before it stopped?' he asked, wiping his hands on a handkerchief he pulled from his shorts.

'Nothing. Well, it had a bit of trouble on the hills. And there was this kind of burning smell. Then it stopped.'

'Oil pressure gauge all right?'

She put a red fingernail to her lip. 'Oil pressure? You mean those little dials and things? I don't know ... maybe.'

He cocked an eyebrow and smiled. 'Maybe?'

'One of them might have gone a teeny bit into the red. But it's a Bentley, for goodness' sake.' She almost said *for Christ's sake*, but held it back. 'Brand new — 1964.'

'Well, even Bentleys need oil, I guess.' He closed the bonnet. 'Better get someone from the dealership to take a look at it. I'll give you a lift back to Nakuru if you like.'

'That's very kind of you. But that'll be taking you out of your way. By the way, where are you going?'

'To the Aberdares.'

'Really! What a coincidence, I'm going to the Country Club too.'

He laughed. 'I'm not going to the Country Club. No, I'll make camp up there somewhere.'

'Oh, what a pity, looks like I'll miss my reservation.' She let her lip pout a little.

'But I can drop you there if you'd rather. It's on my way.'

She inclined her head and gave him one of her

most radiant smiles. 'Why, thank you, kind sir. I'm Diana, by the way. Diana Hartigan.'

'Kip Balmain,' he said, apparently unfamiliar with her husband's name. 'Pleased to meet you.' He shook her hand with a firm grip. 'Anything you need to take out of there?' he said, nodding to the car.

She opened the boot and he loaded her suitcases into the Land Rover. 'What are you going to do with the Bentley?' he asked.

'Leave it to rot,' she said. Seeing his expression, she added, 'I'll contact my husband from the Country Club. He'll send someone for it.'

Her suitcases bounced around on the back floor as he tried to guide the Land Rover around the potholes.

Diana studied him in profile as she pretended to peer past him at the herd of gazelle that bounded from the road as they approached. He could be a teenager, but was obviously older. 'How long have you been a game warden?' she asked cheerily.

'Just over four years.'

'Like it?'

'Yes.'

'What's so funny?'

'Nothing. It's just that everybody asks the same question. As if they're surprised a person could actually enjoy working with animals.'

'Not me. It takes a real man to resist all that great white hunter nonsense. I admire you for it.'

'Well, thank you, Mrs Hartigan, I appreciate it.'

'It's Diana, please.'

'Diana.' He wrestled the vehicle through the bends, making fast gear changes as the diesel laboured up the escarpment. Perspiration stained his underarm and there was another wet patch on his chest.

He must have sensed her thoughts. 'Sorry it's so hot in here. Land Rover hasn't quite cottoned on to air conditioning.'

'I don't mind,' she lied.

He caught her eyeing him and seemed embarrassed by her frank appraisal. 'So, um, how long will you be at the Country Club?' he said.

'Three or four days. Until I get bored.'

'Your husband joining you?'

'No, he can never drag himself away from his damn cattle.'

'I see.'

'What about you? What takes you to the Aberdares?'

'Work. There's a report of a lion.'

'A lion? Surely there are plenty of lions in the Aberdares?'

'Of course,' he stammered. 'But this one's a man-eater.'

'I thought they only happened in books.'

'They do. Mostly.'

She decided to change the subject. He seemed uncomfortable talking about himself, but she was anxious to learn more about the shy young man before he disappeared. And she did. By the time they drove along the Country Club's first fairway, she had learned he was living in bachelor's digs in Nairobi with a friend who was obsessed with becoming a fashion photographer, that he had a mother living quite nearby in Nanyuki but didn't plan to meet her on this occasion, and that he hoped to start up his own safari operation one day.

Kip pulled into the visitors' parking bay and carried her suitcases to reception.

'Ah, Mrs Hartigan,' the manager beamed. 'Welcome back.'

'Thank you,' she nodded.

'I have reserved your usual bungalow, madam. Unless you prefer to have one closer to the lodge instead? It looks like there may be rain coming.'

'No, thank you. That will be satisfactory.' She indicated Kip standing behind her. 'And a bungalow for Mr Balmain too.'

'Certainly.' The manager spun the book around and studied the list.

Kip looked startled. 'Not for me, Diana. As I said —'

'Nonsense, Kip, you saved me from a fate worse than death — I'm talking about walking into Nakuru in these shoes. Besides, it's too late to find your camping spot or wherever you sleep, and it's my fault.'

'It's no problem, really, I've set up camp in the —'

'I insist.' She turned to the manager. 'Would you believe it? This young man rescued me from the wilds and now he won't even accept my simple thanks?'

The manager shook his head in sympathy.

'I could still be out there, wandering in the jungle, a prey to some dreadful man-eater.' She winked at Kip. 'Please put Mr Balmain's room on my account.' She put her hands on her hips and threw her head back in mock defiance. 'And I'll have no further arguments.'

Kip stood in his underwear ironing his trousers. He was glad he'd packed his black slacks. He usually made do with shorts and a pair of canvas rainwear pants while out on bush work in the high country. They kept out the cold as well as the rain. He lifted and studied his trousers, shook the heat out of them and pulled them on.

The shirt was another matter. He had never dined at the Aberdares Country Club, but assumed a jacket and tie would be expected. Bad luck; his open-necked long-sleeved shirt was the best he had. At least it was clean. He'd packed the shirt for the cold mountain nights but it was unlikely he would be cold in the bungalow. The housekeeper had arrived soon after dark with a bowl of fruit and a vase of flowers, then set a roaring fire in the open fireplace. The bungalows were solidly constructed from local stone. His three rooms — bedroom, dressing room and bathroom — were already comfortably warm.

He slipped into his shoes, tucked in his shirt and combed his hair, still wet after his hot shower. In the mirror he looked presentable.

Diana Hartigan. He couldn't quite understand what was happening out there on the Nakuru–Thompson's Falls road. She was a married woman, an attractive one at that, older than him by maybe ten years, and seemed to be taking a keen interest in him. Maybe he was misreading the situation — it wouldn't be the first time. Perhaps she was just being friendly; appreciative of his assistance.

He checked the mirror once more before heading to the bar, where Diana had said she would meet him at seven for an eight o'clock dinner.

Kip was still nervous when he arrived at the bar, and had two whiskies before Diana appeared at seven-thirty. She wore a green, body-hugging dress. Her red hair bounced and shone in the glow of the firelight.

'My, my,' she said, 'don't you look handsome.' She made as if to flick a speck off his shoulder, but patted the flap on his button-down shirt pocket instead.

He raised a hand to check it himself, and she smiled. 'I'm sorry, a force of habit. My husband is always such a slob. You look great. What are you drinking?'

'Whisky, but I think I'll change to beer.' The whiskies were having an effect. 'You ... look nice too,' he added, and immediately felt like a bumbling schoolboy, out to impress.

She didn't seem to notice. 'Thank you, Kip.' She smiled and cast a glance around the bar. A large leather armchair was vacant by the fire. 'Would you like to sit by the fire for our drink?'

'Yes, that'd be ... great.' He'd nearly said *nice* again. 'Can I get you something to drink?'

'Please, a G and T.'

'Now tell me, Kip,' she said as he joined her on the sofa, 'why aren't you going to visit your loving mother while you're so near her?'

'I wouldn't say *loving*,' he said, and immediately regretted it. He must have had too much to drink already. 'I shouldn't have said that.'

Diana took a sip of her gin and tonic, her eyes smiling over the top of her glass. 'I love your candour, Kip,' she said. 'It's very ... appealing.'

'I mean ... what I meant to say was, we don't see much of each other these days.'

'No need to apologise. I couldn't *stand* my mother. She was such a bore. Never let me do anything I wanted. Perhaps that's why I always do what I want these days.' Her laugh was low and sexy. 'Now I've shocked you.'

'Not at all.' He covered his lost composure by taking a gulp of beer.

'Then if we aren't talking about our mothers, tell me about your plans for your own business.'

'Mrs Hartigan, and sir, your table is ready. At your convenience.' Kip hadn't heard the waiter approach.

'Thank you,' Diana said. 'I'm perishing hungry. Why don't we continue this at the table?'

He followed a step behind her, trying to appear nonchalant but feeling awkward and uncomfortable in his casual clothes. Waiters smiled and nodded unconvincingly as he passed. He felt sure that if he hadn't been there with Mrs Diana Hartigan, he would have been asked to leave.

Kip knew of her husband, Hugh Hartigan, although he'd tried not to appear impressed when he learned of Diana's connection to him. Hartigan was the biggest landowner in Kenya, with numerous holdings — the largest being in the so-called White Highlands, near Eldoret — but he was also one of Kenya's human dynamos. There was seldom a day when Hartigan's name was not in the national papers concerning some important industrial or political matter.

The dining room was dimly lit and cosy. A candle flickered on each white linen-covered table, half of which were unoccupied. The waiter showed them to a place by a window that overlooked the courtyard, now lit by lanterns in tree branches or on poles set in the lawn. From his late-afternoon exploration of the grounds, Kip knew that beyond the courtyard large bougainvillea vines tumbled down the grassy slope to the tennis courts and pool. Peacocks paraded themselves on the lawns and, as dusk arrived, he'd seen baboons and impala creeping from the edges of the golf course.

The waiter slid the chair under Diana as she took her seat. Kip sat before he had a chance to do the same for him.

He looked around the room. It had three crystal chandeliers with flickering yellow lamps made to look like candles. Wood-panelled walls matched the dark wood of the maître d's rostrum, as well as the balustrade that separated the two sections of the room.

Diana smiled.

He smiled too, and swallowed.

'So ...' she said. 'You were about to tell me what you really want.'

'I was?'

'Yes, for the future. Your business plans.'

'Oh! Yes, my business plans.' He settled himself, shook out his crisp white napkin and placed it on his thigh. 'Well, plans are probably a bit of a grand description. I would say I have a ... a desire to run my own tour company.'

'Desires are important. We should always have something to desire.'

The waiter appeared and carefully unfolded Diana's napkin, delicately placing it on her lap. He looked down his nose at the napkin on Kip's knee, then bowed slightly to Diana. 'Would you like to order pre-dinner drinks, Mrs Hartigan?' he said, handing her the wine list with a saccharine smile.

'Yes, I think we should. Kip?'

Kip shrugged. 'Mm-hmm.'

'I think we should just have some wine,' she said, scanning the selection.

Kip remained noncommittal, arranging his cutlery on the starched tablecloth. He had never tasted wine.

'Yes, some wine. A bottle of your St Emilion Bordeaux, please. 1958.'

'Certainly, madam. An excellent choice.' The waiter clicked his heels and departed.

'You were talking about your desires, Kip. I'm all ears.'

'Yes, well, that's really it. A game safari. But it needs capital. I need a truck, camping gear, probably a four-wheel drive. An assistant.'

'You'd have plenty of competition out there. Seems like every ex-hunter runs a safari operation these days. What would make your offering any better than the next man's?'

'The ecological experience.'

'Ecological?'

'Ecology. It's a new science: the study of nature, and why living things are where they are. At least I think it's new. I've only just started to read about it in the natural science magazines.'

'I see, but where's the connection with your safaris?'

'My safaris would be an ecological experience, away from the tourist crowds.'

'You mean outside the parks and game reserves?'

'Exactly.' She surprised him by what appeared to be a genuine interest in his idea. 'Away from the tourist crowds and into a close encounter with nature.' He was beginning to warm to his topic. 'You're right about the competition — there're plenty of operators out there. I see them every day in my job. Large groups, poorly equipped. They dash about in Land Rovers while their clients tick off the big five as they go. A pack of amateurs in it for a quick quid.'

'If I may interrupt, madam?' The waiter hovered. 'The menu.' He placed two large folders on the table. 'May I advise you about our chef's specials this evening?'

Diana looked across at Kip, who was chewing the inside of his cheek. 'No, not just now, thank you.'

Kip watched him go.

'You don't like him, do you?' She was smiling at him.

Kip smiled too. 'Does it show?'

'Yes. And I agree with you. A pompous arse, if you'll excuse the language.'

Kip shrugged.

'But let's not worry about him. Go on with what you were saying.'

'In my operation, I'd have small groups. No more than two or three couples. And because we won't be in national park reserves, we'd be able to walk everywhere.'

'Walk?'

'Of course. It's the only way to study animals.'

'But you're talking about using private property, aren't you? Where are the animals, apart from a few gazelle, on a ranch?'

'I'd involve farmers in it — people who are sympathetic to conservation. Yes, conservation. It's a bit of a fringe movement at the moment, mainly in Europe and America, but it's the coming thing. When farmers realise that, with proper management, they can run a farm *and* make some ready cash from tourists, they'll get interested.'

'Farmers and conservation? From what I've seen of my husband, I think you might have your work cut out for you. But getting back to your clients . . . What accommodation will you use?'

'Tents.'

'Tents!'

'You can't experience the bush behind timber and glass. It's got to be canvas.'

'Hmm,' said Diana, tapping her lip. 'Two or three couples, you said?'

'At most.'

'Then I presume you'll have to charge a pretty penny to make your margin ...'

'Well, yes, I would. But I haven't done any detailed calculations yet.'

'And these well-to-do clients are going to be sleeping in tents?'

'Yes.'

'Then they had better be luxury tents.'

He thought for a moment. 'I guess you're right. Luxury tents. Let's call them five-star tents.'

She chuckled. 'Now you're talking. I could see myself enjoying one of your safaris in a five-star tent.'

The waiter arrived with a napkin over his arm and a wine bottle cradled in his hands like a newborn child. 'The St Emilion Bordeaux, 1958, madam.'

Diana made a *what can you do?* shrug for Kip's benefit. 'Thank you,' she said to the waiter, who removed a corkscrew from his pocket, unfolded it with a series of brisk motions, then arranged the napkin around the bottle with infinite care.

Diana shrugged again.

'Here, let me help you,' Kip said, taking the bottle from the startled waiter. 'We haven't got all bloody night.' He smiled at Diana. 'Excuse the language.' And to the waiter, who remained at the table, unsure of what to do, he added, 'Go on, you can go.'

Diana laughed. 'Well done,' she said as the waiter retreated in disarray.

Kip had the cork out and the glasses filled in a moment.

'Cheers,' she said.

He liked her smile. 'Cheers,' he replied.

'No, wait.' She caught his hand before it reached his glass and held it. Her touch was soft and warm. 'A toast,' she said. 'A toast to the tents.'

He clinked her glass as he'd seen done in the picture theatres. 'To five-star tents,' he said, meeting her smile.

The wine was aromatic, sending waves of taste to the back of his throat and into his nose. He tasted it again, then studied its colour — a rich, deep red that revealed other facets as it caught the light.

'You know, Diana, I've never had wine before.' He had no idea why he felt he needed to share his secret with her. Maybe he had started to feel good about the evening.

'There may be many things that a young man like you has yet to try.' She took a sip, watching him over the rim of her glass. 'Don't leave it too late to start.'

'Come up for a cup of hot chocolate before bed,' she had said. Kip knew the hot chocolate was a subterfuge, and didn't care. He sat on the cane sofa while Diana 'freshened up', shifted in his seat, and tried to quieten his half-erection.

The night had been filled with firsts. This was his first visit to an exclusive club. The Aberdares Country Club was a place for wealthy landowners, like Diana's husband. And although its outdated interior wasn't to his liking, and he could have happily strangled one or two of the starchy waiters, being there was like a visit beyond the rainbow.

He'd also had his first glass of wine. It took some time to become accustomed to the flat, slightly acid taste, but by the time the second bottle arrived, he had acquired a liking for it.

Diana was also the first real woman who had shown an interest in him. The fact that she was older and married made the excitement special.

She came out of the bathroom wearing a silk wrap caught at the waist. She said something about the light being too bright and switched it off. Her robe became transparent in the backlight from the bathroom. She came towards him and the firelight danced in her hair.

'You're such a dear boy, Kip,' she said, standing over him to stroke his hair. Her robe parted slightly and he raised his hand towards it but paused. She took it in hers and placed it on her breast. His fingers cupped the smooth, warm flesh and he gently pressed it. He could hear her breathing.

Her nipple grew hard under his fingertips and he lifted his lips to kiss them each in turn.

'Oh God,' she murmured, holding his face and pressing him against her.

Her hands slipped from his cheeks to his shoulders, where she grasped him and indicated she wanted him on his feet. His lips met hers as he rose and his hardness pressed into her gown. She rubbed her hips along him and he thought he would die with the pleasure of it.

While he lost himself in the sensations of her lips and her groin rubbing against him, she was pulling at his shirt, and then he tore open his belt and released his pants, which fell to the floor.

They stumbled together to the side of the bed, he continuing to seek her lips as she was tearing at his underwear.

Her gown was gone when they fell onto the bed, and when her fingers curled around him, making him gulp for air, he was on her, and in her, and the room disappeared.

Afterwards he lay on his back, Diana curled under the crook of his shoulder, staring into the space above the bed. The fire was dying, but its last flames made flickering pictures on the ceiling.

Kip Balmain was twenty years old, no longer a virgin, and, for the first time in his life, deeply in love.

CHAPTER 20

1973

Kip sat on a rock at the edge of the Esoit Oloololo Escarpment, his arms wrapped around one shin and his chin resting on his knee. Below him, the Masai Mara stretched to the horizon, where the sun was making its sally into the day. The rains had come and the Mara's blackened earth was covered in a sea of green. Only the occasional patch of yellow, where the fires had somehow spared islands of grass, broke the monotony. Fire and rain — the essential ingredients of life on the African savannah.

A scattering of black dots converged into a bold line leading to the rambling ribbon of foliage that was the Mara River. The wildebeest were moving to rejoin the million-strong herd returning to the Serengeti, where they would calve in the rain and the relative safety of the short-grass plains.

His tour group had seen the best of the migration in the four days he'd had them in camp. The wildebeest numbers were up again this year. Zebra and other antelopes too. All six of his clients had captured great shots of the crocodiles in attack as the herd made their crossing. He'd also been able to deliver on Kipana Tours' proud promise. They had seen elephant and buffalo herds, quite a few lions

— including a kill — two leopards and a solitary rhino. The mandatory big five — an achievement few other safari operators were able to accomplish.

After breakfast he would take the group for one last safari before Abu drove them back to Nairobi and their five-star hotels. This would give Kip time to visit Kevin Grainger to get his permission to start work on the timber amenities block. Kip had trouble keeping capable chefs once they saw the canvas-covered kitchen. The amenities block would be a small concession to his philosophy of a totally tented camp.

The Graingers had given Kipana Tours a lease on the strip of land along the escarpment six years ago, just after he and Diana Hartigan had started the tour business in partnership. Kevin Grainger had been only partly convinced in the early days, but since then had become an enthusiastic supporter of Kip's ecological safaris.

He would need Diana's signature on the lease too. Apart from providing most of the start-up capital, she had taken little interest in the operational side of the business, which was just how Kip liked it, but at times like this, when he needed her involvement for business purposes, it was difficult to reach her. The lines were often out of order to the ranch at Eldoret. Fortunately, she was frequently in Nairobi, and a phone call to the Mathaiga Club, the Hilton or the Norfolk would generally find her.

Thoughts of Diana brought back memories of their time as lovers. Kip could still vividly recall the wild times they'd shared. He was an inexperienced but enthusiastic student; she, a patient teacher. Through nine erotic months they'd made love in cars, hotels, standing in the rain. Even under the gaze of a herd of elephants on the banks of the Ewaso Ngiro River. He took great delight in finding different ways to bring her to orgasm, exploring combinations of touching, feeling, sucking and, when they had both reached a point of no return, penetration. They would then sleep, or at least he would, but she would awaken him with her tantalising mouth, and he would play his *can't wake up* game until his arousal put an end to it. The second time was generally a more robust session, until he came with a moan of relief and, oddly, regret.

Through all that time he could never quite bring himself to believe that this beautiful and sophisticated woman could be interested in the gormless youth he had been back in 1964. Ultimately, his doubts were confirmed when Diana abruptly announced it was over between them. He was rocked to his core. At the time he thought it was probably because she had found someone new. Fortunately, they had already decided to go into business together. It was odd to see their wild sexual liaison turn into a companionable business relationship. For many months he could not put the vivid recollections of their passion behind him. When he had finally consigned them to distant, pleasurable memories, he realised he'd had more than merely a physical attraction to the vivacious redhead. He had loved her.

'Good morning, Kip. A penny for your thoughts.'

Samantha Williams, an attractive thirtyish blonde, was looking very fetching in short khaki trousers and matching blouse.

'Good morning, Mrs Williams.'

'Now, now,' she chided. 'I thought we had an understanding. It's Sam, or Samantha.'

'Of course, Samantha. Good morning.' She had been flirting with him from day one. Her husband, who ran a beef-processing plant in the US midwest, either didn't notice or didn't care.

'Isn't this just wonderful?' She joined him on the rock, her long, tanned legs almost brushing his shoulder. 'Wow.'

Kip climbed to his feet and dusted the seat of his pants. 'I thought you people might like one last safari before you head off home.'

'Oh, how I hate that word — home. I just love it here, with all these ... these animals, and beauty.'

Kip smiled. 'All good things must come to an end.'

'Must they?' Samantha gave him one of her practised pouts. 'You won't forget your promise to look us up when you come down to Nairobi, will you, Kippy?'

Kip tried to suppress a wince. 'I'll certainly try, Samantha.'

'Don't forget, we leave on Tuesday.'

'I won't.'

'I want you to see ... *we* want you to see our shots of our wonderful safari.'

'That would be nice.'

'Oh, I'll have to get them processed in time. Do you know a Kodak place?'

'I do. Where are you staying?'

'Oh, Kip, have you forgotten already? At the Hilton, of course.'

'Right. Then see Mo down in Kenyatta Avenue. A couple of doors down from Wabera Street.'

'I *do* hope we can catch up, Kip.' She placed a hand on his forearm. 'I have had such a *marvellous* time. I simply must buy you a drink, or something, in appreciation.'

* * *

Diana watched Kip stride across the Mathaiga Club's parking lot towards the main entrance. He'd changed since that first day they'd met on the road to the Aberdares. No so much physically — although he'd filled out a little; no longer the gangly twenty year old, as awkward as a pup. Now he was more confident. It showed in the way he carried himself: tall, and able to look any man, or woman, in the eye.

A moment later he appeared at the door of the lounge. He looked around for a moment, then smiled when he found her sitting at the window.

He took her hand as she stood, holding it for a moment, then kissed her on the cheek. 'Diana, you look sensational.'

She smiled. 'Liar,' she said, taking her seat again. 'But thanks for saying so. You're not bad yourself.'

No matter that their affair had ended over six years ago, and regardless of how many weeks between visits, when Kip appeared, he always had the same effect on her — it was as if she was standing too close to an electrical storm.

'Really,' he added. 'You look like a woman expecting her lover to arrive at any moment.'

She signalled to a waiter to give herself time to compose herself. 'How did you guess?'

'I knew it. You're here on another of your little trysts.'

After they'd broken up, Diana had allowed Kip to believe she continued to have affairs, so he wouldn't suspect the real reason she'd had to break it off with him.

'Anyone I know?' he said, smiling.

'I'm not the kind of girl to kiss and tell,' she said with a coquettish smile. 'So behave yourself.'

The waiter arrived with a cocktail list. He was a

tall man, with tight wiry hair, greying at the sides. His ears had large holes pierced in them.

She handed the cocktail list to Kip without looking. 'A Harvey Wallbanger, please. Fresh oranges.'

The waiter nodded. 'Certainly, madam. And sir?'

She watched Kip as he ran his finger down the list, knowing he would order a beer anyway. That was the problem — she knew him too well. Knew too much about his habits. Like when he finished making love, he would release a big sigh, roll onto his back and immediately fall asleep. She'd tried to consign the memories to history, but their days together remained the most passionate and fulfilling ones of her life. It was the reason she'd had to let him go: she was falling in love, and that would never do.

'Hmm, I think I'll just have a Tusker,' he said.

The waiter nodded and headed back to the bar.

'I know, I know,' he said with a smile. 'It's just that they all sound so good. Too sweet for me, anyway. Make me puke.' He remained smiling at her. 'You really do look well, Diana,' he said as the pause in conversation grew. 'How's Hugh?'

'He's well. He sends his love, and wants to know when you're coming up home.'

'God, yes. It must be three months! Last time was when he was helping me with the Laikipia proposal to the department.'

'Naughty boy.' She shuffled a cigarette out of its packet. 'But he's in London at the moment. Family affairs.'

He held a match for her.

'So, you're ready to start on the new buildings?' she said, taking a deep draw.

'Yes. As I said on the phone, Grainger's happy with the changes in our lease — oh, the papers are in the car for your signature — then I'll send the plans to a few builders in Kisumu for a quote.'

She nodded. 'Good.'

The drinks arrived. Kip took the Tusker before the waiter had a chance to pour it for him. Diana smiled. *Some things don't change*, she thought, but she had teased him enough.

'How are things going with the property up north?' she said. 'What's his name, that rancher fellow?' Diana had made the contact with the rancher through Hugh. She'd not seen the property, north of Thompson's Falls.

'Nolan.' He took a sip of beer and replaced it on the table. 'Everything's going well. Should be able to start organising things for around June. After the wet.'

'This is the one you've been waiting for, isn't it? The one that finally allows you to run your own show, without game wardens sticking their noses in?'

'That's it.' He smiled. '*Real* eco-tours.'

'You haven't changed, Kip. Always the idealist.'

'Am I? I prefer to call it fulfilling a dream.'

'I'll drink to that.' She took a sip of her Harvey Wallbanger. 'Ugh! This isn't fresh orange! Honestly, this place is going to the dogs these days.'

Kip searched for the waiter. He was nowhere in sight. 'Here, let me take it back for you,' he said, reaching for the glass.

'No, Kip, it's all right.' It wasn't the done thing to go chasing a waiter at the Mathaiga Club. 'Really. It's fine.' Knowing Kip's dislike of cant, he would probably give the waiter a dressing-down if the man tried to lord it over him. The Mathaiga Club waiters were notorious snobs. 'Tell me about the place. I've never seen it.'

'You should go have a look at it, Diana,' he said, his face alight with excitement. 'The place is huge — more than fifty thousand acres. Up there on the Laikipia Plateau you can see for ever. The Ewaso Narok runs through the place. There are plains animals, cheetah, even lions.'

'And Nolan's happy about you traipsing in with truckloads of sweaty tourists?'

'Nolan ...' He smiled. 'He's a funny character. One of the old school, but he's had ... what's the word? An awakening? He's happy to go partners with us. Wants to undo all the years of hunting. Just like Hugh did a few years ago. To get it back to what it used to be like — wildlife everywhere.'

'And make some money too, perhaps?' She said it as a joke, or perhaps to tease him for his idealism, but then she saw he had taken her seriously.

'Yeah, that too, I suppose.' He was deflated.

She cursed herself — he had taken it the wrong way, and she had spoiled his vision. 'I don't mean ...'

'No, you're right, Diana. I've got to make sure we can turn a profit in this. It's all very well to work on conservation, but it has to pay. The roads are shit up there on the Laikipia, and who knows how many will brave a tent —'

'Kip.' She put a hand on his arm. 'You've made Kipana Tours work for us so far. You'll do it again. If not' — she shrugged — 'it's not a big financial commitment. As you say, Nolan is happy to offer the place on a profit-share. What have we got to lose?'

He nodded. She could see he was mollified. Pleased that she had circumvented the issue of money, she tried to lighten the conversation again. 'It sounds beautiful, Kip. When were you up there last?'

'The place was dry. Must have been three months ago. Just before the rains. It'd be green again by now.'

'It's not far from your old home in Nanyuki, is it?'

'No.' He reached for his glass and took a sip from it. 'But I go up through Thompson's Falls. It's shorter.'

'Have you been back home since you came to Nairobi?'

Another sip of beer. 'No.'

'Why not? Your family must miss you.'

'I will, it's just ... been a bit busy.'

It wasn't the first time she had tried to learn something about his childhood, and failed. He always appeared uncomfortable talking about it and she didn't want to force the issue.

'Come on,' she said, 'finish that beer. If you can stand the starched napkins, I'll buy you lunch.'

She knew there was only so much a person could do for another. Eventually, he would have to untangle whatever it was on his mind. If not, one day it would smother him.

CHAPTER 21

It couldn't have come at a worse time. Sister Mary Augustine made some changes to the classes for the 1973 school year and Rose found herself in a class with none of her friends. Taller than her classmates, including most of the boys, she felt gangly, ugly and awkward. One of the boys called her *twiga* — giraffe — and it stuck.

She was too shy to make new friends, and sought out her old ones, making matters worse with her new classmates, who started saying she was too proud — a damning condemnation within a small village like Panyiketto.

She tried to make herself less conspicuous by letting her shoulders droop, and walked with her eyes fixed on the ground. The nuns would have none of it and almost every morning, as the entire school paraded past the flag after assembly, Sister Augustine would shout from the podium, 'Rose Nasonga! Straighten your spine, girl. You're slouching again.' This led to more teasing from the boys. '*Twiga, twiga,*' they'd whisper.

She was a natural at sports. Her long legs were ideal for the running track and netball court. As a youngster she'd excelled, but by twelve years old she loathed the limelight of the winners' dais. She tried to become average, coming third or fourth in the foot races, and deliberately missed every second shot at goal.

The boys noticed her two small breasts that she could not conceal under her school blouse, and made smutty remarks behind their cupped hands as she passed. They would release a torrent of laughter when she was almost out of earshot that made her quicken her step. Then she began to worry about her health. Every few weeks she would develop a pain on each side of her waist. It was similar to the pain she got if she had been running too hard, but was lower in her abdomen, and came and went at odd times. She didn't like to trouble her mother with such trivial matters — she had enough on her mind with the running of the farm — and so she kept it to herself, promising to mention it if it persisted.

One day she found small bloodstains on her underwear. At first she thought it was coming from her bottom, but in the next attack she confirmed it was from her front. Somehow this was much worse. She was horror-struck. It validated her greatest fears: she was a freak; a gangling, awkward freak, now with bleeding privates to boot. She kept the problem to herself, hiding the evidence by hand-washing her underwear during the night.

The attacks occurred for a few days and were suddenly gone. When they passed, she tried to convince herself there had been a spontaneous cure. But they returned a few weeks later. And then again the following month.

On the third occasion, when Sister Augustine called her up to the chalkboard — a task Rose always dreaded — the students behind her began to giggle as she walked from her desk to the front of the class. By the time she reached the board, there was general pandemonium. Sister Augustine ordered the children to be quiet and get on with their exercises, then gently led Rose from the classroom.

Outside, the nun told her that she had a stain on the seat of her tunic. Rose slid her dress around to find the evidence of her illness for all to see. Tears brimmed in her eyes. How could she ever go back into that classroom?

Sister Augustine took her hand and patted it. 'Now, now, dear, it's nothing to get upset about. Is it your monthly visit?'

Rose stared at her.

'Hasn't your mother told you about your monthly visit?'

Rose shook her head.

'Your monthly visit ... when you get your period.' The nun was getting impatient with her silence.

Rose wanted to be helpful — Sister Augustine was trying to be kind — but she had no idea what she was talking about.

'Come with me then,' she said, and led Rose around the small block of schoolrooms to the annexe where the three nuns had their office.

Rose felt very uncomfortable in the nuns' room. It was out of bounds for all students. She felt as if she was desecrating a sacred territory. She stood rigid while Sister Augustine rummaged around in a large, black cotton bag — the type that all the nuns carried each day to school.

'Ah, there we are,' she said, pulling a small brown-paper-wrapped package from her bag and handing it to Rose. 'You can have this,' she said. 'It's called a pad. When your period is coming, you put this inside your underwear. It will stop the blood from staining your tunic.'

Rose was indescribably grateful. Her tears threatened to overflow.

'Now, now,' Sister Augustine said. 'Don't cry. You should be happy — it means you are becoming a woman.'

Rose stared at the nun in horror and immediately burst into tears.

There was an expectant hush in the Nasonga family home. George had been called back from boarding school, so everyone knew it was something important. Rose could barely remember the last time they'd held a family conference. It had been after the police came for Adam because he had been poaching ivory in the game reserve on the other side of the Nile. But her big brother had already run away, and nobody had seen him since.

Before their mother called them into the house, there had been much speculation among the siblings about the reason for the conference.

Macmillan said it was to tell them Papa was about to join the army.

George said it was to tell them Adam was dead — killed in the wilds of Zaire.

Rose thought it would be something about their *rwot*, who'd had his head chopped off by the soldiers, but then Akello pointed out it couldn't be that; he was dead, and nothing more could be done.

Rose sat on the hide rug beside Akello. Dembe and George — still in his smart school uniform — were seated behind them, while Macmillan, now the oldest male child in the house, claimed the only other chair.

Mama was at Papa's side, watching him stir his tea.

As far as Rose knew, theirs was the only family that held family conferences. One day she asked her father why. He told her he believed in democracy and peace, and that's what would reign in his household.

Rose didn't understand him. All she knew was that if no other family held family conferences, she was not about to admit to them at school. At thirteen, she was painfully aware of her flaws. She didn't need to reveal that even her father was different.

All eyes were on Zakayo, who had been stirring his tea for a long time. Finally he shifted his chair to face them, giving the signal he was about to speak.

'Children,' he said, 'we have some news, your mama and I. You know about the trouble in the town, with the soldiers ... well,' he glanced at Doreen, 'we have decided to leave Panyiketto.'

Rose looked at Akello, whose eyes had widened like an owl's.

'We will go to Kenya,' he said, and looked around them to gauge their reaction.

Rose was stunned. Panyiketto was home.

'To Kisumu,' he added. 'At first.' Then he nodded, the signal that he had said what he had to say and others could now speak.

George was first. 'But what about school? How will I finish school?' George had begun to develop a deeper voice, but on this occasion it failed him halfway through and he ended in a childlike squeak.

'You will finish school in Kisumu. For the time being I need you here at home, to help your mother with the *shamba*.'

'But —'

'George.' Zakayo silenced his son with a look. There was a limit to the degree of democracy he would permit. 'Rose and Akello will not be here.'

The two younger children again exchanged glances.

'I am taking them to your sister in Kisumu,' he continued. 'While I am there I will make certain arrangements for the rest of you. Meanwhile, you will help Macmillan with the work in the gardens.'

Dembe, as usual, had sat quietly throughout the discussion. Rose was surprised when she spoke.

'Papa, I want to come with you.'

'Of course you will come with us, Dembe, after I get back from taking the younger ones.'

'No.'

The others looked at their sister. She had never spoken to their parents in such a manner.

'No,' she repeated. 'I must come with you. I won't stay in the village and hear all the whispers.' She raised defiant eyes to her father. 'Yes, I hear them. *Poor Dembe*. But they say it with pity in their eyes. What life do I have here now? Who will even look at me, knowing what I have done?'

'You have done nothing,' Zakayo began, but Doreen put a hand on his arm, which stopped him. They exchanged glances, and Zakayo said he would think about it. Rose knew then that Dembe would be with them when they went. What followed was a host of details on what they would take, what they would leave, and when they would go. But Rose heard very little of it.

Kisumu was a place she had only imagined in her dreams. Her sister's letters described a city even bigger than Pakwach in faraway and prosperous Kenya. The thought of leaving her small school and its many irritations pleased her. The journey itself made her head swim with excitement.

* * *

Rose could not feel sad about leaving Panyiketto. Then, on the bank of the river, as Papa's friend brought his small boat onto the bank and they were told to climb in, she began to cry.

Eleven-year-old Akello saw her, and cried too.

Rose held her mother until her father gently told her they had to hurry. She tried to think of something to say to her mother, but Akello claimed her, and Macmillan gave Rose a hug as if he meant to suffocate her. George was more reserved, finishing his embrace with an embarrassed smile.

Their father held the boat while the three children clambered in among the fishing tackle and ropes. They waved and shouted until the bend in the river removed them from sight.

The boatman whispered something to her father and he told the three of them that they must lie down in the boat and keep out of sight.

'But, Papa,' Akello said, 'we won't be able to see the town as we pass.'

Their father hesitated for a moment before responding. 'Exactly, Akello. I don't want any of the co-op members to see me go. They will be pestering me for this and that. And I have no time for it.'

'But —'

'Silence. We are getting near. Keep your head down until I tell you to come up.'

But Rose took a peep over the side of the boat when her father wasn't looking. She could see a flagpole and a circle of tents. One of the big trucks had just arrived and soldiers surrounded it. People climbed out from the back under the barrel of the soldiers' guns with uncertainty in their step. A soldier on the riverbank looked their way but she hid her face.

They were well out into the Albert Nile when their father told them they could sit up again. The river was nearly a mile wide.

'Over there on the left bank,' their father said over the murmur of the motor, 'the bush stretches for many miles. When your mother and I married, white hunters came here to shoot the animals. Elephant, lion, everything.' He thought for a moment and corrected himself. 'No, it was even later than that. After Adam was born. Now, it's forbidden; it's a game reserve.'

'Now only poachers like Adam can shoot in there,' Akello said cheerfully and their father went quiet.

They kept close to the left bank because, further out, the wind made small waves that splashed into the boat. Rose studied the swampy foreshore to see if she could find any sign of wild animals. Akello said he saw an elephant, but she didn't believe him.

As the Albert Nile narrowed, Pakwach came into view. Rose and her young brother had taken the bus to Pakwach with their father when she was nine. He had taken them to the station to see the train come in, but they had waited an hour and it didn't arrive. Akello had cried and Papa bought them both a treat from the Indian sweet-seller on the platform.

This time they would board the train and, her father told them, they would stay on it all the way to the Kenyan border, three hundred miles away, at Tororo.

Most people in Panyiketto had never been more than twenty miles from the village, and here she was, only thirteen, and about to take her first journey on a train. It made her feel important.

Rose had a good feeling about this journey; she thought it would help her grow up quicker.

* * *

It was midnight. Zakayo was pleased to see that Rose and Akello were finally asleep, slumped in uncomfortable positions on their seats. Dembe had fallen asleep soon after they boarded. Neither the rocking of the train nor the incessant stops seemed capable of stirring them.

The Ugandan rail network was grinding to a halt, due to years of neglect and the more recent disruptions the Amin government had caused in all its agencies. Their carriage was second class, according to the chipped gold lettering below the guttering. In the days when the wood panelling had been nicely varnished and the brass polished, it might have been appropriate. Now the varnish was cracked and the brass baggage racks — those that had not been ripped from the wall — were tarnished black. The railway had given up replacing torn upholstery many years ago. The bare bench seats now provided were not made for a journey of fifteen hours.

The train was late leaving Pakwach. Zakayo had expected that, but from then on it moved only reluctantly forward, spending long periods at rest between stations. Once it inexplicably reversed for several hundred yards.

The younger children were unfazed by the frustrations. Akello could barely remain seated in his excitement, moving up and down the aisle between the bench seats, and opening the window to put his head out. Only when his eyes were raw with the cinders did he concede defeat.

Rose tried to maintain her relative sophistication, but her face glowed with the adventure of it. Her questions were endless until she finally succumbed to sleep, about half an hour after Akello.

The children's excitement had been a diversion. Now, being the only one awake in the carriage, and with time to think, Zakayo's thoughts returned to his plans to save his family.

Amin hated the Acholi and the Lango for their part in Obote's attempts to recapture Uganda. Zakayo felt it was only a matter of time before the madman embarked upon wholesale slaughter. Already over a thousand Acholi soldiers had been murdered in their barracks.

And then there was Amelia in Kampala, with little Itema, and now expecting another baby. Although not an Acholi, she had no family to protect her. He had to return to Kampala as soon as possible and try to find more secure accommodation.

His immediate concern was to get into Kenya with the three children. Since Obote's failed attempt, the border with Kenya had come under close attention because of Kenyatta's allegedly covert support for Obote. Zakayo knew that the train service to Kenya now terminated at Tororo, near the border, but he hoped to be able to cross to Kenya and resume their journey to Kisumu by a Kenyan bus or train service.

Dembe moved in her sleep. Zakayo watched the involuntary twitches caused by her dreams. The cloth she now used for the incessant wiping of her hands threatened to fall from her grasp. He tried to remove it, but her eyes flew open and she grabbed it from him, falling immediately back to sleep — perhaps she had not even awoken. The habit had developed since her attack. It worried him.

Dembe had always been a peaceful, happy child. She had drifted into her relationship with her fiancé with no apparent passion or overriding imperative to marry. He rather thought her view of the impending marriage had been just another part of the peaceful continuum that had been her life to that time.

The guilt he carried because he had not been there to prevent the outrage weighed heavily on him. He made a vow to give his 21-year-old daughter every chance to recover from her ordeal. Whatever the cost.

CHAPTER 22

Zakayo awoke as the train jolted to a stop. The morning sun sent shafts of pain into his gritty eyes. He ran his hands over his face and blinked at the grimy carriage window, which was a translucent wall of yellow light.

Rose and Akello were sprawled on the seat, asleep. The other passengers were stirring, preparing to get off for refreshments. He couldn't see Dembe, and had a moment of near panic until he saw her coming through the carriage, wiping her hands on her cloth.

'Where are we?' he asked as she resumed her seat.

She shrugged. 'I don't know.'

Zakayo lifted the window a fraction and peered out. The cracked wooden sign said 'Tororo Station', and in smaller letters, 'Elev: 2950 ft above sea level'.

He leaned over to the others, and gave them a shake. 'Come on, you two. It's time to get up.'

Rose and Akello were instantly awake, stretching and squinting through the window with sleep in their eyes.

'Where are we?' Rose asked, rubbing her eyes.

'At Tororo. Nearly there. So, let's see if we can get something on the station for breakfast.'

They joined the crowd on the platform.

'What's that smell?' Akello said, wrinkling his nose.

Zakayo recognised it instantly. So as not to alarm them, he began to construct a plausible lie, but the thump of distant artillery and muffled explosions made it superfluous. 'It's the army,' he said, noticing for the first time the plumes of black smoke rising over Tororo. Beyond them loomed Mt Elgon, the extinct volcano that marked the Kenyan border.

'What are they doing, Papa?' Rose asked.

Zakayo guessed that Amin was conducting military operations near the Kenyan border to send Kenyatta a salutary message.

'I don't know, Rose,' he said. 'Just some army practice. Don't worry, it is far.' He looked over the collection of ramshackle railway buildings. Strangely, there were no food-sellers to be found. 'Let's not eat here. We'll soon be at the border. They will have much better food there.'

Forty minutes later, as the train rolled into the small border town of Malaba, the railway tracks became lined with soldiers.

Dembe screwed her piece of cloth into a tight ball. Zakayo could think of nothing to say or do to calm her, but her agitation made him nervous. He had expected that his passport and a small cash bribe would see them through. Individually, the children only had a letter signed by a chief in Pakwach — a friend of Thomas's. He hadn't considered that the military would be in charge of border control, and now wondered if their simple travel papers would satisfy them.

The train inched into the station, almost came to rest, lurched and finally jolted to a dead stop. The conductor and stationmaster were shouting that everyone should disembark. The Nasongas gathered together their bags and parcels and stepped onto the station. Troops were everywhere. Dembe made a soft mewing sound like an animal caught in a trap.

At the end of the platform, the passengers were separating into two streams. The majority followed the rail line. In the distance was a row of ugly buildings — the border control point.

A smaller group headed towards the town.

Zakayo gathered his family around him, took one final look at the soldiers assembled around the immigration checkpoint, and guided them towards the town.

Rose had never seen so many bananas. Inside the truck's cab with the driver were her father and Dembe, while she and Akello had to endure the spiders, the uncomfortable seat and the indignity of being perched on a rocking mountain of Busia bananas.

Akello didn't seem to care. He hadn't stopped smiling since the truck driver offered them a ride an hour ago. They had been walking all morning.

Her father had struck up a conversation with the driver at the roadside stall where he had finally agreed, after much complaining by Rose and Akello, to rest and take something to eat. In the time it took to finish their chapattis and tea, her father had learned from the driver that he was from Busia, another border crossing into Kenya, and that it was similarly infested with soldiers.

The man said he was a Baganda, with no great love for either Obote or Amin. He had complained how difficult it was to sell his bananas since Amin had expelled all the Asians. Incompetents and thieves had taken their place, he said. So he had to drive all the way to Jinja, and sometimes Kampala, to sell them at a reasonable price.

Rose was glad for the ride, but she had lost the feeling of importance she'd enjoyed on the train. The artillery fire and the soldiers around Tororo made her nervous, but it was Dembe's shaking and crying that had made their father decide to abandon a land border crossing and to enter Kenya by ferry from Jinja.

Dembe had acted very strangely since the soldiers attacked her. Her injuries had mended, but Rose often heard her older sister weeping in the darkness of the bedroom they shared. Rose loved Dembe, and felt pity for what had happened, but since the accident she had dominated her father's attention to the exclusion of all others. When Rose heard that her father planned to take just her and Akello to Kisumu, she was thrilled by the thought of the adventure, but also by the prospect of having almost exclusive access to her father. Now, with Dembe there, it was just like at home — her father doted on her, as if it was his fault that the soldiers had attacked her.

'Look, Rose!' Akello was pointing from his perch at the rear of the truck. Over a stand of papyrus stretched a body of water with no end to it. It ran to the horizon like a sheet of flattened metal, engraved near shore by the effects of a light breeze, but as bright as polished silver in the hazy distance. Even in the enormous Albert Nile south of Pakwach, the furthest she had ever previously travelled, the water was never so vast.

Rose knew about Lake Victoria from her school assignments. She remembered that the Victoria Nile flowed out of the lake near Jinja and, after many miles, flung itself down the Murchison Falls. After joining Lake Albert, south of her home town, it became known as the Albert Nile.

The rivers were given their names years ago by Englishmen. In Panyiketto, the people still used Acholi names for them, but at school they had to learn the English ones. It had something to do with a queen of England and her husband, who for some reason was not the king. Anyway, she thought, it didn't matter, because further north the river became the White Nile as it entered the Sudan.

Soon they began to climb a winding road until they were high above the lake. Now she could see a number of headlands, and a narrowing where the drowned ancient hills formed large islands. But still the lake prevailed, extending far beyond them all towards Kenya, and Kisumu.

They left the lake behind a hill on the outskirts of Jinja. The road ran on and on, beyond clusters of grubby petrol stations and cheap ramshackle hotels, through a sea of corrugated iron shacks with packing-case window shutters. Eventually, they passed what seemed like real houses, with brick or timber walls, and a few miles further on the buildings rose three or four storeys above the road.

Rose forgot her embarrassment at riding on a banana truck and stared at the shopfronts with bright printed clothing on display.

Akello gawked at the tall buildings. In one block, women were hanging washing on lines strung in the small space of a balcony. In the next, people were seated at desks behind open office windows.

The progression from squatter settlement to town centre was reversed as they continued to the other side of Jinja, where the lake again came into view. The truck drove onto a very long bridge over a river that Rose guessed was the Victoria Nile. The wind dashed off the lake, buffeting the pair of them on their banana mountain.

The truck came to a halt alongside a row of cheap hotels. Zakayo was deep in conversation with the driver as Rose and her brother scrambled down from the back. They were near the river, and from somewhere downstream came the roaring of water confined too tightly by its surroundings.

Zakayo and the driver held their handshake while a few final words were exchanged, then the driver patted her father on the back, waved goodbye to them, and, with a crunch of gears, rumbled onwards down the road.

Later in the afternoon, after their father had found them a small hotel to spend the night, he took them for a walk along the river. They found a noticeboard proudly proclaiming the site as 'The Source of the Nile'. She and Akello spent the rest of the afternoon arguing if it were possible to have the Nile begin where a lake ended, and what about the rivers feeding the lake?

Soon after first light the next morning, they were on the ferry wharf. Rose itched from a dozen insect bites, but the warmth of the calm morning air, and the sun rising over Lake Victoria, restored her spirits and her enthusiasm.

She still had the mystery of the source of the Nile on her mind, and asked her father how anyone knew where a river, more than a thousand miles long and flowing through three countries, began. He said that a journey of a thousand miles began with a single step.

Her father often made strange pronouncements like that, and they generally left her feeling inadequate. But this time she understood. Her journey, which began in Panyiketto, which was already receding like the memories of childhood, had seemed a thousand miles. Her next step, across the lake and into Kenya, would complete it.

He recognised her voice of course, but decided to play the game. 'Could I speak to Mr Williams, please?'

'Who's calling, please?'

'It's Kip Balmain from Kipana Tours.'

'Kip! I thought it was your voice. How are you?'

'I'm fine. Look, Abu found a lens case in the back of the minibus with your husband's initials on it.'

'Oh, so *that's* where it went.'

'I have it here, so if you put him on, we can —'

'He's in the shower right now, but I'll tell him. He'll be so relieved. Would it be too much trouble to bring it around in an hour, say at four?'

'No trouble at all.'

'Room 600. Come straight up.'

'Fine. I'll see you then.'

At three-fifty he left his hotel and strolled through the gardens to his car. He liked the Fairview and its position on the hill. It was cheap, quiet, and close enough to Nairobi's bustling centre to walk if he had to.

He paused at the open car door and inspected the sky. When the rains ended, Nairobi's sky became bright blue, bluer than anywhere else except perhaps for the Great Rift Valley. In spite of its congestion, its squatter problems and its growing crime rate, Kip liked Nairobi. It was virtually on the equator, but at around six thousand feet the climate was perfect — warm in the sun, cool in the shade.

He whistled as he drove down the hill on Haile Selassie. He appreciated his Nairobi days between safaris. There were enough of them to have some fun, but not so many that he missed the Africa he loved.

More than anything, he enjoyed being in the bush. Each wildlife adventure was different. He even found it interesting dealing with his clients. But to Kip, the essence of Africa, the thing that made it special for him, was the feeling he had when looking out over the savannah — the sensation of endless space. A few days in the city made his return to it all the more significant, so while in Nairobi he made the best of it. If he were lucky, there would be a client worth seeing when the safari ended. Some were more interesting than others, like Samantha Williams.

It was surprising the number of women who seemed to think nothing of jumping into bed with a pleasant stranger. Kip had read somewhere that it was a holiday attraction. He smiled; he had certainly chosen his profession well. He made it a rule to stay out of his clients' beds while on safari. A tented camp was an intimate environment, and in a very short time everyone knew what was going on. Anything passing between him and a client — an exchange of glances, a seemingly innocent conversation — would soon be noticed by all.

Moi Avenue was the usual confusion of pedestrians running the gauntlet across four lanes of traffic. When Kip reached the Hilton, Henry, the parking major-domo, lifted the barrier and Kip saluted him. The former Maasai warrior smiled and doffed his top hat, revealing his closely shaved head and pierced ears with holes large enough to carry a Coke bottle.

'*Jumbo, bwana,*' he said when Kip had parked the car at the kerb.

'*Habari, mzee,*' Kip said, using the formal title for 'gentleman'. He extended his hand and the towering Maasai took it African style: a clasp of hands, then thumbs, then palms again.

'*Karibu.* Welcome, *bwana.* You are back,' the Maasai said.

'I am.' Kip complied with the Kenyan tradition of verbally circling each other with a few obvious observations before easing into a conversation.

'And you are well, Captain Kip?'

'Yes, Henry, I am well. And you?'

'*Mzuri.*' The black man nodded and turned to survey the passing traffic. '*Sasa.*'

The word 'now', indicated the meat of the conversation was approaching. Averting his gaze was also a signal, to indicate that Kip could avoid commenting on the next question without the embarrassment of eye contact.

'You are here for one of your clients, ah?'

'One of my *ex*-clients,' Kip said with overstated emphasis.

'Hmm, and would this ex-client of yours be an ex-lady client, *bwana*?'

Kip slapped the black man on the shoulder. 'Henry, that's confidential client information.'

'Heh, heh, heh.' The chuckle came from deep in Henry's chest. 'As you wish, Captain Kip. *Kwaheri.*'

'Bye, Henry.'

Room 600 was a suite. Kip knocked on the door and waited for a few moments. When he was about to knock again, the door swung open. Samantha was wearing a loose cotton dress that almost reached the floor. The embroidered flower pattern worked in gold thread disclosed its Ethiopian origin.

'Kip!' she said. 'So nice to see you again. Come in.'

'Samantha.' He took her offered hand. 'Thank you.'

The sitting room was large. The bedroom and *en suite* were off to one side. There was no sign of her husband.

'A drink?' she asked. 'I'm having a gin.'

'Thanks, just a Tusker for me. Is Mr Williams in?'

'No, he had to go to the airport with some of our luggage. We are *so* overweight, you wouldn't believe it.'

'Well done,' he said as she handed him his beer.

She raised an eyebrow. 'What do you mean?'

'I mean you've given us maybe two hours, possibly three.'

'Why, Mr Balmain, you're a bit sure of yourself, aren't you?' Her smile was like a cat contemplating cream.

Kip shrugged. 'If I've misunderstood, I can always apologise. If not, and we're going to make love, I won't have wasted any time.'

Smiling, she took his drink and put it with hers on the side table.

He swept her to him, crushing his lips to hers before she could speak. Her tongue searched his and she nibbled at his bottom lip, while he held her to him with a handful of hair in his grip.

They broke apart. She was gasping for breath and started to tug at his belt. He pushed the dress from her shoulders and it fell to the carpet, revealing her naked body.

He knotted his shoelaces in his impatience. She tried to drag him to the bed, but he persisted with the shoes another moment before he tore them from his feet.

He went for her breast with a hungry mouth. Samantha held him by the shoulders and, as he came up to meet her lips, she pushed him over and went down on him. He gasped and again reached for her hair.

He ran his fingers through her blonde mane as she worked on his erect penis. She had lovely hair, but it didn't have the thick texture of Diana's.

CHAPTER 23

The MV *Victoria Nyanza* ploughed through the low swell of Lake Victoria. Its sedate pace irritated Zakayo, and added to his acute impatience to get the children into Kenya. He had managed to buy their passage and clear the Ugandan part of immigration formalities in time for yesterday's eleven o'clock departure, but at noon cargo was still being loaded, and it wasn't until four in the afternoon that passengers were allowed to board.

He stood at the rail watching the water stream by in a widening wake. His thoughts went back to his last voyage, at the end of the war, when he was full of hope and plans for his life in Uganda.

Long before he boarded the ship for home his plans had gone awry. The Russians had trouble finding his regiment so he was held over in Germany for weeks longer than the rest of the POW camp. When he finally arrived in London, he went to the Ploughman's Arms to find his Australian friend, returning each day for a week. Eventually his orders came, and he left without finding him.

His hand went to the piece of painted wood that he had worn around his neck almost from the time Ernie had thrust it into his hands as he was leaving. He'd later sent letters to Ernie's squadron, but he heard nothing in reply. Either his letter to Ernie, or Ernie's reply — if there was one — somehow got lost amongst the debris of war.

At the time, Zakayo had thought it immensely important to contact his friend. It was a matter of honour. However, as the years passed, he found that his recollection of the intensity of their friendship in the camp had waned. He came to the conclusion that extraordinary times forged extraordinary bonds. Although he continued to think fondly of Ernie, the years had weaved a different perspective around their relationship. Perhaps they'd both been misfits, cast together in circumstances where each found reassurance in the other's oddness.

When he finally came home to Panyiketto, Doreen was waiting. They'd married almost immediately. In the early years he'd been content on the farm. When the children arrived it was an added blessing.

It wasn't until he went to Kampala that his equilibrium was shaken. There was so much excitement in the city, so many possibilities. He was enticed by its extravagance — as a child might be drawn towards forbidden fire. He was just sixteen when he joined the British Army and, although he went willingly to war, he felt he had been robbed of his youth. When he came home from the war he was still a relatively young twenty-one, but he had squandered his early years on a dream to become a man of the world — a dream that became a nightmare. When his eyes were opened in Kampala to what he had missed by going to war and marrying immediately afterwards, he wanted to repossess his youth and enjoy himself.

Akello tugged at his shirt.

'What is it?' Zakayo asked, a little more gruffly than intended.

'When will we be there, Papa?'

He could see the shoreline of the gulf that sheltered Kisumu from Lake Victoria's main body of water. 'Not long. Go find your sisters.'

It was a further hour before Kisumu came into view. Zakayo looked at his watch. It was nearly four. He had hoped to find his daughter, Grace, before dark, but now doubted it.

The majority of the passengers were Asians, ethnic Indians like Patel, who had been rounded up in a final sweep to expel even those who claimed Uganda as their only home. Like Zakayo and his family, they were hoping Kenya would take them in.

'It is bigger even than Jinja,' Rose said.

'No, it's not,' replied Akello. 'Jinja is the biggest town in Africa.'

'Don't be silly, Akello,' she said in a voice that was meant to convey the authority of knowledge. 'Kampala is bigger than Jinja and Kisumu.'

'How do you know? Just because you —'

'Hush now,' Zakayo said. 'Collect all your things.' He marshalled his three charges into a good position near the gangway, where the early crush of people confirmed their eagerness to escape the confines of the ship following an oppressive night and day on board.

The immigration offices were surrounded by barbed wire. The Kenyan officials wore uniforms and carried guns. Dembe began to fidget with her cloth again. Zakayo put a hand on her shoulder, but she seemed unaware of it.

At the entrance to the large hut where it appeared their papers would be processed, they were told to wait. About a hundred passengers from the *Victoria Nyanza* stood in the remaining sunlight while the officials picked those to be processed. After some time, it seemed they were choosing those who carried a lot of luggage, or whose women wore the more expensive saris.

As the numbers dwindled, the sun began to set, and Zakayo's apprehension grew.

The bar of Kisumu's Grand Hotel had nothing to recommend it except its superb view. The varnish on its wood-panelled walls had long ago lost its lustre, the surviving leather-covered bar stools were cracked and in parts holed, and the vinyl-covered replacements for those too tattered to repair were a different shade of brown. But the steel-framed windows opened onto a garden sloping downward for a hundred yards to the shores of Lake Victoria. Enormous old bougainvilleas climbed the granite boulders that rose like ramparts to defend the garden from the prevailing winds.

Kip and Harry perched on stools at the end of the bar near an open window. The breeze did more to cool them than the idly turning ceiling fan.

The barmaid put down two beers and waited while Harry sorted through some coins in the palm of his hand.

'Do you have two bob, Kip?'

'Just give her the ten, Harry.'

'Nah, then I'll have a pocketful of change, won't I?'

Kip dug into his pocket and put the two shillings on the bar.

'Thanks, sweetheart,' Harry said when the girl swept the money into her hand and headed to the till. Nodding after her, he added quietly, 'She's sweet on me, that one. Fancies my body, she does.'

'Sure she does, Harry.' After eight years of Harry's fantasies, Kip no longer bothered to disillusion him. 'But go on with your story.'

'My story? What story, ol' darlin'?'

Kip shook his head in half-hearted annoyance. 'For chrissakes, Harry, keep your mind above your navel. You were telling me about the job you picked up last weekend.'

'Oh, yeah!' He took a sip of his beer. 'Harry's at this wedding, see, takin' the usual happy snaps of the bride, the groom, mum and dad, when I sees this absolute stunner of a bridesmaid.' He pulled his stool closer to Kip. 'And I say to her, "A girl like you should be a model."'

Kip ran a hand across his eyes. 'You said what?'

'Yeah, I know, I know. But then she says, "Do you really think so?" And then she goes on to tell me how a lot of her friends have said the same thing. So I say, "What you need is a portfolio", and she says —'

'Cut to the chase, Harry — did you or didn't you?'

'I did.'

'You did?' Kip's mouth hung open.

'Well, you know, I arranged a follow-up at my studio.'

'Oh.'

'So, we're in my studio and —'

'Studio? You mean the dark room at your office?'

'It's not the dark room, Kip. As I keep telling you, it's the equipment storeroom.'

'Right. Aren't you worried that one of the partners might find out about your moonlighting?'

'And I say to her, "Sweetheart, why don't you place yourself in a more comfortable position?" And what do you reckon — she storms off.'

'Really! Even allowing for your usual style, Harry, that seems a bit defensive of her.' Kip thought about it again. He knew Harry fairly well. *Place yourself in a more comfortable position* didn't sound right for him. 'Are you sure that's exactly what you said?'

Harry took a mouthful of his beer. 'Yes. Well ... Harry might have been a little more direct. I mean, it was for a fashion shot, for chrissakes.'

'So you said, "Sweetheart, why don't you take all your clothes off?"'

Harry sighed. 'Something like that.'

Kip smiled and shook his head. He'd learned that lecturing Harry was pointless, so he saved his breath.

'But you're right, Kip. What Harry needs is a proper studio.'

'What Harry needs are better lines.'

Kip looked at his watch. 'Hugh should be along at any moment,' he said.

'Hugh? Hugh Hartigan?'

'Yes. He said he'd join us for a drink.'

Harry lit a cigarette. 'I never managed to work it out with you two,' he said, shaking the match out.

'Hugh and me?'

'Yes. I mean, there you are, bonking his wife, and next thing you're like father and son.'

Try as he might, Kip had been unable to keep the affair with Diana secret from Harry, who was his flatmate at the time. Harry was not the kind of man who could abide a mystery. He'd searched and questioned until he had all the pieces of the puzzle and, ultimately, the answer: Kip Balmain was having an affair with the wife of the most powerful white man in Kenya.

'I don't know how many times I have to correct you, Harry. I finished it, or at least Diana did, long before I met Hugh. It was over in less than a year, and it never started up again.'

'You really had balls to begin it.'

'I was young and stupid.' Kip sipped his beer. 'It taught me a lesson. No more getting serious with married ladies — I can't handle the rejection.'

'Not that you've had to worry too much about that in your time, ol' diamond. And now, after — what is it? Six, seven years — you have this friendship with the bloke. Doesn't that make you feel, you know, a bit weird?'

'You mean guilty? It does at times. If Hugh wasn't the kind of person he is, it wouldn't bother me as much.'

Kip continued to ponder the issue, unsure of how to describe the mixture of guilt and relief he felt: guilt because he'd intruded upon a marriage that had survived for many years despite Diana's affairs, and relief that he and Diana hadn't jeopardised what had become, for Kip at least, a very warm friendship with Hugh.

Harry put his cigarette on the ashtray and lifted his beer. 'Harry doesn't feel guilty about having sex. Never,' he said.

'No? What's your feelings?'

'Gratitude.' He took a mouthful of his Tusker. 'Sheer gratitude.'

Kip laughed. 'Ah, here's Hugh.'

A tall, greying man stood at the door of the bar, squinting into the early afternoon light that shone through the window behind them. Kip waved him over. Hartigan's stiff knee forced him to walk more erect than most men of his age, and it made him look a little taller than his five foot ten.

Kip stood and took his hand. 'Hugh, good to see you.'

Hartigan pulled Kip to him and gave him a bear hug. 'You too. Where've you been hiding? Haven't seen you for months.'

'Oh, you know ... You remember Harry Forsythe?' He touched Harry on the shoulder.

'Yes, I do,' Hartigan said. 'The newspaper man.'

'Photographer. Freelancing these days. Nice to see you again.' They shook hands. Harry asked Hartigan what he was drinking, and then went to the bar to order.

Hartigan looked Kip over and beamed his pleasure at seeing him. 'You're looking well, Kip,' he said, arranging his stiff leg under the table.

'So are you, Hugh. I'm glad we could catch up while I'm here.'

'Indeed. I think the last time was when you came to the ranch for Diana's birthday.'

'That's right, and by the way, happy birthday to you.'

'Oh, blast. These days I'd rather forget them. You must have been speaking to Diana.'

'I was, but I remember it from the last time.'

'Well, that's very kind. You know, we really should catch up more often. We're beginning to act like my family — only getting together at birthdays, funerals and weddings.'

Harry returned with the drinks. 'Who's getting married?' he asked.

'Nobody,' Kip replied. 'But it's Hugh's birthday.'

'A birthday?' Harry said. 'That's great! Happy days, Hugh.'

'Yes, many more of them, Hugh,' Kip said, lifting his glass in a toast. They all clinked glasses.

'How old?' Harry asked.

Kip winced. Harry was being Harry, but Hugh

didn't seem to take offence. 'Rapidly approaching seventy,' he replied with a sigh.

'Bloody frightening thought, isn't it?' Harry said, putting his glass down and reaching for another cigarette.

'What is?' Kip asked.

'Galloping old age.'

'For chrissakes, Harry, Hugh said he's nearly seventy, not about to kick the bucket!' Kip shrugged his apologies to Hugh, who just smiled.

'No, I'm not just talking about Hugh. It's about all of us. I'm approaching middle age and you, what are you, Kip, twenty-eight? The big three-oh is approaching.'

'Take no notice of him, Hugh. The man's a born pessimist. I'm sure you'll have a great birthday. What do you have planned?'

'Nothing really. I was hoping you and I could get together for lunch. A few drinks. And Harry too, if you're free.'

Harry accepted immediately.

'I'd love to, Hugh,' Kip said, 'but can we make it this evening? I've got to see my builder this afternoon.'

'Oh, is that for Mara Escarpment Lodge? It's finally happening, eh?'

'Yes. *Hakuna haraka*,' Kip replied.

'I know what you mean. "No hurry" seems to be the popular excuse for everything. I hate to sound like an old colonial, but the country is slowly sinking into a morass. The only things for certain these days are tea money and endless delays.'

'Hugh, you're right, you *are* an old colonial.' Kip smiled, patting the older man on the back. 'You just don't know how to deal with the modern Kenyan businessman. You can't expect *bwana* this and *bwana* that any more. If you deal with them as in any other business relationship — rationally, professionally — you'll find it goes a long way towards fixing the problem.'

'What do you mean, you don't have the timber?' Kip spluttered. 'You told me it was on its way three weeks ago!'

The building foreman shrugged. 'It's the shipping line ... these Ugandans, ah?' The implication was that this fact closed the matter.

Kip eyed the foreman. He was a lanky old Luo who, like Kisumu, had seen better days. 'Tell me, my friend,' he began, trying to keep his annoyance from escalating, 'why would anyone want to order timber from Uganda these days?'

'But ... we always get our timber from Uganda,' the Luo said with raised eyebrows.

'The country's in a state of civil bloody war! Why not buy it from here in Kenya? Don't we have timber? Why would anyone want to deal with Uganda? They have never been reliable, and now they're led by a bunch of madmen.'

The Luo looked at the order form on the desk as if it might hold the answer. '*Sijui,*' he said finally.

Kip had had enough. He was talking to the wrong man. '*Wapi bwana?*' he asked. He decided the manager would hear about this.

The Luo shrugged again. 'Nairobi.'

Kip rubbed his forehead for a moment to give him time to control his temper. 'Let me see that order,' he said, taking it from the foreman's hands.

It had been placed six weeks ago. He jotted down the order number and noted the name of the shipping company. His timber was scheduled for shipment on the MV *Victoria Nyanza*.

'*Kwaheri*,' he said as he stormed out the door. It was after five o'clock, but with luck the shipping agent might still be in his office.

As the sun sank into the lake, the Nasonga family's shadows stretched across the golden compound, through the barbed-wire fence, to eventually climb the wall of a warehouse a hundred yards away.

They were the last of the passengers to be processed and had been waiting for thirty minutes since the previous family were sent through the exit gates. The Indian man had looked back at Zakayo as if he were about to speak. Perhaps he would have under different circumstances, but he led his family away without a word. Meanwhile, from inside the immigration office came the sound of laughter. Zakayo imagined the officials had accumulated a good stock of fine old brandy confiscated from the Asians.

An official came out of the office laughing, and threw an empty bottle into the lake. He was tall and hatless. His hair was cut very short, revealing an angry scar on his scalp. He ran his eye over the family, lingering on Dembe for some time, then he grunted to Zakayo that he should enter. Zakayo motioned to his children to stay where they were.

The uniformed man at the desk had red-rimmed eyes and his neck overflowed his collar. The other four were picking over a collection of items on a table behind him. He looked up at Zakayo and then to the papers in his outstretched hand. Instead of taking them, he grabbed Zakayo's wrist and turned his hand to expose his watch, which was old but had survived numerous mishaps since the end of the war.

The official flicked through the pages of his passport and scanned the letters verifying the status of his children. 'An Acholi,' he said, smiling. 'From the north, isn't it?' He looked up at Zakayo, who nodded.

'Tell me, Acholi, how does an ignorant peasant like you get to own such a fine watch?'

One of the men behind him guffawed.

'I bought it many years ago, sir. It is old, and almost finished. As you can see.'

'And where did you buy this watch?' The man who had laughed asked the question. He was the same official who had called him into the room. Zakayo noticed that the scar on his scalp curved under his ear to the side of his face.

'I bought the watch in London,' he answered.

'Lying dog!' the scarred man said, coming up to him and smashing the back of his hand into his face.

Zakayo reeled back. His head rang like a bell.

'Where did you get the watch?' the official repeated. His breath smelled strongly of whisky.

'I'm sorry, sir. I bought this old watch in a second-hand shop in Kampala.'

'Hah,' the man said and nodded to the man at the desk.

The seated official continued to inspect the travel papers but flicked his index finger to indicate that the watch should be placed on the desk.

Zakayo hesitated an instant, but the fat man looked up from his passport, this time without his smile. Zakayo unfastened the band and placed the watch gently on the desk. The official casually tossed it onto the table behind him.

'Ugandan money?' he demanded.

Zakayo was expecting this, and pulled out a wad of small notes and a handful of coins.

Again the official's bloodshot eyes coldly appraised him. For a moment Zakayo felt panic that he might order him searched. His other money was in his shoe.

The official scooped up the money and made an almost imperceptible gesture to dismiss him. Zakayo hesitated, unsure if he had been cleared to leave.

The tall man at the table said, 'Spot check.'

The fat one lifted an eyebrow in question.

'Spot check, boss. The others have no passports. Maybe we should make a spot check to be sure.'

His colleague nodded, and said, 'Yes. You are right.' Turning to Zakayo he said, 'Send in your daughter, Acholi.'

Zakayo looked from the seated official to the man behind him, who was smirking. 'But, sir —'

A look of pure fury crossed the tall man's face, but the senior man said, 'Don't worry, Acholi, it's normal practice. No one will hurt your precious daughter.'

Still he hesitated before seeing the anger return to the official's eyes. He backed away, the scar-faced man following him to the door where he stood as Zakayo descended the stairs to his family.

Dembe was rigid with fear, as if she knew of some terrible sentence that had been passed on her. She rubbed her hands with her cloth and her lip was white where she bit it to keep from sobbing. Zakayo knew the sight of a uniform made her hysterical. He couldn't ask her to go through the procedure, no matter how inoffensive it was.

The official wanted a spot check of his daughter. He didn't say which one, and Rose would be better able to cope with the immigration officer's questions. He took her by the hand and led his younger daughter up the steps to where the tall man and another waited.

Taking Rose's wrist in his hand, the scarred man pushed Zakayo back. 'Spot check,' he said. The door slammed in Zakayo's face.

He stood there for several minutes in an agony of indecision. He didn't want to antagonise the officials; after all, they'd said it was a routine procedure.

From inside came the sounds of furniture being pushed around and a muffled cry. Zakayo burst through the office door.

Rose was sprawled forward on the table among the cash, watches and jewellery, her hands pinned down, her dress over her head. The tall man stood behind her, his trousers down around his ankles.

'No!' Zakayo screamed.

The Kenyan official at the door hit him with the butt of his gun.

CHAPTER 24

The meeting had begun well enough, with Kip enquiring about his shipment of timber from Uganda. He even remained patient as Samuel Njui, the managing agent for the shipping line, clearly annoyed at being held back after normal closing hours, shuffled papers and, after ten minutes, declared he couldn't find the consignment note.

'No,' Kip said to the suggestion he should come back in the morning. 'I am going down to Nairobi first thing. All I want is confirmation that the timber is on board. Nothing more.'

'Well,' Njui replied, 'as I have just explained, I can't find the papers, so I can't tell you one way or the other.'

Kip started to lose his patience. 'You are a shipping agent, right? I don't know much about your business, Mr Njui, but I imagine it has a lot to do with papers — papers that tell you where things are, or should be.'

Njui stonewalled, glaring at Kip.

'So how the hell can you stay in business if you can't tell me if a consignment is or isn't on a ship that's sitting outside your fucking office window?'

At that stage Kip was merely annoyed. Samuel Njui had been rude, unsympathetic and annoyingly bureaucratic. But then Njui accused him of being an old colonial with a high-handed attitude and suddenly Kip was apoplectic with rage — at Njui, and at himself because he was unable to articulate an appropriate retort.

Finally he made a reference to incompetence hiding behind racism, spluttered a few swear words and stormed out of the office.

Standing at the car door with his ring of keys in his hand, he tried to regain his composure. The sun had sunk into the silver-grey waters of the lake. The evening was still — the interlude of oppressive heat before the onshore breeze brought some relief to the remnant heat of the day. He rubbed the small bit of wood he kept attached to his key ring between his thumb and forefinger. Feeling the squiggly lines of paint on it always seemed to calm him.

The lake made soft lapping sounds against the sea wall. Overhead, a pelican came in for a landing under the floodlights on the wharf. It dropped onto a warehouse roof, tucked its wings into a tidy position and settled for the night.

Kip was about to climb into the car when a bedraggled group came out of the darkness into the circle of light outside the agent's office. They were typical travellers, with an assortment of bags and parcels tied with string. But the man had fresh bloodstains on his shirt, and the three with him, a boy, a girl and a young woman, shuffled along as if afraid to be separated from him by more than inches.

The young girl glanced at Kip, or, more correctly, through him, as they passed. There was something about her, about the whole family, that spoke of despair. Normally, he would have let them pass, not for lack of pity, but in recognition of reality.

Whenever he had been driven to offer help in similar circumstances, he'd invariably found the issues were so complex, or hopeless, that he could offer nothing but sympathy. The experiences had left him feeling sad and inadequate.

'*Ngoja*,' he said, bidding them to wait until he joined them at the edge of the light.

The man lifted his face to Kip. His eyes were bleary and blood oozed from his head wound. Kip was about to use the customary greeting of *habari* — literally, 'How is your news?' — but under the circumstances it rang hollow. Instead he asked if he was all right. '*Umzima?*' The answer was obvious but he could think of nothing else.

The man was only partially conscious. Kip looked at each of the others, probably his children, but they avoided his gaze.

'I'd better get you to hospital,' he said to himself.

'Yes.' The younger girl answered him. She was tall for her age, but Kip thought she could hardly be more than thirteen or fourteen. It was unusual for a young girl to be so forthcoming with a white adult male.

'My father needs a doctor,' she went on.

'Yes, of course. Let's get him into my car.'

Kip steered the man towards the Land Rover and helped him into the back seat. The other two children joined him, leaving the young girl to sit in the front with Kip. She seemed removed from the situation, as if she were simply an observer rather than a participant in the drama. Kip felt as if he was in the presence of a person sleepwalking. He was afraid to speak in case his voice intruded and she awoke in fright.

The hospital's casualty section was a shambles. They waited for hours for a doctor. By then the boy had fallen asleep on the floor beside his older sister, who dozed in her seat. The other girl, the one with the faraway look in her eyes, sat beside her father, who moaned from time to time and put his head into his hands. It appeared to Kip to be a cry of sorrow more than of pain. Apart from a grunt in reply to most questions, he remained uncommunicative.

Kip decided to risk breaking into the girl's barrier of silence. 'Were you on the ship from Uganda?'

She made no response, and he was about to repeat the question when she nodded her reply.

'How did your father get hurt?'

This time the girl remained silent and expressionless.

'Did he fall down?'

Again, nothing.

He thought he'd try another tactic. 'What's your name?'

She turned to face him. She was quite pretty with large, intelligent but, at the same time, sad eyes. She appeared not to have understood the question.

'What's your name?' he repeated.

'Rose,' she said in a small voice.

'Rose. It's a pretty name.'

Her eyes held his again, but she did not appear to hear or understand.

'A rose by any other name would smell as sweet,' he added lamely, trying to break the uncomfortable silence.

Her expression did not change. Kip thought she was in some kind of trance, then, without a murmur from her, tears rolled down her cheeks.

Zakayo slowly pushed his chair back from the table and rose to his feet. He touched a fingertip to the bandage on his head, which had loosened as the swelling reduced. Another day and he could take it off.

'What is it, Papa?' Grace asked. 'There is more to eat. Sit, I'll bring it.'

'No, Grace. I've had enough.' He tried to raise a smile for her sake. '*Asante sana*. I'm just going outside for a walk.'

He had to escape the atmosphere in Grace's house. His eldest daughter was polite, her husband very hospitable, but Zakayo found it stifling.

The sun assaulted him immediately he stepped outside, but he forced himself towards the lake where he could find some silence, and some time to think.

Rose had not said a word to him about the attack on the wharf, but he felt her eyes follow him whenever he came into the room. He had planned to raise it with her, to try to explain what was in his mind when he let her go inside to the guards, but the words would not come.

He crossed the sports ground. Wispy tufts of grass clung tenaciously to the rock-hard surface. A dust eddy swirled around him as he walked through the bare goal mouth. Ahead was a line of trees that defined the pitch's boundary and the edge of the lake.

He found the rock he had favoured each time he had made the journey to the lake over the last four days. A large eucalyptus shaded it, and small waves lapped against its base with a soothing regularity. He settled himself on its rounded dome and, as he had on each previous visit, tried to find a foothold in the wall of regrets that now loomed, blocking his best intentions for the happiness and security of his Panyiketto family.

Perhaps he had been too young to marry; too immature to accept the responsibility of fatherhood.

Doreen had often told him he should spend more time with the children, especially Adam, who, she warned, needed a father's presence in his troubled life. Zakayo had ignored her. But these days he sometimes awoke from dreamless sleep thinking of his lost son, wondering where he was.

He blamed himself for Dembe's rape. He could have been there with her — with them all, for they had all been at risk and were saved only by circumstance — but he wasn't.

And Rose. What madness had made him think he could sacrifice one daughter to save another? He was disgusted by his cowardice. Fear was no excuse, but even if it were, he could not admit it to Rose.

In his other life with Amelia, he had no such regrets. He prayed that he would be a better man for her, and a better father to Itema.

His life was torn between two worlds competing for his time. He could not satisfy both, nor could he abandon either, but with Amelia and Itema at least he had another chance to get it right.

PART 4

MAINA

CHAPTER 25

1982

The Assistant Minister for Provincial Administration and Internal Security, the Honourable Maina Githinji, sat back in his chair, rested one leg over the knee of the other, and folded his hands behind his head. Opposite him sat Barry Costello, the Deputy Consul General at the American Embassy.

'Please don't misunderstand, Mr Costello, the government of Kenya is not opposed in principle to the United States sending observers into the Northern Frontier Zone. As you know, our countries have been co-operating in matters of security for many years.'

'And my government is very appreciative of that fact, Mr Assistant Minister.'

'But one of the objectives of our exercises in the NFZ is to show the Somalis we are capable of defending our own soil.' Githinji sat forward to study a mark on his trouser leg, and brushed a speck of dust from it. Satisfied with the result, he sat back and resumed his pose with his hands behind his head, exposing an expanse of white shirt over his ample girth. 'And that while we have powerful friends, such as the United States,' he gestured with an open palm towards Costello, 'we are able to do so without their assistance, if necessary.'

'Yessir, as I have said, an excellent idea.'

'So, under those circumstances, we don't want a lot of US army personnel in the neighbourhood, do we?'

'Quite right, Mr Githinji, you don't want the US to be seen at all. That's why I thought it would be useful if we had this little chat, off the record.'

'Off the record? As you are probably aware, Mr Costello, I am relatively new to my portfolio here in National Security, but I understand that if a foreign country's forces are to be committed to the field, it is usual practice to have intergovernmental agreements *on* the record.'

'Yessir, but I am not proposing that the US send regulars into the NFZ.'

'No?' Githinji raised his eyebrows.

'No. In fact, in these, ah, delicate times, I thought, that is, *we* thought, it would be better to keep our presence discreet.'

Everybody in the intelligence community knew Costello's real job was head of the CIA in East Africa, but Githinji wanted to play the game. It was better to plead ignorance and be persuaded to the CIA's cause, than to be co-operative at the outset. 'Hmm, most irregular, Mr Costello.'

'Mr Githinji, may I speak frankly?'

Githinji nodded. 'Of course.'

'Our intelligence people are very interested in an Ethiopian-backed group. They are against the present oppressive government in Mogadishu, and we are trying to establish contact with them.'

'Hmm, I see.' Githinji examined his shoe and, taking his handkerchief out, gave its already high sheen a buffing. 'Please, go on.'

'We, that is, our intelligence people in Washington, want to send an operative up north to facilitate that contact.'

'I appreciate your candour, Mr Costello, but I don't see why the Kenyan Government needs to be involved with the movement of individual American citizens. Why, we have hundreds in Nairobi as we speak; thousands on safari in all parts of the country.'

'Indeed, Mr Assistant Minister. I only want to be sure that there is no misunderstanding should our operative be searched en route to Marsabit. I understand the officials at Isiolo can be very, ah, enthusiastic at the checkpoint.'

'And for good reason, Mr Costello. We must know how many tourists are going into that region. And their identity. The Somali *shiftas* are very fierce. My God, they are ruthless! We warn tourists about the danger, but what can we do? At the end of the day, we don't want to have any western embassy chasing us if one of their nationals goes missing up north, do we?'

'No, sir. It's just that —'

'No need to labour the point, Mr Costello, I understand perfectly. You would like me to do you a favour. No, no! It's perfectly all right. You are asking a friend, in this case the Kenyan Government, for a little hospitality. It is no problem to us. We are a very friendly country, as I am sure you are already aware.'

'That is very kind of you, sir. Very kind.'

'Now, if you give my assistant the name of your — what do you call him? Your *operative* — I will make sure our people at Isiolo do not look too closely into his travel luggage.'

'Thank you, Mr Assistant Minister. We are indebted.'

'Not at all.' Githinji rose to see him to the door.

Before stepping into the outside office, Costello said, 'Have you seen our new VIP guest accommodation in Mombasa yet, Mr Githinji?'

'No, I don't believe so.'

'Oh, well you should. It's on the waterfront at Nyali Beach. I think you would enjoy it. We have a fifty-five-foot launch, and a crew of the navy's finest.'

'It sounds very interesting.'

'Perhaps you and Mrs Githinji would like to be our guests.'

'An inspection tour. Yes, I believe we would enjoy that.'

'I'll make all the necessary arrangements with your assistant if you wish.'

'Thank you.'

'Good day to you, Mr Githinji.'

'Yes, good day.'

'I thought we were going to the Mathaiga Club, Diana,' Kip said as the taxi drew up outside the Norfolk Hotel in Harry Thuku Road. 'This end of town is not the place to be these days.'

'Kip, don't be silly. The riots were weeks ago, and anyway, the university is closed.'

Kip fumbled in his pocket for the taxi fare, but Diana beat him to it.

'Good afternoon, Mrs Hartigan,' the Norfolk doorman said, opening the car door.

'Afternoon, George,' she replied.

'I wish you wouldn't do that, Diana,' Kip whispered as she took his arm to climb the few steps.

'What?' she said, feigning innocence.

'You know damn well.'

'Oh, don't be so old-fashioned,' she said. 'Come on, you can pay for the drinks if it makes you feel any better.'

They sat at a table overlooking the street, Kip still chafing about the taxi fare. 'And I'm really not happy about being at this end of town.'

'Kip Balmain! You old fart. How old are you now? Thirty-eight? I can remember when you faced a charging rhino and didn't flinch.'

'Diana, don't exaggerate — it was a buffalo, and I did flinch — but I don't go looking for trouble either.'

'Trouble! What trouble? A few rioting students aren't going to bother us.'

'It's not the students I worry about; it's the General Services Unit. They don't seem to care where they point their semiautomatics.'

'What's all the fuss about anyway? I mean with the students.'

'It's the new legislation to make us a one-party state.'

'So what? It's been all KAAB since way back anyway.' The Kenyan Association of African Brethren had been the ruling party since independence.

'I know, but now it's official. Can't say I blame the students for being upset.'

The waiter arrived and Kip ordered their drinks. 'The service here has gone off,' he said after the waiter had left. 'I don't know why we couldn't meet at the Mathaiga Club, as we usually do.'

'It's boring and stuffy, and besides, we have to meet some people here later.'

'We do?' Kip sighed. 'I was hoping to get out to the National Parks headquarters later.'

'Don't worry about that. Relax. You can go to Langata tomorrow.'

'Yes, ma'am.'

Her laugh was the same deep throaty chuckle of eighteen years ago, when they'd first met on the road to the Aberdares Country Club. 'This is important. Hugh's bringing some people he met through the American Embassy. It's something about surveys around Marsabit. They want us to be their guides.'

'No problem. The office can arrange all that for them.'

'But they want us — you, actually. And they're prepared to pay.'

'Diana, I can't just charge off to Marsabit. There's the office to run.'

Business had boomed in recent years. Kipana Tours offered an ecologically sound, high-quality wildlife experience, and it was proving more popular than Kip and Diana had ever hoped.

It had been Kip's idea that discerning tourists would become disillusioned with the type of mass-market tourism that Kenya was promoting. His experience in the true wilderness game reserves of Tanzania, while training to be a game warden, had introduced him to the delights of wildlife in a natural environment and without the intrusion of half a dozen tourist-laden minivans jostling for the best photographic vantage point. However, unlike Tanzania, where the state-run tourism industry suffered from the laissez-faire attitudes of socialism, Kipana Tours also offered five-star accommodation and service.

To offer those kinds of tours, Kipana had to strictly limit their number of clients. The greatest risk for Kip and Diana was that people might not be prepared to pay the price they had to charge to cover the cost of running such an exclusive service.

As it transpired, Kip learned there were people who not only wanted to enjoy an authentic wildlife encounter, but would only do so if not in private, then with a minimum number of similarly minded people. Kip realised that the wealthy had always exploited a simple rule to ensure this condition was met: they went for the most expensive offering on the market. Diana made use of· her and Hugh's network of millionaires to find sufficient clients.

'Harry can look after the office for a few days,' she countered now.

Kip had to admit she was right. Harry had first become involved with Kipana Tours doing promotional shots on a contract basis. Then he started handling the advertising and did stints as a part-time marketer. As his knowledge of the business grew, he became indispensable to the rapidly growing company, filling a number of roles from occasional tour guide to truck driver.

'Okay, it's true, Harry could fill in, but why me specifically?'

'Don't know. I imagine we'll learn more when we meet them.'

Thirty minutes later, while Diana was momentarily away from the table, Hugh Hartigan's Jaguar arrived. Hugh was sitting in front with his driver.

Kip admired Hartigan. He had arrived in Kenya on a shooting safari after the war, and decided to settle. Since then he had made and lost more than one fortune in various ambitious projects, and now, according to Diana, was turning his attention to minerals. He had boundless energy and charm, and his generosity was legendary. Most knew of his financial support for local charities, but it was his generosity of spirit that appealed to Kip; with the same energy he applied to his business interests, Hugh held nothing back from his friends.

It made Kip wonder why Diana continued to have affairs. It wasn't because he was jealous, although deep inside he was still very much in love with her, but because they threatened to hurt Hugh. Kip had to continue to remind himself of his hypocrisy, and he lived in fear that Hugh might learn about their past, or that he might inadvertently reveal his real feelings for Diana. He was sure it would break Hugh's heart.

Hartigan pulled himself out of the passenger's seat, ignoring the doorman's assistance. Three others followed him out of the Jaguar. The first was an American; Kip guessed his nationality by his checked shirt and striped tie. The second, in a bush shirt and cotton slacks, looked like a tourist, but was more likely a businessman with enough sense to wear comfortable clothes in the tropics. The last was a black woman. From her stylish, pinstriped dark skirt and pink blouse, he could see she was also from out of town. She strode purposefully up the steps to the veranda, beside the men.

'Hello, Kip,' Hartigan said, stepping forward to take Kip's hand in his.

'How are you, Hugh? Long time.'

Hartigan drew him in and threw his other arm around his shoulder, giving him a bear hug. 'It is, my boy. Too long.' He kept his arm over Kip's shoulder and added, 'You look well.'

'Thank you, Hugh. You're a ball of muscle yourself. As usual.'

'Hah!' The older man slapped his midriff. 'Look at this! Flab. Too many hours on the books and too few on the horse. But where's Diana? I'd like to introduce you both to my friends here.'

'She's just —'

'Ah, there she is.'

Diana came sweeping up to give Hartigan a peck on the cheek. 'Hello, darling,' she said.

Her husband kissed her hand. 'Darling, and Kip of course, I'd like you to meet Miss Eva Deloite, John Demitrio,' he indicated the striped tie, 'and Kevin Armstrong.'

Kip shook hands with the two men, nodding a greeting. He hesitated at Eva. Since equality had become the consuming social issue of the day, he was always uncertain how to proceed with Western women, but she extended her hand and took his in a comfortable grasp.

As they ate lunch, Kip learned that the two men worked for the same large American mining conglomerate, and Eva was from the US Department of Industry. A deposit of what they called 'rare earths' had been found north of Marsabit, and their visit was to determine what was available to support a mining operation.

When discussion turned to the infrastructure, Kip told them they would have to take everything they needed. 'There's not much there. Water, food — everything's scarce. Marsabit is a small town at the edge of an enormous wilderness. It would make your old west pale into insignificance. The road was bad when I was last there in 1979. Really bad. In the last three years they've had some terrible weather. It may be almost nonexistent by now.'

'Why not fly there?' Diana asked.

'No. Can't do,' Eva said. 'Part of our study is to evaluate the road network.'

'Then we drive,' Kip said. 'You know we'll need some paperwork to get us beyond Archer's Post, don't you?'

'Yes,' Demitrio said. 'The embassy people have been working with someone in the government.' He was a dark, heavy-set man with an aggressive thrust to his jaw.

'We all have our clearances,' said Hartigan.

'Are you going too, Hugh?' Kip thought the older man had given up field work.

'Yes. We may be able to offer local support if the project goes through.'

'Me too,' Diana said, grinning.

'You? Why are you going?'

'Because it's there, silly. And I've always wanted to see the wild north, but Hugh wouldn't take me.'

'And for good reason,' Kip said, turning to Hugh. 'So, why now, Hugh?'

Hartigan shrugged and rolled his eyes.

'I see,' Kip said. 'Well, we can stay in our Laikipia Lodge for the first night, but I've got to say that after that it's all downhill. Not our usual Kipana standards; we'll be sleeping rough under canvas.'

'We'll manage,' Eva said, crossing her long legs. Kip noticed again that she had a very direct gaze, holding him with her eyes for a moment longer than customary.

'I reckon you'll need about five days to cover the area you're interested in. Would a Tuesday departure be okay with you people?' He looked around the table. There were nods from all.

The man in the bush shirt, Kevin Armstrong, said, 'What do we need to bring?' He was angular and wiry, with a crew cut that made him look like an ageing college kid. He had been silent to that point.

'Only your personal stuff. Sensible clothing. What you're wearing is okay. I'll arrange all the camping gear, food and water.' Kip turned to Diana. 'I really wish you'd reconsider.'

'Well, too bad. I'm coming.'

'This isn't just another safari. There are plenty of *shifta* bandits up there. The army have had no real impact — they strike at anybody they think might be worth robbing, then scoot back over the border. A tourist was hurt a couple of months ago.'

'But the Kenyan army don't have what we have.'

'What's that?' he asked.

'Kip Balmain,' she said with a cheeky grin. 'The great white hunter.'

CHAPTER 26

The Westlands Inn was always dimly lit and poorly patronised. It was one of the reasons it was chosen for meetings of the Karuri Group. Another was the kitchen, which was known to offer the best *nyama chosa* west of Nairobi.

Making barbecued goat a feature of the menu in the *mzungu* heartland required either courage or naivety. That the restaurant had survived at all was due to the patronage of *wazungu* from surrounding white neighbourhoods who wanted to impress their friends and overseas visitors with their knowledge of African cuisine. They were people who would find nothing unusual about a dozen black businessmen enjoying the *nyama chosa* after work. But the Karuri Group were not just businessmen. They were all rising stars in their professions, and all Kikuyus.

The group borrowed their name from Karuri wa Gakore, the last of the great Kikuyu chiefs, who had fifty wives when he died in 1916. Karuri was formed following the death of Jomo Kenyatta — Kenya's first president, and a Kikuyu. Many of the tribe rose to positions of power and influence under the *Mzee*. With his passing in 1978, Kikuyus — particularly the young bloods — began to fear that the new president, a Luo, would rob them of their chance to follow in the successful footsteps of their elder brethren.

The youngest members were from the air force's air cavalry unit — men who favoured crew cuts and wore dark glasses at night. They were well educated, trained to take control in tight situations, and flew the flashy F-5 interceptors. They were impatient to make their mark on modern Kenya, and their egos made them prime candidates to do what must be done when the time was right.

Githinji, at forty-two, was about the oldest member of the group, but an important one because of his position in the Office of the President. It was his access to privileged information that had prompted him to call the group together that night, to discuss the disturbing news that the parliament had passed a bill declaring Kenya a one-party state.

'The army are about to make a show of force in the north,' Githinji said, speaking softly in Kigikuyu for added secrecy. 'Most of the units will be dispatched progressively over the next few weeks, so as not to draw attention to it. By the time they are all assembled, the standing force in Nairobi will be little more than telephonists and floor-sweepers.'

'How long will they be there?' someone asked.

'Probably just long enough to show the Somalis we are capable of looking after ourselves, and to impress the Americans that we can do our share of the fighting, if it comes.'

'Then, is this the time?' another man asked. It was the question in everyone's mind.

Githinji looked around the circle of faces. 'It is not for me to say. But those of you who are thinking about lighting the fire,' he looked at the young men of the air force, 'can do so knowing the army will be at least a two-day journey from Nairobi.'

Maina Githinji sat in his darkened sitting room feeling a mixture of excitement and fear. The boulder he had started rolling months ago was finally gathering momentum. Initially it had faltered at pebbles put in its path by the many doubters, but now it had found a direction.

Earlier that night he had given it a bold shove, but it was not his wish to be seen as its prime mover. It was for others to rush in its wake. He must remain at a safe distance and await his call to leadership — real leadership, unlike the scraps that the party had tossed him following President Odhiambo's rise to power.

Under Kenyatta, Maina's star had risen rapidly. Although the president had denied involvement with the Mau Mau, Kenyatta had great sympathy for the ex-freedom fighters. People like Githinji, who had taken to the forest in the bad days and showed some ability, were not forgotten by the *Mzee*.

Now there were Kikuyu leaders who had seen their chances crumble when a Luo rose to the presidency. If he were removed, they would fill the void with energetic young Kikuyu men like Githinji. By the time the boulder had run its destructive course, Maina Githinji, the boy who years before had fled into the jungle filled with misery and rage, would take his place among the powerful.

He had fought for that place and it had come at a terrible cost. There was blood on his hands — bad blood. He had tried to put the vengeance and hate behind him, but although nearly thirty years had passed, one memory would not fade, no matter how he tried to erase it.

It had been a night troubled by persistent rain, but finally the rain had cleared as the squad neared their target.

Dewdrops clung like pearls to the drooping fan-shaped fronds of the young borassus palm. Maina sat below it, ignoring the chill that invaded his body. He was tall for his age, and no longer a boy. The massacre of his family and neighbours had hardened his heart, and six months in the jungle had hardened his body.

Field Marshal Kimathi signed that they should again edge forward. They had marched all night to be there before the dawn and, as the birds came to life with a song to welcome the sun to the forest, they were almost in position to attack. Below them the hamlet was wrapped in a veil of mist. Like a ripe melon, it was ready to be slashed open.

The crisp morning air carried the raw scent of mouldering vegetation and wood smoke — an aroma Maina knew well. He would rather it was a white settlement they were about to attack than one of their brother Kikuyu, but Dedan Kimathi was not a faint-hearted man when it came to the fight for land rights and independence. An obstacle of any kind must be destroyed. The villagers below had demonstrated misplaced loyalty when they gave shelter to a number of the hated Home Guards — black traitors led by *wazungu* thugs in Meru. They had to be punished. The Movement needed to win back their misguided brethren in a hurry, otherwise they would be starved, or bombed, into submission.

The young orphan's mind was fertile soil for Kimathi's uncompromising doctrine of death to the invader. The field marshal had taken a liking to the wild boy who came stumbling from the forest howling like a wounded animal. Rather than trying to soothe the painful memories of his family's death, Kimathi had fanned the flames until Maina was consumed with hatred.

Maina got to know Kimathi, and soon learned that behind his leader's idealism was a man torn apart by a clash of cultures. While decrying the impositions of the white man in his homeland, his abuse of power and the injustice perpetrated by his every instrument of government, Field Marshal Kimathi went nowhere without his copy of the Bible and *Napoleon's Book of Charms*, which he used to divine the best strategy to employ in battle.

Secretly Maina was afraid of Kimathi. He was a fearful sight. With long matted dreadlocks, he looked what he was — a creature of the jungle. But more than his appearance, Maina feared him because of his erratic and violent behaviour. Kimathi could inspire allegiance by his charismatic leadership, but if that failed, he would attack disloyalty with utter brutality.

About a month after he joined the camp, Maina sat enthralled by a speech Kimathi was making about the glory of the Mau Mau cause. The field marshal began to pace among his audience, drawing their rapt attention with him as he diverged into a tirade against traitorous Kikuyus — men who dared to break their sacred Mau Mau oath. As he continued pacing, he began to circle a particular group. Without a word of warning, Kimathi grabbed a *panga* and hacked off the head of a man sitting two places from Maina, splattering the boy with blood. Kimathi threw the head and the *panga* into the bush, using the dead man's case as an example of disloyalty.

The brutality of the act thrust Maina back into the violent world that had wiped out his family. He wanted to flee, but he had just witnessed the consequences of abandoning the cause. His instinct for survival told him he must choose a side, and a child's logic said that there could be no middle ground. Whereas he had previously been intent on revenge, the boy-man now believed that he must not only unequivocally follow Kimathi's orders, he must leave no doubt that he was the most enthusiastic of the field marshal's followers. He would be Kimathi's wildest of the wild; the cruellest of the cruel. From then on, whenever Kimathi used his rhetorical skills to whip the mob into a bloodthirsty frenzy, Maina would almost froth at the mouth. He imagined the hooded face of his family's murderers in every enemy, black or white, and he would change from a twelve-year-old child into a bloodthirsty killer.

Now, poised above the next victims of Kimathi's war of attrition, Maina convinced himself that it was the cool morning air that sent a shiver down his spine. He unsheathed his *panga* and felt its fine edge to calm himself.

Kimathi signalled that they should creep forward again.

As they reached the edge of the forest, a shriek of alarm fractured the still of morning. A woman, going to relieve herself in a pit latrine, had spotted them. Kimathi yelled a war cry and fired into the nearest hut, signalling the start of the attack. Soon the village was in pandemonium. The guerrillas torched the huts and slashed or shot anyone who ventured from them.

Maina rushed through the village screaming like a demon. A boy his age dashed from a hut towards the safety of the bush. Maina felled him with a cut across his legs and hurled himself upon him, raining *panga* blows on his head and body.

A woman holding a baby ran past. Maina saw her from the corner of his eye and slashed at her as hard as he could. She screamed and her arm hung loose from a thread of skin and sinew. Blood gushed from the wound, covering her baby, which had fallen to the ground. Maina gave a yelp of glee and slashed again, severing her throat. The woman collapsed and was silent.

He held his *panga* aloft over the infant as it cried and waved its arms and legs. Then he plunged it into its chest.

In his darkened sitting room, Maina tried to stop his hands from shaking. The boy in his memory was now an alien creature to him. He could not conceive how he had become such an uncontrollable animal.

Over the years, he had driven the vengeance and the hate from his heart. But the ambition to win his rightful place in the leadership of the country he had helped to free from the tyranny of the colonialists had not been vanquished.

CHAPTER 27

Harry knew he should have taken Waiyaki Way. Every time he tried to use a clever short cut to Kip's apartment he got lost. It was no wonder really: the apartment was so new the road wasn't shown on any of Nairobi's street maps. He was following a promising dirt road, but swore as it came to an abrupt end. Swinging into a three-point turn, he sent the gravel flying as he retraced his path.

Five minutes later he drove through the open security gates at Kip's apartment block.

'Where's your bloody security guard, Kip?' he said at the apartment door.

'Hello, Harry,' Kip said. He wore a cotton open-necked shirt and a pair of denim shorts. Even his bare feet were tanned. Harry always felt pasty in comparison.

'Hello, matey,' he replied, a little embarrassed by his rudeness. 'But I mean, the gate's wide open, your security intercom's still not working ... Don't you know we have a crime problem in this city?'

'Don't worry about it. It's all being fixed — so the agent tells me.' Kip waved Harry through to the sitting room and went into the kitchen. 'Anyway, the crooks don't know we're here yet.'

Harry walked onto the balcony. 'You're probably right,' he said over his shoulder. 'Harry had a helluva job finding you again.' Kip's apartment was on the top floor of the three-storey block. Below, the terrain ran down through a tangle of vines to a hidden watercourse. 'Look at this — not another house in sight. You could be in the bloody jungle!'

'That's what I like about it.' Kip placed two chilled Tuskers on the glass top of the cane coffee table.

'But why so far out of Nairobi? With all your money you could be on an acre block in Mathaiga.'

'Mathaiga! Are you kidding? Boring. Anyway, what makes you think I have a lot of cash? Everything goes back into Kipana Tours.' He took his seat. 'Sit down, Harry, you're getting too excited. Relax. Have a beer.'

Harry joined him. 'Cheers,' he said, taking a mouthful. 'Ah, at least you have electricity for the beer.'

'Now what's this "marketing proposal" you have for me?' Kip said.

Harry flipped a cigarette from his packet and lit it. 'I want to use the Mara Lodge for a Peugeot promo.'

'You do? Why?'

Harry blew a stream of smoke over the balcony. Kip tolerated cigarette smokers so long as they didn't foul the air in his immediate vicinity. Harry thought he was a bit of a pain in that regard. He was the only friend he had who didn't smoke, and the only person he knew who had such rules. 'I've been talking to my old agency. They've just won the Marshals Motors Group account, and Barbara wants to knock their socks off.'

'Ah, the lovely Barbara ... Isn't she the one who always gave you a hard time?'

'Yeah, Balls-for-Breakfast Barbara.' Harry shook his head at the memory. 'Bloody dyke,' he muttered. 'So she wants to, you know, impress Peugeot with her innovative approach.'

'What's that got to do with us? And how come you and Barbara are so close these days?'

'Actually I'd rather wring her neck, but you see the pain I go through for the company's sake, don't you?'

'I do, Harry. And I just want you to know you're still on the company's Christmas card list.'

'Thanks, pal. And for your information, I've got an agreement with Barbara to get joint billing on this part of the Marshals account. Newspapers, glossy magazines, the works.'

'Hmm, sounds interesting.'

'I thought you'd like it. Anyway, this is what I have in mind. We set up on the escarpment out at our place near the Mara.' He spread his hands to indicate the panoramic backdrop of the Masai Mara National Reserve. 'Big sky. The savannah stretching for ever. The 504 — a beautiful piece of work — looking like a million bob, and a chickibabe, as cute as a button, in the driver's seat.'

'And that's it?'

'No. Hell, no. Nothing in advertising is that simple.' He spread his hands again. 'Then we go down near the river, maybe there's an umbrella tree — real Africa, you know — and there's the Peugeot again, this time with the young lady on the bonnet or the roof, something like that. I'll work it out when we get there.'

'So why do you need me? Sounds like you'll have it all done in an hour or two.'

'An hour! Are you kidding? This is a day, day and a half, easy.'

'Okay, a day or so, but still, why do you need me? Diana's roped me in to chaperone a group of Yanks up north some time next week.'

'Don't worry, we can have it done by then. The shots around the camp will be fine, but I'll need you in the Mara, otherwise I'll get hassled by the wardens about getting out of the car for the river shots and stuff. You know how they are. They'll want a little tea money here and there.'

Kip frowned and Harry held his breath. Kip could be tricky if there was any hint of bribery being needed. He was a stickler for everything being above board.

He sighed. 'Okay, Harry. When does it happen?'

'That's my boy, Kip. I knew I could count on you.' He slapped him on the shoulder. 'End of the week. Maybe Friday, Saturday? I've found a little honey for the model. A real knockout.'

'One of your many conquests, Harry?' Kip said, smiling as he lifted his beer to his lips.

'No, but I wouldn't mind.'

The girl he had in mind was young, only about twenty-one or twenty-two her agent said, which was just what the brief called for. Harry had met her at her agent's office. The prospect of an overnight stay with her was the best part of the assignment.

'She's fairly new on the modelling scene.' He removed his notepad from his pocket. 'Do you mind if I give her agent a call from here? We can sort out the shoot days before I go.'

Kip motioned to the telephone in the sitting room. 'Be my guest.'

Harry dialled the number. The Indian's voice came on the line.

'Hello, Gupta. It's Harry Forsythe from Kipana Tours.'

The agent remembered him. Harry liked that.

'Listen, we talked about that new girl of yours for the Peugeot piece up at the Mara? Well, I've decided to use her.' He rocked back and forth on his heels, smiling at Kip as Gupta prattled on. 'That's right. Standard rates, overnight. Yes, yes. Expenses included.' He stuck his pencil in his mouth and fished in his pockets to find his notebook again. 'Yeah, yeah. The usual deal. I'll pick her up at your office at, say, nine o'clock Friday?'

He raised his eyebrows in a question for Kip, who shrugged and nodded that it was all right with him.

'Okay. Confirmed. At your office, nine o'clock, Friday. Done.'

He went to replace the receiver but remembered another question. 'Gupta? Gupta? Oh, there you are. Give me her name again, will you? I wrote it down somewhere and it's gone.'

He scribbled in the notebook. 'Nasonga. Rose Nasonga. Got it.'

Harry was right. The model was beautiful. Tall. Slender. Legs all the way to her short mini-dress. Kip guessed the magazines would describe her as *willowy*. She had expressive dark eyes and her mid-length hair, which must have been straightened, clung to her well-shaped head in soft waves, instead of the recently fashionable Afro style.

'Rose, this is my friend Kip. Kip, Rose.' Harry looked like a cat in charge of a canary.

'Pleased to meet you, Rose,' Kip said, taking her hand.

'Me too.' But she didn't look pleased at all. She barely met his eyes before turning away from him to peer down into the Great Rift Valley. Kip imagined it was a beautiful model's way of dealing with the lecherous public. Or perhaps she was practising the aloofness they all seemed to have when on the catwalk.

The wind rushed up the escarpment and threatened to lift her tiny skirt. She pushed it down with both hands.

'Oops! Be careful, sweetheart,' Harry said. 'Don't go showing all your charms until Harry's ready.'

Harry chuckled, as he did when trying to take the edge off a joke that had fallen flat, but she ignored him and gave Kip a look of disapproval, as if blaming him for the gust. For a moment Kip felt the ridiculous urge to explain himself.

'And what do these two guys do?' he said, indicating the two young men. He wasn't particularly interested, but he needed a diversion to cover his discomfort.

'Well,' Harry said, 'this is Gakiha, my lighting man, and Michael, my assistant. And this' — he pointed to the car with a theatrical gesture — 'is our star. The Peugeot 504 — the French car built for Africa.'

'Is it?' Kip asked.

'You'd better believe it. Why, I'll have you know, young man' — Harry began to mimic a carnival spruiker, a pretend cigar between his fingers — 'that Peugeot has won more rallies, more East African Safaris, than any other car. The world's roughest test of a stock car. Yessir. Cars have to plough through hub-deep mud, dodge angry elephants and smash through the scrub to finish the gruelling three-thousand-mile course.' He was directing his act to Kip but it was obviously for the model's benefit. 'Yes, indeed. Last year only sixteen out of eighty-five cars finished — five of them Peugeots!' He dropped his act with a laugh. 'Or something like that.'

Rose didn't seem interested in Harry's antics, and was filing her nails. 'Very impressive, Harry,' Kip said, walking away. 'I guess I'll leave you to it. Unless you need me up here?'

'No, me ol' darlin'.' Harry followed him to the car. 'I'll take a few rolls here and we'll come over to the camp when we're ready to go down into the Mara.'

'Tell me this much, Harry,' Kip said, scratching his chin. 'Why are you trying to sell a city car in the bush?'

'It's Marshals's brief,' Harry said. 'Peugeot — the car for Africa.'

'Okay, so why the girl?'

'Sex sells.'

'Hmm,' Kip said, looking to where Rose was touching up her make-up.

'See you soon,' Harry said, turning on his heels. 'C'mon, people, let's go. We've got some beautiful pictures to make.'

Kip climbed into his Land Rover. The model intrigued him. There was something going on behind her eyes, and he had the uncomfortable notion he should know her from somewhere.

Kip had brought them to a place on the river that he knew well. He sat on the mudguard of his Land Rover, watching Harry, camera in hand, leaping around the model like a pronging gazelle.

'A little higher, sweetheart,' Harry said. 'That's it!' *Snap!* 'Now, tilt your head back. Hold it.' *Snap!* 'Great. Good girl.' *Snap! Snap!* 'Now, drop that

shoulder strap a little more, darling. Beautiful.'
Snap!

Kip had little knowledge of the art of photography, and none about the world of fashion, but from what he observed, Rose and Harry worked in perfect harmony, like a pair of ballroom dancers, he leading her into a series of intricate steps, and she following, faultlessly.

What interested him most about the girl was her ability to switch off all expression when Harry asked for what he called a 'really serious' shot. In those moments, sometimes minutes, while Harry flittered around her, she was a vacant space. Her eyes were open, she would move and pose as required, but her soul was absent.

'Just a few more, sweetheart,' Harry said as he reloaded the camera.

They had been taking shots for over two hours, with pauses for Rose to make wardrobe changes. For this series of shots she was wearing skin-tight cotton jeans.

'Let's see ... what about one with you kinda stretching across the bonnet?' Harry indicated the line. 'Sort of pointing to the Peugeot motif on the grille. That's it. No, wait.' He moved her leg a little further behind her, his hand lingering longer than Kip thought necessary. Harry was being Harry.

'There you go! Now, hold that a moment.' *Snap!* 'That's it.' *Snap!* 'One more.' *Snap!* 'A little bit of cheese for Harry? That's it. Hold it.' *Snap!*

Harry lowered his camera and squinted into the western sky. 'Hmm, okay, that's it. Pack it up, Michael. We've lost the light. That's all for today.'

Turning to Rose, he drew her to him by a hand under her arm. The model turned away without giving Kip a clue as to what Harry had said.

'She's hot for me,' he said as he joined Kip at the Land Rover.

'She is?' Kip answered. 'How did you figure that out?'

'Oh-ho, Harry can see it in the body language. It's more about what she doesn't say than what she does.'

Kip decided to let it go. Experience suggested it was futile to talk sense to Harry under such circumstances. But then he thought, maybe he's right. Maybe the girl was feeling a rapport with him. They seemed to work well together.

'Where's she going?' he asked, nodding at Rose, who was heading towards the river.

'She said she was hot in the jeans and wanted to slip into her lighter slacks.'

'Hmm, she'd better be careful.' Kip glanced down the path in the direction she had taken, and decided against following her. 'What now?'

'Back to camp. A drink or two.' Harry rubbed his hands together. 'And let's see what the night brings.'

A scream came from the river. Kip leaped from the Land Rover and raced through the bush towards the cry. He arrived at the bank in time to see a crocodile disappearing into the muddy water. Harry arrived a moment later. Rose was cowering against a tree, her jeans clutched to her chest in a defensive gesture. She was sobbing.

Harry let out a low whistle. 'Holy ...!' he said. The girl was almost naked in a pair of very brief panties and bra.

Rose dragged her eyes from the swirling water, dashed to Kip and clung to his arm. She turned her head away from the water, burying her head into his bicep. When this didn't seem to reassure her, she flung her arms around his neck and held him like a python.

'It ... it's gone,' Kip said. 'Harry, get the big towel from the back of the Land Rover.' He patted Rose on the head. 'There, there,' he said lamely. 'Harry?'

Harry was rooted to the spot. 'Right. Right you are,' he said, and dashed off.

When he returned, Kip wrapped Rose in the towel and led her back to the car.

Rose lay in the darkness, staring up at the canvas ceiling. The breeze from the Great Rift Valley moved it gently in and out like the chest cavity of some huge beast that had swallowed her whole. Beside her, Harry snorted, smacked his lips, and rolled to the other side of the bed.

She had been awake for hours, and she knew it would probably be hours more before she finally succumbed to sleep. It wasn't the incident with the crocodile that had disturbed her, although the episode from her childhood had come vividly to mind the instant it lunged at her. What unsettled her was the reappearance of Kip Balmain after all these years. He hadn't changed a scrap from the young man who had rescued her in Kisumu in 1973.

It wasn't surprising that he didn't recognise her. The incident ten years ago in Kisumu wouldn't have been important to him and had probably gone from his memory. He didn't know she had just been raped, and nobody in her family had felt inclined to enlighten him.

In time, Rose had been able to deal with the trauma of the rape, but not with the way her family had reacted to it. Only Akello was blameless, and that was because he was genuinely unaware of what had happened. Her sister and father had their own ways of dealing with it. Dembe suspected what had happened inside the immigration office, but couldn't bring herself to ask. Grace — the constantly serene Grace — probably assumed the others had done all that was possible to restore her younger sister's mental equilibrium, and was therefore anxious to avoid unsettling Rose with any superfluous mention of it. Her father was so shocked by it, he didn't want to believe it had happened. He acted like a man who'd had a great injustice done to him.

Kip was unaware that he had rescued her that night; unaware that he had made a major impact on her life with his simple act of kindness when he helped her family in a crisis. He had simply assumed that the Kenyan border guards had robbed them. As she was to learn from others during her years in Kisumu, it wasn't uncommon. And he didn't recognise her now, of course, because she was no longer a fresh-faced thirteen year old. She sometimes imagined that her whole appearance had changed that night on the Kisumu wharf. Certainly her perspective on life had.

Ten years on, and what had become of her? Her father had never returned as he'd planned. The letters that reached them from Uganda told of the waking nightmare of a country trapped in the grip of a maniac. It was unsafe to move out of the north. The Acholi kept to their villages while Amin's thugs from West Nile waged a genocidal war against them and their cousins, the Lango.

Only some of the letters from their parents arrived, passed from hand to hand through a network of people they didn't know. Many lost their way, or the bearers lost their lives somewhere during the five-hundred-mile journey. There were long periods when they heard nothing, then another message would appear and the four of them would try to piece together the parts of the story that had been lost in transit. The letters were like loose pages fallen from a book and blown into their hands. The story was disjointed and, in time, even the characters faded into unfamiliarity.

Rose and Akello continued to write, but when it became obvious that none of their letters reached Panyiketto, Rose quit.

Dembe finally married, but the old Luo who took her to his farm at Karasuk, a hundred miles away, might as well have taken her to the moon. They only saw her every few years, although she sent letters to Kisumu from time to time. They seldom made happy reading.

Abandoned by her parents, and impervious to Grace's attempts at discipline, Rose ran wild.

At sixteen she met an Indian with a camera who called himself a photographer. He paid her to allow him to take 'fashion' photographs of her. Soon she was gracing his bed as well as his studio, where she modelled for clothing labels, fashion accessories, even products on special at the supermarkets. As her Indian photographer told her, she was a natural at modelling. She had devised a switch to turn off her emotions so that holding a pose and maintaining a certain expression came easily. It was a trick she had learned soon after her attackers threw her out of the Kisumu immigration office. People like Harry called it 'The Look'. To Rose, it was simply survival.

She saved her money and at age eighteen, had informed Grace that she was leaving Kisumu to work as a model in Nairobi. Her sister protested, as she usually did, but they both knew Rose would get her way.

Work came slowly at first, but eventually she could afford a flat of her own, rather than suffer under the strict dictates of the YWCA's hostel. With money and freedom, Rose was able to do as she pleased. Nairobi's bars and nightclubs were a world removed from her earlier life. She learned to smoke and drink. At parties she tried *bhang* and, although the weed made her feel slightly queasy on an empty stomach, she enjoyed the heady release it gave her.

It was fun to tease prospective clients and employers, letting them think they were manipulating her. Meanwhile, she was working on a plan of her own. She could see what the modelling competition offered in Nairobi. She would soon rise to the top of that tree, then go looking in the wide forest for taller ones to climb.

She slipped out from under the single sheet that covered them and pulled on her robe. Harry was still snoring as she slipped through the flap of canvas.

On the porch step she sat and lit a cigarette.

The light was still on in Kip's *banda*, which, like hers, consisted of a timber floor, four posts and a heavy canvas fly straddling a lighter canvas tent. It gave the tourists the thrill of camping without denying them hot water and flush toilets. His light shone green through the mosquito netting on the roll-up canvas shutters.

She knew men well enough to know if a man was interested in her. It was an important skill for her, for if they were, as was generally the case, it gave her power over them. In Kip's case she wasn't sure. It worried her; not because it meant she had no control over him, but she wanted him to like her.

She imagined it had something to do with the fact that he was her hero from so long ago. Whatever the reason, it unsettled her not to know.

Tomorrow would be the last opportunity to assess him because she had no intention of seeing Harry on a regular basis. She had told him she had a boyfriend in Nairobi, but would keep the photographer keen enough to arrange other on-site shoots, which always paid well.

In the morning she thought she might prevail upon Harry to take her to Kisumu. The offer of another night with her, this time in an air-conditioned hotel, should be enough to convince him. And it would give her the chance to see her sister again.

CHAPTER 28

Grace's house was not grand, even by Kisumu's standards, but compared to her previous dwelling — their family home in Uganda — it was quite an improvement. Electricity and tap water were luxuries for most people in Panyiketto. As the taxi pulled up at the gate, Rose noticed there were insect screens fitted to the louvred windows. Her brother-in-law was usually up-country with the railway, and too busy when at home to attend to matters of that kind. Rose suspected her sister had had them fitted using the money she earned from selling her hens' eggs.

She paid the taxi driver and told him not to wait. Harry would come later to pick her up when it was time to head back to Nairobi.

Little Doreen sat in the front yard, playing in the dirt with an old gardening tool. Rose scooped her up and nuzzled her nose into her niece's fat cheeks.

Grace swept through the front door like a ship in full sail, and they embraced. Rose stepped back to examine her sister at arm's length. 'Pregnant again, Grace?'

'As usual.'

'You should tell that husband of yours to stay away for longer.' She shook her head. 'I swear, Grace, you have five already.'

'I know, but what can I do? But come inside. I'm so glad you're here. I have a surprise.'

Grace was still beaming when she sat Rose down in the sitting room. She took a seat opposite, but couldn't contain herself. She stood to announce her news.

'What is it?' Rose asked.

'Papa.'

'Papa?'

'He has come!' Grace said, clapping her hands like a child. 'I couldn't get in touch with you to tell you. Akello knows. He's on his way.'

Rose had spent so many hours praying for this day, she could only stare at her sister, trying to digest the news. She was a child when he'd left them there. 'Where ... where is he?'

'Gone to wait for Akello at the station. He went an hour ago and will be back very soon, I'm sure.'

'And Mama?'

'In Panyiketto. Papa has been stuck in Kampala these last three years because of the fighting. Oh Rose, it's so lucky you've come. He can only stay a day more and then he'll go back.'

'To Panyiketto?'

'To Kampala. He doesn't know when he can reach Mama and George and Macmillan. But he hopes it will be soon.'

Rose was unsure how to take this news. Her heart told her to be glad — she loved her father and wanted him back. She wanted the whole family back together again, but her modelling career promised so much. Instinctively she felt her father would disapprove of her new life in Nairobi. She was suddenly afraid.

'What have you told him of me?'

Grace's smile melted and she took her seat opposite Rose, who now feared her instincts were correct.

'He was ... surprised.'

'Surprised? By what?'

'By you not being here.' Grace stopped her before she had a chance to ask the next question. 'I told him you had a good job and that you were in a nice place in Nairobi.'

'And ...?'

'And he went quiet.'

'He said nothing after that?'

'No.'

Rose clasped and unclasped her hands. It had taken years to reshape her life after her father had left them in Kisumu. The decision to go to Nairobi had been hers alone. Grace had been reproachful during the years when Rose ran wild, and reluctantly accepted her decision to begin a life of her own. Dembe, who seemed to have no strong opinions on anything, had said nothing, while Akello had never stopped being Rose's greatest supporter in everything she did.

If her father was angry that she had not stayed in Kisumu as he had ordered, it was his fault for not returning as he had promised. How many years could she wait to do something with her life?

It was not possible to return to Kisumu. She was no longer a child.

She fumbled for a cigarette and stopped herself. She looked at her watch. Perhaps Harry would come before her father arrived.

Zakayo stood in the doorway, looking grey with fatigue and much older than how Rose remembered him when he had said goodbye ten years before.

Akello swept her into his strong arms as he always did, and crushed the breath from her. '*Sista*,' he said. 'Look! Papa has come!'

When she peered over Akello's shoulder, she saw her father's broad smile, but when his eyes met hers, his face dropped. He appeared to be feeling awkward, and turned his gaze to the wall.

She went to him. 'Papa,' she said, reaching her arms to him. He hesitated, then took her in his embrace. Rose was surprised that he no longer towered over her. He seemed to have shrunk.

He held her for longer than she'd expected considering his apparent mood, but when she looked up at him he had a stern expression. 'So you are here.'

The phrase could be taken in two ways. It could be the usual statement of the obvious that people used as a greeting, but she chose to answer it as the accusation she felt was his intention.

'Yes, Papa, I … I'm up from Nairobi … doing some work here.' There was no point in delaying the issue.

'From Nairobi is it?' He scowled, making his weary face appear more haggard. Where had his smile lines gone?

'Yes, I —'

'And why were you not here to greet your father when he arrived after all this time?'

'Papa, I —'

'Did I not order you to stay with your sister?'

This was not like her father. Her memory of him was as a strict parent, but he would always listen to what any of his children had to say before condemning them. Had he forgotten his own rule: only democracy and peace would reign in his household?

'Well,' Kip said, extending his hand, 'everything seems to be coming together nicely, Eva. I look forward to seeing you tomorrow morning.'

'Me too,' she said, taking his hand and holding it a moment more as she asked, 'Can I buy you a cold drink?'

'That would be great, but I really should get back to the office. Got plenty of prep work for our safari.'

'All work and no play makes Kip a very dull boy,' she said with a twinkle in her eyes. 'It's too early to eat and too late to go sightseeing.' She held his eyes with hers as she had at the Norfolk on their first meeting. 'Besides, I can't stand drinking alone.'

'Well . . .' he said.

Kip had seen numerous naked black breasts at the traditional dances he arranged for the entertainment of his clients, but seeing them emerge from a crimson bra was more exciting than he could have imagined.

Eva's skin was warm, brown silk. She shivered as he ran a finger along her shoulder and down to her nipple.

Her tongue darted inside his mouth and played with his tongue as she pulled his shirt from his back.

She was everywhere. Her hands were on him one moment, then helping him undo his belt the next. He was naked before he had a chance to slide her bra and blouse from her shoulders. She pushed him towards the bed, planting kisses on his mouth as she slipped out of her crimson bikini panties.

He was accustomed to taking control at that point, but Eva pinned his arms to the pillow and lowered herself slowly down onto his erection.

'And look at your face. Is this my daughter? Is this my daughter of twenty-two years? What is this muck you have here?' He wiped his hand across her face. Make-up coated his palm. 'A painted whore!'

'Hello-o-o?'

It was Harry. Rose hoped the earth would open and swallow her whole.

'Anybody home?' Harry appeared in the open doorway. 'Ah, there you are, sweetheart. Thought old Harry was lost.'

Zakayo stared at him. He opened his mouth to address him, but turned to Rose and asked her who he was. They had been using English to that point. Now he spoke in Lwo, the language of their home.

'He is my photographer,' she said, deciding to keep it simple, but the word did not translate well. It could be taken two ways, and the moment she had uttered it she realised it could mean that Harry was her procurer.

Zakayo's anger grew. Rose knew her father understood what she meant, but he deliberately misunderstood it to belittle her. 'Your pimp, is he?' he said. The Lwo word shocked her. It sounded like the worst schoolyard filth she could remember.

She glanced at Harry, who looked bemused by the obvious tension in the room. 'Harry, I'm sorry, but could I have a moment more with my family?' she pleaded.

'No troubles at all, my sweet. I'll, you know, mooch around in the, um, garden for a spell.'

She used the moments it took Harry to retire outside to regain her composure.

'Papa, I'm a grown woman now. How long should I have waited for you before I could find my own life?'

'It is not for you to question me. Your place is with your family.'

'And what about you? Where is your place, Papa?'

It was her tone, or perhaps that she dared to retaliate, rather than her question that startled him. 'What! What did you say to me?'

From the corner of her eye she could see Akello fidgeting, trying to find a comfortable place to put his hands. She knew she was treading on dangerous ground merely by calling into question his actions.

'I asked you: where is your place? Why have you been away from Mama for so long? Three years. Where is your place that you can leave your wife and family to fend for themselves, without so much as a visit?'

Her father's eyes widened in his rage. He had trouble breathing. For a moment Rose thought he would strike her, but she stood her ground, her heart pounding in her chest so hard she felt it would burst.

'I have heard enough. You will send this ... this man away, and you will be with your sister. As I ordered you.'

Her father's face was a thundercloud. She had never seen him so angry, nor so unreasonable. She looked at him for a long moment, tears welling in her eyes. She did not know this man. It was pointless trying to explain anything to him.

She turned her back on her father and stormed out the door.

Harry was out on the street, picking at the flaking paint on the garden fence.

'Harry,' she commanded.

'Yes, blossom?'

'Get me out of here.'

CHAPTER 29

Before leaving for Marsabit, Kip wanted [ ] organise a briefing session, so the Hartigans offe[ ] to treat the Americans to lunch. Afterwards, [ ] and the overseas guests shared a taxi to the Hilt[ ] leaving Diana and Hugh free to return to [ ] Norfolk, where they had a suite in the historical [ ] wing.

'Well, thanks for the ride,' Kip said after th[ ] had climbed out of the taxi. 'I guess I'll get back [ ] the office for a bit of paperwork. Are you people [ ] clear about tomorrow?'

They nodded. Demitrio looked at his wat[ ] 'There's some time before the stores close,' he sa[ ] and pointed at Armstrong's shirt. 'I'd like to get [ ] one of those neat shirts, Kevin. Where'd you buy i[ ]

'Oh, it's just a block or so. Let's see . [ ] Armstrong craned his neck to see over the passe[ ] by. 'Hell, why don't I take you? I could use anoth[ ] one myself.'

'That'd be great,' Demitrio said. 'Eva? Wan[ ] join us?'

'No thanks, guys. I'll take a rain check.'

'Fine. See you at dinner. So long, Kip. See yo[ ] bright and early tomorrow.' The men shook Kip[ ] hand, and disappeared into the heavy pedestria[ ] traffic surrounding the Hilton's entrance.

He found Diana sitting on a canvas director's chair, a leg curled beneath her, with a white wine in her hand. They were staying at Kipana Tours' premier accommodation, Laikipia Lodge, en route to Marsabit.

'A penny for your thoughts,' Kip said, joining her in the clearing under the stars. The others in their party were in the open-air dining room, thirty yards behind them.

'Actually, I was thinking about you.'

'Me?' He dragged another canvas chair towards hers and sat down.

'Yes, I was wondering how you got on with Eva, after you left us at lunch yesterday.'

'You don't miss much, do you?' he said, smiling.

'It's just that I know the signs after all these years. She was devouring you with her eyes.'

Kip smiled. He had met other attractive black women in his life, many of whom he'd found sexually enticing, but Eva was the first he had taken to bed. 'We've been friends for too long, Diana.'

'We have. And don't change the subject. How was it?' Diana never stood on ceremony with Kip. It was one of her most attractive traits.

'Hmm ... not bad for a clerk.'

Diana chuckled.

Kip watched her green eyes sparkle in the light of the moon. 'But we have, haven't we?'

'Haven't we what?' she asked, still smiling.

'Been friends. For ages.'

Her eyes met his, then she turned her face away. 'Yes,' she said, looking at the stars.

The silence hung in the still, warm air.

'You used to live over there somewhere, didn't you?' She nodded towards the savannah, which spread outward like a golden sea under the full moon.

He followed her eyes to the east. 'When I was a kid I knew the family who lived at the other edge of these plains. They had about twenty thousand acres.'

'Outside Nanyuki.'

'Yes.'

'You never talk about your childhood, whereas I have filled hour after boring hour regaling you with my childhood dramas.'

'They're not all that boring.'

He could feel her eyes on him.

'You've never been home, have you?'

He took a sip of his wine and placed it on the ground at his feet. 'Nope.'

'Do you mind if I ask why?'

'You can ask, but I'm not sure I'll be able to answer you.'

'Because you don't want to?'

He hesitated before responding. 'Because I can't. I don't know why.'

'You lived with your mother, right?'

'Yes, and an aunt.'

'I thought she lived alone. I didn't know you had an aunt too.'

'Well, I don't think she was really an aunt. She was ... how can I describe it? My mother's ... lover.'

'Oh, I see. That must have been difficult for you to understand.'

'That was the least of my worries, believe me.'

'And your father? What about him?'

He shifted in his seat and reached for his glass

again before answering. 'I know nothing about my father.'

'Is he still alive somewhere?'

'I don't know.'

'Surely your mother had something to say about him, even if it was just a lie?'

'Nothing,' he said.

One of his earliest memories was asking his mother why he didn't have a father. Marie had seized him by the arm and hissed that he was never to ask that question again. It must have been years later, when he was about seven, that he'd dared to try again for an answer. Her response on that occasion had taught him to avoid the topic altogether.

'I felt safe enough to ask her on my fourteenth birthday. This time she just said, "You have no father". It was just before I ran away.'

Diana placed a hand on his knee. 'It must hurt not to know if you have a father out there somewhere.'

'It does. It's why I don't know how to answer the question: do I want to go home? On the one hand I have no wish to be reminded of that nightmare with those two women. On the other, I feel there's a huge question mark hanging over my life. *Who am I?*'

He stood and took a couple of paces into the darkness. 'Do you have any idea how unsettling that can be, Diana? I mean, I've imagined a dozen scenarios — that my father ran away because he didn't love us, that he fell in love with another woman. I even imagined that he died, or suicided. Any of those answers would satisfy. They may not be the best answers, but they fill the void. They give closure to the question: *Who is Kip Balmain?*'

'I believe it's always best to confront your demons. Would it be so hard to go back to face her again on those issues?'

Kip came back and took his seat beside her. After a moment he said, 'Yes.'

Kip met the security guard as he reached the most easterly point on the perimeter of the lodge's security fence. '*Jumbo*,' he said as they approached one another.

A broad smile flashed in the darkness as the guard passed. '*Mzuri, bwana.*'

Patrolling the area before retiring was an old habit that Kip found difficult to break. The security guards knew of the boss's strange habit, of course, and were no doubt amused by it, but Kip found the walk, and the African stories told in the sounds of the night, soothing.

The lights of the lodge were on his right. Over his left shoulder, in the inky darkness, loomed Kere-Nyaga: Mt Kenya.

The deep rumbling of a buffalo's warning bellow came from over the hills to the north. He imagined the sound clinging to the cool earth as it rolled through brittle dry-season grass for miles, before arriving as a whispered reminder of the ever-present danger in the darkness surrounding him. A predator, probably a lion, was on the prowl, threatening the young and vulnerable. The bull's gutteral call was a reminder of his intention to fight to the death if necessary.

From closer to hand came the high-pitched barking of zebra, and the sniggers of stalking hyena.

Kip's conversation with Diana had troubled him, as thoughts about his childhood often did. It wasn't the memories of the loveless life he'd endured as a child. It wasn't even dealing with the outright cruelty, nor the feeling that his mother had simply tolerated him because he was a convenient source of cheap labour. It was his inability to even begin to tackle the mystery of his father.

He understood part of the problem, which was his reluctance to confront his mother on the subject. He could go only so far in rationalising the situation. He told himself he was no longer physically afraid of her. Even in the last year or two of his life at Nanyuki he had lost his fear of the *kiboko*, with the result that Marie had stopped threatening him with it.

At fourteen Kip had been physically and emotionally self-sufficient. He could have remained at home for some time longer than he did, tolerating the estrangement between mother and son, but on the day she had so spitefully told him he had no father, he'd realised that finding the truth about him was the only reason he'd stayed. It was only much later that he realised the return path, over burned bridges, would be very difficult, and that he'd lost the link to finding his father, or at least finding out why he'd abandoned them.

It was never going to be easy to prise the story from Marie; now it would be near impossible. Being abandoned by her labour force would have surely increased her spitefulness.

A lion's roar shook the night and intruded upon his thoughts. It would be Bluebeard — the alpha male of the local pride — warning off pretenders to his throne.

He looked above. The stars could be plucked from the sky. It was time to get some sleep — the day following would be one of nightmare roads, heat and dust.

Kip kicked a stone in annoyance. It rolled into the fence wire with a metallic ping. Something in the brittle undergrowth beyond the boundary made a scuttling sound, and then it was quiet again.

He was annoyed because he had so often reached this point, but had been unable to come to a resolution. It made him feel ineffective, and he hated it.

CHAPTER 30

Kip drove slowly through the shambles that was
Isiolo, avoiding the donkey carts and scavenging
goats that claimed the road as their paddock. Apart
from an impressive mosque with filigreed windows
and a stone minaret, corrugated iron appeared to
be the building material of choice. There were
numerous small, corrugated-iron pubs with names
like Miami Beach and Nice Hotel, a sizeable
corrugated-iron general store with a tattered
billboard announcing 'Weetabix — with added
riboflavin', and so-called beauty shops where
women in short skirts leered from under
corrugated-iron verandas as they passed.

He glanced over his shoulder to where
Armstrong and Demitrio sat in the cramped fold-
down seats in the back of the Land Rover. 'Are you
guys okay back there?'

They answered that they were fine.

'We'll be stopping at the checkpoint on the other
side of town. It'll give you a chance to stretch your
legs.'

The Isiolo checkpoint — a galvanised-iron boom
gate beside a tin shed — sat astride the dirt road on
the town's northern edge. Two strips of four-inch
steel spikes across the road made sure all vehicles
came to a stop. A sleepy policeman came out of the

corrugated-iron office with a clipboard under his arm.

'*Habari*,' Kip said in greeting.

'*Mzuri sana*,' the cop replied with a yawn.

Kip took the clipboard and filled in their names. Under 'Purpose of Visit', he wrote 'tourists'.

The guard, meanwhile, was peering into the back of the Land Rover, stalling until his tea money was offered. Kip ignored him. He hated the petty graft that nearly every public servant demanded for doing his duty. He had heard the arguments about poor pay that some used to excuse, even to justify the practice, but Kip would have none of it. He completed the paperwork and stood leaning against the mudguard.

The guard circled the car. Hugh Hartigan came up to Kip and whispered, 'Give him the ten bob for chrissakes, Kip.'

'Bugger him,' Kip replied. 'He can earn his money like I do.'

'*Bwana*,' the cop said, pointing to one of the bags on the roof rack. '*Asante sana*.' There was a sarcastic note in his voice.

'Oh gawd,' Hugh muttered. 'Here we go.'

Kip pulled himself onto the rear foot rail and yanked down the bag, dropping it at the policeman's feet.

The cop's smile faded as he squatted to unzip the bag. After sliding his hands among the clothing items he stopped, looked up at Kip with an expression of amazement, and withdrew a revolver from the bag.

Kip's mouth fell open. He searched his passengers' faces for a sign, an explanation. He had assumed they all knew that possession of a hand weapon was a serious offence. The Kenyan authorities were particularly nervous about hand weapons. Crime was becoming a major problem in the city and they didn't want tourists' handguns turning up in local crime scenes.

Kevin Armstrong appeared quite calm. He had indicated some knowledge of Africa as they travelled north, giving Kip the impression that it wasn't his first time in the country. Surely he wouldn't be so stupid as to carry a gun.

John Demitrio, on the other hand, was cracking his knuckles and fidgeting with the ostentatious gold ring he wore. He had a nervous disposition — a condition that might have led him to conceal a weapon.

The guard held the snub-nosed Colt between thumb and forefinger as if it was a bomb. 'Lieutenant!' he shouted. '*Kuja upesi!*' Then he drew his own gun, pointing it unsteadily at the six foreigners.

The officer, an obese man with sweat stains under the armpits of his khaki shirt, ambled out of the shed scratching his buttocks. '*Shauri gani?*' he asked, then saw the weapons in his colleague's hands. '*Hakia mungu!*'

The two policemen went into a huddle, casting sideways glances at the travellers. The first one kept his pistol pointed in their general direction.

Kip whispered out the corner of his mouth, 'Who belongs to the weapon?'

Nobody replied.

The fat cop walked to the Land Rover where he retrieved the clipboard from the bonnet. He ran a finger down the list and then hurried into his office. When he returned he demanded, 'Who owns this bag?'

Again nobody spoke.

Kip was furious. He couldn't remember who owned the black leather bag, but when he found him, he would tear strips off him.

'It would be better if you admit it. I ask again, who owns this bag?'

'I do.'

'And your name is … ?'

'Eva Deloite.'

The officer turned his back on the group, said a few whispered words to his young assistant, and returned to his office.

Kip looked first at Eva, who remained unperturbed by the whole affair, then back to the policeman, who replaced the Colt under the clothing and zipped the bag closed. 'Go,' he said in a fractured tone. 'Just go.'

Kip didn't waste time doing what he was told. After fifteen minutes of furious driving, during which the Land Rover bounded into and over potholes, he hit the brakes and slid the car to a halt under a large baobab tree.

He turned to face Eva in the back seat. 'Well?' he asked.

'Well what?' she said, blinking at him in wounded innocence. 'A girl has to take care of herself out in the wilds, doesn't she?'

'How … ? What … ?' Kip spluttered.

'I told you the other day I was nervous about travelling up here. Don't you remember? When you dropped me at the Hilton?'

'I remember. But what's that got to do with carrying a pistol? How did you get it into the country in the first place?'

She shrugged. 'I just had it in my suitcase. I don't know what the big deal is anyway. He let us through, didn't he?'

'That's another thing. By all rights you should have been thrown into gaol. And all of us with you.' He looked at Hugh, who shook his head in disbelief.

'Well ... I guess it's because he's a brother.' Eva gave him a wide smile. 'You white folks could never understand that.'

Behind the stainless steel doors, the New Miami disco throbbed with sound. Maina Githinji adjusted the collar of his open-necked Hawaiian shirt so that it sat neatly over the lapels of his black jacket. The bouncer gave him a quick once-over, but Maina ignored him. He pushed both doors wide open, allowing a gust of chilled air to escape into the tepid Mombasa night. The tall black woman with him followed.

Maina had taken up Costello's offer of the launch, making it known that he intended to take a day or so for a complete rest from official business. It was a subtle hint that Costello shouldn't try to use the opportunity to get more concessions for his CIA man's involvement in the troop movements in the Northern Frontier Zone.

He parted the curtains and ambled towards the bar through the stroboscopic lights. The dance floor was pulsating with bodies. There were tourists from several different countries, and a group of four Kenyan cowboys who were hogging the bar, cracking jokes at every passing female. 'Kenyan cowboy' was the derogative term for white Kenyan males whose immaturity and self-consciousness led to their loud and obnoxious behaviour, usually resulting in a brawl, and more so when they were in the minority.

Maina caught the attention of the owner, who was on the other side of the dance floor. As he approached, Maina beckoned his girlfriend to him. Raising his voice over the music, he said, 'Here, darling, get yourself a drink, ah? And a beer for me.' He pressed a five-hundred-shilling note into her hand, and she wandered off in the direction of the bar.

The Kenyan cowboys nudged each other as she approached. One said something to her, but the tall black woman ignored it. Maina smiled. When she passed they exchanged whispered comments, and a roar of laughter followed.

'*Jumbo*, Maina,' the owner said, taking his hand in the clasping African handshake. '*Karibu*, *bwana*.'

'*Asante*,' Maina said. 'How are you, Charles?'

'I'm fine. What about you? You're looking great!'

'Well, I could lose a little weight,' Maina said, patting the bulge under his Hawaiian shirt, 'but otherwise I'm fine.' He looked around the crowded bar, nodding in approval. 'Quite a crowd, my brother. Business must be good.'

'Not bad. Not bad, if I say so myself.'

'Even Japanese tourists. Very trendy, *bwana*.'

'Ha ha, Maina. You are nothing unless you have Japanese tourists in your club these days, *si ndio*?'

'Yes, and you have so many. Well done.'

'Oh, thank you, my friend. But what brings you to Mombasa? You should have called, and I would have arranged a girl for you.'

'I brought my own this time.' Maina nodded to the girl at the bar.

'Wow, where did you find that, man?'

'She's okay,' he said dismissively, but was pleased by Charles's reaction. It would have been difficult to think otherwise. The girl looked sensational in her clinging dress and long braided hair.

'Are you staying at our hotel, my brother?'

'No, I've got the American Embassy's launch for a few days. Why don't you come down tomorrow, we'll have a few drinks. We should talk.'

'Love to.' Charles chewed the inside of his cheek. 'Look, brother, about that silly business with the commissions ... I want you to know I had nothing to do with what those other guys did. I was happy to send the money.'

'I understand, Charles, but we need to talk about it, yes? That's why it would be good if you could come down to the boat tomorrow to have a chat. Just a friendly chat.'

'Sure. Sure. I'd love to come. Hey, *bwana*, I'll be there. I want us to remain friends. I just wanted you to be aware of my situation.'

'Situation? Charles, I don't know what you are talking about. It is perfectly clear. We had a business arrangement — I talk to my friends, and we arrange a lease on the marine national park. A business arrangement. That is the only situation I know.'

The nightclub owner fell silent.

'Ah, here are the drinks,' Maina said as his girlfriend came back from the bar. 'Thank you, my darling. Oh, Charles, won't you join us?' He smiled, trying to cover his look of smug satisfaction as he noticed that Charles was looking a little grey. 'Of course you will.' He dived a hand into his pocket again. 'Here, Rose, get Charles a strong scotch.'

Rose loved loud discos — the louder the better. When she mixed the music with some *bhang*, and maybe half a bottle of whisky, she could let herself go.

Maina Githinji was a good dancer, although he was terribly vain. He really danced by himself, playing to the crowd. His partner — in this case, Rose — was incidental. After meeting him only a month ago, between dates with Harry, she had already learned his habits, his likes and dislikes. It was a skill she had developed to survive.

She knew Maina liked to dance with her because they looked good together; he made use of her as he would a fashion accessory. She let him take the limelight and played up to him as if she were captivated. She didn't really mind. It was an act, like a modelling assignment. She could play the part, or hold the pose, for as long as was needed to accomplish what she wanted. For the moment, all she wanted was a good time, and the escape that marihuana and alcohol could achieve.

When Maina had asked her to go to Mombasa with him, she'd hesitated briefly, then agreed. The idea of spending two nights and three days with Maina was offset by the promise of escape from the depressing memory of her reunion with her father. Unlike Harry, Maina was not afraid to throw money around, and he enjoyed a good time. It was exactly what Rose needed at the moment.

Rose enjoyed a good time too; the bad times would return to haunt her soon enough. She let the flashing lights and the music of Michael Jackson carry her away.

She loved Michael Jackson, and so did the DJ at the New Miami, who played tracks from his latest album throughout the night. She wanted to dance to every one, but the scotch turned Maina's mood. When he refused to join her on the floor, she danced on her own, gyrating to the compelling beat of 'Billie Jean' and 'Thriller', without inhibition. It made Maina angry and jealous, but she didn't care. The more she danced, the better she felt.

He was silent throughout the taxi ride back to the dock, and on board he became rough with her, pushing her to the bed and covering her with his whisky breath.

Later, she squirmed from beneath his heavy thigh, which he had left lying across her midriff when he had finished. The effects of the drugs were evaporating. In the darkness she listened to Maina's snores and the lapping of the waves on the hull for what seemed like hours, before she finally fell asleep.

The heat and gentle rocking of the Land Rover on the rutted murram road lulled everyone into a torpor. Even Kip had difficulty keeping alert at the wheel. Beside him, Hugh Hartigan had slumped down in his seat and his head lolled from side to side.

Conversation had died shortly after passing the square-headed mountain of Ololokwe, near Archer's Post. It was also the last time they had seen another vehicle — an Abercrombie & Kent four-wheel-drive minivan, which was speeding south, probably returning from one of the stylish lodges at Samburu National Reserve.

With the shallow muddy waters of the Ewaso Ngiro behind them, they began a gentle climb into the Sagererua Plateau — a land of swirling dust devils, low grey hills dotted by termites' nests that shimmered in the heat haze, and little else but myrrh and sansevieria bushes.

Kip had spent six months in Marsabit when he was with the National Parks and Wildlife Service, and knew the road and its surrounding landscape well. The desert wildlife fascinated him. It was different to that in the more fertile south, but they were in the heat of the day now and there wasn't much to be seen.

He glanced over his shoulder. His passengers were hunkered down against the heat, resting or sleeping as best they could. He kept the Land Rover at twenty-five miles per hour, which reduced the chance of a blowout on the rocky corrugation sections.

A herd of pinstriped Grevy's zebra sauntered from the dirt road into the surrounding savannah. First one, then another of the more skittish ones, bolted as the car drew closer. Finally they all thundered off in a cloud of dust.

Some time later he saw a long-necked gerenuk, standing on its hind legs to reach the upper leaves of a stunted shrub, but then the desert seemed to close a door against the searing heat and he saw nothing more. It would be late afternoon before the heat abated and the desert animals reappeared. By then he hoped they would have already set up camp in the Marsabit Reserve.

On the horizon directly above the line of road, a plume of dust hung in the ice-blue sky. Kip watched it approach for some time before it dispersed. The vehicle must have stopped for some reason, as there were no turn-offs on that section of road. He decided to stop on the next ridge to give his passengers a break, but when he reached it, the vehicle that had raised the dust — a large khaki truck — came into view.

Kip thought it odd that the vehicle was facing north, its tarpaulin-covered rear section turned towards them, as he was sure it had been heading south when he first saw its dust cloud.

He eased off the accelerator.

The most ominous sign was that the driver had stopped on a culvert over one of the rocky creek beds that had been carved deep into the plateau by the many years of brief wet-season rampages. It was one of the only impassable sections of road for miles in either direction.

Kip let the car roll down the slope from the ridge, and drew to a halt a hundred yards short of the truck.

'What's happening?' Hugh asked, stirring from his doze in the passenger seat.

'I'm not sure.' Kip lifted his peaked cap and scratched his scalp. 'This character's picked an odd place to tinker with his truck.'

'Where's the driver?' Diana asked from the rear seat.

'Don't know that either.' Kip scanned the surrounding countryside. It was rocky and covered with the gnarled scrub typical of the dry north.

'Look!'

The covering canvas was flung aside. Men with rifles appeared in the back of the truck. Kip gunned the motor and swung the Land Rover off the road and into the bush on the right. A bullet pinged nearby.

'Hang on!' he said as the heavy vehicle bounded and bounced over the rocky ground. They crashed through the scrub. The diesel roared in protest under the load. Kip searched the ridge to his right for a break that would allow them to escape south, but it was a wall of stone, thirty feet high. The only gateway to the south appeared to be back on the road.

He could see nothing in the rear-vision mirror except the back of Armstrong's crew-cut head peering through the back window. 'Can you see them?' he yelled over the roar of the engine.

'No. I think we've lost them,' Armstrong said.

The going was getting rough. Kip stopped the Land Rover to listen. In the silence, Eva whispered, 'Who are they?'

No one wanted to utter it, but Diana said, 'The *shifta*.'

Kip could see nothing in the mirrors. 'Anything?' he asked Armstrong.

The undulations in the savannah concealed the road from view.

'Nothing. Yet.'

If the *shifta* could hear them, they could find them. Kip cut the motor and there was silence in the cabin as they all strained to listen for the sound of an approaching truck. Kip used the time to examine the rocky creek bed below them. It was a last-chance choice if the *shifta* were still in pursuit.

Armstrong shouted, 'Here they come!' The canvas canopy bobbed above the scrub about a quarter of a mile away.

The Land Rover roared into life and leaped forward, tearing through the constraint of the foliage. With barely a pause at the creek bank, the car plunged downwards. Armstrong gave a yelp of pain from the rear section. 'Hang on!' Kip added belatedly.

The creek bed was deep enough to conceal them, but its path was winding and the boulders were almost more than the four-wheel drive could master. A number of times they came to a shuddering halt, requiring Kip to throw the car into reverse and try another path. From the depths of the creek bed they had no way of knowing if the diversion had worked. Kip drove on in the hope that they could lose the truck, get back to the road, then outrun it in the easier going.

There was a sudden explosion and a cry of pain. Kip's vision was lost in the crazed glass of the windscreen. Another bullet finished it off and crystal granules of glass flew into his face.

Ahead and above, the *shifta* trained a line of gun muzzles at them. Kip waved out his side window. 'Don't shoot! *Hapana!*' His Swahili almost failed him. 'Stop!'

'Hugh! Hugh!' Diana was leaning over the seat, her arm around her husband, who had slumped sideways. Hartigan opened his eyes but they were clouded in shock. From beneath Diana's protective arm, blood soaked through his shirt.

Above, the *shifta* rebels looked down their rifles at them.

CHAPTER 31

Maina came out of sleep with an aching head and an incessant noise in his ear. 'Sir,' it said, 'you must wake up!' A hand lightly shook his shoulder.

If he had felt well enough he might have been inclined to clout the man, but his head throbbed. He needed sleep.

'Sir,' the voice persisted, 'I have a message from Deputy Consul Costello in Nairobi.'

Costello. The name was vaguely familiar. Githinji ignored it.

The hand shook him rudely. It was too much. Maina threw the sheet from his shoulder, rolled over and stared at the white man in navy uniform standing over him. 'Who are you?'

The man stepped back and snapped to attention. 'Sir, I am Ensign Ferguson of the USS *Tarsal*. The young lady on deck informed me you were here. I hope you don't mind me intruding, sir, but I have an order from our embassy in Nairobi to contact you immediately.'

'Why?' Maina's head nearly split with the effort to sit.

'Mr Costello advises that your president needs you back in Nairobi immediately. We were asked to find you, sir.'

The new president hardly acknowledged Maina until something went wrong.

'What time is it?' he asked, rubbing his eyes.

'Eleven o'clock, sir.'

Maina groaned.

'Sir?'

Maina raised his bloodshot eyes to the ensign, noticing for the first time the envelope in his hand.

'Yes?'

'I have been ordered to pass on this telex message, and to offer you the services of our helicopter, sir.'

Githinji opened the envelope. The telex read: *Three Americans attacked by* shifta *vicinity Marsabit, including friend we discussed. Imperative we speak before any public announcement. Three Kenyan civilians also held.* Six names were listed at the bottom of the sheet. The message was signed Costello.

Now he remembered the name. Barry Costello was the CIA plant in the American Embassy — the man who had so generously offered him the navy's launch for the weekend.

'Go.' He waved his hand at the ensign.

'Thank you, sir.'

The girl was sitting on the deck staring out to sea. She wore a pair of crisp white shorts and a red and white polka-dot halterneck top. 'Rose — get your clothes on,' Maina said. 'We're leaving.'

She made no protest, simply picked up her beach towel and went below.

The ensign stood on the wharf beside a jeep, a picture of youthful health and quiet efficiency.

The hangover's fog cleared a little. Maina pulled the message from his pocket and read the six names again. Hugh Hartigan's name had registered immediately, of course. Diana, he presumed, was his wife. He tapped at the third name: *Rupert Balmain*. It was strangely familiar, yet he couldn't recall why. It would come.

The helicopter flight to Nairobi raised Rose's spirits. She watched the landscape below them change from a dark-green coastal frieze to miles of the yellow fabric of the grasslands, here and there patched with the mottled colours of dry-country scrub. As they neared Nairobi, the Athi Plains spread like a pale-green tablecloth, stained by the blood-red volcanic soil of newly hoed vegetable gardens.

Maina said he could not see the president in his beach clothes, so they landed at Wilson Airport and he shoved her into a taxi, while he drove to his office in another.

Rose was at a loose end, and wondered if she should go home to have a nap before deciding what to do for the coming night's entertainment. On a whim she directed the taxi driver to her brother's apartment.

Akello opened the door wearing only his underpants, and waved her in with a weary smile. He had grown from a scrawny kid into a well-built, six-foot-something young man. His job at the casino paid little, but his charm earned him a lot in tips. His apartment reflected it, with a black leather lounge suite, a teak dining setting and walls hung with modern prints.

'You look tired,' she said.

'So do you.' He walked behind the kitchen bench, which opened onto the sitting room. 'Coffee?'

'Thanks.' She sat on an arm of the sofa and watched him search for a cup for her.

'Where were you last night?' he asked. 'I thought you were coming to the casino for a drink?'

'I've been down to Mombasa for a couple of days.'

'*Kweli*? Who with?'

'Oh, nobody special.'

'How was it?'

'I had a ride home in a helicopter!' she said, trying hard to conceal her excitement.

'Wow! How did you manage that?'

A young blonde came from the bedroom, pulling up the straps on a long black evening dress. She put an arm around Akello's shoulder and kissed him on the cheek. 'Bye, honey,' she said, giving Rose a smile as she passed on her way to the door. 'I'll see you around, okay?'

'Okay, bye,' he said. 'A helicopter, huh?'

'Who was that?' Rose asked.

'Just a friend. She got lucky last night.'

'Obviously.'

'I mean on the tables, you terrible lady,' he said, smiling.

She shook her head in resignation. 'Honestly, Akello. Night after night. Why don't you get a regular partner?'

'Why don't you?'

She let it go unanswered. She never discussed her boyfriends with Akello, nor was she keen for him to meet them. In most cases they only lasted a month or two so it wasn't really worth the effort.

'Who was the *mzungu* I saw you with at Bubbles last week?' he asked.

'I don't know. Just someone.' She studied her fingernails. 'Did Papa have anything to say after I left Grace's house?'

'Um, well he said he still loved you.'

'Good.'

Akello never could lie very well. She knew her father would not have sent his love, or any other message. He had too much pride.

'And he said he might try to get back to Panyiketto.'

Rose studied her brother's face in profile. He avoided her eyes as he shook the creases from his black trousers.

She stood and walked to the window with her coffee. The traffic dashed by on Chiromo Road.

'Why don't you write him a letter?' Akello said. 'He says the post is much better these days.'

'No.'

'Rose ... *hakia mungu* ... It can't do any harm. Just try to explain everything to him, okay?'

'Akello, you heard what he said about me. You know what he's like. I told you that this would happen if he ever learned I had left Kisumu. And it's true. You don't know him like I do.' She put her cup down and turned her back to him at the window. 'No amount of apologies will ever be enough for him.'

'Just try one more time. I'll send a note too, so that —'

'You're not listening, baby brother. Papa will never forgive me. I've got to learn to live with that.' She turned back to face him. 'And you should too.'

The security guards saluted as Maina's car drove through the high steel gates of State House. A uniformed man opened the car door, and another showed him into the comfortable lounge that served as the waiting room to the President's office.

Maina sat for a moment, then stood again. Above him hung a large portrait of the smiling is necessary. But on no account are you to agree to exchange the prisoners. Kenya will show no weakness towards Somalia. We take no part in any of the nasty business they play. It will never end. The Hartigans have themselves to blame for this. They make themselves a target for extortionists. Besides, he and his wife have been nothing but trouble for us — agitating for conservation all over the country. You'd think they owned the place. Don't worry about them. And this ... this Balmain person ... it's his own fault. He's nobody. We warn tour operators to stay out of the Northern Frontier. It's on his own head.'

The conversation paused while an assistant came in and poured the drinks.

'Mr Costello has offered any help the embassy can provide, but the Americans must not be seen to be involved.' The President stood, signalling an end to the meeting. 'Maina — I'm counting on you.'

President, but from one angle the artist had, unwittingly perhaps, captured the calculating coldness behind the eyes.

Waiting for the President never failed to unnerve Maina. He was the last senior Kikuyu member in the Office of the President; one by one, his Kikuyu colleagues had been weeded out of their positions in the government. They usually learned of their fate at meetings like this, when they would be summoned to State House on some routine matter, only to learn that they had been accused and found guilty of a crime that required them to tender their resignation or be guaranteed a gaol term. Some said the enigmatic President Odhiambo — a member of the Luo tribe — was merely keeping his promise of sharing government appointments equitably among all tribes. But Maina and most Kikuyus believed it was a conspiracy to render the Kikuyu, the most numerous tribe, politically impotent.

The door to the President's office swung open and the Permanent Secretary came out to meet him. 'Good morning, Minister,' he said with a faint smile and a weak handshake.

'Morning, Gerishon,' Maina said with a nod of acknowledgment.

'The President will see you now.'

Maina followed him into the office where he found Barry Costello sitting at the desk opposite the President. His unease increased.

'Good morning, Your Excellency,' he said.

'Ah, Maina! Come in, my friend. You've met Mr Costello of the US Embassy, I believe?'

'Yes, Excellency.' He took Costello's hand. 'Mr Costello. Nice to see you again.'

'Likewise, Mr Githinji.'

'Sit, gentlemen. Please sit.' The President indicated a chair to Maina. 'Mr Costello has been briefing me on the hostage situation in Marsabit.'

'Hostage?' The word slipped out before he could suppress it. Costello had mentioned nothing about hostages in his telex. And he could have. He glanced at Costello, who was smiling innocently. 'I mean, I have only just now rushed back from an appointment in Mombasa, Excellency. I've had no time to be briefed by my people.'

'Good,' President Odhiambo said. 'They know nothing, and that's how I want it to stay for the moment.'

Githinji tried not to show his surprise.

'I'll let Mr Costello tell you about the Americans. Mr Costello?'

'Thank you, Mr President.' Costello leaned towards Maina. His smile disappeared immediately. 'Two of the people are middle managers of a medium-sized mining company working out of Nevada. The company specialises in the mining of small deposits of rare chemicals in hard-to-reach sites.' He glanced at the president before adding, 'They are not important in the context of this operation.'

The President was sitting in his high-backed chair with his elbows resting on the arms. He idly drummed his fingers under his nose.

'The third American is the agent we discussed in your office on the fourteenth of this month. She is a member of our intelligence community, sent here to make contact with the Free Somalia Movement, now headquartered in Addis Ababa. We believe she made contact with the FSM before the group was taken captive. We expect that the *shifta* know her identity. They are demanding that we — that is, the Kenyan Government — hand over one of their imprisoned leaders, and others whom you've had in detainment for the last twelve months, in exchange for the three Americans and three Kenyans.' He stopped abruptly and turned to the president, nodding that he had finished.

The President waited for a moment, then said, 'The Kenyans are all white, and include Hugh and Diana Hartigan. The third is someone called Rupert Balmain, known as Kip.' The president leaned forward. 'He comes from up near Mt Kenya, at Nanyuki. I believe that is your home town too, Maina.'

It was not something Githinji had ever mentioned to anyone in the party. He worried why the President of Kenya would bother to know his birthplace.

The mention of Nanyuki in connection with the name Kip Balmain hurled an ancient memory at him. He pictured a fair-haired boy, large green eyes — or were they blue? An ill-fitting hat. He stood, hands shoved in the pockets of his oversized shorts, his head tilted at a quizzical angle, as Maina agonised over his orders to sacrifice the *mzungu* boy in the interests of the Movement. It could be no one else. The coincidence momentarily stunned him.

It must have shown in his expression. President Odhiambo asked, 'Are you all right, Githinji? You look unwell.'

'I'm a little dry from the flight, Excellency. Perhaps a glass of water ...?'

'Certainly.' The President buzzed the intercom and ordered cold drinks.

'*Sasa*, this is what I want you to do, Maina. You must get this woman out of Marsabit. Do whatever

CHAPTER 32

'Where are we, Kip?' Eva's voice came from beside him in the semi-darkness of the moonless night.

'I'd say we're north of Marsabit. About a hundred miles at a guess.' He couldn't be sure of the distance, but while they'd been bound and guarded in the canvassed rear of the truck, he had felt the climb up Mt Marsabit and down the other side. He guessed they'd reached the black basalt of the Dida Galgalu — the Plains of Darkness — which lay halfway between Marsabit and the Ethiopian border town of Moyale.

He adjusted his sitting position against the incongruous loquat tree that formed the centrepiece inside the thornbush enclosure. Eva was at his shoulder, also using the tree as a back rest. Hugh was the only one given a bedroll by the *shifta*. He lay on the other side of the tree, beside Diana. Occasionally he moaned, and she whispered comforting words to him. Hartigan had lost a lot of blood. Kip had pleaded with the rebels to release the women and let them take Hugh back to Isiolo. They had ignored him.

It troubled Kip that the *shifta* hadn't simply robbed them and released them — which was their usual practice — but had taken them north. Now, many things that previously didn't make sense started to come together.

First there'd been the revelation that Eva carried a hand weapon. When the *shifta* found the gun in their search, it was puzzling that they didn't appear surprised. Then, shortly after they'd arrived here, Kip heard the unmistakable squawk of a radio and a babbled conversation in Somali. Their captors were no ordinary thieves.

'What's going on here, Eva?' he asked softly.

'What do you mean?' Her tone was measured, cautious.

'First it was the gun and the way the guards let you through at the border. That seemed more than odd. Then I remembered you made a radio-phone call from Laikipia Lodge.'

'Are you in the habit of eavesdropping on all your guests?' There was a note of annoyance in her voice.

'No. Our operator told me you'd asked to set up the call yourself. He thought it unusual that a tourist could tune a VHF system.'

'Well, I'm not a tourist.'

'And not a clerk in the US Department of Industry either.'

There was silence from her side. He could hear her breathing. When she adjusted her seat to a more comfortable position, he caught a tantalising whiff of her perfume.

'They plan to hold us hostage in exchange for a few of their people.'

'How do you know that?'

'I heard them receiving their orders on the radio.'

'And you speak Somali too. Not bad. Beautiful *and* talented.'

'I do my best.'

'And why would the Kenyan Government agree to this exchange?'

Again she paused before answering. 'Okay.' She took a deep breath. 'I'm going to need your help on this. So here goes.' She leaned closer to him; his heart thumped as her breast brushed his arm. 'I'm working for the US Government.'

'Why don't you just say CIA?'

'I don't like using CIA. It sets up preconceived ideas. Let's just call me an agent, shall we?'

'If you insist.' He shrugged.

'I'm here to make contact with a group in Addis Ababa who share certain common interests with the USA.'

'Why?'

'They have information we need.'

'No, I mean, why you? A woman. Not that I'm against women, but this seems to be a tricky assignment for a female. I don't think these Somalis have much sympathy for affirmative action.'

'We're dealing with Somalis and Ethiopians. I speak Amharic, a little Orominya and Tigrinya, several of the lowland Eastern Cushitic dialects as well as Common and Central Somali.'

'I see.'

'And, of course, Arabic, French and Italian.'

'Of course. Um ... point taken. Go on.'

She paused to collect her thoughts again. 'So my task is to make contact. My government believes the information from this group will be vitally important for our future dealings with Somalia and, to some extent, Ethiopia.'

'So that's why the US will be keen to secure your release.'

'Yes.'

'And do you have that information?'

'No.'

'Then let's tell the *shifta* and get the hell out of here.'

'If they think I don't have any useful information to trade they will kill us.'

He tried to read her eyes in the light of the stars, but it was impossible. She seemed to have a lot of confidence in what she was saying, and he didn't see any reason to disbelieve her. 'You said you'd need my help?'

'Yes. The Kenyans have launched a major military exercise along the Somali border. The US has a number of observers with them. If you're right about our position, that's only about a hundred, hundred and fifty miles east of here.'

'So? That's still a long walk.'

'I've activated a radio beacon that the commander of the US contingent should be able to receive at that distance. His orders are to track it down and pick up the information.'

'What do you mean, "activated a radio beacon"?'

'A miniature transmitter, sending out a specially encoded signal.'

'From where? The *shifta* took everything from us.'

'It's hidden in my hair clip.'

The small clip held her braids above her ears.

'So what we need to do is be ready to make a break when they arrive.'

'You make it sound easy. How are we going to get Hugh out of here?'

'We don't.'

'I can't —'

'It's either leave him or we all die. Sometimes you have to make a decision. Not everyone survives in this world. You, of all people, should know that.'

He was silent, wrestling with the cruel logic of it. 'Survival of the fittest, Kip. That's Africa, isn't it?'

Maina sat at his desk, mulling over his options. He felt he was compelled to use the GSU rather than the army. If he needed the army he would have to go through the Permanent Secretary of Defence, who was a scheming Luo and liable to watch him like a hawk, hoping for a blunder.

The General Services Unit was an instrument of internal security and nominally under Maina's control, but its commander, Colonel Gabriel Opiyo, was a veteran soldier with powerful friends in the party. He was virtually unmanageable. Maina suspected he had ambitions to replace him as the Assistant Minister of Internal Security, and was plotting behind his back with that in mind.

It also had occurred to Maina that President Odhiambo might have chosen him to lead this action hoping he would fail, thereby giving him the excuse to sack him. And it was odd that he had ordered him to keep the action secret from others in the government and his own department. It was a technical breach of procedures — a sacking offence. On the other hand, he could hardly deny the president's request for secrecy. If he did, he could be accused of disloyalty — the most common charge laid against those removed from office.

Maina slammed his pen onto the desk. He hadn't fought his way up through the party to let his position be stolen from him — especially in these turbulent political times when change was afoot. He would rescue the CIA hostage from the *shiftas* as ordered, and he would do so without the so-called assistance of the Americans. He would allow nothing, and nobody, to steal his victory from him.

He picked up his telephone. 'Get me Colonel Opiyo,' he ordered.

For the next ten minutes, he fidgeted with the pencil on his desk and fumed. He knew that Opiyo would deliberately delay contacting him, but used the time to plan a process that would prevent the commander from employing his usual brutal tactics to resolve the hostage situation. He knew it would be difficult. Opiyo had no incentive to cast the minister's performance in a good light.

The pencil snapped in his fingers. If he couldn't control Opiyo, then his career, and the hostages, were doomed.

Kip pulled off his T-shirt and folded it into a pad. The sun was gold, clinging to the eastern horizon, but he felt a taste of its approaching strength on his bare back. He tilted the bucket, poured some water onto the cloth, and carried it, dripping, back to where Diana sat beside Hugh under the loquat tree.

'Here,' he said, handing the wet pad to Diana.

She looked up and smiled her thanks.

'Why don't you take a break? I'll sit with Hugh for a while.' He lowered himself to the ground beside her.

'I'm okay. Thanks anyway.' Diana pressed some water from the shirt and patted her husband's forehead with it.

'How is he?'

'The bleeding is slowing but I think it's getting into his lungs. He's had some terrible coughing fits, which start it bleeding again.'

'Yes. I heard him during the night.'

Within twenty-four hours, the 68-year-old Hartigan had suddenly begun to look his age. Kip was shocked at his appearance. Always a robust,

sun-drenched man, his skin had turned pale, almost parchment-like, and his breathing was shallow.

'I don't know how we're going to move him,' Kip said, thinking out loud.

'Move him? What do you mean?'

He told her about Eva's plan. 'I'll have to work something out. We can't move him if it means he loses any more blood.'

'You're not supposed to talk about the patient within his hearing,' Hugh croaked.

'You're awake?'

'I am now,' he said, swallowing hard to clear his throat. The effort made him wince. 'Had a weird dream, about elephants. They were like my cattle, and I had this tribe of Maasai who milked them for me.'

'Sounds like just another of your schemes,' Diana said, smiling at him.

'Ah, my darling. You've heard them all, haven't you.' He reached an unsteady hand for hers.

'How do you feel, Hugh?' Kip asked, shifting his position to Hugh's side.

'I'm not bad for an old bloke.'

Kip felt the jab of his bunch of keys in his thigh and shifted them to his other pocket before taking the damp shirt from Diana's hand to pat Hugh forehead with it. 'Glad to hear it.'

'Kip, what *is* that damn thing on your key ri I've always wanted to ask.'

'Just a piece of wooden junk.'

'You've had the bloody thing for as long a known you.'

'It has something to do with my family. these days I'll find out what it is.'

'You know what it looks like to me?'

'What?'

'It looks like ...' Hartigan's voice caught in his throat and, in attempting to clear it, he brought on a coughing fit. He couldn't regain control of his coughing, and a film of blood appeared on his lips. Kip picked up a tea mug and rushed to the bucket of drinking water.

When he returned, the bandage on Hugh's chest was bright red, and he lay with his eyes closed, exhausted by the spasm.

Diana shot a glance at Kip. She had panic in her eyes and Kip reached across to pat her hand. As he did so, Hugh opened his eyes.

'Ah, Kip. That's just was what I was about to say,' he croaked with a wan smile. 'I was going to ask you to look after this wonderful woman for me.'

'You're not getting out of that contract just yet, my darling,' Diana said, forcing a smile.

Hugh sighed in feigned exasperation. 'There she goes again. Pinching my authority.'

Kip was feeling trapped in the moment. 'I'll get some more water,' he said. He couldn't handle the fact that Hugh was dying, and was afraid that his emotions would soon overwhelm him.

'Kip. Stay.' Hugh placed his hand on Kip's. His fingers were icy. 'There may not be another chance to say this, and I don't want to die leaving you to torture yourself.'

Kip risked a glance at Diana, who seemed resigned to letting Hugh have his say.

'Diana and I have had an ... an arrangement during our life together. That grenade did more than just bugger up my leg. When it happened, we were engaged, and I know I should have called it off, but right then I needed Diana more than I ever did. It was selfish of me, I know, but Diana agreed

to marry me. And she's been everything to me that I could possibly want.'

His breath came in shallow, difficult gasps.

'But there was a condition I put on our marriage. It was done on the strict understanding that, for the sake of both of us, when she needed, she would discreetly find someone, somewhere, to satisfy her physically.

'I have no doubts when she tells me the men she has occasionally brought into her life have meant nothing to her. Until she met you. Then, poor darling, she had to let you go. She was falling in love. And that would never do.' He paused to swallow, and flinched with the pain of it. 'She ended it, not at my insistence — I knew nothing of it at the time — but because of her own ... determination to stick with our agreement ... So you see, she has been faithful to both of us.'

Kip swallowed the lump in his throat and covered Hugh's hand with his. 'Hugh, I would never do anything to hurt you.'

'And you haven't,' he said.

'I didn't know you then, and I couldn't know how it would go, with Diana and —'

'You're not listening, dear boy. You have nothing to feel guilty about ... I'm just glad, so glad, that ... Kip, you've been like the son I never had. Oh gawd ...' He began to chuckle, but it became a cough. He took a breath and started again. 'I sound like someone in a fifties movie.' He swallowed hard, fighting back the urge to cough.

'Hugh —'

'Shhh, Kip, this is my scene ... I don't have to give you my ...' He stopped to draw a painful breath. '... My blessing. Your future is for you to decide, but I ... well, I suppose all I really wanted to say was ... don't let that conscience of yours … get in the way of whatever might … might happen between the two of you. Okay?'

'Hugh … I —'

'Okay, Kip?'

'Okay, Hugh.'

The older man closed his eyes, and for a moment Kip thought he had dropped into sleep, but his chest was no longer labouring under the effort of breathing. 'Hugh?' Kip touched him on the cheek.

'Hugh!' Diana felt for the pulse in his throat, then covered her face with her hands.

Kip lifted Hugh's cold grasp from around his fingers and placed the hand on Hugh's blood-soaked shirt, before taking Diana into his arms and holding her while she sobbed.

CHAPTER 33

They buried Hugh in the rocky ground above the camp while the *shifta* looked on with dark impassive eyes.

It was a Saturday. Diana recalled that on Saturdays it was Hugh's habit to go riding with friends. They were an eclectic crowd of landowners, lawyers and others who, in one way or another, had a connection with the land. Early in their marriage, Diana had joined him on one or two occasions, but she'd soon realised the group were of another world. They were of Hugh's generation, and they shared a collective memory of their earlier lives. They seemed to have a different language, requiring only a word or two from one to be immediately understood and associated with the pertinent story by the others. Hugh's first wife featured in a number of these recollections, leading to an embarrassed silence. It didn't worry Diana — Hugh's first wife had divorced him five years before Diana met him — but it was another reason for her to be otherwise occupied on a Saturday.

So it became with many of their routines. She and Hugh pursued different interests, coming together at the end of a day, or a week, of not seeing each other, but with contentment in the renewed company. Their lives settled into two parallel paths, seldom overlapping. She thought perhaps it was this arrangement that now left her feeling not only sad, but sadly empty — as if she had lost a close friend.

She wondered how other people handled the death of a spouse, but immediately dismissed it. There would be endless variations. She imagined it all depended on how long one had been given to prepare for the event. With Hugh nearly twenty years her senior, she'd always known he would leave her a widow one day. But she had not been prepared for the death that came so brutally, so suddenly. She was as much in shock as grieving.

Kip had checked on her regularly in the two days since Hugh's death, asking if she needed anything, and fussing about her comfort. He avoided talking to her about Hugh, however, and she had no idea how he felt about her husband's deathbed disclosure that she had been secretly in love with him since they'd met.

Maina cursed himself for agreeing to Gabriel Opiyo's request that they hold their meeting in the GSU headquarters; it was home turf and all the paraphernalia of Opiyo's power would be on display. But Opiyo played the clock, knowing the Assistant Minister was under pressure to resolve the hostage situation, and Maina agreed to meet in Opiyo's office because he was in a hurry to get to Marsabit.

Maina resolved to keep the meeting brief and to the point, affording Opiyo no opportunity to play his power games. Immediately he entered Opiyo's office, which was resplendent with insignia, flags and sundry mounted weaponry, he curtly shook the colonel's hand and immediately launched into his plan.

'Colonel Opiyo,' he began, taking the chair on the other side of Opiyo's vast desk, 'in the interests of time, let me come straight to the point. We are dealing with a difficult situation, as you know. The presence of foreign nationals complicates the operation, so, as the Assistant Minister, I am forced to impose some constraints upon your GSU operations in this case.'

Opiyo's smile was icy. 'Of course, Assistant Minister. The GSU is at your service. As always.'

'Excellent. Then here is what we must do. I understand you already have a strong squad on its way to the north. You are to order them to find and surround the *shifta*, and contain them until I arrive. I have certain options available to me to stop this matter escalating out of control.' It was a lie, but he thought it unlikely that Opiyo would be aware of the President's orders about not dealing with the Somalis. What he hoped he could do on arrival was to offer the rebels their own freedom in exchange for their hostages. 'I am flying to Marsabit in an hour.'

'I assure you, Assistant Minister, my commander is capable of handling the situation. Under my orders, of course.'

'I'm sure he can, Colonel, but I am instructing you to tell him to find, surround and contain the *shifta*. There is to be no exchange of fire unless it is absolutely necessary.'

'As you wish, Mr Githinji.'

'There is a helicopter on standby for me in Marsabit. You will call me at the administration post when your GSU people are in place. Understood?'

'Perfectly, Mr Assistant Minister.' Opiyo's smile revealed nothing.

Maina didn't trust him, but his hands were tied.

Kip had learned nothing new from his visit to the *shifta*'s leader other than that the arrangements to free their colleagues were progressing. The leader said nothing about the fate of his five hostages if these negotiations failed — he didn't have to.

Eva maintained her earlier belief that the Americans would come to their assistance, but admitted that if there were no sign of them within the next twenty-four hours, she would have to assume the radio signal had not reached them. She had no other idea of how they might get out, other than to wait for the Kenyan authorities to act. Kip felt anxious about being caught between a heavily armed, ill-disciplined military team and the desperate rebels.

The Westerners had been under the eyes of the *shifta* riflemen on the rocks above their thorn *boma* for three days. Although they were allowed to move freely within the confines of the thorn barricade, Kip felt trapped. When he wasn't pacing the perimeter like a caged lion, he sat brooding on the death of Hugh Hartigan.

Apart from attending to matters of her comfort, he had been avoiding Diana, and he was unsure exactly why.

He hated the feeling of helplessness her grief brought him. He'd had no experience in comforting friends or relatives after the death of a loved one, and he hovered around her, desperately needing to do something to ease her pain, but totally bereft of the means.

There was also the guilt about his affair with Diana, which always increased when in Hugh's company, but now, perversely, seemed worsened by his death.

Perhaps he was trying to avoid the most unsettling revelation of all — the news that the reason Diana had ended their affair was because she had fallen in love with him.

Kip had tried to reconstruct the atmosphere of those days, to retrospectively find the clues he had missed eighteen years ago. He couldn't recall any sign that his love was reciprocated; she had concealed it very well. He wondered if there was any of that love remaining after all this time.

'How are you, Diana?' he asked now, on his return from the *shifta* leader's tent.

She looked up at him from her seat at the base of the loquat tree. 'Won't you sit with me, Kip? Please?'

'Of course.' He sat and they both stared out over the *boma* fence into the rock-strewn semi-desert of the Dida Galgalu. Kip waited for her to speak.

'I'd always imagined caring for Hugh as he grew old,' she said, eventually. 'It used to frighten me. I'm not a very caring person. But now that he's gone, I feel cheated of the opportunity.'

When she had been silent for a few minutes, he could hold back no longer. 'Why didn't you tell me how you felt about me?'

'I couldn't.'

'Why did I have to learn about it from Hugh? Why couldn't *you* tell me?'

'Because it was impossible to love you. I couldn't do that to Hugh. Never.'

'I understand that, but why didn't you tell me the reason you ended it?' He remembered the weeks of anguish in which his mood swung wildly between rage and depression. 'It drove me crazy. I thought you dumped me for someone else. I began to think I was some kind of lovesick adolescent, totally missing the point. I felt stupid.'

She put her hand on his. 'Kip, oh Kip, I'm sorry. Don't you think it tore at me too? I had to turn my heart against you. I had to force myself to forget you so I could carry it off. I couldn't tell you. How could you continue to be my friend if you knew I loved you?'

'*You* managed it.'

'Yes ... and it was the hardest thing I ever did.'

'I know how it was for you and Hugh now, but I can't help thinking that we've both wasted the best years of our lives — you in a marriage that was like brother and sister, and me ... what have I been doing? Screwing around, looking for that missing something, hoping I'd recognise it when I found it.'

'I can't say I have wasted my life. Okay, Hugh and I didn't have a sexual relationship, but we had something that most married people never achieve. We had intimacy. Sometimes I think sex and intimacy are mutually exclusive. I could talk to Hugh about anything. I mean anything — even my affairs. He trusted me. Totally. It was one of the reasons I could never leave him. He gave me permission to be myself.'

'Is there anything left, Diana?'

'You mean after all these years of denying you? Of pretending you were just another feckless young man?'

'Yes.'

'Kip, I'm too old for you.'

'That's not true.'

'I've seen some of the pretty young things you take to bed.'

'You bloody well have not.'

'Well, I've imagined them.'

She gave his hand a squeeze, but didn't face him.

'You haven't answered me,' he persisted. 'Do you still love me?'

He covered her hand with his.

'Diana?'

She turned to him, and her eyes began to fill up. 'With all my heart.'

Eva joined Kip in the shade of the loquat tree where he was stripping the bark from a piece of foliage. 'We need to talk,' she said.

'Hello, Eva,' he replied.

'I don't think there's a chance in hell these guys are going to get what they want from the Kenyans,' she said.

'I agree.'

'I've been watching them. They go off to pray a few times a day.'

'I've noticed. I also noticed, when we went to bury Hugh, that there's some thick scrub out past that *kopje*.' He nodded to the granite massive rearing thirty or forty feet beyond the *boma* fence.

'What about the thorn fence?'

The thornbush was stacked around them into a six-foot-high barricade in what would have once been a cattle enclosure, fifty yards wide.

'I've put aside a couple of the bigger pieces of firewood, using them as fireside seats. If we could get a couple more, we could throw them onto the thornbush and maybe squash it down enough to climb over.' He squinted up at her. 'Have you given up on your CIA buddies?'

She picked up a pebble and tossed it around in her hand. 'They would have been here by now.'

'Then I reckon it's time for Plan B.'

'When?'

'The sooner the better. I get nervous at the thought of the Kenyan army rushing in here, guns blazing.' He looked out over the surrounding boulders. 'This afternoon, at evening prayers.'

'I'll see if I can get the guards to bring more wood.'

He nodded in agreement. 'I'll tell Diana about our plans.'

Eva walked casually towards the gate to try for the firewood.

Kip rested his back against the tree and closed his eyes. He should have been exhausted — the last seventy-two hours had been a constant drain on him, and he was apprehensive about their planned attempt at escape — but he felt rejuvenated, as if he'd been suddenly transported back eighteen years, to when he and Diana were so immersed in each other that the universe simply did not exist outside their sphere. It was the time before his multicoloured world had lost its sheen, the day Diana told him, *It's been great, Kip, but I'm sorry, it's time we took a break.*

He slipped his hands behind his head and sighed. Eighteen years of denial, and eighteen years of remorse — first for losing Diana's love, and then for tainting his friendship with Hugh. But it was time to end the interminable guilt trip about Hugh, and for them to explore their old feelings. If they could find the lost spark of their love, and rekindle it, they could start their lives over again, perhaps leave Kenya, and their old memories, behind.

He found himself vaguely troubled by the idea of leaving Kenya. While it wasn't his country of birth, it was the only one he called home. A memory of Nanyuki rushed out of his past. It was surrounded by all the usual frightening childhood images, and the unsettling void that symbolised his father. He couldn't flee the country without putting that mystery to rest. He promised himself that he wouldn't start his new life without solving the riddle of his past.

He turned away from the anguish that awaited him in Nanyuki, and let his mind wander into the life he and Diana might soon share, before drifting into a dreamless sleep.

He opened his eyes and inhaled the hot dry air off the desert. He guessed he'd been asleep for less than an hour, but he felt good. Patches of intense blue sky peeped between the dark green spears of the loquat tree. The sun had edged into its lower boughs, allowing shafts of sunlight to splash his face.

In spite of their perilous situation, the chance that he and Diana might renew their love gave him courage. The loquat tree and the dancing shafts of sunlight made him reluctant to rouse himself, but he sat up and rubbed his eyes.

The flash of sunlight again caught the corner of his eye and he realised it came not from the afternoon sky, but from the east, in the direction of the *kopje*. He scanned the granite's outline, waiting for the reflection to return. In a moment it flashed again. Some fool was stalking them wearing a pair of silvered sunglasses. He was on the next-to-top boulder. Kip watched as he lifted his glasses to sit on the top of his camouflaged cap, then raised a rifle.

Kip followed the soldier's sightline to the *shifta* guards. Beyond them was Diana, rinsing some clothes in the disused cattle trough.

'Diana,' he called, trying to keep the urgency out of his voice. 'Diana!' This time a little louder.

She turned towards him and he signalled frantically for her to come. She waved back.

One of the guards stood to investigate his call. Kip knew it would give the sniper on the *kopje* the target he needed. There was no time to wait. Kip leaped to his feet and sprinted across the compound towards her. A second guard was now taking an interest; he reached for his weapon as Kip charged directly at him.

Rushing towards the barrel of the *shifta*'s gun, Kip waved for him to hold his fire. He had no time to negotiate — he had to get to Diana.

The *shifta* put the rifle to his shoulder.

Diana shouted, 'Kip! For God's sake, stop!'

The crack of a high-velocity bullet ripped the air. The *shifta* guard was spun off his feet and fell to the ground. In the next several moments, the silence of the afternoon was shattered by the stutter of automatic gunfire and the crack of rifles.

Diana dashed towards Kip, and her body shuddered in the crossfire. She fell ten paces from him.

Kip dived to the dirt and gathered her in his arms, lifting her head and turning her face towards him.

He lay with her, holding her, rocking her, pleading for her to not die, but he knew she was dead before he even reached her.

The telephone in the Marsabit office rang once.

The deputy provincial commissioner grabbed it. 'Yes?' he snapped. After a moment he said, 'It's for you, Minister.'

Maina took the phone. It was Opiyo. 'Yes, Colonel. What's the situation?'

He listened to the GSU commander's silken voice. It all sounded perfectly plausible. Regrettable, but plausible.

The GSU had no choice but to vigorously defend themselves from an unprovoked assault by the *shifta*.

One civilian female, white, was deceased.

One civilian male, dead prior to the action.

All *shifta* terrorists had been eliminated.

No GSU casualties.

CHAPTER 34

Harry just loved Florida 2000. He loved the climb to the second-floor bar, where the girls would loiter in the stairwell, chatting him up, and where the more adventurous would run silken fingers over his groin.

He enjoyed the music. The DJ played Isaac Hayes and the Bee Gees, Sister Sledge and the Village People. In Florida 2000 you could find a quiet corner to enjoy a beer or make small talk with a particular lady, or you could be in the crush of bodies on the dance floor or at the bar, surrounded by the trendsetters of Nairobi, people who had made it in business or politics — the power-brokers, the money-makers.

Tonight it was duty as well as pleasure. After many weeks, he had finally persuaded Kip to join him for a drink. After the Hartigans' funerals, Harry had hung around Kip's apartment whenever he could, but Kip let him know that he didn't need a minder and asked him to let him have some time alone. Then Kip had avoided him for weeks, refusing to return his calls. Harry abandoned his attempts to reach him by phone and simply appeared that evening on his doorstep, and refused to leave unless Kip agreed to go out for a drink with him.

The two men reached the head of the stairs. Before them was a throng of gyrating bodies, lashed by strobe lights. On the far side of the dance floor, the bar was six-deep with people queuing for drinks.

'Harry, I'm going,' Kip said, and headed back down the stairs.

'No, no. Kip, hold up.' Harry grabbed him by the elbow. 'Come back here. We've just arrived —'

'And I'm just leaving. Can't handle this, Harry. I thought we were going out for a quiet beer, not this … this …'

'But Kip, ol' diamond, this is what you *need*. You can't sit around in that apartment of yours, day and night. You've got a life to live —'

'Harry, I appreciate what you're trying to do, and maybe in another week or so I'll be ready, but —'

'Kip, listen. Listen to Harry. This,' he made a sweeping gesture around the darkened night club, 'is … well, let's just call it shock therapy. Kip, don't look at me like that. Harry knows what he's doing here. A drink or two, and we can go. Can't be fairer than that, can I?'

Kip eyed him for a moment then shook his head in defeat. Harry slapped him on the back. 'That's my boy.' Kip didn't appear convinced, but Harry gripped his elbow and led him across the floor to the bar.

There was a group of marketing people he knew that might be fun, and a few familiar faces from the up-and-coming ranks of government. He recognised Maina Githinji in one cluster of faces. He had a cigarette in one hand and a whisky in the other. Beside him was Rose Nasonga. Harry hadn't seen her for months.

Kip was looking like a gazelle caught by the stare of a leopard — ready to spring for the exit at any moment.

'Kip, ol' darlin',' he said. 'How would you like Harry to introduce you to the government minister who sprang you from that trap in Marsabit?'

Harry had forced him into it, and Kip knew it was a mistake the moment he set foot in the nightclub. But when Harry said he could introduce him to the government minister who had been responsible for the disaster that led to Diana's death, he was suddenly glad he'd come. He followed Harry through the press of people at the edge of the dance floor.

In her high heels, Rose stood half a head taller than the women around her. The white silk sheath of her dress covered her from its high neck to just above her knees. She watched him approach with the haunted, intelligent eyes he remembered from their first meeting in the Mara. She held herself aloof from the two men huddled in conversation at her side.

Harry greeted her. 'Hi, Rose,' he said, taking her hand.

The two African men broke off their discussion and turned to Harry.

'Hello, Maina,' he said, nodding to the first man, then greeted the other, Bethwel Muraya. They exchanged handshakes. 'This is Kip Balmain,' Harry said, stepping back to usher him forward.

Kip hesitated to extend his hand, wondering which of them was responsible for the GSU's reckless handling at the *shiftas*' stronghold, but he decided to wait his time and shook their hands in turn.

'Kip, you remember Rose, I think?'

'Yes. Hello, Rose.'

She had a strange, sad look in her eyes, like a pup lost in the rain. 'Kip,' she said, hardly moving her lips.

'Kip Balmain?' the man called Maina said. He seemed amused by the sound of it. When it became obvious he had nothing further to add, and simply stood there grinning, Harry hastened to fill the gap. 'So-o-o, a good crowd tonight — even for a Saturday, ah?'

Bethwel, a bespectacled man in a white shirt and black suit, looked over the crush and nodded absently. He was Kip's guess as the minister. The other one, Maina, somewhat heavyset and probably in his forties, looked too young.

'Kip Balmain,' Maina repeated, still grinning. 'Didn't I read that name somewhere recently?'

Harry answered for him. 'Yes, Kip was one of those hostages up Marsabit way.'

'That's right!' Maina said, nodding. 'It was in all the papers, wasn't it?'

'That's it,' Harry said, smiling broadly.

Kip turned his attention back to Bethwel, who had remained curiously outside the conversation although it had been a big event involving him. Kip wanted to draw him in, to trap him into an admission. It was unusual for a politician to forego an opportunity to put himself in the limelight. Unless, of course, he felt guilty about it.

'Two people died,' Rose said, almost to herself.

Kip heard her, and said, 'Yes … they did.'

'Two of your friends,' she added.

Something in her voice said she understood how he felt.

'Yes,' he said softly, surprised that it still hurt so much.

'I read that you were something of a hero, Mr Balmain,' Maina said over the top of their conversation.

Kip ignored him, trying to maintain the connection with Rose. With her few words she had touched on something inside him that needed to be expressed. He searched for it, sensing he would lose it at any moment.

'Absolutely!' Harry added. 'Kip got two of the *shiftas* with one of their own rifles.'

'Magnificent,' Maina said. 'And how did you develop these skills, Mr Balmain? I mean, are you in the security business? Or are you one of these mercenaries I hear are running all over Africa at the moment?' His laugh prompted Harry to join in.

'No,' Kip said, trying to remain polite. The man was annoying him. Although he appeared to be sober, he was acting quite strangely, like a person who'd had too many drinks to realise he was being rude.

'Perhaps you have some experience in the hunting profession then? Where were you raised, Mr Balmain? Was it in the deep bush?'

Kip gave a tight smile. He was beginning to lose his patience with this person who seemed determined to force the conversation in an unwanted direction.

Harry must have sensed his mood and tried to calm Kip's hostility. 'That's right, Maina. Kip was raised up Nanyuki way. On the edge of the jungle.'

'Mt Kenya. That's Mau Mau country, isn't it?'

Kip had had about enough, 'I wouldn't know about that, Mr ...?'

'Githinji. Maina Githinji.' Again, that smile.

The memory of a childhood friend — a Kikuyu playmate with that name — came to Kip in that instant. Not so much a friend, but a force in his life. He had been killed by the Home Guards in a terrible night of reprisals against the Mau Mau for murdering a white family. The coincidence that brought together these childhood memories and the more recent, but equally violent, deaths of his friends unsettled him.

'I think I'll get a drink,' he said, and went to the bar without risking another word.

Maina had enjoyed the sport. It was particularly pleasing to find that Kip remained ignorant of who he was, even after Maina was forced to reveal his name.

He wondered if he would have recognised Kip had he not been introduced. His hair had darkened from the snowy-headed blond he was at age eight, but his eyes held the same intensity, and the glint of stubborn determination had not been lost. Back then, it gave Maina the impression it was not his size that prevented the young Kip Balmain from retaliating against his childish taunts. He also never understood why he preferred the company of a bullying, heartless Kikuyu boy, four years his senior, to being with white kids. Maina always knew there was something deeply personal driving this *mzungu* boy. Perhaps he would have the opportunity to learn more about him now that their paths had again crossed.

His game with Kip added a touch of amusement to a night promising high drama. Earlier, Bethwel Muraya had told him that his contact within the Air Cavalry Unit had warned that, with the Kenyan army on manoeuvres along the Somali border, the young bloods would launch their bid for power very soon, even as early as later that night. They would seize the barracks first, then the radio station, where they would make their announcement of the new government. They would play Bob Marley songs over the air as a signal that the coup had begun, and was going as planned.

Maina had suggested to Bethwel that they go to a public place to ensure they were not associated with the action, in case it failed. He looked over the crowd of unsuspecting revellers, dancing like ignorant fools. Rose had been pestering him for a dance, but he was too distracted by what might soon happen to bother with her. By now she would normally be dancing by herself — and annoying him by it — but she was strangely subdued.

His inside knowledge of the possible coup gave him a feeling of power. He itched in anticipation of what might await him in the morning. There might be an invitation to take a leading role in the new Kikuyu government — one prepared to reward the freedom fighters who had made the break from colonialism a reality.

He would have liked to continue his game with Kip, but he had disappeared. He hoped there would be another occasion to exercise his power over him. It amused him to tease his old playmate as he had when they were children — to play him along, to psychologically pinch and poke him, keeping his identity a secret until a time of his choosing, when its revelation would annoy him further.

Rose wanted to follow Kip to the bar. She could see he needed help. But she didn't, because she knew it would annoy Maina and, from past unpleasant experiences, she knew that if Maina was displeased he could become quite unpleasant. Seeing her walking after another man, especially a white man, was almost guaranteed to make his blood boil.

But it wasn't Maina's temper alone that prevented her from going after him — she was about done with her relationship with him anyway; he had taken his spite out on her once too often. She didn't follow Kip because she feared his intensity. She was afraid she would be drawn into his vortex of anger and frustration, and was uncertain of her ability to deal with it.

Harry wandered off to find Kip, and Maina and Bethwel went into another huddle. Rose couldn't care less about being included in their conversation — they generally talked about government matters, and who was presently winning the ear of the President — but it annoyed her that they acted as if she wasn't there.

'Rose, get us a drink,' Maina said, emerging from his private discussion. 'What do you want, Bethwel? Another scotch?' He sunk a hand into his pocket and thrust a five hundred at her. 'Two scotches.'

She ignored him.

'Rose, two scotches,' he repeated.

'Get them yourself,' she said.

Maina opened his mouth, and then closed it again without a word. She could see his jaw tighten and the veins on his temples stand out. She had surprised even herself with her impulsive gesture, but it was done. She folded her arms and stuck her chin out. *Let him make a scene, if he dares.* She was emboldened by being on neutral ground.

Just as she thought he might strike her, Harry rejoined them.

'I don't know where the hell Kip's gone. Looked all over. Did you people see him come past here?' He looked from one to the other. Nobody answered.

Maina hadn't taken his eyes off Rose, who decided to stare him down, just once, before she got shot of him.

'No? Oh, well . . .' Harry sipped his beer. 'By the way, Maina, I was hoping you'd tell Kip you were his saviour up there in Marsabit. I reckon he'd have been really pleased to meet you. Probably would've bought you a bottle of champagne for saving his life . . . Maina?'

Maina dragged his gaze from Rose and looked at Harry. Rose felt she had been under the flame of a blowtorch, and had almost conceded defeat before Harry intervened.

'If your friend's life is worth one drink, he now owes me two, Harry.'

Harry's smile faded, unsure if Maina was joking or not.

'I could have killed him years ago, but took pity. Last month it would have been even easier. All I had to do was to do nothing.' He snapped his fingers in Harry's face. 'Like that, he would have been gone.'

Maina jerked his head, indicating to Bethwel that they should leave, and departed without a word to Rose. *Good riddance*, she thought.

Harry's mouth hung open. 'What . . . ? What the hell was that all about?' He turned to Rose. 'Rose? What was that about?'

Rose shook her head, not unhappy to be seeing the last of Maina. 'I don't know, Harry. And I don't care.'

CHAPTER 35

Maina refused Bethwel's offer of a lift and walked unsteadily to his Volvo. He was still fuming from Rose's impudence, and roared out of the car park, sending a hail of gravel over the security guard.

He headed for home along Moi Avenue, then decided to try one of the small taverns out along Ngong Road. He had the urge to find a girl for the night, and the illegal bars attracted the type of woman who would be impressed by the offer of a drive in a Volvo.

He swung into Biashara Street to cut across town, before noticing the mob of about a dozen young men, obviously drunk, blocking the way. They were trying to jemmy open the steel security screen on a shop specialising in hi-fi systems. Maina dropped the car into reverse, but another group of about twenty approached from behind. At first sight he thought they were carrying lanterns, but a sputtering flame flew through the darkness and a bottle smashed against the wall of a nearby shop, sending a ball of flames exploding into the night.

Maina felt the heat on his cheek and a stab of panic in his heart.

He had never forgotten the night his siblings burned to death in his family's hut in Nanyuki. Large fires, even campfires, frightened him. The atmosphere of violence, the mob — there was a chilling similarity to the night his family was attacked.

Another Molotov cocktail hurtled towards him. It exploded on the boot of the car.

In a panic, he hit the accelerator. The Volvo responded immediately, leaping forwards with a squeal of rubber. It roared down Biashara Street towards the mob attacking the shop door, some of whom had spilled onto the street. His headlights picked up terror-filled eyes before the young man hit the windscreen, shattering it. Maina felt, rather than saw, a second hit, but he would stop for nothing. He roared down the narrow street, flames trailing behind the black Volvo.

He needed to escape. Speed would extinguish the fire.

He took the corner into Kenyatta Avenue on two squealing wheels and roared away, the flames chasing him into the night.

'Hey, Kip, ol' diamond. There you are! I was looking all over for you. Where've you been?'

'C'mon, Harry, let's get out of here.' Kip had found Harry sitting with two heavily made-up young women at a table in a darkened alcove.

'Out of here? Hold on, ol' sweetheart, it's only ... what time is it?' Harry extracted an arm from around one of the women and squinted at the luminous numerals on his watch. 'It's only ... shit, it's only three-thirty.'

'We've got to go, Harry. An emergency. Excuse us, ladies.' Kip grabbed Harry by the elbow and eased him out of the alcove seat.

'What for?'

'I'll explain on the way.'

Outside in the fresh air, Harry became more coherent. As they walked to his car he asked Kip what the emergency was.

'I took off for home an hour or so ago,' Kip began.

'You walked? Are you stark, raving mad? It's a jungle out there.'

'I had to get out of the nightclub — driving me mad. So I started to walk. Up near the Parklands Club, I came across a huge mob — they were burning cars and breaking into houses.'

'Were the police there?'

'No sign of them. So I cut down towards Chiromo Road. A block away it was worse. I saw a bunch of thugs cut down an old Indian guy with *pangas*.'

'Jesus!' Harry said. He tipped the security guard and opened the car. 'You were lucky to get out of there alive. When these guys start in on the Asians, there's something serious going on.'

'It was like a war zone, Harry. Maybe there's something about it on the radio.'

Harry flicked the switch. 'I Shot the Sheriff' was playing.

The motor coughed into life and Harry eased his old Peugeot through the congested car park.

'You notice there's not a single taxi around?' Kip asked.

'Hmm, strange. We should have asked Maina if he knew what was going on.'

'Maina?'

'Yeah, he's the Minister for Internal Security.'

'Maina is? I thought it was the other guy. Damn! I knew I didn't like him for a reason.'

'Why not?'

'It was his fucking GSU who blasted the shit out of us at Marsabit.'

'Oh, my God, ol' diamond, be careful with Maina Githinji.'

'Stuff him. I'd like to wring his fucking neck.'

'If he gets something against you —'

'Better take Valley Road, Harry,' Kip said.

Harry swung the car into Kenyatta Avenue. The street was deserted, except for a *matatu* that sped across their path at an intersection. As was typical with the small, privately owned buses, music belted from its high-powered speakers. They were tuned to the same radio station as Harry's. 'Buffalo Soldier' shattered the otherwise quiet night. The *matatu* roared away along Koinange Street, leaving the avenue deserted again.

'What is it with Radio Kenya tonight?' Harry asked. 'Since when have they been Bob Marley fans?'

'Turn right, Harry.'

'Oh shit! You should drive, Kip. I always get lost trying —'

'What's that? Harry, look — a car's in the ditch up ahead.'

Harry pulled in to the side of the road. The car, a late model Volvo, had been badly damaged by fire and had obviously hit the guardrail before ending in the ditch. Steam spiralled from the cracked radiator.

Kip rolled down the window. 'Are you all right?' he asked the man sitting in the ditch, holding his head.

The man looked up. It was Maina Githinji.

'You!'

'Steady, Kip,' Harry cautioned in a soft voice. 'Remember what I told you about this guy.'

'I don't give a —'

'Hold on, Maina!' Harry yelled. 'We'll give you a hand.'

Githinji was muttering incoherently. He was either drunk or concussed. It was just as well, as far as Kip was concerned — he might have been tempted to take up the matter of the GSU with him.

Harry helped him into the back seat of the car, and then fussed about, making him comfortable. 'He doesn't want to go home,' he said when he resumed his seat behind the wheel.

'Why not?'

'Don't know. Something about wanting to stay out of the way for a day or two. I'm gonna take him to my place, after I drop you off.'

'Did he say he knew anything about the girl?'

'Rose? I don't know.'

Kip turned in his seat, leaned over and shook Githinji roughly by the shoulder. He let out a moan.

'Where's the girl?' Kip demanded. 'Where's Rose?'

'There,' he muttered.

'There? Where?' Kip said, shaking him again.

'Ohhh,' he moaned. 'Florida 2000.'

'You rotten —'

'Kip!' Harry caught his arm. 'Careful.' Shaking his head, he added, 'For my sake, if not for yours.'

Kip snarled, but Harry shushed him and pointed to the radio. The presenter was making an announcement: '...*has been removed from office. The constitution has been suspended and all instruments of government are now in the hands of the Provisional Government of Reconstruction. A spokesman for the Provisional Government has appealed to the public for calm. There will be another broadcast within the hour.*' After a moment's silence, Bob Marley's 'One Love' came on.

'So that's it,' Kip said. 'A coup d'état. Someone's lost patience with our Luo president.'

'Sounds like we'll have to keep his head low for a few days.' Harry nodded towards the back seat.

Kip looked over his shoulder. Githinji was slumped across the seat. 'I wouldn't be surprised if your friend here had something to do with it.'

For the remainder of the trip to his apartment, Kip sat in silence, stewing.

'Thanks, Harry,' he said, leaping out of the car and heading for the garage.

'Where're you going, Kip?' Harry asked out the car window.

Kip slid behind the wheel of the Land Rover and gunned the diesel.

'Kip?' Harry shouted, but the four-wheel drive roared out the gate.

The destruction of property that had begun in the Asian enclave of Parklands earlier in the night had spread to the city by the time Kip returned. Nairobi was beginning to look like Beirut in the 1970s. Scattered gangs were wrecking cars, smashing windows and trying to prise the iron grilles from them. Uniformed security guards were among the looters. Fire bells rang, and burglar alarms wailed unanswered throughout the city.

When Kip turned into City Hall Way, he almost ran into a large mob blocking the thoroughfare. A rock thudded on the Land Rover's roof and bounced to the road. The mob advanced in a mass. Kip dropped the gearstick into reverse and screamed backwards for a hundred yards before spinning the wheel and roaring back towards Kenyatta Avenue.

He circled the city centre, trying to find a safe approach to the Florida 2000 nightclub on Government Road. Stones thrown by gangs hidden in the shadows of Uhuru Park pinged from the car. A bottle smashed on the roof post above his window. At the roundabout on Haile Selassie Avenue he brought the Land Rover to a halt and tried to read what lay ahead.

An eerie pre-dawn light touched the top fronds of the palm trees and washed the shopfronts of Government Road's grand boulevard in a golden glow. It reached towards the entrance to the nightclub, but failed to breach the shadows under the shop awnings. As far as he could make out in the poor light, there was a shifting mass of people around the entrance. It could be patrons milling while awaiting taxis, or it could be more looters. He decided to take a closer look.

Kip turned off the lights and let the car creep along the double yellow lines in the middle section of the boulevard. The triple carriageway afforded ample width to manoeuvre out of trouble, should it occur. He approached the front of the nightclub, straining to see into the shadows. A shout went up and a fusillade of projectiles rained onto the car, shattering his passenger window. Bottles and glasses exploded into crystal fragments all around him. He hit the accelerator and sped away, stopping in a quiet section a couple of blocks away to reconsider his strategy.

In the brief glimpse he'd managed as he passed, it appeared that the nightclub staff, having herded the remaining patrons into the street, were trying to secure the doors against a threatened invasion by the looters. The guests, who appeared to include a number of women, were being manhandled by the drunken thugs.

Kip decided he had to give it one more try and headed back down Government Road. He hadn't been discovered as he mounted the footpath at the end of the block. Ahead he could make out the mass of shadowy bodies and hear the clamour of voices punctuated by shrieks and screams.

He reached under the seat and picked up the tyre lever. He hefted it in his hand, then laid it on the seat beside him. He revved the big diesel motor and the Land Rover roared down the footpath, headlights and two overhead spots on high beam, and Marley's 'Concrete Jungle' blasting out at full volume. Revealed in the headlights were attackers and victims. All fled from his path. Clustered around the nightclub doorway was a sea of bodies. Kip blared on the horn. Faces loomed from the darkness, eyes widened in fright. People scattered in a panic.

Kip knew he had just moments to find Rose, if she was there. A flash of white silk caught his eye. She was struggling with a man in the doorway beyond the entrance to the nightclub. Kip flung the door open and ran to her. He pulled the thug off and belted him with a solid right cross. 'C'mon!' he yelled.

Rose stood petrified in the headlights. 'Rose! Get in the car!'

Still she couldn't move. Kip grabbed her roughly by the arm and she screamed and lashed out at him with fists and feet.

'Shit!' he said. 'Rose, it's me. It's Kip!'

She stopped attacking him, but Kip took no chances. He slipped under her guard and tackled her around the waist.

Opening the door he flung her across the front seat, but was grabbed from behind before he could clamber in. Rose let out a scream. Kip swung a backhander at his assailant as another came at him with a broken bottle. Kip lifted himself in the car-door opening and kicked both feet into the man's chest, hurling him to the footpath.

Rose screamed as someone lunged at her through the broken passenger window. Before Kip had a chance to react, she grabbed the tyre lever and jabbed her attacker in the face. He cursed and fell back.

Kip gunned the motor. People scattered ahead of them. He knocked over a cluster of garbage bins, then crashed through a bus shelter onto the road.

The Land Rover took the roundabout at Haile Selassie Avenue on two wheels.

CHAPTER 36

Kip came quietly from his kitchen carrying two steaming mugs of hot chocolate. He waited beside the sofa where Rose sat resting her head in her hands.

'Here's your chocolate,' he said when she failed to notice he had returned.

'Oh! Thanks. Thank you.' As she took it, he noticed her hands were trembling.

Kip sat on the opposite side of the coffee table, watching her. She had replaced her torn dress with his bathrobe, which she incessantly rearranged, adjusting the cord and smoothing the fabric over her legs.

'How's the hot chocolate?' he asked, acutely conscious of how inadequate he was when it came to offering words of comfort.

'It's very nice. Thank you.'

'You're welcome.'

The silence stretched into minutes while they each took nervous sips at their scalding drinks.

'You're welcome to stay here tonight, you know.'

'I'll be all right. I'll just get a taxi. It's not far.'

'Well, I don't think there's a taxi to be found. I haven't seen one all night. I can drive you, if you wish.'

'No, I . . . I'll . . .' She let her words trail off.

'I can drive you. That's not a problem. Where do you live?'

'Near the Aga Khan Hospital.'

'Parklands? Oh ... Parklands is not a good place to be right now.'

She raised her questioning eyes to him.

'I was there earlier tonight. Gangs roaming everywhere. They're looting the Asians.' He placed his cup on the coffee table and studied his hands as he said, 'You can stay here. It'll be all right. I mean, you can take my bed. I'll sleep out here.' He threw her a glance, and found her studying him. He hurried on, 'You don't have to worry about, you know, about —'

'I know. I'm not worried about that. You ... you seem like ... If it's not too much trouble.'

'It's no trouble at all. Really.' He sat back, pleased with the outcome of their conversation, but vaguely unsettled by how he had handled it.

The silence extended again.

'I'm sorry about my friend, tonight,' she said as she again tucked the robe around her body.

'Your friend?'

'Maina.' She looked up at him. 'Maina Githinji. He was so rude, when he knew you didn't want to talk about what happened up there in Marsabit.'

'I didn't know he was your boyfriend.'

She ran a hand over her head, pressing an imaginary loose hair into place. 'He's not. Not any more.'

Kip grunted his approval.

'Anyway,' she went on, 'it was rude of him to tease you like that. He has no shame.'

'The funny thing is, I felt I wanted to talk about it. Not with him, of course, but you seemed so ...'

One of the last conversations he'd had with Diana

came to mind. 'A very dear friend once told me that it's healthier to talk about things that are hurting you. I don't think I agreed with her at the time, but now I'm not so sure. What do you think?'

She hesitated. 'Sometimes.'

He felt he was handling the whole matter badly, bringing the earlier events of that evening unnecessarily back to her mind.

'Well, all I'm saying is, I appreciate your words earlier tonight,' he said. 'It was a tough time, the first couple of weeks after the funerals. I didn't know what to do. There was no one to talk to about it.' He rubbed the rough palms of his hands together vigorously, studying them after he had done so. 'When I think back on it now, I realise that simple little exercise — talking to someone — could have helped me a lot.' He turned to her. 'Do you know what I mean?'

She considered this for some time, then she nodded. 'Yes,' she said. 'Yes, I do.'

Rose lay alone in his bed, engulfed by the smell of him — his soap, his aftershave, his body. They weren't unpleasant smells, but she was bothered, not only by the intimacy that his aromas conjured in her imagination, but by the thoughts he had stirred in her mind.

When Kip said that by just talking to someone he would have been better able to cope with his pain, he had struck a chord. She had instinctively known this at age thirteen. If she had been able to talk to her father, to anyone, about the rape in Kisumu, she felt she could have escaped the worst of its consequences.

When they arrived that first time at Grace's house, she had waited in vain for a chance to unburden herself, but it never came. A day or two after the incident, and it was as if it had never happened. The incident became something that could never be mentioned. So far as she was aware, her father had said nothing to ban the topic from family conversation, but her father's strong will pressed upon all of them. They complied with the unspoken rule without discussion and without dissent. It was not the African way to challenge your father.

Rose's silent resentment had grown. She'd found herself condemning her father for numerous sins. She missed her big brother, Adam, and was sure it was her father's indifference that made him run away. He'd never supported Adam, and seldom spent time with him. She had convinced herself that her father had never shown Adam — or any of them — enough love.

Her father should have been her saviour in Kisumu, but it was Kip who was her real hero, although he never knew the extent of his kindness. It was ironic that while he didn't recognise her as the girl he had helped that night, she had never forgotten him — the kind stranger who showed concern and sympathy.

The confusion of guilt and pain surrounding that night was a tangled mess. Somehow she blamed her father — not only for that night, but for the aimless way her life had drifted since.

She wondered if it was her father's denial of the rape that had caused her intense resentment against him. It seemed to have built without her being aware of it. Years later, his concern about his daughter becoming involved with a man, a white man at that, twenty-something years her senior, had been a trigger to her pent-up emotions. Although her father's concerns were understandable, she had lashed out at him. Was it because of his disapproval, or was it revenge for the years of enforced denial of the rape?

There had been a moment earlier that night, as she and Kip reached tentatively towards each other, when she was tempted to reveal to him who she was; to tell him about the rape, and how dreadful it was, but how much worse it could have been had he not taken the time to help the African family he thought had been the victims of a simple robbery. But she had foolishly let it pass.

Rose felt she had missed a rare opportunity to unburden herself, but there was one redeeming outcome from the night, with all its drama and terror: she at last understood her relationship with her father. And she determined that if the opportunity ever arose, she would correct the omissions of the past, even if it meant another confrontation with him.

Kip awoke from a dream in which he was running away from a murderous mob in a *matatu*. Instead of the usual blaring radio, the bus had an annoying bell that rang incessantly.

He half opened an eye and scanned the lounge room. The phone was ringing and the strong light of day streamed through the window. He sat up and ran his fingers through his hair before lifting the phone.

It was Harry. 'Are you okay?'

'Yeah, I'm okay.'

'Well, I was a bit worried.'

'What time is it?'

'A little after midday. Are you sure you're all right?'

'Of course I'm all right.' He looked around the

apartment for any sign that Rose was awake. The sound of running water came from the bathroom. 'Why?'

'Did you hear the BBC news?'

'No, what?'

'Most of the Kenyan cabinet has been evacuated to a British navy ship off the coast of Mombasa.'

Kip wondered how the British knew so much about what was happening in Kenya.

'Parklands is a war zone,' Harry continued.

'You've been there?'

'No, just got up. It's on the news. Mobs are running wild, raping, killing. Hundreds dead, they say.'

Kip folded his arms and cocked his head to one side, appraising Rose's outfit. He covered his mouth to conceal his smile, before he said, 'It really doesn't look all that bad.'

Rose looked down at the shorts caught at her waist with a belt that almost went twice around her. The bundle of khaki material might have been made from an unwanted tent. It hung below her knees. 'Are you sure? What about the shirt?'

The neck of the white T-shirt was so wide it looked like she was wearing an off-the-shoulder gown.

'Now the shirt ... I've got to say the shirt is ... well, the shirt is just fantastic.'

She saw him smiling behind his hand. 'Oh, no! You're teasing! That's it! I can't wear these.'

'I'm sorry. I couldn't help it. It's just that, you being a fashion model and all ...'

He was pleased to see she was beginning to smile too. In an instant, the tension of the previous night evaporated.

'Maybe I could repair my dress.' She lifted the piece of white silk and turned it to examine the damage again. 'No. Look at it — my best dress. It's ruined.'

'The shorts and shirt will be fine.' When she looked dubious, he added with a shrug, 'Who's going to see you in the car anyway?'

They had already been through the discussion about whether it was wise for her to go home while the city was still in turmoil, but Rose was adamant. As a compromise, they'd agreed she would return to Kip's apartment if the neighbourhood was still unsafe.

'Well ...' she said, not in the least convinced. 'Shall we go?'

'If you insist. Just let me give Harry another call. He may have heard something on the radio.'

As the phone rang out, Kip decided he should get a short-wave radio. He couldn't receive the BBC, and the local station, which had mercifully discontinued its Bob Marley musical tribute, had nothing to add to its earlier announcements from the Provisional Government of Reconstruction.

Harry didn't answer the phone.

'Hmm, maybe it's okay. Harry's gone out.' He looked at Rose again, and smiled. 'Now that you've got your party clothes on, I guess we can go.'

When they drove through Westlands, the rising column of dense black smoke they had watched in silence since leaving Kip's apartment appeared above the road dead ahead. A mob was congregated around a burning tyre in the roundabout near Museum Hill. Kip did a U-turn back to the Sarit Centre, then took to the back streets.

Rose was fidgeting with the hems of her shorts, folding and refolding them.

'Are you sure you want to do this?' he asked.

Rose hesitated before answering. 'Yes.'

'Isn't there a girlfriend you can stay with?'

'I've been thinking about that, but they all live out this side too. Anyway, I've got no clothes.'

They drove on in silence through leafy residential streets, some of which had cars upturned on their well-kept grass verges. Destruction and debris marked the passing of the riots. In one street, where high-walled, razor-wired compounds were in the majority, the scent of death seemed to hang in the air. Through the twisted iron gates of some enclosures, small groups of mourners could be seen. Elsewhere, in the older, more modest parts of the suburb, residents stood in the smouldering remains of their dwellings, stunned into silence by a night of terror that had come without reason or warning.

As they approached the Aga Khan Hospital, Rose directed him, saying she lived in a small flat behind a grand old stone building, originally the residence of an English surgeon, but now shared by two Indian families.

As he swung the Land Rover into her street, they almost drove into an angry mob that had a group of Indians in a cowering huddle in the centre of the tarmac. Kip slammed on the brakes and, for a moment, considered trying to somehow disperse the mob, but Rose began to whimper in fear. He slammed the car into reverse and roared away.

CHAPTER 37

Later that night, at Kip's apartment, Rose sat on the sofa at the window, her feet curled under her. Outside, the black void of the uncleared bushland tumbled down to the creek.

The electricity had failed soon after they arrived back from Parklands. Kip made scrambled eggs on a gas ring he used for camping. They ate in the semi-darkness of candlelight.

'Here's your coffee,' he said and took his to the chair opposite.

'What's happening to this country, Kip?' she asked.

He sighed. 'I don't know. At times like this I feel we're not far removed from the jungle.'

She studied him from behind her coffee cup. The candlelight etched the frown lines deeper into his brow. 'Do you think of Kenya as your home?'

He looked a little surprised. 'Yes, of course.'

'Not England?'

'Certainly not England. If anything else, it would be Australia. I was born there.'

Australia didn't register any image for Rose. In school, history and geography classes had been dominated by lessons on the British Isles, and little else.

'What about you?' he asked.

'Me?'

'Yes, where is home for you?'

She had to think about it. Panyiketto was impossibly distant, both in time and space, yet Kenya had always seemed a temporary place — somewhere to live while the rest of her world caught up to her. She had not seen her mother in nearly ten years. Her father was now estranged and ignoring her. The possibility of reconciliation was increasingly remote. She felt like an orphan; Akello her only living relative. Where was home?

'Um,' she stammered, 'Kenya, no, I mean Uganda.'

Kip looked at her, bemused. 'Which one is it?'

'Kenya,' she said with an embarrassed smile. 'Sometimes.'

'I'm glad we got that cleared up,' he said with a teasing smile.

She felt compelled to explain. She didn't want him thinking she was a scatterbrain. 'It's been a long time. I was born in a little place near Lake Albert. That was home. Then Idi Amin made it bad for us ... for all of us ...'

She was suddenly crying. Not great sobs, but a quiet torrent of tears that would not stop. In the poor light it took Kip some time to realise it. He stammered in embarrassment. 'Look ... Rose ... I'm sorry. I didn't mean to upset you. I'm such a thoughtless dope.'

Her tears continued, but now she began to laugh as well.

Poor Kip became totally confused. His frown lifted and he started to smile at her amusement. Then he stopped himself, afraid perhaps that he had misread her emotions again.

This made her laugh and cry some more. How could she explain that, far from being a thoughtless dope, of all the people she knew, he was the only one who showed any compassion at all.

Harry answered the call on the second ring. 'Yes?' he asked, breathlessly.

'It's Kip.'

'Oh. What's up?'

'That's what I wanted to know. What have you heard?'

'This morning the BBC started reporting that there's fighting out near Karen, between the new chaps and what they called "forces loyal to President Odhiambo".'

'What about the city, and Parklands?'

'Don't know about Parklands, but the city was spooky yesterday. Nobody about.'

'I rang you yesterday and, when you weren't in, I thought it'd be safe to go out.'

'It was Maina. He drove me mad all day, making a million phone calls, until I agreed to drop him in town. I was glad to be rid of him. Is Rose still there?'

'Yes. She wants me to take her back to Parklands again.'

'Again?'

'Tried yesterday, but there were thugs all over. We couldn't get to her flat. I haven't a clue what's going on — we've got no power out here. Have you?'

'Went off for a while, but ... hold on. There's something coming over the BBC now. Listen to this.'

The jumble of background sounds cleared as Harry put the phone near the radio. Kip heard the scratch of static, then a distinguished radio voice came on: '... *situation grew worse overnight, before the General Services Unit, Kenya's special paramilitary force, under the command of army*

*veteran Colonel Gabriel Opiyo, took to the streets
to quell the rioting. Analysts believe this may mean
that the government is winning support from the
only significant force presently in Nairobi, and that
if the GSU can gain control, the undecided military
elements, now on exercises in the north of the
country, may fall in behind them on their return.*

'*Meanwhile, unconfirmed reports are that the
rioters are raping and looting the Indian residential
and business areas of the city and surrounding
suburbs. Our roaming reporter has seen evidence of
dozens, perhaps hundreds, of murders and ...*'

Harry came back on the line. 'The GSU are
Maina's chaps. That must have been why he was so
frantic yesterday. Getting them mobilised.'

'Or trying to get on the bandwagon,' Kip added.

'So, what are you going to do?'

Kip looked across at Rose, who was trying to
make sense of the conversation. She was wearing
another of his shorts and T-shirt ensembles. 'Rose is
all dolled up, so I suppose we'll try to make it to
Parklands again.'

The GSU sergeant waved them to a halt at the
roadblock. He peered at Kip through the driver's
window, then at Rose, whose oversized shorts
weren't so obvious while sitting down. He slung his
rifle over his shoulder and circled the car. Kip
watched him in the rear-vision mirror as he looked
into the back compartment. Before they left his
housing compound, Kip had carefully removed
everything that might be attractive to the
wandering eyes of a poorly paid soldier.

The sergeant and his platoon were stationed at
the Forest Road intersection near City Park — the
once-beautiful parkland that gave the suburb its

name, but was now a vast wasteland populated by muggers and the homeless.

Returning to where he'd started, at Kip's window, the sergeant growled, 'Papers!'

Kip reached into the glove box and handed the ownership logbook to him. The GSU man opened it, giving Kip a frown. Kip avoided eye contact, watching a truck being searched on the other side of the intersection.

The sergeant thrust the book of papers back at Kip, who folded them and calmly returned them to their place.

But the military man was not yet satisfied. He stared at Rose before asking her in Swahili, 'Sister, why are you with such an ugly *mzungu*, ah? Why not one of your own people? Are we not good enough for you?' He wore a humourless smile.

'It's not like that, sergeant,' Kip answered for her in Swahili. 'I am the young lady's employer, and I am escorting her home to her husband.'

The GSU man raised his eyebrows in begrudging acknowledgment of Kip's fluency.

'Her employer is it?' he drawled. 'And what kind of work do you give this pretty one when her husband is not looking, my friend?'

Kip ignored the innuendo. 'I am in wholesale, sir,' he said, with a bland expression. 'We import hardware items from Indonesia.'

The sergeant grunted. It appeared he might have been thinking of something further to say, then abruptly waved them on without another word.

Kip gritted his teeth as he engaged first gear and moved away. 'Bloody GSU,' he muttered. 'Think they own the place.'

'At least all the gangs seem to have run away,' Rose said.

'Seems so. Is this your street?'

'Yes.'

He drove past the corner where the mob had held their hostages the previous day. He imagined they'd forced the families to produce their hidden valuables.

He parked outside the old mansion, and he and Rose stepped over the smashed wrought-iron gate.

'Wait,' she said, pointing. The door to her small flat was ajar.

'Who has a key?' Kip whispered.

'Only me. The landlord makes me leave it above the window ledge when I'm not here.'

'Could it be the landlord then?' he asked hopefully.

'No.'

Kip groaned. 'Wait here. I'll go in first.'

Rose waited on the lawn.

At the door, Kip paused and pushed it a little further open. A short hallway, with two doors opening from the middle of its length, had a closed door at the far end. He took a few tentative steps before turning back to Rose, who stood with her knuckles in her mouth.

As he moved in, the front door closed behind him. He peeped into the first room. It was a bedroom, brightly lit from the front window. The other door led to what appeared to be a spare room.

He moved towards the end of the hall and grasped the door handle. It made a rattle as he turned it. He peeped into a sitting room through the gap in the door. It had a sofa lounge and two chairs on one side. On the other was a dining table.

'Oh, shit!' Kip said, seeing a black African man of around sixty seated at the table, watching him with interest. He had an open book before him.

'Are you the landlord?' the man asked.

'No, I'm bloody well not the bloody landlord. Who are you?' Kip's heart was thumping in his chest.

'Papa?' Rose said from behind him. 'Papa!' she repeated.

'Rose,' the man said, his voice catching in his throat. 'Rose. My baby, you're safe.'

She hesitated until he stood and opened his arms to her.

She rushed to him, knocking over the chair as they embraced. After a moment, when he had blinked away the tears in his eyes, he held her at arm's length and said, 'Your brother told me you were a fashion model.' He looked from her outsized T-shirt to the shorts that ballooned from her hips. 'Is this the best Nairobi fashion can do?'

Kip laughed with them, relief replacing his anxiety. He should have known the man wasn't a thief — there was never a thief so blasé.

It was only after much more hugging and excited conversation in a language Kip didn't recognise, and they all sat down and Rose made tea, that it became apparent that her father, Zakayo, hadn't been expected at all. He told them he'd come to Nairobi to take Rose back to Kisumu to see her mother, who, with most of the other members of her family, was now out of Uganda.

This news brought on more excited chatter from Rose. She apologised to Kip for resorting to their native tongue. 'I still lapse into Lwo whenever I get excited. Papa speaks good English, so there's really no excuse.'

Kip was able to follow the remainder of the story, which was that Zakayo had found out where Rose lived from her brother, but when he arrived in the neighbourhood searching for his daughter, the riots had erupted. He had found the key, and even though members of the mob had invaded the small house, they'd let him be.

Rose seemed pleased about her father's visit, and the news of her family awaiting her in Kisumu, but Kip sensed there was something unresolved between her and Zakayo. He decided it was best to leave her alone to work it out.

'I'd better go, Rose,' he said, fumbling in his pocket for his car keys.

'Please stay. I'll cook something.'

'You seem to be in good hands now.'

She stood as he prepared to leave. 'Well ... thank you then,' she said.

He twirled his key ring self-consciously.

'Thank you for everything,' she added, taking his hand, then, as an afterthought, stood on tiptoe to kiss him on the cheek.

Kip nodded, smiled, and said, 'My pleasure.' Then he added, 'No problem. *Hakuna matata.*'

'*Hakuna matata,*' she repeated, smiling happily.

Kip turned to her father, extending his hand. 'Nice to —' He stopped abruptly when he noticed Zakayo staring at the key ring in his hand.

'Papa, what is it?' Rose asked.

Zakayo said nothing but, standing slowly, he pulled a leather cord from inside his shirt which held a painted wooden object. He took Kip's ornament and placed it beside his own. The two broken ends came together. The colours were identical. The patterns matched, even down to the wavy lines that joined at the broken edges, which fitted together perfectly.

Kip had never known what the wooden object, inadvertently stolen from his mother's bedroom chest, was supposed to represent. To him, it was just a piece of painted wood. Now that the curved part was added to it, he recognised it immediately. 'A tiny boomerang!' he whispered, almost to himself.

'Yes,' Zakayo agreed. 'An Australian boomerang.'

Kip stared at the man — a man from central Africa — holding an icon from the country of his birth. It was a bizarre coincidence. What connection could Zakayo have with his mother? With his childhood? Or with his father?

In the presence of two people who surely could have no possible connection with his past, Kip had found the most important clue to his existence.

PART 5

ROSE

Zakayo strolled along the shores of Lake Victoria, wrestling with memories of his idealistic youth. The reconstruction of a little boomerang — an alien object that Zakayo thought he alone in all of Africa might know by name — had dragged them back to mind.

When he and Ernie had shared their dreams in the prisoner of war camp, Zakayo's single, abiding desire was for a peaceful life. He'd felt Uganda was a paradise, and all that was needed for utter contentment was the peace and prosperity that was promised when the European war was won. But the Empire disintegrated, and a British-trained madman called Amin began the Ugandan wars, shattering Zakayo's peace and splitting his Panyiketto family between their home and Kenya.

When another soldier — this time a brother Lango from the north, Apollo Milton Obote — returned to power by defeating Amin, Zakayo scarcely had time to savour the heady taste of peace before the National Resistance Army, under Yoweri Museveni, decimated the countryside in yet another bloody civil war, trapping Zakayo in Panyiketto. Museveni was a formidable enemy and, in his attempts to defeat him, Obote's regime became even more vicious than Amin's.

Before the latest bloodshed began, Zakayo had managed to send Amelia and their two children back to her Banyoro home to the northwest of Kampala. But he'd never had the chance to join them there, where, as far as he knew, they still lived with her father.

One family united; another torn asunder.

With most of his Panyiketto family now together, Zakayo should have been content in some part. Only Macmillan, the born farmer, remained behind in Uganda.

He wondered what had happened to the Africa he knew when he was a young man.

He sighed, knowing he should send the melancholy memories back to where they had been hidden before the boomerang dragged them back to mind. Instead, his thoughts returned to the matter of the boomerang itself.

Most of his idle moments had been consumed trying to solve the mystery since he had found the other half of his, that is, Ernie's, boomerang in Kip's hands. He retraced, not for the first time, the circumstances leading to his ownership of it.

Ernie had said that he'd broken the boomerang and given half to his wife. That half was now in Kip's hands — a young man who'd made no mention of Ernie. He'd said it had come from his mother — an unmarried woman living in Nanyuki, of all places. Why had it not been in Sydney, or some other Australian town? It would have made more sense.

Kip was about the right age to be Ernie's son, but in the wrong part of the world. And if Kip was Ernie's son, the woman calling herself Kip's mother must be Ernie's wife. But where was Ernie, and why didn't Kip know Ernie's name?

Zakayo wondered if his old friend could have come to Africa at some point, bringing his wife's half of the boomerang with him, and somehow it had fallen into Kip's hands. He remembered promising to return his half to Ernie, but having failed him. He felt bad.

Could Ernie have come to Africa looking for his toy boomerang? Zakayo dismissed the idea. Even Ernie would not be so silly. But he might have come to Africa for another purpose altogether. Maybe he came for a holiday, and decided to stay in Kenya?

His head began to swim. It was too difficult a mystery to solve after all these years. Instead, he turned his mind to his daughter's impending visit. It would be the first time Rose had seen her mother and brother George in nearly ten years.

Rose enjoyed the renewal of her ties with her family, but she had hoped it would be like the old days in Panyiketto, when the family gathered together and enjoyed each other's company. It wasn't. Everyone had changed.

Her mother, Doreen, had always been careful in giving her approval to those closest to her. To some extent this could also be said about how she gave her love. She could be difficult to please, as the children soon learned if the work in the garden was not done properly. Rose supposed it hadn't been easy for her, raising a family and running the farm while her husband was away for long periods in Kampala. It wasn't always that way. Rose remembered happy days in her early childhood when her father and mother laughed a lot. It seemed that, with the years, her mother had become even more reserved in her affection, and most things Zakayo now said or did seemed to annoy her.

Dembe, poor Dembe, who had never recovered from the soldiers in Panyiketto, was constantly fretting about her five children. She would hardly let them out of her sight. Her husband, always silent, often brooding, had not bothered to come to Kisumu this time.

Unlike Dembe, Grace did nothing to control her rabble. When Rose lived in her sister's house, she'd likened her nieces and nephews to a pack of young jackals, for ever playing boisterous games. It appeared that Grace had finally given up on the role of disciplinarian. Her husband had never attempted it in the first place.

Of all the family, George was least changed. He was still the studious, determined young man he had been in Uganda. He intended to resume his interrupted studies as soon as possible. There was no room in his life for romance. His bachelorhood was assured for years.

Of her missing brothers, Macmillan was still living on the family farm in Panyiketto, now with a wife and two children. Adam, who nobody had seen since 1972, had been everyone's favourite when she was a child, but they seldom mentioned his name these days. So far as she knew, there was not a Ugandan family who had not been affected by Amin's bloody rule and the civil wars that followed his ousting. Many had lost more than one member of their family; some had lost all. Adam's disappearance was initially because he was caught poaching, and ran away to avoid the consequences. But Rose had little doubt that the upheaval that had set the country ablaze with violence had ultimately taken him from them. The legacy lingering from those years was the torture of uncertainty. Not knowing the circumstances of his death was more painful than the certain knowledge of it.

Her youngest brother, Akello, had been unable to get away from his croupier's job at the casino, but had promised to join them on the weekend. He and Rose planned to travel back to Nairobi together.

Grace declared it was time to eat, and began to pile food onto the plates. The chatter died away as everyone became absorbed in their meal. In the silence, Grace asked Rose what modelling work she was doing.

'I started on a set of magazine pieces for Athi Tours. They come out in *Bwana* magazine next month.'

'*Bwana* magazine? That's a men's magazine, isn't it?' her father asked.

'Not really, Papa. It's a magazine for people interested in photography and travel and such.'

'Yes — a men's magazine,' he said dismissively.

'How long is the job?' Grace asked, deliberately diverting Rose from responding to her father's jibe.

'A few sittings ... except I don't think I can finish it.'

'Oh, why?' her sister asked.

Rose hesitated. 'I'm going to London.'

'London?' her mother said.

Rose hadn't planned to announce the news. In truth, she hadn't decided whether to accept the offer or not.

'Yes,' she answered. 'London.' She caught the look of surprised dismay on her father's face as she spoke.

The table came alive with her siblings' enthusiastic support. Grace prattled on about London fashions; George raved about the museums and libraries she could visit. Her parents remained silent.

Zakayo cut across the conversations with: 'I thought you would join us in Kisumu, now that our family are all together again.'

'W-why did you think that, Papa?'

'Because ... when I found you in Nairobi ...' He frowned, as if trying to recall their meeting during the riots. 'Because ... we are family.' To Zakayo, it seemed this was the only necessary explanation.

'We can be family while I'm in Nairobi. Akello is there too.'

Her father gripped the edge of the table and tightened his jaw. 'And who is paying for this holiday?'

'It's not a holiday, Papa, it's an employment opportunity.'

'Employment opportunity?' he sneered. 'That's a good name for it. Who provides this ... this *employment opportunity*?'

'It's a photographer ... no, a photography company. I won a competition run by *Bwana*. The prize is a trip for two to London.'

'Aha! And who is the two?'

'Akello,' she said defiantly. 'If he'll come.'

'Isn't that perfect? My playboy son and my run-around daughter. In London together.'

'What do you mean by that?' Rose demanded.

Her father folded his arms and scowled at her.

'You went to England when you were sixteen!' she spat at him.

'There was a war on!'

'And were you so fond of the British that you would fight their wars? You volunteered.' She pushed her plate away. 'You went because you wanted to do something with your life. Well, so do I.'

Zakayo placed his palms on the table. Leaning forward he said, 'I do not approve of this running around, Rose.'

'You do not approve?' she said, her words dripping with sarcasm. 'When have you ever approved of anything I have done, Papa? When have you ever stood up for me?'

'Don't talk nonsense.'

'Nonsense? What do you call it when it is rape, Papa?'

'What?'

'Look at Dembe!' She pointed at her sister, who had been attending to one of her children. She looked around the table like a night creature caught in a spotlight. 'And look at me. Where was your approval of us when we were raped? Where was your support then, Papa?'

'There will be no talk of this at the table!'

Rose was fighting back tears. 'Then when?'

'This is not a fitting discussion to have at the table.'

'The trouble is, Papa, there has never been a fitting time to discuss it, has there? You just hoped it never happened to us. But it did, Papa. Dembe and I have been raped, and when we needed you ...' she brushed her hand across her eyes, '... you thought it wasn't a fitting discussion. Ever.'

'Rose.' Her mother spoke for the first time. 'That is no way to speak to your father!'

Rose stared at her in disbelief. She ran her eyes around the table. It was clear nobody thought the matter was 'fitting'. Even Dembe; no, especially Dembe, who had turned her face away and fussed over her child.

Rose pushed back from the table. Her chair toppled, and she ran from the house, crying.

On the bus, Rose sat with her elbow against the window, resting her head on her hand, as the Kisii tea plantations rushed by. In the hour she had spent waiting for the bus, her anger had subsided and a profound sadness descended. She had again lost her family.

She'd half hoped that one of her siblings, perhaps it would be sensible George, would find her at the bus station and speak kindly to her. They would bring word that her father was repentant and wanted his daughter back home; that it was only his love for her that made him speak so imprudently. But nobody came, and she boarded the bus without a backward glance.

The incident had decided the issue for her. The idea of leaving everything and going to London was very exciting, but simultaneously very intimidating. She would now work on Akello. She felt if her young brother were with her, all would be well.

She rationalised that while the modelling competition, which was actually just a bathing suit contest, had been something of a gimmick for *Bwana*, the modelling offer might lead to real opportunities to break into the London fashion scene with all its glamour and excitement. If not, she could return to Kenya, no harm done. At least she and Akello would have enjoyed a free round trip to England.

By the time she disembarked at the bus terminal in Nairobi, she had convinced herself it was a good idea to go to London.

CHAPTER 39

The wide, golden savannah of the Laikipia Plains ran north to the horizon under an endless blue sky. A line of wispy white clouds marked where land and sky converged over distant Sudan. Rising dust clouds followed the tracks of a herd of zebra a mile or two to the southwest. In the southeast, the Aberdare Ranges rose blue–green and misty.

The vaulted *makuti* roof of Laikipia Lodge loomed directly ahead. The traditional thatched palm shelter covering the main building had been the logo of their company from its earliest days, when Kipana Tours — Kip and Diana tours — had little to offer but enthusiasm and ambitious plans.

Kip drove the long-wheelbase Land Rover into the lodge's parking area. The troop of baboons, who had made Laikipia Lodge their private domain, scattered ahead of him, scampering through the lodge's public areas and dispersing into the surrounding gardens. They were a constant nuisance, requiring Kip to employ people to prevent them stealing food and anything else of interest, including cameras and handbags.

This visit, Kip had given the entire staff a few days' break. Apart from the *askaris* patrolling the compound's perimeter twenty-four hours a day, he was alone.

Having deposited his tour group of important businessmen and minor celebrities at the airport for a flight to the next leg of their gold-plated safari — the exclusive Mt Kenya Safari Club — he had nothing demanding his attention until the next group arrived in a few days. Now, standing under the awning that opened onto the open-air dining area, he contemplated how to keep himself busy so that the churning mass of memories and questions brought about by the discovery of Zakayo's half-boomerang did not consume him.

Kip went to the bar and came back with a can of beer to find the baboons occupying the pool area. He clapped his hands and made *shoo* sounds at them. Some of the juveniles trotted a few paces away before settling to pick at titbits hidden in the grass, but the huge alpha male sat defiantly on a table overlooking the pool. Rippling muscles under its bristling olive mane made it shimmer in the sun.

Sitting under the umbrella of a poolside table, Kip sipped his beer and eyed the alpha male. The baboon stared back, raising its eyebrows in a passive-aggressive display.

Kip thought of all the questions he should have asked Zakayo, but had been too astonished by the coincidence of the boomerang pieces to think of at the time. They had both explored the obvious — comparing owners of their respective halves. Kip didn't admit to stealing his half, simply saying it had belonged to his mother, Marie Balmain of Nanyuki. Zakayo had asked if Kip or his mother knew the owner of his half — an Australian pilot by the name of Ernie Sullivan. Kip hadn't wanted to confess that he knew nothing of his early life in Australia, because asking such questions of his mother was forbidden, so he'd simply said no — which was the truth.

He could have — should have — asked Zakayo in which city his friend, Ernie Sullivan, had lived. Somewhere in his story must lie the clues that would enable Kip to decipher his early life. Could it be that Ernie Sullivan was his father? Or maybe he was a friend of his father's. Living under those circumstances, the men must have shared many details of their lives. But he hadn't thought to ask.

His mother would surely know of Sullivan. He should simply jump in the Land Rover, and drive to Nanyuki immediately. He had the time, and his mother's house was a mere hour away. But he squirmed in his chair at the idea of it.

He thought he should speak to Zakayo again, and this time extract every last thread of his story. Then he could confront his mother.

In his heart he knew he was simply stalling the dreaded visit to Nanyuki.

He finished his beer and, as he stood to fetch another from the bar, made a half-hearted effort to scare off the baboons. Again, they ignored him. The alpha male yawned contemptuously at him, revealing the fearsome set of fangs that made an adult baboon a good match for a leopard. Kip swore at him, and went to the bar.

His cowardice for not wanting to confront his mother with the evidence of the boomerang irritated him. He hated indecision. Worse than that, if he couldn't overcome this weakness, how could he ever find the courage to tackle the intimidating secrets that the boomerang implied?

He pulled a beer can from the refrigerator and slammed the door. The sound of breaking glass came from inside, and a pool of foaming liquid formed at his feet.

'Shit!' he said. Opening the door, he found the shattered remains of a beer and a bottle of expensive French wine. 'Shit,' he said again, and stormed out to the terrace.

The big baboon was shredding the palm-frond umbrella on its table, throwing the pieces into the pool.

'Get out of here!' Kip roared, shaking his fist.

The baboon turned and nonchalantly walked away. Kip, infuriated, searched for a missile. There was nothing within sight. The baboon turned towards him and showed its teeth.

Kip hurled the beer can at it, catching it full in the face. The big male let out a surprised shriek and bolted for the fence, leaping over it in a single bound. Its outraged screeching continued intermittently for an hour, giving Kip some satisfaction as he wrestled with his own infuriating frustration.

It was a week before Rose saw Akello again. Without knowing, they had crossed paths on the Kisumu–Nairobi road, he on his way to sister Grace's house to join the family, and she in full flight from them.

Rose knew he would have heard everyone's version of her argument with their father. She was still sad and upset about the day, especially having so recently renewed the relationship with her father, and she needed to talk to Akello about it. In the week following her return, she either missed him at the casino or he was not at home when she called.

By the time Rose finally caught up with her brother, it wasn't her father she wanted to discuss, but her trip to England.

Akello was in a rush to go to work, but he let her in as he continued to dress for the casino.

'You will come, won't you, Akello?' she pleaded.

He was ironing his black silk trousers under a wet towel. Steam billowed around him. 'Tell me again — how did you get these tickets to London?'

'A contest.'

'Oh, that's right, run by that naughty men's magazine ... what's it called? *Stud*, or *Dick*, or ...'

'It's *Bwana*. And you know it. And it's not a *men's magazine*, as you call it, there's plenty of photography and camping, and other things. You make it sound awful!'

She put on a hurt expression, which Akello ignored, continuing to run the iron over his casino uniform.

'Lucky for me it was not *kaka asije akaona nyonyo yako*,' he said, quoting a Swahili joke.

'Stop it! There was no chance you were ever going to see your sister's titty in that magazine!'

Akello just laughed at her. 'My, my, my. What a face!' He pulled his trousers on and tucked in his ruffle-front shirt. 'Okay, no more joking. Tell me.' He picked up his keys and wallet from the coffee table and began to stuff them into his pockets. 'C'mon,' he said. 'Tell me. Otherwise I am off to the casino.'

'It's two return tickets to London,' she said, pouting.

'And what happens after that?'

She sat forward, unable to contain herself. 'Then, the best part! I have a contract with a fashion studio. Do you know what that means? My face in Europe. Europe! Think of it, Akello. How many models from Africa do you know who have made it in Europe?'

'Europe? I don't know ... Is Iman an African?'

'Is Iman an African! Don't you know anything? Of course she is.'

She caught his smile as he pulled on a sock. He couldn't resist teasing her, and had done so since they were children together.

'I wonder if she got her start in *Bwana* magazine too,' he said.

She pulled a face at him.

He ignored it. 'So . . . no first class? No five-star hotel in, what is it? Piccadilly?' He finished tying his shoelaces and stood to check his reflection in the window.

'No, but we'll be all right. We can find something cheap until I get my first pay.'

'Hmm,' he said, turning to check the back of his shirt where it was tucked in. 'Is this shirt too bunched up?'

'No. And when I get paid we can get something better.'

'Did I tell you I met a very interesting lady at the casino last week?'

'By interesting, you mean she took you to bed.'

'Cynthia. An English lady. You should have seen her suite in the Hilton.'

'What has any of this got to do with London?'

'Nothing, except she also invited me to visit. She says she has a wonderful apartment in London, and wants me to give her a call if I ever go over there.'

Rose's jaw fell open. 'You mean you'll come?'

'Are you sure this shirt is okay?'

'Akello, I swear . . . I'll kill you if you tease me any more. Will you come or not?'

'Okay,' he said at last.

'Okay? You mean it?' Her voice rose with excitement.

'I said okay, didn't I? Just one thing . . .' He held up a finger to halt her from leaping at him from her chair.

'What?'

'No showing your titties. I've been peeping at them since I was ten and, to be honest, I'm getting bored with them.'

She threw a magazine at him and then rushed to embrace him.

On her way home Rose couldn't keep the smile off her face. London. It was the escape she needed to make a new start in her life. The family reunion had not delivered all it had promised. Apart from the terrible row she'd had with her father, her siblings had grown up and grown apart in the process. They would always be dear to her, but apart from Akello, the bond they had shared in their childhood had loosened.

Papa was another problem altogether. She despaired of ever coaxing him into the twentieth century. For all of his knowledge of the world and its ways, gained from his daily study of newspapers and his travels to Europe during the war, he was still an old-fashioned African man at heart.

Unlike her recollections of their early life together in Panyiketto, when he prided himself on his modern ideas about discussing matters with the family, he now insisted on keeping to the old customs where he was the head of the family and no dissenting voice could be raised. These days he made all the decisions for Mama and everyone else in the family. About the only African male custom he seemed to have resisted was keeping a village girlfriend hidden away somewhere.

Family matters aside, she was also happy to be able to make a new start in her personal life. For some reason she had managed to assemble a tawdry list of ex-boyfriends.

She realised she had been smiling to herself as she walked, but she didn't care about the curious looks she received. She felt happy. London would be a bright new beginning.

CHAPTER 40

Rose climbed the dimly lit stairs and searched the nameplates along the corridor for the fashion agent's office. She was beginning to feel she had the wrong address. The neighbourhood, and the building, did not match her impression of the London fashion industry.

The train trip from the flat she and Akello had rented on the other side of the city had taken longer than expected, and she was late. Shivraj Patil — 'Call me Shiver' — had given her directions over the telephone, but she had disembarked at the wrong station. She had yet to come to grips with the tube, and the maze of coloured lines on the map that was intended to help people find their way. It was difficult enough to purchase a ticket, with coin slots and change machines, and then another series of slots to steal your ticket if you were not careful.

She tapped on the door under the tarnished brass sign: 'Xanadu Fashion Agency'. After a moment she tapped again, before tentatively opening the door.

The office space was brighter than the corridor, but the dirty window glass blocked what little light struggled down between the buildings.

'Mr Patil?' she asked the back of the person's head. He was sitting behind a desk with his feet on the windowsill.

'Huh?' he said, swinging about to face her. He had red-rimmed eyes, which he rubbed vigorously while trying to focus on her. His crumpled grey shirt was opened at the top button, and the pale blue tie that held it partially closed at his neck had a gravy stain on it. 'Oh! Morning ... afternoon,' he said, sitting upright and sliding the knot of his tie tight against his throat. 'Shivraj Patil.' He extended his hand across the desk and, with the other, thrust a business card at her.

'Good afternoon. I'm Rose Nasonga.'

'Pleased to meet you, Rose. How can I help you?'

'Don't you remember? I talked to you on the phone on Wednesday. You gave me directions.'

'Oh! Yes, of course. How can I help you?'

'I'm here because of the prize.'

'Prize? What prize?'

'The modelling prize run by *Bwana* magazine ...'

'*Bwana*?'

'Is this Xanadu Fashion Agency?' She looked around the office as if searching for evidence. There were photos of attractive women on the wall. 'The sponsor was Mr Sivalingam Sritharan.'

'Oh! *Bwana* Magazine ... Sritharan ... And you are ...?'

'Rose Nasonga.'

'Rose Nasonga. Ye-s-s-s. And how is old Sri?'

'I think he is well, but we really didn't —'

'And you're a model? Now I remember.' He nodded as he ran his eyes over her. His grin revealed a gold-capped canine.

Rose tucked her feet under her chair and patted her skirt into place. She was uncomfortable in the silence, but didn't know what further to say. She had assumed everything would be ready for her to start work immediately. 'Mr Patil —'

'Shiver,' he corrected, still studying her and tapping his gold tooth pensively.

'Shiver ... I was hoping you would have something for me to —'

'Stand up, sweetheart,' he said, raising his arms as he stood. 'Up, up!' He came around from behind his desk, waving his hands in the air. 'C'mon, let's have a look at you.'

Rose did as she was told.

Patil spun his hand in a circle. She turned, trying to make a professional revolution.

'Tall,' he said. 'Nice and tall.' He sucked on his thumbnail. 'Okay, sit.' He resumed his seat opposite her. 'Stoke Newington.'

'I beg your pardon?'

'Rooters footy club. Stoke Newington. Fundraiser.'

She blinked her incomprehension.

'A fiver an hour and what you make on the side is your business. No questions asked.' He scribbled something on a scrap of paper before shoving it across the desk at her. 'Saturday night. Look beautiful, and ring me next week.'

'Mmm, darling ... that was wonderful.' Cynthia stretched full length on the bed and sighed. 'Just like Nairobi.' She rolled towards Akello, running her hand up his arm to his shoulder then down to caress the tight black curls of his chest hair. The bedclothes lay in a tangle at their feet.

Akello smiled. He had been in London for a little over a week. After seeing a few of the sights he gave Cynthia's office a call. Her secretary took the message from 'Mr Akello of Kenya Safaris', and an hour later they were in bed together. That was three days ago. Since then they had made love more than a dozen times.

Even when they weren't making love, he was having a good time. There was the food and excellent room service in the hotel they used for their sessions together. And yesterday Cynthia had sent him shopping for a wardrobe more suitable to the climate. He'd bought a tailor-made suit in Jermyn Street, and enough casual wear to fill a suitcase in the market at Camden. Akello decided he would enjoy London very much.

'Let me see that wonderful weapon of yours,' she cooed, bending to tenderly kiss his penis. 'Oh look, he's lifting his head again. What a marvellous little man ... sorry, big man, but let's finish the champagne first. I need a breather.'

Akello climbed unself-consciously from the bed, his manhood at half-mast as he refilled their glasses.

Cynthia giggled. 'We really must share you around. You're too good to be true, and my girlfriends deserve a treat, poor darlings.'

Akello laughed with her and came back to the bed with their glasses. He ran his eyes over her body as she lay curled up like a lion cub in the sun. He had seen better bodies, but in his twenty years he had learned that important matters should be judged on their results rather than on their prospects. Although Cynthia admitted to being twice his age, and may have even been a little more than that, he didn't care. He particularly enjoyed her enthusiasm, which, given her age, was quite impressive, but more important than that, she appreciated what he did for her. He could bring her to a climax several times in an hour until she was panting with satiated pleasure. He basked in her compliments.

'To London,' he said, clinking her glass.

'To sex,' she said with a wicked smile. She kept her eyes on him over the rim of her glass. 'I think we should do that, you know,' she said, reaching over him to place her glass on his side of the bed. Her breasts brushed his chest, making him rise again.

'Do what?' he asked.

'Share you around.'

'You are making a joke.'

'Why not? You can obviously give all I can take, and some of the inadequate lovers I've known have said I'm insatiable.' She laughed. 'So why not let me introduce you to some other appreciative pussies?'

'I like your pussy best.'

'Of course you do, darling, but why not try a few others? Honestly, there is not one of my girlfriends who wouldn't climb over broken glass to get some of what you're offering. And they can be very generous.'

'Generous?'

'Very generous. In fact, a very good friend of mine is celebrating her divorce on Saturday. I think you might be just what she needs.'

Akello smiled and sipped his champagne.

Rose lost her way, but it wasn't hard to find the Rooters Football Club when she eventually arrived at Stoke Newington, fifteen minutes late. The club's entertainment centre was massive, and stood forth from the neighbouring shopfronts like a garishly decorated palace in a row of windowed boxes.

The team colours were obvious. Red and yellow stairs led to a first-floor doorway festooned with red and yellow streamers. A burly doorman directed her into a large but low-ceilinged room, lined with gaming machines. A few men stood around in dimly lit corners, obviously early arrivers for the night's festivities. At the head of the room was a low platform with a lectern and microphone on it. A red and yellow banner hung above it with the proud claim: 'Rooters — We Never Stop'. On the lectern hung a more modest sign: 'Rooters Fundraiser 1982'.

The carpet may have once been chequered red and yellow, but it was so badly stained it appeared as a nondescript orange–brown. Rose's shoes had the tendency to stick to it as she walked towards what the doorman had said was the manager's office. The door was ajar, and she nudged it open to peep in. A man in a red reefer jacket, with black slacks slung below his belly and a yellow pocket-handkerchief, was addressing two young women wearing swimsuits.

'. . . what I'm sayin' is, I want youse girls to sell as many tickets as you can. And drinks. Be accommodatin' like. You've been around by the look of you, so you know —' He stopped, noticing Rose in the doorway. 'Who are you then?' he asked, taking a long draw on his cigarette.

'Rose Nasonga, from the agency.'

The manager squinted through a curl of tobacco smoke. 'Agency? You mean Can-a-doo, the wog, ah . . . what's-'is-face?'

'Yes, Mr Patil. Xanadu.'

'That's 'im.' He blew a cloud of smoke in her direction. 'Haven't seen you here before, have I?'

She felt like covering up as his narrowed eyes explored her body.

'You're a bit of orright for the likes of 'im.'

She realised his continuous squinting was not caused by the smoke, but was a facial characteristic. It made him look suspicious of everything she said. To fill the silence she said, 'Sorry I'm late.'

'And so you should be. I've just been sayin', youse girls ought to look smart out there and collect the money for the raffles and the like real quick. Also — hey, where's your suit?'

Rose stared at him. 'Suit?'

'Yeah, suit. Swimsuit like. What you gonna wear?'

'Wh … Mr Patil didn't say anything about a —'

'Don't worry about what 'e said, you've gotta have a swimsuit or summink, don't ya?'

The other two girls were wearing costumes. The first was a blonde with large breasts that overflowed a one-piece swimsuit that seemed at least a size too small. The other — an auburn-haired black woman — wore a two-piece suit that revealed a road map of stretchmarks. Rose was mortally self-conscious about the scars she'd received from the crocodile attack when she was a child. She only posed bare-legged if she could somehow conceal her left leg.

'Never mind,' the manager said. 'I'll give you one for the night. Now, what was I sayin'?' He tapped a dirty fingernail against his bottom lip. 'Oh bugger it, the other girls'll tell you the rest. Now get out of 'ere the lot of yer.'

Akello checked the large brass number on the front door against the slip of paper Cynthia had given him, then stepped back to look at the impressive façade. Two stucco lions stood rampant on the portico, and the doorknocker, which he could just make out in the streetlight, was a lion's head made of brass.

There was a light on in the hall, and another on the first floor, but his instructions were to take the driveway at the end of the hedge and follow the picket fence to a rear door. His feet crunched the quartz screenings, which reflected enough moonlight to illuminate his path. At an opening in the hedge, he found a gate in the picket fence and lifted open the catch.

A dog barked from somewhere beyond the neighbour's high garden wall. He felt like a felon, creeping around in the night. Everything was dead quiet. A tingle of anticipation ran up his spine.

The high trees in the back garden obscured all the moonlight, but dim light shining through a leadlight panel in the back door showed him the way. He ran his hand up the sides of the wrought-iron grille that enclosed the rear porch and found the button. From deep inside came the sonorous sound of a two-tone gong.

He waited for what felt like an age, and was about to press the button again when a shadowy figure approached the leadlight door panel. There was a click and the sound of a slide bolt slipping then clicking into place. The door opened.

The woman was invisible in a halo of backlight. Akello swallowed and smiled. He could make out blonde tips on a head of hair that fell to slender shoulders. Her waist was a little thick, but not overly so.

When she spoke her voice had just a hint of a quaver that might have been nerves. 'Mmm, Akello. Do come in.'

Rose stood gripping the sink with both hands to stop them shaking. She heard the kitchen door open behind her and she spun around, ready for battle.

'Just ignore 'em, sweetheart,' the auburn-haired black woman said, puffing a cigarette into life from a lighter that she then tucked into her swimsuit bottom. 'You just get 'em all the more excited if you carry on a treat like that.' Her English accent was so broad, Rose had trouble understanding her.

'It was horrible.'

'Yeah, ain't it a bitch? Be thankful you've got something they want. I can't remember the last time someone tried to grab *my* tit!'

A group of drunken patrons had made lewd remarks within Rose's hearing. When she ignored them, they tormented her about the scar on her leg. When one of them grabbed at her, she'd fled in tears.

The other woman took a deep draw on the cigarette, eyeing Rose as she exhaled. 'Christ, you're shivering like a stiffy in a snow storm, aren't ya? They was just teasing you. Forget it.'

'I can't ... I won't go back out there.' She struggled to hold back more tears.

'You're new at this, are ya, darlin'? By the way, I'm Gloria.'

Rose wasn't sure what 'this' was, but it was certainly unlike any modelling assignment she'd ever had. 'Yes,' she said, blowing her nose on a tissue.

'Not even from around 'ere, are ya? Where're you from, sweetheart?'

'U-Uganda, um ... Kenya.'

'Hmm, Africa?'

Rose nodded.

'Thought so. Patil has been getting a few new-uns from over there. How long you say you been 'ere?'

'Three ... three weeks.' Her heart had stopped racing and she began to regain her composure.

The blonde burst through the kitchen door. 'Christ, they're a frisky bunch!' She looked at Rose. ''Ere ... what's up?'

'This 'ere's ... what'd ya say your name was, love?'

'It's Rose.'

'Come again?'

'Rose. My name is Rose.'

'Right. This 'ere's Rose. Rose, Wilma. She's one of Shiver's new girls.' Gloria indicated with a nod in Rose's direction. 'From U-bangi, Kenya.'

'U-bangi?' Wilma asked with a wide smirk.

'U-betcha!' Gloria answered, and the two women burst into laughter.

Rose didn't catch the joke. Added to her tearful outburst, it made her feel childish.

Gloria laughed so much she began to choke on her cigarette smoke. After hacking away for a few moments she tried to apologise. 'Sorry, Rose ...' She paused for another paroxysm. Her eyes streamed with tears, sending a cascade of heavy make-up down her cheeks. 'It's an old one, but a good-un, eh?'

Rose looked from Gloria to Wilma, then back again. 'Yes, very.'

Wilma took a tray of sausage rolls out of the oven and dealt a dozen to each of three platters. 'We'd better get our arses back in there. C'mon, you two.'

'Right you are. Be there in a sec,' Gloria said.

Rose bit her lip. She was trapped in a terrible situation. She couldn't storm home from her first assignment — she would never get another — but to return to the ordeal in the function room was more than she could stand.

Gloria put a hand on her shoulder. ''Ere, girl. Why don't ya 'ave a snort of this.' She pulled what looked like a lipstick capsule from beneath the band of her suit and ran a line of white powder along the bench. 'It'll 'elp settle yer nerves.'

If he'd been asked, Akello might have chosen a good English beer rather than the thin and tasteless French wine that Liz continued to pour for him. The more he drank, the drier his mouth became.

She asked him what he thought about the wine, and when he told her, Liz replied, 'It's a chablis, my dear. It's meant to be dry.'

She played sweet music on the stereo system, and brought out plates of tiny dry biscuits with strange concoctions of meat and various coloured pastes. One serving was of small black spheres that tasted like fish. These made him even thirstier. He washed them down with the chablis.

Just when he thought dinner would never arrive, it didn't. Liz took him coyly by the hand and led him to the upstairs bedroom.

Rose made use of the lipstick container a few times during the night — she couldn't recall exactly how many — but Gloria said that next time it would be *her* treat.

Rose guessed she meant that next time she would have to supply the white powder she sniffed. She didn't mind. The night was more bearable, and whenever the men pawed at her she would laugh at them and concentrate on the red and yellow banners.

Akello learned that at two o'clock on a Sunday morning in London, taxis were difficult to find. He also learned something about women.

Perhaps it only applied to English women, but in the future he would be more careful when answering a direct question. His honest opinion about the wine was the first of several that seemed to displease his hostess.

Liz had climaxed twice in the two hours they spent together, but he left her feeling unfulfilled. There was nothing he enjoyed better than pleasing a woman. He was a lover who was constantly alert to his partner's needs. In many cases he was able to help them discover pleasurable sensations they had previously not experienced. His was a talent largely god-given, but still it required concentration and a selfless attention to where his partner was in her climb towards a climax. It was not always easy. When he achieved it, all he asked for was a little recognition of a job well done.

Cynthia had said Liz was getting over a nasty divorce, and he felt it might be the reason she hadn't thanked him.

He left the posh house in Knightsbridge with a hundred pounds in his pocket, but an empty feeling in his heart.

CHAPTER 41

The old Maasai woman's face was like a leathery mask as she rocked, eyes closed, beside the small fire in her hut. When she opened them and found Kip sitting opposite her in the smoky dimness, she showed no surprise. Instead she smiled as if she was expecting him.

Naisua was the *laibon*, the spiritual leader and chief, of the village near the Loita Hills, just northeast of the Masai Mara. Hers was a unique position, for no other female had ever been made a *laibon*. But Naisua was a unique individual. Her piercing black eyes sparkled with intelligence, and her tiny frame seemed to pulse with energy. Kip had heard accounts from men not given to exaggeration that she had the gift of magic passed down to her from the Great Laibon, Batian. They had known each other since he was a young game warden in the Masai Mara.

Kip extended his hands across the fire to her. '*Sopa*,' he said, using the Maa salutation.

The old woman gently spat on his hands and arms — a sign of endearment and a blessing — before taking his hands in hers. 'You are welcome, young Kip,' she said in English. 'You have come.'

'How are you, Naisua?'

'I am old, too old,' she said with a sigh. It was her familiar complaint. Embarrassed by her age, she felt she was a burden to her tribe, but she was greatly respected by all the Maasai, and dearly loved by those in her *enkang*.

'But age brings wisdom, old one.'

'We Maasai have a proverb: *We begin by being foolish, and we become wise by experience.* I already have too many years for wisdom. Do you know, Kip, I was a girl when the *mzungu* railway crossed our land.'

'I have heard it said.' Kip doubted that the old woman, as ancient and frail as she appeared, could be over ninety years old. But some said she had learned her English from her lover, one of the railway engineers.

Kip knew it was considered impolite for a Maasai to ask the reason for a visit, and he would not keep the old woman in suspense any longer than necessary. 'You will wonder what brings me to your *enkang* today, old one.'

Naisua smiled. 'I have known you since you were an *olaiyoni* in the Wildlife. I can guess, but I will let you speak.'

Her teasing reference to him as a 'big boy' in the National Wildlife Service was not too wide of the mark. He'd been quite young when he first met Naisua. Duty had forced him to threaten her about her *moran* killing the reserve's lions for their initiation ceremonies. And it was the reason he was here today.

'I've heard some talk among the rangers, old mother. They say that your *moran* are killing lion again, and they are not happy.'

She cackled at him. 'So the lion are still of your family?'

'No, not any more, but I come as a friend to warn you. The rangers are not so easy these days. Killing lion is a serious offence.'

'I know.' She nodded. 'You mean well, and I will speak to them.'

'It is good that you do, Naisua. So ... that is all I have come to say, and I must leave you now. I am going to Laikipia this afternoon.' His resolve to challenge his mother about the boomerang had been a long time coming. He didn't want his courage to slip by delaying it any more than necessary.

She struggled to her feet, ignoring his helping hand, and followed him into the morning light. 'Tell me, young Kip, what do you know of this slimming sickness that comes from Nairobi?'

'Slimming sickness? I have never heard of it.'

'Our young people are coming home sick. The women cannot fatten them. They puke and grow thin.'

'What do the clinic people say?'

'Clinic? The service is finished.'

'What do you mean, finished?'

'The doctor was old. He left us to return to Mombasa. Nobody has come to replace him.'

'What does your big man say of it?' 'Big man' was the Maasai way of describing their member of parliament.

'Hah! What does he care of the Maasai? He's a Kikuyu. From Nairobi! Pah!'

'Still, it is his responsibility. What is his name?'

'His name ... his name? Oh, this old head of mine ... I cannot think of it. Maybe I never knew it. He has not been to our *enkang*. Nor any other, so far as I know.'

'Why not speak to Mr McMahon at the mission in Narok? He seems able to get the ear of the officials. If not, let me know.'

He reached his hands for hers. She took them, and held them with a strength that belied her frailty. 'Laikipia is a place of great sorrow,' she said.

Kip was unsure why she raised Laikipia in this way, but he was quite certain that he had not mentioned the reason for his visit to Nanyuki. He saw his reflection in the bottomless black pools of her eyes.

'The Laikipia was our home until the British forced us to leave to make way for *wazungu* farms and the railway. I was little more than a girl, but I carried my first-born from the Laikipia Plateau.' Her eyes glistened. 'My family nearly died. Thousands of others did. The Laikipia is a place of great regret for the Maasai.'

Kip's knowledge of the history of the resettlement of the northern Maasai to the Loita Hills and the grasslands of the Great Rift Valley was vague, but he thought it must have been at least eighty years ago. He felt sure Naisua was letting her imagination run wild, but her expression was intense as she looked up at him.

'When you reach Laikipia, you must harden your heart, my son.'

Kip could only nod.

'Go with *Ngai*, young Kip,' she continued, squeezing his hands.

'And you, old mother.'

The road that followed the Ewaso Narok from Laikipia to Nanyuki was seldom used. Tourists travelling from Mt Kenya towards the Lerochi Plateau might take it, but would soon regret it.

Although the road crossed the Great Rift Valley, it did so where the valley flattened and widened into a grass-filled expanse. The road was rough and the landscape desolate and boring. It had none of the grandeur of the Rift nearer Naivasha, where the continental drift had torn the land apart, leaving a gaping scar two thousand feet deep and forty miles wide, and where the escarpment bounded down in a series of breathtaking leaps. The geological force had spent its anger by the time it had reached Nanyuki, but an implacable wind buffeted the rolling plains as a reminder of the land's former temperament.

As Kip edged around the many potholes, and boulders exposed by years of flooding, he realised this tortuous track was the one he had always imagined he would take when he eventually went home to Nanyuki, and his mother. The symbolism was not lost on him. Like the mental journey to arrive at the decision to confront his mother, the Ewaso Narok track was slow and painful. It was shorter than the route through Thompson's Falls, but took longer. After twenty-four years, Kip was in no hurry.

Many of the Thompson's gazelle, which spread across the plain in thousands, stopped to gape in wonder at the Land Rover, their tufts of tail twirling like halved propellers. A mother rhino stared defiantly at him until he was almost upon her, then trotted off, tail aloft, her calf at heel.

Directly ahead rose the broken tooth of Batian, the snowy peak of Mt Kenya. As it drew nearer, memories of his childhood returned. He began to tremble. Soon he was shaking so violently he had to stop the car. He folded his arms over the steering wheel and hugged it. With his head resting on his forearms he struggled to regain control. He was in his treehouse, unable to breathe for fear the sound would divulge his presence. Below him his mother slapped her palm with the *kiboko*-hide whip.

He flung open the car door and kicked at a rock on the road. Then he snatched up another, and flung it as hard as he could towards the mountain. The wind moaned around him. A cloud passed across the face of Mt Kenya. Batian, the ancient and powerful magician of the Maasai people, looked down, displeased.

Nanyuki had lost nearly all of the flame trees and jacarandas from its main street. The few remaining were surrounded by deep ruts where the lorries had become bogged during the wet.

The electricity authority had erected a substation where the billboard pointing to the Equatorial Hotel — 'Have a Drink in Each Hemisphere' — used to stand.

In a much shorter time than Kip remembered, he was there.

The pub was closed. The sign above the veranda, with its shadow-relief font in two tones of blue, was cracked and faded, and a torn, half-drawn blind waved in the draught from a broken window.

A wisp of smoke rose from the flue above the kitchen at the rear of the building. He parked the car beside the hotel, which seemed remarkably smaller than he remembered, and walked around it towards the back door

When she opened the door, the sight of her stern expression made his heart leap with the same adrenaline that had infected his childhood. But she had aged, and in the wrinkles of her cheeks and forehead, the thin scraggy neck, and the dullness of her eyes, he saw a woman whose strength had clearly burned out long ago.

She squinted, momentarily blinded by the daylight behind him. As recognition dawned, her expression turned from shock to something resembling joy, before retreating into a resigned sadness. 'You've finally come,' she said in a rasping voice.

'Hello, Mother,' he said.

She looked up at him again, and turned from the door, leaving it open for him to enter behind her. She walked with a stoop, pausing to cast a backward glance to confirm that he had followed her, then she sank heavily into her chair with a sigh. 'You've finally come,' she repeated, nodding. Her hair was thinning and streaked with grey.

'Yes. It's been a long time.'

'A long time.' She nodded, staring at the floor.

In the ensuing silence, he studied the room. It had changed little, except that now the door to her bedroom was standing ajar. The large four-poster, with the picture of the Virgin Mary above its bedhead, rose like a monument in its cool, dark interior.

'How are you, Mother?' he asked.

She eyed him before answering guardedly, 'How do you think I am? I'm like any other old woman. There are good days and bad.'

He had forgotten her Australian accent. Memories came of a ship sailing under the Sydney Harbour Bridge, and shadowy recollections of open-sided tramcars and double-decker buses.

'And Aunt Kathleen?' He looked around, as if she might be concealed somewhere in the kitchen.

'Died. Fourteen years ago.' She spat it out as if to hurt him with the news.

For some reason he felt guilty for not knowing. 'I'm sorry,' he said, then added, 'What … How did it happen?' Kathleen, he recalled, had always been the fitter of the two.

'Went to clear a block in the furrow, up near the off-take at the river.' She gave him a reproachful look. 'Your job — if you were here. Damn fool woman found a leopard cub. Should have known the mother wouldn't be far away. She bled to death just after I found her.' She seemed angry rather than sad, as if she were blaming Kathleen for leaving her alone for fourteen years. 'I suppose you'll want tea?'

'No. I'm okay, thanks.'

'Going to make one anyway.'

She placed her hands firmly on the arms of her chair and raised herself to her feet. He could almost feel the pain of arthritis in her grimace. How she managed the daily chores of collecting wood and drawing water made him wonder about her livelihood.

'The hotel's closed,' he said, stating the obvious. 'How are you managing?'

She lifted the plate on the stove and slid the heavy kettle onto the flame. 'Been doing a bit of knitting, taking in some mending.' She put the teapot onto the table with a clatter. 'For all you care,' she added spitefully.

He had felt sorry for her, seeing her struggle with the lid of the tea container, but the malice she bore for a world not constructed exactly to her liking reminded him of the much younger woman who could turn from cool to malevolent in a heartbeat. It was the most chilling of her characteristics, and meant Kip was never at peace in her presence.

'Who's Ernie Sullivan?' he asked abruptly.

Her hand froze for a moment on its way to the teacups hanging behind the stained-glass sliding doors of the dresser. She lifted two floral-patterned cups from their hooks and put them carefully on the table before answering. 'I've never heard of him.' She turned her back on him and opened a drawer. After rattling around among the cutlery she came back to the table with a pair of teaspoons.

Kip pulled his key ring from his pocket and showed her the half-boomerang. 'I found the other half of this.'

'The boomerang!' Her hand flew to her mouth and she slumped into her chair. 'I'd forgotten the boomerang. So that's what happened to it — you took it.' She said this without rancour. 'He broke it on the wharf and gave me the half when he was leaving for England. He said it meant he had to come home, because a boomerang always returns.' There was a faint hint of amusement in her eyes. 'He was always talking nonsense like that.' She drifted off into some reverie of her own.

'Who is he?' he demanded.

Her sour expression returned. 'He's your father!' she hissed, with venom in her voice. 'Your father, who said he loved me and, behind my back, had it off with some tart somewhere!' She slammed her hand to the table. The cups rattled on their saucers. 'You were dumped in an orphanage because the woman who bore you was already married.'

'So . . . so you're not my mother?'

'No. I am *not* your mother. And you . . . you have no father, because your father went off to war, having . . . having put his *cock* in that bitch and made her pregnant.'

The crude expression shocked him almost as much as the revelation that she wasn't his birth mother. Kip hadn't heard her swear in all his life. Her ferocity made the word more obscene.

Questions tumbled through his head. He had difficulty containing himself. 'Where is he? Who is my mother?'

'Some tart on the same ship that brought your father back from pilot training in Canada.' She curled her lip. 'An American tart, with a husband in the US navy.'

'How do you know all this stuff?'

'From her letters. The air force sent them to me, all neatly bundled together, after they thought he'd died over Germany.'

'And he didn't? He's not dead?'

'I don't know, never saw him again. But he didn't die in the war — that much I know.'

Kip's head was spinning as he tried to digest it all. His real parents had burst into life like characters in a movie, or the people in a book about his life — people who'd had no existence until then. He tried to see their faces, but nothing appeared. They were motionless players. The only action that he could ascribe to the character who played his father was that of breaking a boomerang.

Marie was pouring the boiling water into the teapot, still cursing under her breath.

'If Ernie Sullivan is your husband, my father, how come we're called Balmain?' Kip said.

'St Patrick's Orphanage, Balmain — that's where your mother put you until your father came back from the war.' She leaned on her knuckles over the table, the tea forgotten. 'That's where he was going to find you, and probably bring you home. I suppose he was planning to confess everything to me — his very patient, very understanding little wife.'

'Are you saying he never even got to see me?'

'I named you after we arrived here — Kathleen and me. Rupert, my grandfather's name, and Laikipia Balmain — the places in your life.'

'Answer me!' he said, raising his voice for the first time. 'Did my father ever get to see me?'

'No! He never set eyes on you. I would never, *ever* let him take enjoyment from his dirty act! I would never let him see the result of his filthy fornication.' Even after all the years, her eyes shone bright with gleeful revenge.

'But that's impossible. The authorities, the orphanage, would never allow a child to be taken —'

'Kathleen ran the orphanage. When I went there to see you, to see the spawn of his lust, she saw how wretched I was, she took pity on me. She comforted me.' Tears welled in her eyes. 'She helped me get you out of the orphanage before he could come back to claim you.'

Kip watched the woman he'd tried all those years to love as his mother, and he was repulsed, horrified by the vindictiveness of her act. How could anyone use a child as a weapon to inflict pain on another human being as she had? He recoiled from the memory of his pitiable efforts to find love in that heart so cankered with hatred as to be hardened shut.

Marie lifted her chin as she said, 'Kathleen was the love of my life. The only one I could trust after what your father did to me.' Then she lowered her head to her hands and sobbed.

Kip reached a hand towards her, but recoiled. Even after all this time, he couldn't touch her with affection.

He had returned to Nanyuki with trepidation, to demand the truth about his father. He'd come with fear and anger. Now he'd overcome both, and, at one point, had even experienced pity. But now, having heard the truth, he felt nothing but disgust.

CHAPTER 42

Akello opened an eye and squinted into the brightly lit room. It was his room — the sitting room in the one-bedroomed flat he shared with Rose.

Rose wasn't up, and he hadn't heard her come in the previous night, although he hadn't flopped into his bed on the couch until after three. He swung his feet to the floor. His mouth tasted terrible. The woman he had entertained last night had insisted he try some *bhang*, or 'marihuana', as she'd called it. It had nearly made him puke.

He went to the bathroom to clean his teeth and, as he scrubbed at them, he poked his head around Rose's open door. 'Are you on shift this afternoon?' he asked through a mouthful of toothpaste foam.

The lump under the pile of bedclothes stirred and gave a soft groan.

Rose was moonlighting at a local supermarket while she waited for work with the agency. Akello knew little about the modelling profession, but he knew enough to realise that Rose's late nights had more to do with partying than with employment. He had paid the last three weeks' rent out of the gifts from his grateful patrons.

As he came out of the bathroom, Rose went in and closed the door behind her. He heard the shower running as he boiled the kettle.

'Tea?' he asked when she came out a little while later, wrapped in her towel.

She stared at him for a second then blinked.

'I said *tea*, do you want tea?'

'No ... no, thank you ...'

'Rose.'

She had turned towards her room, and paused before facing him.

'What are you doing to yourself? Look at you! You're skinny like a jackal. Don't you eat when you go out?'

'I eat. Don't worry.'

'Don't worry? Hey, look at me.' He caught her by the arm as she was about to leave. 'Are you taking these slimming drugs?'

She pulled her arm away and glared at him. 'Leave me alone!' she snapped.

Her venom surprised him. 'You're not looking after yourself,' he added lamely.

'Don't you give me any of your preaching, little brother. I don't get paid to go to bed with wrinkled old women.'

He had always shared his secrets with Rose, and he trusted her because she had never judged him by them, nor thrown them back at him in an argument.

She stormed off to her bedroom before he could conjure a reply.

Her door slammed.

Akello stood staring at it. This person with puffy eyes and a snarl in her voice was not the sister he knew.

No matter how many times she walked down that dead-end lane, Rose always felt frightened. It was claustrophobically narrow and the concealed doorways and dark steps down to unseen cellars could hide anything or anybody.

Gloria had been her introduction to this dealer, Jonesie, but since then Rose had made a few contacts of her own. They were cheaper, but not always easy to find as they sold their stuff on the street for extra cash and would disappear from time to time to spend it. Rose had no time to go looking for them today; she had one of Shiver's private parties to attend. As a hostess she was expected to be bright and bouncy all night. It was only eight o'clock and she already felt down. She needed a lift then a little coke to add the sparkle.

She heard the bolt slide on the other side of the door. The familiar rattle followed as the chain took up its slack, then a white face, with lips too pink for a man, appeared at the narrow opening. 'Well ... Black Velvet. Back again?' he said with his asthmatic chuckle.

The door closed then opened to admit her into the darkened hall. He led the way into the room he used as his office — an eight by eight cube with a narrow table and chairs on each side. He began to make small talk, but she cut him off and told him what she needed.

'In a rush tonight, sweetheart?' He cackled again. The image of a hyena came to her mind. His pasty white skin was mottled with some kind of rash, and his bronchial complaint tended to make him pant as he spoke.

'How much?' she asked, looking over his hand at the calculator.

'Let's see, a dash or two of speed and a few more of coke ... you're going to be a busy girl tonight, Velvet, eh?'

'How much?' she repeated, as the calculator flashed green figures at her.

'Sixty quid, Velvet, my dear. Special price.'

'Special price? It's twenty more than last time!'

'Supply and demand, Velvet. There's been a bit of a shortage on the street. What can I say?' He smirked at her.

She looked in her wallet but she knew she only had fifty. 'I . . . don't have it,' she said, looking into his eyes.

He licked his full pink lips. A ripple of revulsion ran up her spine.

'Well now, that's a bit of bad luck, eh?' He smiled, revealing tobacco-stained teeth. 'What can be done, eh? What can be done?'

'Can I owe you? I'll get paid tonight.' She tried to smile but it must have been unconvincing.

'This is the second time you've needed a little help-out, isn't it? What have you got, sweetheart?'

'I can give you forty. Forty tonight and the other twenty tomorrow, okay?'

'You could reduce your order.'

'No. I want to take it all.'

'I suppose I can stretch a point for a friend.' He smirked. 'But why don't you be a little more friendly now and then, eh?'

She snatched the packets from his hand and pushed the forty pounds across the table. 'Th-thanks, Jonesie. I appreciate it.'

'Sure you do, darlin'. Sure you do.'

She stuffed the packets into her handbag and went to the door, waiting while he hovered over her, fumbling with the locks. His breath almost made her retch.

In the alley she took a deep breath. It was filled

with the smell of the accumulated garbage of the neighbourhood.

Rose stumbled a few paces away, and clung to the railing of a set of stairs leading below street level. At the bottom, a person lay face down next to the door. She stared at the body in horror, afraid that it might move, then equally afraid it wouldn't. There was no sign it was breathing. She thought she should be able to see some kind of movement, even a twitch. An instinct told her the person hadn't moved, and would not move, for a long time.

She folded her arms around her chest and hurried down the alley to the street.

Kip loved the mornings in Laikipia, when the sun wore a blush of pink and the sky held a hint of green — a tint that a watercolour artist might use as a wash for a coral seascape. And mornings that followed a clear night — a night when nothing, not a cloud, not a speck of dust, intruded between the Laikipia and the stars that filled the black and infinite universe — were the best time to enjoy the air of the high plateau. Heavy with dew, it caressed the skin, and cleared the head like a drop of fresh lime let fall on the tip of the tongue.

Mornings always lifted Kip's spirits, and on the morning following his encounter with Marie, he arose early and drank deeply of the fragrant brew. He stretched, and threw off the despondency of the previous day.

By the time he drove through Rumuruti, the sun had peeped over the shoulder of Mt Kenya and golden fingers of sunlight crept into the shadows on the savannah. A silver mist hung low to obscure the villagers who shuffled about in their patched woollen pullovers or second-hand army greatcoats. A few who recognised the car gave Kip a wave, their smiles flashing behind a breathy cloud of vapour.

In Naivasha he stopped at Bells for a breakfast of tea and toast, and a chance to think. Marie's revelations had drawn him tantalisingly close to his quest to discover who he was. Finding his father was the first step. He would do whatever was necessary. Zakayo Nasonga was the key.

He didn't know where in Kisumu Zakayo lived, but Harry could at least give him directions to his daughter's house. It meant going east to Nairobi before retracing his steps to the west, but a telephone call would not do. With luck, he would be on his way to Kisumu by noon.

Heavy lorries had already started to rumble along the cratered tarmac through the town. He quickly finished his meal, wanting to beat them to the beginning of the climb up the Great Rift Valley's escarpment. Sitting behind a convoy of dead-slow trucks, trying to coax some acceleration out of the Land Rover before the next tear-arse vehicle came roaring downhill, was a test for his nerves he didn't need.

By ten o'clock Kip had left the breathtaking panorama of the Great Rift Valley behind and was coasting down through the tea plantations of Limuru towards Nairobi. The easier going gave him time to reflect upon how his life might change with the disclosure of the story of the painted wood.

It had been 'the painted wood' throughout his childhood, and would probably remain so, even though he now knew it had been a miniature boomerang before Ernie Sullivan had made his romantic promise.

For his entire life, there had been a void where his father should have been. Now he knew he was Ernie Sullivan's son. But Ernie Sullivan, the person, eluded him. As a child he had fitted various faces to this invisible person. Usually, they were movie stars. For a long time Johnny Weissmuller was the image the young Kip had constructed for his father. Weissmuller's characters of Tarzan and Jungle Jim not only had the physical and moral attributes Kip wanted in his father, they inspired a love of the African bush that Kip carried into adulthood. Then, as maturity forced him to abandon such fantasies, the vacant space had returned. Now, at least, the faceless person had a name.

He realised he didn't have the same sense of emptiness about his mother, his real mother, as he did for his missing father. He would probably never know who she was, and he didn't expect he would ever meet her, but he could accept this. The space of mother had always been filled by Marie, and knowing that Marie was not his mother left no sense of loss.

As for Marie — a woman wronged by an unfaithful husband — she had showed more humanity in crying for Kathleen, her lost lover, than she'd ever shown in her life. As she wept, she was just another vulnerable human being, wounded by life and impoverished by death. But Kip could feel no pity for her. Outrage at her monstrous crime swamped any such emotion. She had stolen his parents from him. She had stolen his childhood.

He could never forgive her.

Harry sat in the passenger seat of the darkened Land Rover. Another lorry roared towards them out of the night. The truck's headlights filled the cabin with a harsh white light, illuminating the lines of tension on his friend's face. He had tried to convince Kip to let him drive home from Kisumu, but Kip, as in most things, was determined.

'Why don't you flash them?' Harry said, as the truck passed, plunging the cabin back into darkness.

'Huh?'

'Those bloody lorries with their high beams. I can hardly see a thing.'

'I guess my eyes are used to them.'

'Well, don't overdo it. And let me know when you want a break.'

'I will, Harry. Don't be a nag.'

When Kip had arrived earlier that day in their Nairobi office, he'd been totally strung out but had insisted on driving immediately to Kisumu. He'd told Harry what Marie had said about his father, and felt that Zakayo could add vital additional clues.

As it transpired, Zakayo could add very little to what Kip had already learned from Marie, except for important information about his father's squadron.

'When do you plan to go to London, ol' diamond?'

Kip dragged his eyes from the road ahead. 'London? As soon as I can.'

'It's Harry's hometown, you know. Wish I was coming with you.'

'Me too, Harry, but someone's got to look after the store.'

Another truck approached, high beams blazing. Kip dipped his lights. When the other driver didn't respond, Kip let him have it with the Land Rover's high beams as well as the spots mounted on the roof rack. The truck came on regardless. Kip swore under his breath, shielding his eyes as it roared past.

'Did you notice how Zakayo kind of clammed up when I asked about Rose?' Harry said.

'Not really. Maybe he knows you're an old lecher.'

'Lecher I don't mind, but what's this *old* lecher business?'

'Rose ... what is she ... twenty years younger than you?'

'Something like that. She's one old girlfriend I'd like to renew acquaintance with.' He couldn't remember when or why he and Rose had split up.

'I think she's got a few problems, that Rose,' Kip said after a moment's thought.

'Does she? I've never noticed.'

Kip had a habit of overanalysing people. As far as Harry was concerned, Rose was just another girl, happy to drift from man to man — as if she was looking for something special, but never finding it. In Harry's world that didn't signify a problem. He decided to let it go.

'How are you going to find the stuff you need to know about your dad?' he asked.

'I've been wondering the same thing. I have a name and a squadron number. I suppose there's a government office somewhere with all the records.'

'The Ministry of Defence would be a good place to start. But then what? They can maybe give you a home address, but it's been what — nearly forty years? What's the chance he'd still be there?'

Kip tightened his jaw. 'Thanks for the encouragement, Harry.'

'Sorry, ol' darlin', but you've got to be realistic. Nobody's going to keep track of those old geezers after all these years. He could be anywhere in Australia. In fact, since his wife dumped him, he might be anywhere in the world. Where would you start?'

Kip shook his head. 'You're right, Harry. He *could* be anywhere. But I don't have the luxury of choice. I've got to try.'

CHAPTER 43

The British Airways jumbo lifted off from Kenyatta International Airport then banked to the left to reveal the Nairobi National Park directly below. It had taken Kip three months, but he was on his way to England. Below, in the Nairobi National Park, he could see giraffe and zebra, wildebeest and buffalo.

This was his first intercontinental flight. There had been many opportunities in the past, but Harry did the trips to overseas client organisations, and before him it was Diana. Kip decided he'd let others do the more glamorous work of business development because the bush was his preferred place of work. In truth, he was afraid of flying.

After vacillating for too long, Kip had finally gathered up his courage. But it wasn't only his fear that the three-hundred-ton aircraft might not defy gravity that delayed his departure. It was a possibility more frightening than that: if he couldn't find his father with the information he now had, where else could he turn?

The mighty engines roared and the cabin began to vibrate as the jumbo climbed out over the Athi Plains. The baggage compartment above Kip's head dropped open with a bang. He didn't know what to do, so he tried to ignore it by casually pulling out the in-flight magazine and turning to the *About Your Aircraft* page. Again he studied the emergency exits diagram.

When the plane levelled out, and the crew rolled the drinks trolley down the aisle, Kip decided he needed a whisky. He seldom drank spirits. In fact, the only whisky he'd ever taken was to calm his nerves when he first met Diana at the Aberdares Country Club.

Memories of the flirtatious Diana on a dirt road near the Aberdares came back to him. Not for the first time he cursed his luck for finding the love of his life already married to a fine man who he was proud to call a friend. And, again not for the first time, he wondered whether, if Hugh hadn't been Diana's husband, they could have been happy together. Now he would never know.

He sighed. Instead of getting on with his life after Diana had decided to end their affair, he'd spent it chasing every available woman he met. When he wasn't chasing them, they were chasing him. The outcome was the same. Looking back on his love life, he could hardly recall a name. He was even unsure of the name of the last one — a British Airways stewardess he'd met while making his booking.

'Good afternoon, Mr Balmain,' another stewardess said. 'Can I get you a drink from our bar?'

She was smiling at him, but not in a provocative manner. She might simply be trying to be friendly. He was fairly sure he had never met the young woman before, but she had addressed him by name. Then he guessed the airline would have names allocated to seats, and he relaxed. She was just proving her efficiency.

'We have red and white wine,' she said. 'Also spirits, soft drinks, and a favourite — Tusker beer.'

He shot a glance at her. Had she said, *your favourite*?

The stewardess smiled sweetly at him, patiently awaiting his order.

'J-just a beer, thanks.'

'Certainly, sir,' she replied, and put a Tusker, a plastic glass and a small bag of peanuts on his tray table before moving on.

Kip poured the beer and chastised himself. He simply had to change his ways; he was becoming paranoid.

Kip couldn't understand what the fuss was all about. To hear some of the white Kenyans back home talk about the Old Country, he'd thought it would be something special. Maybe his expectations were too high, but he found London a bleak, sunless place, predominantly grey in colour, and expensive — far too expensive to be worth the money.

He had spent the first day searching for a reasonably priced hotel. By mid-afternoon he realised London had no such thing, and settled for the Royal National Hotel, which, in spite of its name, was neither royal nor national. It was a rambling maze of small rooms, and the continual stream of new arrivals in the foyer were from all parts of the world.

Early on the second day he equipped himself with maps, a list of government addresses he'd pulled from the telephone directory, and a day pass for the tube.

The Public Records Office in Kew told him they couldn't help, and that the service records, which might, were at Innsworth, Gloucester. Or there might be something useful in the World War II records at Hayes, Middlesex.

At Hayes he was asked why he wanted to search their records, and when he told the administrative assistant that he was searching for his father, Ernie Sullivan, she asked to see some identification. The name on his passport was Rupert Laikipia Balmain, but he pleaded the case that Ernie Sullivan was his stepfather, and that it was his ailing mother's wish to find the final resting place of her dearly beloved husband before going to her own reward. The assistant relented, but he then found that Hayes housed only British Army records, not those of the Royal Air Force. But he had won the administrative assistant's sympathy. She suggested he should try Innsworth, which held the RAF's records, but warned him that the RAF were very tough and that he should get a copy of his mother's marriage certificate as proof of his bona fides.

Kip had no chance of doing that, so instead he tried the Royal Air Force Museum in Hendon, which held officers' records from private collections. Ernie Sullivan did not appear among them. In frustration he recounted the litany of his travels to the museum curator. She wasn't a particularly sensitive person and bluntly suggested he try the Commonwealth War Graves Commission in Maidenhead.

Quite a few Sullivans had died in the service, but there was no clue that Ernie was one of them. From what Kip had found to date, he was beginning to wonder if Ernie existed. Innsworth would be the decider.

He bought a white shirt and tie, and had a photograph taken at a studio near the hotel. With his passport-size photo in hand, he found a printer in Earls Court who agreed to print his photo on a business card.

'What name do you want on the card, sir?' the printer asked.

'Sullivan. Um, Kevin Sullivan.'

'Right you are. Address and telephone?'

Kip constructed an address and phone number in Oxford.

'You've come a long way to find me then?' the printer said with a smile.

'Yes, er, no . . . I'm in the city on business.'

'Right. Your title?'

'Title?'

'For the card. What's your position in the company?'

'Oh, I'm Managing Director.'

'M-a-n-a-g-i-n-g D-i-r-e-c-t-o-r.'

Kip guessed what the next question would be, and realised he hadn't prepared for it. He had constructed an elaborate scheme by taking the unusual step of using a photograph on a printed card to identify him. He hoped that the novelty of it, and a suitable story about leaving his passport at home, would carry it off at the RAF records office.

'And the company name for the card?'

Kip stalled. The printer waited, pencil poised.

'Graphic Printing.'

'G-r-a-p-h-i-c P-r — So you're a printer, Mr Sullivan?' he asked with a surprised look on his face.

'Mmm,' Kip answered evasively.

'Then . . . why don't . . .' The printer's smile, and the question, trailed off.

'A printer? Me?' Kip had a laugh in his voice. 'Hell no, I'm . . . This is just a little joke I'm playing on a friend of mine.'

'Oh-ho, I see.' The printer's smile returned. 'You folk in Oxford go in for some elaborate jokes, don't you?'

'Well, if you knew this friend … but it's a long story.'

'I'll bet, so … that's about it. When do you want them?'

'As soon as possible. I've got to get back home to Oxford.'

They agreed he could collect them in two days.

Kip left the shop, taking a deep breath. He wondered about his ability to carry off the next phase of the deception at the military establishment if he had so much trouble lying to a printer.

Three days later, at the RAF's Personnel and Training Command Headquarters in Innsworth, Kip ran his finger down the microfiche image of past serving officers in Squadron 149, and found *Sullivan, Ernest Horace, Ft Lt.*

His father was a real person — with a name, rank and personnel number — but there was no clue as to how he could be found.

CHAPTER 44

It was going to be a long, difficult night at the bar. Rose decided she would need a little help, and waited while Jonesie wrapped her cocktail of cocaine and heroin in a greaseproof-paper satchel. She tucked it away in her handbag before following him to the door, and waited while he fiddled with the lock.

'You know, it's none of my business how you use the stuff,' he said, 'but it might be more economical ...' He shook his head as if to admonish himself. 'Here I go again, being too helpful ... but it might be more economical for you to use a pipe or, even better, a syringe.'

She looked at him, wondering if she could believe anything he said. 'Why?'

'You get more for your money, so to speak. Saves you in the long run.'

'How?'

'Well, when you snort, it gets into your lungs and that's all very fine, but next breath, half of it comes out again.'

She studied him warily. Anything to save money was important. Her packages, every two or three days, were costing about a day's earnings at the bar — if she was lucky with tips.

'Look, don't take my word for it, give it a try for yourself.' He went back to his table and pulled a sealed syringe from the drawer. 'There you go. Compliments of the house. And there's a room out the back I sometimes let my good customers use.'

The fragile plunger and sliver of silver sat in her hand. It looked so hygienic wrapped in its clear plastic shroud.

'I don't know how.'

'Nothing to it. C'mon, I'll show you if you like.' He came around the desk to her with a package containing a piece of rubber tubing and a spoon. 'Sit there. Won't take a sec.'

'I don't like injections.'

'Not really an injection. Just a prick, if you'll pardon the expression.'

She hesitated again.

'Look, makes no difference to me. As I say, it's your business if you want to waste your money.'

'What's that for?' she said, indicating the rubber tube.

'Helps find a vein, that's all.'

She looked from the tubing to the parcel in her hand.

'Jesus, Velvet, I haven't got all fucking day. Do you want me to help you or not?'

Maybe he was a little homesick, but as Kip moved around the city, his eye was drawn to every black face he passed. It was some kind of conditioned response that led him to believe a black face might be someone he knew from home. Eventually he got used to the idea that in London there were many black faces, and many more in every shade of brown.

It came as a surprise, therefore, when he saw someone who really was familiar.

He had been killing time, seeing the sights and doing some desultory shopping, when he took a

414

breather in a small bar in the Paddington area. A conversation in one of the booths behind him grew louder and caught his attention. In profile the young black woman looked remarkably like Rose Nasonga. Whoever she was, she was involved in an argument with her male companion. There were a few other drinkers in the bar, regulars by the look of them, but they ignored the couple.

Kip dismissed the girl as another case of mistaken identity, but the argument turned heated and the man — a pasty-faced individual — was on his feet, shaking a fist at the girl. The others in the bar, including the staff, still ignored them. When the man grabbed the girl by the hair, her face turned, giving Kip a better view.

Kip put down his beer and, with a glance at the other customers, walked over to the booth. 'What's going on, folks?'

The man looked from the girl to Kip. 'Who the hell are you?' he demanded.

Kip had his eyes on the girl. He was almost sure it was Rose, but she had a hand over her face, hiding it from his view. 'The question is, who is the young lady?'

She looked up at him then, and although she appeared quite different to when they'd last met, he knew she recognised him by her expression.

The man kept hold of Rose as he said, 'What are you, one of her tricks or somethin'?'

Kip took the wrist of the hand holding her hair and crushed it in his grip.

The man's full pink lips formed an insipid smile that withered under Kip's gaze. He released Rose, but drew himself up to his full five and a half feet and, with a show of defiance said, 'Are you going to pay what she owes me then?'

Kip remained expressionless. 'I think you should leave now.'

The pink lips formed a number of protests, which were not uttered. The man left, muttering curses under his breath.

Kip slid into the seat opposite and studied her face. She had always been fine-featured and slender, but now she looked tired and drawn. 'Rose. I thought it was you! What the hell are you doing in London?' he asked.

She kept her eyes down, studying her hands. For a moment he thought she might try to fob him off, perhaps humiliated by the incident. 'Hello, Kip,' she said, raising her face to really look at him for the first time. Her eyes were deep wells of resignation. 'I could ask you the same thing.'

'Who was that bloke? And what was that all about?'

'The landlord. A misunderstanding,' she said, attempting a smile. 'So why *are* you in London?'

He decided to let the issue drop. 'I'm here ...' He was about to construct a lie to conceal the real reason for his visit, then, for some reason, felt it time to change his childhood habits. 'I'm here to find my father.'

'Here? In London?'

'Well, this is the only starting point I have. I've found out he was in the RAF — the Royal Air Force — and I was hoping to find his address from their records. But I've had no luck so far.'

'Don't you have family that can tell you all that?'

Again he hesitated. He remembered the time at the nightclub when Rose had seemed to understand his loss following the death of Hugh and Diana. In all his life he had never had the opportunity to discuss his childhood with another human being, let alone disclose the truth of his abduction to Kenya. It must have been the homesickness, because he was tempted to tell Rose, a person he hardly knew, everything.

'I never knew my father's real name,' he began. Once started, he didn't stop talking for half an hour. He told Rose about his childhood, and how he could never win his mother's approval for anything he did. Of how she never seemed able to express an ounce of love for him. And he told her of his father's affair with a married woman, and how a woman had taken him from the orphanage with nothing but revenge in her heart. When he explained how Marie and Kathleen had conspired to steal him away from his father, Rose covered her mouth in horror and tears filled her dark brown eyes.

'I'm sorry,' he said, suddenly realising that the story he had lived with all his life might be too much for the unaware. 'This is ... this is not your concern. I suppose I got a bit carried away —'

'How could a person be so cruel?' she asked, dabbing her eyes with a paper table napkin.

'Years of practice,' he said with an ironic grin.

'How can you joke about it?' she admonished him.

'There's not much else I can do. I've tried prayer. Tears. I've even begged for forgiveness when I didn't know enough to realise I'd done nothing wrong.'

'Have you found him?'

'No.'

She put her hand on his. 'I'm sorry, Kip.'

Her gesture suddenly made him embarrassed. 'Hey, enough about me. What have you been doing over here? When did you arrive? Where are you staying? Can you believe what they charge for accommodation around London?'

She slipped her hand back. 'I've been doing some modelling work,' she said, smiling modestly.

'Wow, congratulations. You must be good at it, huh? I mean, to make it in London.'

'I wouldn't say I've made it . . . yet. But things are coming along nicely.'

'That's great, Rose. I bet your father's pleased.' He wondered why Zakayo hadn't mentioned it.

'He is. Very pleased. And proud.'

'I'll bet.' Kip nodded and smiled. The conversation had hit a wall for some reason.

'Why don't we, you know, have a meal together some time?' he suggested. 'I've got 'til Sunday. It's the earliest flight available.'

She hesitated, as if she was on the point of refusing, and he began to compose something to ease them out of the awkward situation he had created, but she agreed.

'Great,' he said. 'That's great.'

They made plans to meet outside his hotel the following night.

Kip had done all the usual things to help time fly. He'd counted the number of different bus routes that passed the front of the Royal National. He'd done an estimate of the number of taxis that called at the hotel, and the number of guests going to and from it in an hour. In between, he'd checked the pub attached to the Royal National in case Rose had mistakenly thought he meant they should meet there, and had walked down to Russell Square, hoping she would arrive by osmosis, or whatever the name of the process was that summoned beings from nowhere.

She was late. Very late.

At nine o'clock he had been waiting an hour and a half so he went to the Royal National's pub and ordered a beer. He was beginning to know his beer in London — a sure sign he had been there too long. Sunday couldn't come soon enough. He needed to be home in Africa.

After four pints, during which time he kept an eye on the front of the hotel just in case, he went to bed.

'Kip?' The voice was small at the end of the line.

'Rose? Is that you?'

'It's me.'

Silence.

'Are you there? Rose?'

'I didn't make it last night.'

'I know.'

'I'm sorry ... I ... Something came up.'

Is that the best you can do, he thought. 'That's okay. I understand.'

Silence again.

This time Kip decided to wait it out. He was annoyed about having his night spoiled. Who was he kidding? He only would have stayed in his room and watched old movies. He was annoyed because he'd been stood up. By a slip of a girl. The silence lengthened. He gave in. 'So ...'

'I'm really very sorry ... There was this ... kind of an emergency.'

'Emergency? Is it something serious? Are you okay?'

'Yes, I'm okay.'

'What happened?'

'Um, it's nothing. I'll tell you later, okay?'

First it was an emergency, then it's nothing. 'So do you want to try for dinner again? Or not.'

'Tonight.'

'Tonight? Okay, tonight is good for me.'

'I'll meet you at your hotel?'

'Why don't I meet you near your place? I don't want you to get lost.' He hoped the sarcasm wasn't too obvious.

'Near my place ... All right ... Why don't you meet me outside Paddington station?'

'Okay. Where, exactly?'

She gave him some directions.

'Done. At, say, eight o'clock?'

'Can we make it nine?'

Nine was late, but he understood it could be a local habit because of the summer's long twilight. 'Nine o'clock it is.'

He hung up the phone feeling pleased that she had rung.

Akello took the stairs at the Oxford Circus underground station two at a time. He walked straight past the schematic map to the cross-connecting walkway to the Victoria Line.

He felt quite pleased with himself for getting to know his way around London so well. He knew at least half a dozen suburbs — the homes or meeting places for Cynthia and her girlfriends — and when he had time to himself, he learned a few more in his shopping trips.

He was also pleased with his new clothes. Starting from the modest pieces he'd bought with Cynthia's initial gift, he had progressively added to his growing wardrobe by shrewd shopping. He liked the markets best. The clothes were very much like the styles he had seen at the movie theatres back in Kisumu, and more recently in Nairobi. Colours — he loved the colours.

The Victoria Line train swept into the platform, and he took a seat opposite an attractive black girl who smiled at him. Akello smiled back, and started his game of guessing the girl's country of origin. He was becoming quite accomplished at picking the Americans. They always chewed gum with an exaggerated action, and they tended to have more teeth than Africans, or blacks from Paris and other parts of Europe.

He caught her eye and smiled. She turned away, but there was a hint of a smile on her lips. His guess was that she was about seventeen, maybe even nineteen.

'Hi, I'm Akello,' he said, putting out his hand.

'Hi,' she answered, brushing his hand with hers.

'I'm thinking, this one's from Paris,' he said.

'Paris, France?' she said, giving him a wide smile this time. 'No way, bro. I'm from Charleston, South Carolina in the US of A.'

'America? That's a wonderful place.'

'You bin there?'

'Not yet. But I am going to go. I am going to go soon.'

'You'll have a ball. It's a gas. I mean it's, like, way out there, you know what I mean, bro?'

'Yes. Sure.' He tried to think of something American to say. 'Sure' was the best he could manage. 'Are you here on a holiday?'

'Yeah, summer vacation. It's a blast.'

'Right on.' He felt he was getting the swing of it. He made a note to remember to say 'blast' like *bl-a-a-a-st* when next he met an American.

'Love your threads,' she said. 'Where'd you get your gear?'

'This? This jacket? Oh, it's nothing much. I picked it up in Camden market.'

'Is that a good place for clothes? I bin lookin' all over. I bin to Harrods, I bin to Marks and Spencer. Honey, I bin everywhere. Let me think now, I bin —'

'Camden market. It's the best place to be. It's a real blast.'

'Right on. I'm a-goin' there, bro. You better believe it.'

They were slowing as the train approached Pimlico station. 'I've got to get off here. What's your name?'

'My name? Camilla is my name. What's yours?'

'I told you, it's Akello.'

'Ay-kello? Ay-kello. What kind of a name is Ay-kello?'

'It's Ugandan. But I come from Kenya.'

'Kenia? Is that near Jersey?'

The doors opened, and he stood to join the departing passengers. 'No, it's in Africa.'

'Oh ...' She frowned, shaking her head at the wonder of it.

Akello gave Camilla a wave as the train overtook him on his way to the exit, but she didn't see him.

He whistled as he walked down Belgrave Road towards Caroline's house in one of the tree-lined back streets. He was pleased he had worn the jacket again. He had worn it once before to Caroline's and she seemed to like it, so he wore it again for her benefit.

The enormous elms that met above the middle of the road obscured the streetlights, but he knew where he was going. Caroline was another divorced friend of Cynthia's, and tonight was going to be different, because Cynthia had said she would be there too. She promised something a bit more exciting for the three of them. He felt a stirring in his loins at the thought of it.

There was no light in the front of the house, which was usual for his visits to Caroline. She asked him to always use the rear door. 'So the neighbours don't get nosey,' she said.

He heard voices from inside and stepped quietly up to the back window. Cynthia and Caroline were in the kitchen, sharing a glass of wine. He decided to give them a surprise and sneak in on them.

He carefully turned the door handle and let himself into the rear hall, which adjoined the kitchen where they were sitting.

'If it wasn't for that marvellous equipment of his, darling, why would we be interested?' It was Cynthia's voice.

'Isn't it amazing?' Caroline giggled. 'No sooner does he come than it's up again, rearing to go.'

'But he's not only big, he uses it so well too.'

'He could be a bit more imaginative at times, but I agree, he's got the essentials down pat.'

'Do you think it's an African thing, or are all black men built like that?'

'I dare say — I don't have a clue. Akello is my first and only black man.'

'Maybe I should try to recruit a little more sophistication next time.'

'Sophistication? Who needs sophistication. Give me a big dick and I'm a happy lady.'

'Well, that too, but maybe next time I'll find someone who can actually carry a conversation beyond football scores and the latest, what does he call it, *reggae* music.'

'I know what you mean. It's nice to have a monkey on a chain, but he should be well trained. And someone who has just a touch more dress

423

sense. Honestly, I thought I'd die last week when he walked in with that ghastly blue thing he wears.'

'You mean the jacket? Isn't it a scream? He thinks he looks so hot in it, too.'

Akello closed the back door, and was careful not to make a sound when he retreated into the night.

CHAPTER 45

Kip came out of Paddington station and found the post office behind the Hilton, just as Rose had described it. The streetlight on the corner of Praed Street was out. Kip angled his watch to catch what light he could. It was just after nine o'clock.

As he leaned against the lamp post, assuming a position of nonchalance, he noticed a figure walking towards him in the semi-darkness of the side street beside the post office. He was more pleased than he wanted to admit when he recognised it as Rose. He waved.

Rose lifted a hand to respond, but a man came from the shadows and, without warning, spun her about and smashed his fist into her face. She staggered back.

Kip sprinted towards them. The man was a solid brute, about Kip's height, but Kip had the advantage of surprise and leaped into his back, sending him sprawling onto the asphalt. He followed up with a couple of quick kicks in the ribs as the thug tried to get up. When he succeeded in rising, the man bolted.

Kip couldn't believe his luck. He wasn't a fighter and, as he'd run down to help Rose, he'd expected to get a hiding for his trouble.

Rose was slumped against the corner of the building, holding her face in her hands. Kip went to her and put his arm around her. She was shaking.

'C'mon, let's get you home,' he said.

She leaned into him and sobbed.

Rose flinched as Kip pressed the cold compress onto her face.

'Sorry,' he said, removing it for a moment to study her eye. 'I think he's caught you just above your eyebrow.' He gently placed the folded towel back in place. 'I hope the bastard broke his knuckle.'

Jonesie's standover man hadn't cut her with his right cross, but Kip told her she would probably have a shiner for a week or so. It was not the news she wanted to hear. It would mean more time off from the Laddies and Lassies Bar, which was her best chance to catch up with what she owed Jonesie. She mentioned nothing about Jonesie to Kip, nor the fact that his standover man wasn't the first warning that he was losing his patience with her. As far as Kip knew, it was a simple mugging.

Tonight's attack was just the most recent of a run of bad luck. A week ago Shiver had told her he couldn't promise her any more work because she was too unreliable. He became abusive and loud when he reminded her she'd been booked as a single act at a club in Chatham, and had let the club and him down by her no-show.

She tried to get him to relent, but then he made the suggestion that he might reconsider if she gave him some 'special consideration'. It wasn't the first time he'd hinted at it, and she was pleased to see the end of him. A few days later Jonesie tried the same thing, but with less subtlety. He said she had to either pay him or blow him. She said she would get the money in a day or so.

She tolerated Jonesie's sleazy manner because he was the only dealer she knew who would extend credit. If she could only hit onto a good modelling contract she wouldn't have to work the late hours. Those late hours, and the type of client she met at her job at the girlie bar, meant she needed something to help her through the night. The coke was good, but it was the touch of heroin that gave the kick she needed these days. Heroin was expensive, and her income was struggling to keep up. If it weren't for Akello, she would be out on the street.

Her unlucky run had continued on her way to meet Kip for dinner the previous night. His was the only friendly face she had seen for weeks, and she was looking forward to his company. A block from her apartment, a man with a cloth cap pulled low over his eyes grabbed her from behind. He took the few pounds she had left to her name, and said that if Jonesie didn't get his money by noon the following day, he would be back. She'd tried to avoid the thug by arranging a later meeting time with Kip, but he had been waiting.

'Hey, I'm sorry.' Kip lifted her chin and wiped away the tears that ran from her good eye. 'You should have told me it was hurting too much.'

She sniffed and said, 'You know what people say — African girls don't cry.'

'Is that so?' He removed the ice pack and studied her eye up close. He wore the same aftershave as the night he'd rescued her from the mob in Nairobi.

'The swelling's going down a little. Maybe I was wrong. Maybe it'll take less than a week.'

He handed her brandy glass to her, and took a sip of his own.

'That's better — a smile. I told you at the corner store that a dash of brandy would do you the world of good.'

'I'm not smiling about the brandy. Or Dr Kip's prediction about my black eye. I'm smiling because you're my hero, and you don't know it. You've just dragged me out of another mess. It's the third time.'

'That's what the great white hunter does in all the movies, isn't it? Anyway, it's no big deal, and — wait a minute ...' He scratched his head. 'What do you mean the *third* time? I count two. Tonight is one —'

'In Nairobi, during the riots was two,' she added.

'That's right. So where's the third?'

She decided it was a night to break down old barriers. She sensed that telling Kip her secret would help. 'The first time you were my hero was in Kisumu, many years ago.'

'Kisumu? Years ago? You mean a few years ago, when we first met at the Mara Escarpment camp?'

'No.'

'No, that can't be right. I didn't go to Kisumu on that trip. Harry took you there.'

She was pleased he was playing the game with her. She let him struggle with the puzzle, becoming increasingly unsure whether to reveal her secret, and wondering whether she wanted the haunted memories, the old fears, to return. She still battled guilt, even though she had been the victim. Her emotions ran the gamut of fear, anger and self-pity.

'I need a clue,' he said after a while.

'It was much earlier than that.' Having started it, she felt caught in her own trap. But she had reached the point of no return. Her heart started to race. 'Ten years ago. I was thirteen.'

'Kisumu ... 1973. Let me see ... I was setting up the kitchen and reception buildings at the Mara camp around then.' He raised his eyes to hers, trying to read a clue in them. 'Kisumu. I had a helluva job getting my timber out of Uganda. Now I remember ...' He folded his arms, tapped his bottom lip with his forefinger and stared at the wall. 'Spent a lot of time at the shipping agent's ...'

'I was with my family. Four of us.'

'I remember!' He swung back to her, the light of recognition written on his face. She smiled to camouflage the tears that welled in her eyes.

'The young girl on the wharf!' he said, pointing a finger at her. 'With her family. There were three of you kids, with your father. Your father! Was that Zakayo all those years ago? My God! But how could I know?' He cocked his head and again stared at the wall as he recalled the scene. 'Three kids with Zakayo ... he said you had just come across the lake from Uganda ... That's right! You had just come across the lake from Uganda, to stay with your sister. That must have been Grace! I met her just a few weeks ago.' He smiled and shook his head. 'What a small world.' He continued to stare into the vision he saw on her apartment wall. 'Ten years ago. Doesn't it fly?'

He grew silent and seemed lost in some memories of his own. It gave her time to surreptitiously dab a tissue to her eyes. It looked as though her confession could be postponed for another day, but he returned to the scene in Kisumu.

'You were the advance guard for the rest of the family. It was in Amin's time. The madness. I thought you were all very brave to make the attempt to get out. You had an older sister and a younger brother with you. Peas in a pod, the three of you. And you were the only one I could communicate with. You were shy, so I tried to make a joke.'

'You made a poem about my name.'

'I did?'

'A rose by any other name would smell as sweet,' she quoted.

'That's right. That's what I said. Must have been my timing. You got upset.'

'It was only years later that I found it in a book. I thought you'd made it up.'

'If I had, I would have done a better job than Shakespeare. It made you cry.'

'That wasn't what made me cry.'

But he was back in the scene on the Kisumu wharf. 'I remember now ... your dad had been bashed. You were all in a state. How did I forget that? I took your father to hospital. I never did figure out what happened that night.' He turned to face her. 'What *did* happen, Rose?' He noticed her tears. 'What's wrong? What did I do?'

'It's not you. You've always done everything just perfectly. You're always there when I need someone. Whether you know it or not, you have saved me at the times I most needed to be saved. That's why I always think of you as my hero.'

'I don't understand. All I did was what anybody else would have done, under the same circumstances.'

'But nobody else did. Nobody else has. It's always you. You don't know what it meant to me that night in Kisumu when you helped us.'

'I can hardly remember it. Your dad had a broken head — I remember that much. What else was a fellow to do?'

'It wasn't Papa that you helped that night, it was me.'

'You? You looked fine, from memory.'

'But I wasn't fine. I was thirteen and I had been raped. At age thirteen, I knew nothing about anything, and the immigration guards raped me, not a hundred metres away from your agent's office.'

In spite of her best efforts, and promises to herself that she would resist, she sobbed into her hands.

She felt his firm touch on her shoulders. 'Oh, no ... Oh, Rose, I'm so sorry. I ...'

She struggled for a moment to regain control, sniffing, and noisily blowing her nose on a tissue. Kip handed her the cold towel again, and she spread it across her face and burning eyelids. She took a deep breath of the cool, damp air of the towel. It made her feel better. She had purged her demon, and now just wanted to put Kisumu behind her.

He still had hold of her shoulders. His hands were strong and warm. It felt good to be close to the strength of him. She removed the wet towel and looked up at him.

He cupped her face in his hands. 'You should get some sleep,' he said, with his sad blue–green eyes holding hers.

And she wept again, this time with relief that his expression was of concern, not of disgust.

In the morning she examined her face in the bathroom mirror. Her skin colouring concealed the worst of her bruising, but her eyes were puffy from too much sleep and the tears of the previous night.

After she had showered, she pulled on a robe and joined Kip in the kitchen. It felt strange to see him there in his T-shirt and slacks, a near-empty cup of tea before him, and seemingly at ease in the chair where her brother normally sat.

She greeted him and asked how he had slept.

'Like a log.' He smiled. 'But I needed a pick-me-up. Hope you don't mind — I made a cup of tea while I was waiting for you.'

'Not at all. I can't believe I slept so long.'

'You must have needed it.' He drained his cup and arose from the table. 'Best cup of tea I've had since getting to London,' he said, brandishing the empty cup. 'Want to join me for one?'

'Yes, please.'

He took another teacup from the cupboard. 'How are you feeling this morning?' he asked as he added boiling water to the cups.

'Much better.' It was true, she felt as if she had been reborn. It was the time of morning when the sun angled between the neighbouring buildings to send a stream of golden warmth into the apartment. Was it the light, or Kip in his bare arms, that lent an air of intimacy to the room? She had an almost uncontrollable urge to stroke his arm as he dunked the tea bags at the kitchen bench. 'I'm sorry I had to burden you with all that stuff last night,' she added.

He shrugged and smiled. 'They tell me it helps.'

'It does. Don't you think it does?'

'I've never tried it.'

'You should.'

His smile hovered on the verge of melting. 'One of these days. When it's needed.'

'I thought you might have gone back to the hotel by now.'

'I wanted to make sure you were okay first.'

'I am. And thank you.'

'Me? What did I do apart from give a friend a little of my time?'

There was an awkward pause. Kip disposed of the tea bags, and placed her cup on the bench beside him. 'Here you go.'

She took it as he took a sip of his own tea.

'Ouch!'

'Hot?' she asked.

'It sure is.' His hand went to his mouth, but Rose took it before he reached it and, replacing her cup on the bench, tenderly touched his lips with the tips of her fingers.

'Careful,' she said, and as her fingers fell from his mouth she let them caress his muscular bare arm.

Kip seemed confused at first, but he retrieved her fingers, and kissed them before stroking his bristled chin with them.

He had closed his eyes, and when he opened them, Rose drew him towards her and kissed him.

The touch of his cool lips on hers sent a ripple of pleasure through her body. He must have sensed it, because when she drew him to her again, he pulled her body to his and caressed her mouth with the tip of his tongue.

When she opened her eyes his expression had changed. He was looking at her, studying her, as if he had found something he had never seen before.

Her arms went around his neck, and his lips pressed hers, before crushing her body to his.

Rose pulled his shirt over his head, and ran her hands over his chest. Her tongue found the little round bud of his nipple, and he muffled a moan.

He led her to the sofa, but she whispered she wanted him in her bed, and when he was there she wouldn't allow him to touch her until she had undressed him.

His hands trembled as he untied her gown to reveal her nakedness, and he drew her to him on the small bed.

As he gently entered her, she thanked all her small gods that Kip, her hero, had saved her yet again.

CHAPTER 46

Serious relationships had always eluded Kip, or else he'd chosen to avoid them. He couldn't be sure which it was, but the fact was, he'd never had one. He sometimes worried that his childhood might have left him so emotionally scarred that his soul had lost the ingredients necessary for love.

It therefore came as something of a shock when he realised there was something special about his feeling for Rose.

It should have been all wrong. Firstly, she was far too young for him — sixteen years younger. When he'd met her, she was with Harry, a man even older than he. Kip had taken the moral high ground and let Harry know he thought it ridiculous. Harry had a great belly laugh, reminding Kip that when he was having his affair with Diana there was a similar age difference. Kip, taken aback, mumbled that it was different when the woman was the older one. Harry had laughed again, accusing him of double standards.

Different backgrounds was another reason Kip thought he and Rose might not be compatible. He could have said 'racial differences', or 'colour', but they weren't entirely it — they were just external differences. The real issue was whether he and Rose had enough common ground inside themselves to build a loving relationship. It was like trying to grow a crop on infertile ground. When people were poles apart, their core beliefs too disparate, nothing could grow. Kip was fairly sure that he and Rose had compatible souls.

They spent a lot of time together. Rose moved a few of her things into his room at the Royal National. Kip deferred his flight home.

In the next couple of days, they raced around London like a pair of children on a school excursion. In the early evenings they would go back to the hotel room and make love in his narrow bed. After a nap, they would rise to share a late supper together.

For three days it was bliss. On the fourth, Rose showed signs of agitation. The crowds irritated her as they shuffled along in the queue to see the Tower of London. At lunch she spilled a cup of coffee, and burst into tears. When they went back to the room in the late afternoon, she didn't want to take a nap.

'I've got to go home for a bit,' she said.

'Sure, Rose,' Kip said. 'Want me to go with you?'

'No. I mean ... you have your rest. I'll be back soon, okay?'

'Of course. Are you feeling all right? You've been a bit tense today.'

'Have I?'

'A little.'

'Sorry. It must be my, you know, my periods.'

'Will you be back later?'

'Why?'

Her sharp response took him by surprise. 'Nothing ... I just wondered if we're going to have supper together when you get back or —'

'I don't know. No, you go ahead. I'll grab a bite over there.'

'Okay.'

They kissed briefly, and she swept out the door without another word.

He turned on the TV and stared at it for ten minutes before switching it off. The incident with Rose was small, but it had disturbed him. Their time together had been idyllic. It came as a jolt that the practicalities of life, or female conditions, could intrude.

He decided to have an early meal and picked up his watch from the dresser. A corner of a pound note protruded from his wallet. He was careful with money — a habit learned when he was a kid struggling to survive alone in Nairobi — and always kept his money tucked out of sight. Flipping open the wallet, he found he was missing about a hundred pounds — almost all he had in cash. He ran through the activities of the day, hoping to recall where he might have miscalculated his spending, but he knew he'd made no mistakes. He had checked his cash at the end of the Greenwich tour — the last of their day. He sat back on the bed, racking his brain for an explanation.

Rose's head pounded as she stood in the doorway facing the cracked paintwork. The slide bolt sounded, and Jonesie's piggy eyes narrowed in the slit of the open door.

'You've got a cheek,' he snarled, but she heard the chain clatter and he let her in.

After he had bolted the door behind her, she quickly said, 'I've brought the money. I've brought what I owe you.'

His expression immediately changed. 'Have you now, Velvet,' he said with a guarded smile. 'Welcome to my office.' He swept a hand to the nearest chair, and took his seat on the other side of the small table. 'Show me the money.'

She fumbled in her purse and put four twenties on the table in front of her.

'Well, I'll be … Velvet, darling, you've found a rich boyfriend at last. And if I might say —'

'I want another package, and your room out the back.'

He nodded and his smile broadened. 'Of course you do, Velvet, of course you do. That's what Jonesie's 'ere for, isn't it?'

His tone was one that would be used with a small child. It made her sick to her stomach, but she held her feelings back. She pushed the remaining notes towards him. 'Here's twenty for the package. The usual.'

''Ang on a sec, sweetheart, that's not enough for your usual. Are you asking for more credit? More credit and not even a kiss-my-arse for my trouble?'

She eyed him in silence.

'Well, it looks like your credit's improved. I suppose I can be nice to you. Again.' He slid open his drawer.

She sat impatiently as he carefully poured the magic powders onto his scales. She hated the way he acted like he was God, dispensing blessings, and the way he measured the quantities with delicate movements of his childlike hands.

He had a syrupy smile on his repulsive red lips as he slid the packet across the table towards her. ''Ere you are, my sweet Velvet,' but as she reached for it his arm shot out and his delicate hand gripped hers like a vice.

'No more screwing with me! Understand?'

The transformation was frightening. Rose had never felt intimidated by Jonesie, but in that moment she had no doubt that this weedy individual could do whatever was necessary to survive in his sordid business.

'I've 'ad it with customers like you,' he hissed. 'You take me for granted and leave me out of pocket. The other night you were just lucky your boyfriend was there. But he's not gonna be around all the time, is he? So this time it's pay or *you'll* pay. Understand?'

She swallowed and nodded.

'Good.' His expression softened immediately and he showed his row of tobacco-stained teeth.

She got unsteadily to her feet and went to the door to the back room.

Jonesie was there already, with his hand on the knob. 'You know, sweet'eart, if you're ever short of cash and you want to avoid all this nasty money business, there are other ways, you know . . . to pay.'

She defiantly stared him down.

'Just offering, is all. Just offering. No 'arm done, eh?'

Kip spent a long time debating whether to go to Rose's house or not. In the end he couldn't bear the waiting any longer. It was after eleven, and if she was still planning to come to the hotel, he worried about her being on the streets of Paddington at such an hour. He walked down to Russell Square and jumped on the train.

At Piccadilly Circus he searched passing faces, wondering what the chances were that they would cross paths at the interchange.

On the Bakerloo Line train, he again tried to find an explanation for the missing cash. Again he drew a blank. He could only assume that Rose was in some kind of trouble — something that she didn't want to share with him. That concerned him too; he'd hoped they'd developed a greater intimacy than that. He felt isolated and hurt.

He hurried up the stairs and out of the deserted station.

A block from her building he saw her. She was heading towards home, arm in arm with a tall black man.

Rose lay fully clothed on her bed, the afternoon sun streaming onto her face. She couldn't remember how she had got home. She grimaced as she squinted at the clock. *Kip*, she thought, but her body felt like lead. She rolled away from the light and threw an arm over her eyes and groaned.

As she lay there, willing her body to revive, she tried to recall what had happened the night before.

There was Jonesie and his needle ... then the rush. She had been carried out over Murchison Falls, the water roaring beneath her as she flew in and out of its billowing spray. Her mother, brothers and sisters, and her father, were there, cheering her on. And Akello, her darling little brother came flying with her, both of them laughing as they did when they were children. They were all together, and they laughed and laughed. It was so good being with her family again.

Time had passed — it felt like hours — and she had become heavy with fatigue, unable to rouse herself. Her dream merged with reality. A telephone rang and Jonesie said, 'Who? Akello? Who the hell are you?' Then she fell asleep until Akello came into her dream and carried her away into darkness.

The darkness persisted until she moved her head. She was surprised it was not as painful as she had expected.

A noise came from the sitting room. She tottered out to investigate.

'Akello? What are you doing?'

'I am leaving, sister.' He was packing folded clothes into a new suitcase. His old one was already packed full, sitting on the floor beside him. 'And so are you. Come on, get packed.'

'Leaving? Going where?'

'Going home.'

She felt behind her for the sofa and dropped onto it. 'Home? Why? When did all this happen? Why didn't you tell me?'

'I've been waiting to find you at home so I could tell you. It's been four days.'

'I was looking for you too, but you were never in when I came by.'

'Well, it's lucky I found that telephone number when I came home last night, because I would have been off to Heathrow without you. But now I'm taking you too. Now hurry, get packed.'

'Packed? I can't leave London! Not now.'

'That's where you are wrong, sister. After seeing you last night in that creepy little fellow's house … I said, that's it! You are coming with me right now.'

'You don't understand. Last night was … last night was the end of it.'

'From what I saw, it will be the end of you too. Now get up. Get packed.'

'No, it's not like that.' Rose couldn't think straight with her brother rushing from cupboard to suitcase, throwing clothes about. 'Sit down, Akello, let me explain.'

He gave her a guarded glance, then reluctantly joined her on the sofa.

She took his hand and patted it. 'I've been taking a little bit of stuff to keep me going at nights, but that's going to stop.' She saw his dubious expression. 'I mean it. I've met someone, a friend from a long time ago. I think we're right for each other, and ... I don't want to leave just now ... until it gels. You know what I mean?'

'Hmm ... maybe.'

'I'll come home, with him, in a week or so. Okay?'

'You promise?'

'Have I ever lied to you?'

'No. And you'll tell me all about this friend of yours?'

'I will.'

He looked into her eyes for a long moment, then said, '*Sowa, haraka!* Look at me sitting making silly talk. I'm late!' He went back to his suitcase.

'But you haven't told me why you're leaving.'

He sighed, flipped the lid of his suitcase closed and sat on it, his arms folded. 'I'm tired of London. There's nothing here for me. This is a cold, dark place. It's not right for a man from Africa.'

'I don't like it either, so stay until I leave,' she pleaded. 'Only a few more days.'

She could see she almost had him convinced, but he shook his head. 'It's here,' he said, tapping his fist into his chest. 'Heartache.'

'Heartache?'

'Don't you remember? Mama would press her fist here, and say, "*Aiya*, the heartache is deep today." Do you remember? Her heartache was always much worse when Papa had been away for a long time.'

She smiled. 'I remember. So ... are you saying that you have heartache too? Why?'

'Ahh, these women ...' But he just stood and slammed his suitcase shut. '*Sasa, kwaheri.*'

She stood and hugged him. 'I'd come with you to the airport, but I have to meet my friend.'

'That's okay.' He hugged her again. '*Kwaheri*, sister.'

'*Kwaheri*.' She walked to the door with him. 'Akello?'

'Yes?'

'Did anyone call this morning?'

'No, why?'

'Just wondering.'

Rose knocked on the door to Kip's room. There was no answer.

At reception she said, 'Can I have the key to 2232, please. My friend has gone out, and I left mine in the room.'

'Certainly, madam. Can I have your name, please?'

'It's under my friend's name. Balmain.'

'Balmain?' The receptionist checked his screen and looked over his glasses at her. 'Did you say Balmain, madam?'

'Yes. Kip Balmain, but he might be registered under Rupert, it's ... you know ... a family name.'

'Yes, madam. But unfortunately Mr Balmain checked out earlier this afternoon.'

CHAPTER 47

Rose had been lying on her bed for nearly an hour, trying to avoid dwelling on the loneliness — the loneliness of an unfriendly city — and trying to keep her mind free of the self-pity that threatened to overwhelm her.

She had examined every inch of the wallpaper, and her eye continued to be drawn to a point in a corner, up near the ceiling, where she had found a spot. She couldn't decide if it was a mark, a hole in the plaster or a small spider. She thought it was probably a spider, and she hated spiders, so she watched it, waiting for it to move. But it didn't.

Every thought of Kip came with a rush of humiliation. He had found out about her theft, and was so disgusted by it that he had left London without even a word of reproach.

But reflections on him were also filled with deep regret. She had been happier with him than she'd thought was possible. During the short period of their intimacy, she'd felt a bond was forming. Every day, every hour, was a reconfirmation of that connection. For the first time in her life she felt she understood love — love with all its ecstasy and joy. And now, love with all the pain of its rejection.

She forced Kip from her mind. She had more immediate problems — no money. She would have to go to the bar to earn something to keep her going. But the thought of that poisonous air, with the hands of drunken patrons pawing her, the effort to keep up a smile for the manager's benefit, and the hours on her feet, were too daunting.

To endure the ordeal she needed to see Jonesie again. To see Jonesie she needed money. The conundrum made her head spin.

She would do what had to be done for the white powder.

In the daylight, the purple door of the so-called nightclub at the end of Chatham Lane in Soho looked tawdrier than under the bright lights of the night. At night, the Flashdance Disco and Niteclub was one of a dozen similar establishments at the lower end of the entertainment spectrum. But it was a well-known fact among the girls trying to make a living in the quasi-fashion industry that by day the Flashdance had a sideline operation that some of the girls used when they needed to earn some extra cash.

Rose pushed open the heavy purple door and peered into the gloom. The room had the odour of stale tobacco and rancid beer. She could see nothing, but a voice said, 'Come in, if you're coming in.'

She hesitated a moment more, then stepped inside. When the door thudded shut behind her, her eyes became accustomed to the light and she saw a bar about ten paces long, with a backlit wall of white glass or plastic where brightly coloured bottles were arranged on shelves. A man in a white shirt was standing behind the bar, a newspaper spread before him.

He paid no attention to her until she was standing in front of him. 'What can I do for you, darlin'?' he said, squinting through the smoke of a cigarette that dangled from his thin and pinched lips.

'I've come to speak to Eddy,' she said in a small voice.

The barman looked her over. 'Oh yeah? And who shall I say is askin'?'

'Rose,' she said, then added, 'but he doesn't know me. Just tell him Gloria sent me.' She could have bitten her tongue — she sounded like a character in a cheap movie.

The barman gave her one more appraising look and disappeared through a swing door at the end of the bar. When he returned he made no further comment and went back to his newspaper.

Rose was beginning to feel she had been misunderstood, when the door swung open again and a large man in an ill-fitting suit approached her. He eyed her suspiciously for a few moments then flicked his head, indicating she should follow him to one of the small round tables at the end of the bar.

'You know the arrangement then, do you?' he said. 'What's your name again?'

'Rose.'

'Rose ... So, do you know the deal, Rose?'

'Not exactly ... Gloria said —'

'Half for you, half for me.' He studied her for the first time, looking from her ankles up her legs — which she had crossed at the edge of the small table — to her breasts. 'You get one free drink for every two he buys.'

'I ... I see ...'

'What do you do?'

'I'm a part-time model,' she said, surprised by his interest.

'Aren't they all?' he said with a cheerless smile. 'I mean, straight sex, continental, fetish, hand jobs, blow jobs ... what is it you do?'

'I don't want to ... I mean ... the last two ... would be all right.'

'Right, you should manage at least twenty quid from every trick. If you can get a better deal, it's yours. Fair enough?'

Rose nodded.

'Good. We'll give you a trial.' He stood to leave.

'When can I start?'

The manager's eyebrows raised. 'In a little spot of bother, are we?'

'No ... it's just —'

He nodded. 'Never mind, I don't need your life story.' He scanned the bar area. 'See that bloke over there in the right-hand corner?'

Rose peered into the gloom. She hadn't noticed anyone when she entered, but there were two men sitting at the tables furthest from the bar, as if they had each been told to sit in a corner. They were both nursing drinks.

'There's a couple of rooms out the back. You can use the one with the orange door. Clean up after yourself, and give the money to Barry at the bar.' He nodded his head as if ticking off another item on a checklist. 'Should have picked you for a junkie. All the good-looking ones usually are.' He disappeared into the back room.

Rose sat for a few minutes gathering her courage. The urge for the powder would not leave her. Her head and back ached. Her skin crawled as if there were burrowing insects under the surface. She knew it would only get worse.

Her chair gave a frightening screech as she stood and pushed it back from the table.

She shot a glance at the barman, who was still reading his newspaper, and then at the man Eddy had indicated. He was middle-aged and wearing a neat pinstriped suit. A felt hat sat on the table beside his beer glass. He seemed clean and remarkably presentable. It gave her the courage to approach him.

At his table she raised her eyes to meet his. He was smiling, or, more accurately, leering at her.

'A-are you looking for a g-good time?' It was the only sentence that came to mind.

'Here you go, sweetheart,' he said, pushing back the table. 'Would you like to have a go at this?'

He pulled aside the flap of his suit coat to reveal his semi-erect penis.

The relief came with a rush. Rose lay back on the couch in her flat and allowed the warmth to spread through her body. Her headache dissolved and her limbs stopped throbbing.

She enjoyed the floating sensation, and soon she was flying over Panyiketto, feeling the moist air from the Nile soothing her face. White clouds floated above her — soft fluffy ones like she'd seen on a TV advertisement advertising fabric softener. *As light and bright as innocence* said the voice on the commercial.

Innocence. Panyiketto was as light and bright as innocence. It was a time when she knew nothing about sex. She didn't even understand her body. *Twiga*, the boys at school called her in those days — giraffe. And there was Sister Augustine, who must have known how self-conscious she was, for she was always scolding the boys for teasing her when she was not admonishing her for slouching. She had explained one of the mysteries of the female body when Rose had started getting her periods. She introduced her to her first pad.

Rose smiled in her half-dreaming state. The nun had given her the pad with instructions to put it into her underwear before school the following day.

At home, Rose had retreated behind the cotton print screen that defined her bedroom and took the package from her school bag. Beneath the brown paper was another covering of white cotton material. She could find no way of unwrapping it further. She took the scissors from her mother's sewing box and carefully cut into the white cotton envelope. It was packed with tiny feathers. One or two drifted away. She captured them and returned them to the envelope.

She thought she understood about the feathers, and vividly recalled the feeling of utter relief that the simple solution had promised ...

Sister Augustine stood erect on the podium. Her colleagues, the two other Sisters of Charity who had accompanied her from Ireland, stood one on each side, clapping their hands in an attempt to keep the children marching in time.

The little ones led the parade, swinging their arms enthusiastically, while the older children followed, looking as if they'd rather be somewhere else. Four abreast, they marched out from assembly in reasonable order. By the time they approached the large fig in the centre of the playground, the lines had begun to waver and many children were out of step, or out of time with the hand-clapping. As usual, when they wheeled around the tree and headed back towards the classrooms, there was general disarray.

The head nun sighed and wondered if she should ask Sister Mary Joseph to spend another session on marching practice. It seemed that nothing was easy in Uganda. Even the simple task of keeping the schoolyard tidy was beyond them. She made a note to enquire which children were responsible for cleaning the schoolyard that week. It was a mess. Small pieces of paper were fluttering around the youngsters' feet and being swept aloft on the breeze.

The parade wheeled at the end of the school ground and, as they approached the podium, Sister Augustine noticed that the paper flying around the marching students was, in fact, feathers. Small white feathers.

When the older children at the end of the column approached, the flurry increased. Sister Augustine's hand flew to her mouth. Rose Nasonga marched past, making a commendable effort to keep her shoulders back and her head high, completely unaware of the blizzard of white feathers in her wake.

CHAPTER 48

1986

The Indian Ocean sparkled as only an ocean under an equatorial sun can. Beyond the reef it rose from deep blue depths to crash against the coral, sending small emissaries of its power to the shore, where they died sedately against the slope of yellow–white sand. In the shallows, a lone tourist attempted to windsurf under the tutelage of a local expert — a jet-black Swahili youth in floppy red shorts. The hotel's manicured tropical garden ended abruptly at the beach resort's white-coral sea wall. Between it and the water, topless female sunbathers and their bronzed partners lay on beach towels, glistening with coconut oil.

Kip rested his head against the back of the deckchair, one bare foot on the white-coral wall and the other on the cool grass of the hotel's lawn. Even in the shade of the coconut tree, the light reflecting from the white sand assaulted his eyes. He closed them, and let the monotonous lapping of the waves lull him into an indulgent daydream.

He had spent the last few days in frustrating meetings with local authorities who were making it difficult for him to get approval for his latest project — a lodge built in the trees above the dense jungle of the littoral forest. It had been Kip's dream to open the rainforest to tourists, believing that when the public became aware of its beauty they would more readily fight to preserve it.

He knew the easy way to secure the approval, but he refused to play the politicians' corrupt game. He had been doing business in Kenya all his life without resorting to the innocuous-sounding tea money. Although he was tolerant of many of the failings of his homeland, he opposed corruption with a passion.

He had heard the economic arguments that endemic corruption would impose an unbearable economic burden on the country. But Kip despised it because it was blatant theft, usually committed against those least able to pay — the vast majority of the population, who were already struggling for the simple necessities of life. The poor suffered petty graft from lowly officials, while their superiors milked the big end of town.

He had come to the beach to relax, but he just couldn't erase the frustration of the last few days from his mind. He knew it was a good project. The Jungle Lodge, as he would call it, would be a blessing for the local tribes at the edge of the Shimba forest. Their small cash-crop holdings of coconut and cashew nut couldn't compete with the local and overseas conglomerates. The lodge would provide employment, and a market for their produce and handicrafts.

Kip tried to be philosophical. He could build his fourth lodge somewhere else, if he built it at all. It wasn't as if he needed the money. His easy acquiescence to the setback vaguely troubled him. It wasn't like him to retreat at the first obstacle. Upon reflection, he realised that the last four years had been one capitulation after another. Since returning from London he had lost a lot of enthusiasm for his life in Kenya.

London was supposed to begin the discovery of who he, Kip Balmain, really was. At the back of his mind, he had lived with the expectation that one day a door would somehow open and his life would be revealed. He had found the opening to his past, with the tantalising hints about his father, but when the door led nowhere, he became more unsettled than ever.

His consolation had been that while he had searched in vain for his father, he'd thought he had found something equally important in Rose, who offered the hope of filling a need to love and be loved that he had lost when Diana died. But it became apparent that it was only he who had thought it important. Rose's betrayal had proved she didn't share his belief.

London had doubly denied him. Since then he had been in a holding pattern, slowly losing altitude. He hated the feeling that his life was running out of steam, but felt powerless to prevent it. For twenty years his business had been a substitute for a life, but now even that was losing its energy.

'I saw you out here without a drink and thought, *Hello, hello — Kip needs a Tusker.*'

Harry's white, hairy legs were unmistakable. 'Hi, Harry,' Kip said as he accepted the offered frosty glass.

'What's up, ol' diamond? Been planning our next assault on the bastions of petty graft?' Harry sat on the wall and took a long draught of his beer.

'No. I took on something simple like solving the mystery of the universe, then I got bored and I switched off.'

'Good idea. I, on the other hand, have been admiring the tits on the beach.'

'There does seem to be a good crop out there this afternoon.'

'Not that Harry's complaining,' he said, licking the froth from his lips, 'but what do you suppose it is about the Germans that make them want to expose their breasts at the drop of a hat?'

'I have no idea. Anyway, what makes you think they're all Germans?'

'Haven't you heard the hotel announcements or seen the notice boards? German! Everything's in German.'

'I hadn't noticed.'

'You'd think if it wasn't English, it would at least be in Swahili.'

'You can't speak Swahili either, Harry.'

'I know. But it would make more sense. How do they know they're on holiday? They may as well be in a bloody Hamburg beer hall.'

A waiter sauntered by. 'Here you go, diamond,' Harry said. 'Another beer for my friend and, while you're at it, I'll have one myself.' The waiter nodded and headed towards the bar.

'What's next?' Harry dragged over a chair and sat beside Kip, facing the beach.

'You mean about the permit?' He sighed. 'Don't know. It's all sounding a bit too difficult.'

'Bullshit. We can get around these local yokels. We haven't done anything new in years. And the demand is enormous! I can sell every bed you give me. Europe, America — they're coming from everywhere.'

'I know, Harry, it's just —'

'Why don't you go to see Maina?'

'Maina?'

'Yes, you know, Maina Githinji. My old pal.'

'I didn't think Maina Githinji had any pals.'

'You know what I mean. I can talk to him and, you know ...'

'Offer a bribe?' Harry was seldom bothered by scruples. Kip envied him.

'No. Of course not.' Harry feigned indignation. 'But I could, if ...' He saw Kip's expression. 'I mean, we could, you know, talk him around a bit.'

'He's in a new portfolio now, isn't he?'

'Yes, he looks after tourism. He's our man.'

Kip reflected upon the last time he had seen Githinji, when he was the Assistant Minister for Internal Security during the coup attempt of 1982. 'Did I ever tell you I once knew a kid by the name of Maina Githinji?'

'No. But it's a pretty common Kikuyu name, isn't it?'

'Probably ... but there's something about him that —'

'Speaking of which — did I tell you Rose Nasonga's back?' Harry removed his sunglasses to polish them on his garish shorts. 'Kip? I said, Rose Nasonga is back in Nairobi.'

'Rose Nasonga, eh?' he answered, pretending indifference. Kip had told no one, not even Harry, about the affair with Rose, or its aftermath. 'When did you hear that?'

'Weeks ago. I meant to mention it. Do you remember her? She used to go around with Maina.'

'I remember her. Is she back with Githinji?'

'Don't think so. That ended before she went to England.'

'How is she? I mean, what's she doing these days?'

'I hear she's back into modelling. Starting all over again. I suppose she didn't do too good in London.'

'I see. Did you speak to her?'

'Not yet, but Harry's not backward in coming forward when there's a model involved.'

Kip waited for him to continue, but Harry had replaced his sunglasses and resumed studying the talent on the beach.

Kip let the issue of Rose Nasonga drop.

About ten kilometres lay between Rose's apartment and Mathare Estate. But the manicured lawns, tended gardens and stuccoed mansions of the Mathaiga neighbourhood through which she drove were a world away from Mathare's sprawling mixture of squatters' settlements and public housing.

Mathaiga had always been the home of the rich, the diplomats and the chief executives of Kenya's largest companies, and while the new estate where Rose lived didn't include mansions, her comfortable apartment, set in an estate carefully designed for the successful Nairobi professional, had everything she needed. The supermarket was neat, clean and always well stocked. Most of her other needs were catered for elsewhere in the shopping centre, even to a choice of restaurants should she need a place to entertain a friend or business associate.

The drive from Mathaiga to Mathare passed through Kenya's socio-economic spectrum — from affluence to poverty; from financial success to desperation. It was a journey of about twenty minutes, but it spanned over twenty years of failure to reduce the disparity between Kenya's haves and have-nots.

The frenetic dash along Thika Road in the press of peak-hour traffic, the *matatus'* high-powered pop music blaring from billowing clouds of diesel exhaust, marked the transition from the beauty and order of Mathaiga to the reality of life typical for the vast majority of Nairobi's population. The roadsides always teemed with people — people waiting for a bus or *matatu*, hawkers carrying or wheeling their wares, people walking to stores and shops to sell or buy.

Mathare was never intended to house the homeless in ramshackle cardboard and iron boxes in its back streets; it just happened that way. It was planned as a dormitory suburb of modest housing to accommodate some of the thousands who worked in the surrounding sheet-metal shops, foundries and furniture factories.

Once, when Rose caught a taxi to the airport for an early-morning flight, her driver took a short cut through the eastern settlements. She had witnessed a side of Kenyan life that few Mathaiga residents could imagine. In the grey light of pre-dawn on Juja Road, a silent army moved in waves through a cloud of mist and dust. The reach of the headlights revealed the determination of the many thousands who walked for hours to places where employment might be found, to save the few pennies that it would cost for public transport. Grim, determined, they were a moving ocean of humanity, wearing the best clothes they owned in the hope that it would impress prospective employers.

As Rose turned into Koma Rock Road now, she clicked the Peugeot's central locking switch. She had no illusions about the risks of driving a respectable car into a squatter settlement. Amid the thousands of honest folk going about their business, trying to find ways to make ends meet, were a small but desperate minority who would beat a person senseless for the price of a stripped car's spare parts.

It wasn't only the whites and the relatively wealthy blacks who suffered the crime wave in the city; everybody was a target, even the poor of Mathare. The little people of the slums did not trust the police — who were either incompetent, corrupt or both — to bring offenders to trial. Any unfortunate caught committing a crime, particularly theft, would face summary justice, which could turn a peaceful neighbourhood into a lynch mob which chased down the thief and stoned or beat him to death. It was this desperation of life in eastern Nairobi that had originally drawn Rose into her work with street kids.

Like any big city, Nairobi had a population of homeless people. Many thousands were homeless children, including children whose parents had been taken by the new epidemic called AIDS, and others who had been turned out to fend for themselves. Many turned to drugs. In Nairobi, petrol sniffing was the cheap and easily accessible drug for the kids on the streets.

Rose understood their condition. In London she had been on a downhill spiral of depression and drug addiction until her guardian angel found her, literally in the gutter.

Rose had been spaced out on some or other drug cocktail, and had wandered into a quiet street where somebody tried to snatch her handbag. She could never recall the attack in any detail, but she remembered clutching at her bag as if her life depended on it. In fact, it very nearly did. She suffered several broken bones, a fractured skull and severe concussion. The man who had found her, Moh Lakhani, carried her to hospital and, during the weeks of her convalescence, helped her find her self-esteem. His next challenge was to convince Rose to join his addict support group.

Rose was initially suspicious of Moh and his great generosity of spirit. She had met too many people in London who would use apparent kindness to subvert her defences. In Moh, however, she had found a true saint. His devotion to his 'family', as he called them, was unconditional and totally selfless.

There were days when she felt she could endure the treatment no longer, and then Moh and the family would be there to encourage her. Without them she would not have had the strength to persevere. Alone, in spite of her determination to kick the habit, she had always slipped backwards again.

A little over a year ago, Rose had come home — in more ways than one. She had returned from London, and had returned to the human race.

Akello took her in until she started to earn some modelling money. During this time she started thinking about helping the street kids. Her brother told her she was crazy to get involved in a hopeless cause. Rose said she knew hopeless — hopeless had been her situation in London until Moh and the family had saved her life.

'But, Rose,' Akello said, 'where would you begin? And how would you protect yourself? Some of these street kids are just little thugs.'

But her experience in London had convinced her that people sometimes needed a helping hand to overcome a problem. Her attention was increasingly drawn to Nairobi's street kids. She decided to do something for them, but Akello was right — she didn't know how to begin.

When she found the Good Shepherd, and Faith, it all became clear.

CHAPTER 49

Rose handed the tiny child back to Faith Mburu — a woman with a mother's kind eyes and very African hips and buttocks. 'Thanks to you, little Charity is getting heavier every time I visit,' she said.

'It's more thanks to you and the food you are sending. All I do is cook it and serve it. Hunger does whatever else is needed.'

'Well, it's working, whatever the reason.'

Rose looked around the Good Shepherd Home. In the year since she'd found Faith, or Faith had found her — she couldn't recall which way it was — she had seen the corrugated-iron dormitories grow to accommodate over fifty street kids. The children, aged from the snotty-nosed toddler, Charity, to older teenagers, were housed, schooled and fed at least one decent meal a day by Faith.

'I am hearing nothing from Nairobi Council about the standpipe,' Faith said. 'I don't know what I can do.'

Mathare had no sewage or reticulated water. Faith collected drinking water from a standpipe over a mile away, and Nairobi River served for washing and cleaning purposes.

'What about Mr Kalonzo, the head of utilities? I

spoke to him last week. He promised to come see you.'

'Promises, ah? Who in the council keep their promises? But I will go to see this Mr Kalonzo.'

'No, let me try again, Faith. You have enough to do.'

'Oh-ho! Look who's talking! This one who has a rush-rush job here and everywhere. No, Rose, this is my problem. You have been too good. Me, or my Henry, we will go to City Way.'

'Well, if I see Kalonzo first, I'll give him a piece of my mind. He promised me that standpipe would be there in a week!'

'Good morning, Rose.' The tall young man paused as he passed the two women.

'Hello, Moses. How are you today?'

'I am very fine, thank you.' He dropped his eyes to the packing-case timber that formed the walkway over the mud near the ablutions block. His shyness was almost palpable.

'How is business?' Like many of the street kids, Moses sold trinkets and second-hand magazines at the traffic lights at peak hour. Without Faith, the next step for homeless children like Moses would be pushing drugs.

'It is also very fine.'

'Good. I'm pleased to hear it.'

'Yes. Thank you very much, Rose.' He dared to raise his eyes to her for a moment before dropping them again to his muddy bare feet.

'So ... good luck.'

'Thank you, Rose. Goodbye, Rose,' he said, and ambled off towards the dormitory shed.

'Bye, Moses.'

After he had gone, Faith said, 'That boy is too old for the traffic lights. The office workers take pity on the little ones. But big boys like Moses have no chance.'

'He tries. And it gives him something to do.'

'And what else can he do, ah?' Faith shook her head. 'I have to keep my *pipa* of petrol locked away. The glue and petrol have cooked his brains, that one.'

'I know. And he's so shy. But maybe he'll get a job somewhere.'

'I hope so. Look at the size of him. Sixteen, and already like a full-grown man. I can't feed the likes of him for ever. He eats the *ugali* of five little ones.'

Rose wandered to the open doorway of one of the iron huts. The bed pallets of the previous night had been neatly stacked along the back wall and replaced by small desks and stools. The younger children were head-down over their school books. Two of Faith's volunteer teachers were patrolling the rows, stopping here and there to help.

The next room, of a slightly smaller size, was set up as a classroom for the older children. Beyond that was the older boys' dormitory, where bunks were mounted three-high in the long, narrow space — the top bunk mere inches from the corrugated-iron roof.

'How many more can you house, Faith?' Rose asked, returning to where Faith was brushing the hair of another preschooler.

'None. I worry about the disease, you know, the TB, and the hepatitis, and whatever we might catch from Nairobi River. Anyway, every bed is taken. I am turning away little ones who come looking for a place. I give them food, but they must go back to the street.' Faith looked up at Rose. 'What can I do, ah?'

Rose put a hand on her shoulder. 'Nothing more than you're doing, Faith. Nothing more without some help.'

Maina Githinji, the junior Minister for Tourism, listened as his secretary went through the day's new business. Firstly, there were the usual requests from the Tourism Board for more funds for their advertising campaign. This time it was to launch a documentary-style film for the European market. Item two was a letter from the National Parks authority pointing out that continued poaching in the parks and reserves was damaging the country's tourism potential, and wanting to know what his department planned to do about it. At the end of the long list, she finished with a reminder that his senior minister, Bonaparte Nabutola, was still awaiting an update on Maina's fundraising plans for the party. Maina thanked his secretary, and curtly told her she could leave the matter for his attention.

The problem was that Maina had *no* fundraising plans.

The usual process was that the member's supporters would organise a *harambee*, or communal benefit, to contribute to party funds. But Maina had no such group of supporters — apart from a disparate bunch of ageing soldiers, who had scattered throughout the country after leaving the forest. His years in the Mau Mau had isolated him from whatever family and tribal affiliations he might have otherwise been able to call upon for help.

In his Mara electorate he was virtually unknown. The recalcitrant Maasai cared more for their cattle than for anything else, including who governed them. Maina believed Kenyatta had chosen his electorate to test his young minister's mettle. The new president's motives in leaving him there were not so clear. Perhaps he was hoping for him to fail.

Kenya's founding president had made concessions in favour of Mau Mau freedom fighters, but when President Odhiambo came to power, the emphasis changed. Odhiambo was not beholden to, and had no affiliations with, the Mau Mau. In fact, they were now an embarrassment to a country trying to put the lawlessness of Mau Mau behind it in the interests of attracting foreign investments.

When Odhiambo declared Kenya a one-party state following the attempted coup in 1982, it made it easy for politicians like Maina to be re-elected. The difficulty was to retain the support of local party officials for his continued candidature. Without a successful *harambee* fundraiser, this would become very difficult. He desperately needed someone with influence among the Maasai.

In his pile of incoming mail was a letter from Harry Forsythe of Kipana Tours, asking for a meeting. Kip Balmain was well connected in the Maasai community. Maina began to see a plan emerging.

Maina Githinji's move from Internal Security to Tourism sent an ambivalent signal about his prospects within the government. Some said the move was a demotion; others said the appointment to the new and important tourism portfolio was a vote of confidence by President Odhiambo.

Maina's suite of offices was on Kenyatta Avenue, in central Nairobi, where Kip and Harry now waited while the receptionist buzzed her boss on the intercom.

'Impressive, eh?' Harry said, indicating the lavish reception area.

Kip followed his eyes to the old Abyssinian wall-hanging, alight with gold thread. 'Not so much impressive as nauseating.'

Harry groaned under his breath. 'Kip, ol' darlin', you said you'd behave.'

'I said I would be open-minded. That's as far as I go, but okay, I'll keep my mouth shut about the minister's grubby taste and waste of taxpayers' money.'

'Good boy. Just leave it all to Harry. I'll do the intros, make a little chitchat, then ease into the need for the minister's gracious assistance in getting our permit.'

'Mr Githinji will see you now,' the receptionist said as she hung up the phone.

'Thank you,' Harry said, smiling sweetly.

The minister's office was even larger than the reception area. Maina sat behind an enormous desk. Above him was the mandatory portrait of the President of Kenya, looking sternly down from a wall devoid of distractions. The recent official suggestion that portraits of the past president were no longer appropriate to hang in government offices had condemned thousands of Kenyatta's portraits to the rubbish bin.

A single notepad, an elaborate desk set and a file, neatly folded back to display the page where the minister was appending his signature with a flourish, adorned the glossy surface of the ebony desk.

'Ah, Harry, Mr Balmain, do come in,' said Maina, waving the men to the chairs opposite him.

'Thank you, Minister,' Harry said, bobbing affably on his way to the indicated seat. 'You remember Mr Kip Balmain, General Manager of Kipana Tours?'

'Of course. Good to see you again.' Maina reached across his desk and the three men shook hands.

Harry began his preliminaries, stepping through compliments upon Maina's advancement to tourism, to Kipana's gratitude, on behalf of the entire industry, for the government's promotion of Kenya as a tourist destination, and how important it was for the industry to continue to develop new tourism sites. By then he was well placed to launch into the reason for their visit, when the minister interrupted.

'We don't see you around Nairobi much, Mr Balmain.'

'No,' Kip agreed. 'I'm generally too busy running the operations. I leave most of the promotional work to Harry.'

Maina's eyes widened. 'Promotional work? You're the GM of Kipana Tours, surely paying your respects to the minister is not considered just *promotional*.'

'What Kip meant, sir, was —'

'I know what he meant, Harry.' Maina's stern countenance softened into a broad smile. 'Can't old friends have a little joke once in a while? No?'

Harry's anguish melted into a relieved smile. 'Oh! Ha ha. Yes ... a joke ... of course.'

Kip was intrigued by the expression 'old friends'. He was pretty sure the minister couldn't even remember him — it had been four years.

Harry turned to Kip, attempting to carry a laugh in his voice. 'A joke between old friends, eh, Kip?'

Kip smiled for Harry's benefit.

'Harry,' Maina continued, 'why don't you let me and my old friend Kip have a little chat?'

Harry's jaw dropped. 'A chat?' he asked, a doomed expression on his face. 'You want a chat with ... with Kip? Alone?'

'If you wouldn't mind.'

'Certainly. Of course! A chat ... with Kip.' He shot Kip a pleading glance before retreating to the door. 'By all means. I'll be just ...' He backed out and closed the door before finishing his sentence.

'He's right, you know, Mr Balmain.'

'Please, it's Kip. He is?'

'About the need for new tourism sites. Sites like the one you propose for the Shimba Hills.'

Kip raised his eyebrows. The minister had done his homework.

'A unique experience for overseas visitors. A chance to generate more foreign exchange.'

'Exactly,' Kip agreed. They were the precise words used in Harry's letter.

'I know all about your problems with the local authorities, Mr ... I mean, Kip. And I'm sympathetic.' He leaned back in his chair and, with his elbows propped on the armrests, began to tap his fingertips together thoughtfully. 'Perhaps we can help each other?'

Kip braced himself for the bargaining about bribe money to begin.

'You're a businessman — a successful businessman,' Maina went on, 'and I am in the business of politics, which is in many ways similar.'

'And no doubt costly for you to keep up appearances,' Kip said, tensing his jaw.

Maina's gaze descended from a point somewhere on the ceiling to rest on Kip. His thoughtful contemplation turned into an expression of confusion. 'I'm not sure I am with you,' he said, frowning.

'We can skip the preliminaries, Minister. I came here expecting to pay some tea money.'

'I think you misunderstand me, Mr Balmain.'

'Do I? It's how all you politicians work, isn't it?' He smiled at Maina's efforts to appear piqued. 'Let's not beat around the bush. Just tell me how fucking much, and we can get on with it.'

'That's been the *wazungus*' constant whine, ever since *uhuru*, isn't it? Guilty until proven innocent. The verdict is always against "the cheating black man". You want to know how much?' The veins on his temples stood out. 'You ask how much? Let me tell you, if I was serious you could not afford my help. Understand me? Your money would be useless.'

'If there's ever been a whine, it's from incompetent blacks such as yourself, who try to dodge fair criticism by branding everyone who disagrees a racist.'

'You dare to come into my office asking for help, then accuse me first of cheating and now for being incompetent?' Githinji's eyes blazed. 'Why you ungrateful ... I could have your business closed. I could have you run out of the country.'

Kip's jaw tightened in determination. 'Just because you're the beneficiary of a corrupt electoral system gives you no say over my life and no right to throw your weight around. I'm a Kenyan citizen. And you are a servant of the people.'

Githinji was fuming now. 'Your servant! Why you ... I am no servant of yours! Look at you! You've not changed since you were a snivelling child. I could have killed you all those years ago!'

'What . . . ? What the hell are you talking about?'

'Back there in the bush near Mt Kenya.'

Kip stared at him.

'Kip Balmain, from the Equatorial Hotel. The little *mzungu* who had no white friends to play with, so he came to the Kikuyu on the Grearsons' farm.'

'You! It *is* you! I thought you were dead. All of you. On that night —'

'On that night when the Home Guard burned my family to death. Is that what you were about to say?'

Kip stared at him. 'Yes,' he said, stunned. The resemblance was there. He just couldn't associate Maina with a child he had thought long dead.

'Well, I didn't die there. Me — I'm here.'

'Everybody searched for you, all of you, but . . . how . . . how did you survive?'

'Survive? Nobody could call it surviving. In the jungle it was a living hell. The Mau Mau made no concessions to a boy.'

'You must have only been about thirteen years old.'

'Twelve.'

Kip recalled that losing his only companion — he could not honestly call him a friend — had left him devastated. When he'd heard the Home Guard had committed the crime — men of his own colour — Kip had felt he must bear some of the blame. White Kenyans were his tribe.

'I . . . was sorry about your family. I'm sorry we couldn't help.'

Maina closed the file on his desk. 'Nobody could help. It was done. It was the times.'

Kip rubbed his chin. 'Look, maybe I've been a bit hasty here. You were about to ask me something and I . . . well, what were you going to say?'

Maina's eyes were still ablaze but he took a deep breath. 'You have some influence with the Maasai in the escarpment region of the Mara. I need some of that co-operation.'

'What do you mean?'

'As you are probably aware, I am the elected representative in the Mara electorate.'

Kip didn't want to acknowledge any interest in local politics. When he made no comment, Maina continued, 'You are an important man to these people.'

'I am an employer, yes,' Kip answered guardedly. 'And we send our tour buses to the Maasai villages for our guests to buy souvenirs.'

'And they do quite well out of it. Therefore, you have influence with them, and their chiefs.'

'Perhaps I do.'

Maina nodded. 'Let me get to the point. There is the matter of a *harambee* for KAAB. I would like you to ask the Maasai chiefs to sponsor me.'

Kip had learned to mistrust power figures at an early age. He was sceptical about Maina's request for help in such an important matter. It was uncharacteristic. 'Why should I?' he asked cautiously.

'As I said before, we are businessmen, you and I. You help me; I help you.'

Kip remembered well enough that the young Kikuyu boy could be manipulative, and he had no expectation that the years in the forest with the Mau Mau had made him less so. But he thought his assistance to arrange a *harambee* with the Maasai was a fair trade for assistance to get approval for the Jungle Lodge. However, it was clear that Githinji was desperate, and it occurred to him that he might be able to press his advantage to win another concession.

'I will see what I can do. I know every Maasai chief, from Narok to the Mara River, personally.'

'Good. That's exactly what I need.'

'You've missed my point.'

Maina wrinkled his brow. 'What are you saying?'

'I'm saying, how many of them do *you* know?'

The minister lifted his pen and studied it. 'They're Maasai. Would you expect them to welcome a Kikuyu?'

'You could try. You could even try listening to their needs. They genuinely need help.'

'What kind of help?' the minister asked warily.

'Basic stuff. Health is a big issue. The clinics are disappearing.'

Maina sat in silence for some time, flipping the pen through his fingers. After a few moments he seemed to have come to a decision. He sat forward and said, 'Tell me who I should talk to.'

Kip nodded, satisfied that Maina had nibbled at his bait. 'There is an old Maasai woman, a *very* old Maasai woman, on the outskirts of the Mara . . .'

CHAPTER 50

Rose slowly put down the telephone and stared at it. It had come: the modelling assignment she had been dreading — and dreaming about.

Harry Forsythe had sounded like the same Harry from years ago. He had hardly even conceded that four years had passed, launching into his spiel and belatedly welcoming her back to Nairobi. Her boss had told her to deal directly with the client, but she had expected that when she rang him, Harry would have changed his mind — as he so often did. But Harry was adamant that she was the right person for the job — a promotional video for Kipana Tours. Kip's Kipana Tours.

It had briefly crossed her mind that she could refuse the assignment. It was a luxury she could only recently afford, having returned from London with very little cash.

It had been difficult to save in London. When she finally climbed out of the gutter and rehabilitated herself, she found her scarred left leg limited the type of assignment she could win. Although the agents complimented her stunning features, and said her story of the crocodile attack in her childhood was interesting, even exciting, they needed perfect legs for catwalk work. She got by on the less glamorous side of the profession, doing studio shots for merchandise, and in-store cosmetic displays.

After returning from London it had taken weeks to secure her first modelling assignment; months to earn enough to move out of Akello's apartment. At twenty-six she was past her modelling prime. It was the eighteen year olds who were in demand as the latest teen fashion trends swept East Africa. Rose accepted every assignment that came her way. She had been on sites from Samburu in the north to Tanzania in the south; from the coast to the lake.

She had not seen Kip since returning from London, and that was by design.

Harry told her he had chosen her for this, his next big campaign, but later admitted it wasn't actually a Kipana campaign, but a Ministry of Tourism video to be shot at Kip's lodge in the Mara. It confirmed her suspicion that it wasn't Kip's idea to engage her. He probably didn't even know she was in Kenya.

Harry said it would be a great opportunity for her — she would be the main presenter. There was no doubt it would be a good contract, but that was not the reason Rose had agreed. She dreaded the moment when she would meet Kip and explain her actions in London, but she ached for the chance to see him again.

When Harry arrived at her apartment in his Land Cruiser, she was already onto her third change of clothing, and made him wait while she threw on another outfit, this time something that wouldn't show the grime of the journey.

It seemed to be to no avail. When they arrived at the Mara Escarpment Lodge four hours later, she felt she looked like a dust devil had hit her.

Then she caught a glimpse of Kip. He seemed remarkably serene, chatting with a group of workers in the gardens by the edge of the pond. She, on the other hand, was a nervous wreck and bolted for her tent to make emergency repairs to her appearance.

Half an hour later she emerged in a pair of white stretch slacks and the pink top she felt best suited her colouring, but Kip had disappeared.

Kip sat in the dust under a full sun, swatting at flies as the conversation ambled from one Maasai *moran* to another about whether they should perform for the *mzungus*' cameras. Debate among the Maasai was a desultory affair, usually conducted without passion, which was fortunate, since the warriors went nowhere without their war clubs, long spears and the cruel, short-bladed *simis* used in close combat.

From long experience he knew the negotiations with the Maasai to help with the promotional video would take time. It wasn't because they were reticent — the young warriors were quite vain, and loved the opportunity to dance and demonstrate their hunting skills — but because everyone had to have a chance to enter into the collaborative process. It was Maasai democracy at work.

Normally he would have been patient, but he was hot, and the flies were worse than usual. But most of all, Rose's arrival at the camp earlier that afternoon had unsettled him. He had expected her, but after four years he wasn't prepared for the effect she still had on him.

She looked better than he remembered her in London's cold grey light. She had added a little weight to the body he could still vividly recall writing in passion beneath him. The extra pound or two would improve the fullness of her breasts and the curve of her thighs. He thrust the vision from his mind as his body started to respond to the image he had conjured up.

He became annoyed, recalling how she'd seen him when she arrived, but had rudely darted away rather than having the manners to greet him.

The silence around him intruded into his thoughts.

'What?' Kip stammered, feeling all eyes around the circle upon him. They were waiting for his response to something that had been said. 'I'm sorry, what did you ask?'

Their leader repeated his question. 'It is agreed we will dance, and we will find your lions. Our first price is three cows and five goats.'

Kip nodded thoughtfully. Their price was well within budget, but he would have to spend another half-hour or so going through the motions of the bargaining. If not, he would not be respected. Since the government had prohibited the Maasai from killing a lion as part of their rite-of-passage initiation, the Maasai were starved of the chance to hunt lion. His request to simply find one, and go through the motions of the kill, was a welcome opportunity.

When the haggling over price was concluded, he would then have the difficult task of convincing the parochial Maasai that they should listen to their representative from Nairobi, whom he would introduce to them in a few days.

Kip sighed and said, 'Ah ... I am sorry, brother, but that price is impossible.'

The leader nodded and exchanged a few words with others around the circle. In a few minutes he turned to Kip again. 'We can talk about this price,' he said, nodding encouragingly, 'but my brothers first want to know how many lions are needed?'

On his drive back to the lodge, Kip revised the points he would raise when the inevitable meeting with Rose occurred. He had already constructed and abandoned a dozen stances he could take, ranging from wounded outrage to aloof disinterest. His latest tactic was to confront the issues directly; to be firm, but not lose his temper. He would be methodical, outlining the events in London, and why he'd had good cause to be upset and leave as he did. Above all he would retain his dignity.

Finding no sign of her as he passed through the reception area, he hastened to his tent. It wasn't that he wanted to continue to avoid her, but he thought he would not be at his best until he had showered and dressed. But Rose caught him by surprise.

'Hello, Kip,' she said, startling him in spite of her small voice.

'Oh! H-hello, Rose.'

'I'm sorry, I didn't mean to sneak up on you. Did I give you a scare?'

'A scare? Me? No, not at all ... I was just ... walking.' He silently cursed himself. *What a pathetic start*, he thought, and he had completely ruined the opening lines where he would be cool, and friendly in a reserved kind of way. 'How are you, Rose?'

'I'm fine. It's good to see you, Kip. You look well.'

'Thanks. You do too.'

In fact, she looked sensational.

'Are you in a rush just now?' she asked.

'Um ... no. I was just going to take a shower. Before dinner.'

'Oh, then I'm sorry. I don't want to hold you up.'

'You're not holding me up.'

'I'm not? But I thought you said you wanted to take a shower?'

'Well, yes, I did but ... What do you want to talk about?' Again he winced inwardly. He had handed the initiative to her. The conversation was not going at all as he'd planned it.

'I have ... I just wanted to ... here.' She shoved a handful of pound notes at him.

'What's this all about?' he said, thrusting his hands in his pockets without touching the money.

'It's the hundred pounds I, um, borrowed from you in London.' Her gaze was on the fistful of notes, rather than making eye contact with him. 'I've had it all this time.'

'I don't want the money. Do you think that's all it was about? The money?'

'Yes. No,' she stammered. 'I don't know. I was all mixed up back then. And when I went back to explain, you were gone.'

'It didn't look like you were going to miss me for long.'

'What do you mean?'

'I mean, I saw you with your boyfriend that same night. Arm in arm like old pals.' He tried to keep the spite out of his voice, but it crept in regardless.

'Boyfriend? I don't know what you're talking about.'

'Rose, I don't know why you stole the money —'

'I didn't steal it. I ... I had an emergency, and there was no time to explain.' Her eyes were brimming with tears now.

'. . . and maybe you had a good reason, but I thought we had something between us back then . . . something important.'

'We did. I felt it too, and we —'

'But when I saw you with that guy, I realised I had been taken for an idiot. You were only interested in what you could get out of me. Thank God I worked it out before I got in too deep.'

Tears rolled down her face. 'How can you say that?' she said in disbelief. 'How can you believe I could be so . . . so . . .' She turned and ran towards her tent.

Faith Mburu walked down the dusty Mathare back street towards her home, so dispirited she could not muster the zeal to chase the neighbourhood children from their play in the pool of putrid water filling the huge pothole running the width of her street. On her good days she would lecture them on the dangers of playing in potholes that carried the effluent of the scores of ramshackle squatters' dwellings in the street. But today she lacked the energy. Trying to convince Mr Kalonzo of the Nairobi City Council to put a standpipe in their street had consumed it all.

It was a never-ending task, chasing children from putrid potholes, because there were hundreds, perhaps thousands, throughout the Mathare area. Each one held a potentially fatal dose of cholera, or one of several other vile diseases. Instead, she resigned herself to treating the diarrhoea and infected wounds when the mothers arrived at her house with their sick children.

Faith continued to think of the Good Shepherd Home as her house even though it was now unrecognisable as such. Six years before, when her own children were small, they began to bring home little friends who had nothing to eat and nowhere to sleep. Like any mother, Faith shared what she had at the table and let them stay the night. But the children would bring them, and others, back again. Soon there were a dozen almost permanent guests crammed into Faith's modest house, and she had room for no more. But still the children came.

Faith and Henry owned a vacant block of land next to their house — a legacy from her grandmother — that they planned to sell to support their old age. With the help of neighbours, she and Henry had transformed their pension fund into a dormitory, kitchen and schoolhouse using materials scrounged from all over Nairobi. It grew and improved to the stage where Faith could not feed her extended family. Then she met Rose Nasonga, and the Good Shepherd Home for orphaned or homeless children was established, with its single asset — the title to a quarter-acre block of land in Mathare — transferred to the Good Shepherd Home Trust Account.

When she got back, the boy, Moses, was waiting for her at the gate.

'Where is she?'

'Where is who, Moses?' she asked, already knowing the answer.

'Rose. Where is Rose?'

'She is not here today, Moses.' His infatuation was becoming a nuisance. He arrived early on the days he knew Rose would come, and didn't leave until she was gone. On days when she didn't come, he would hang around, disturbing the other children's studies until Faith chased him away. 'Don't you have something else to do other than standing around the gate like a beggar?'

'But she said she would come on Tuesday. It is Tuesday already and she is not here. She said she would come.'

Moses had probably overheard the conversation she'd had with Rose about coming on Tuesday. Since then, Rose's plans had changed. 'She's on safari for a few days, Moses. Now go away and don't disturb these children in their studies.'

'On safari? Where? She said she would be here.'

'Never mind where, she's not here.'

Moses looked panic-stricken. Having pity on him, she said, 'She's up at the Masai Mara with a man who takes movie pictures. Now go.' Faith shook her head and walked up the path, past a classroom where a chorus of childish voices droned through the seven-times table.

Moses wrung his hands as he watched Faith walk towards the house. His mind was in a turmoil. How could Rose forget him and go away with someone else? What would she be doing with him at the Masai Mara?

He had no idea of what might be at the Masai Mara, but he imagined a beautiful place with flower gardens, and waterfalls, and people serving drinks beside a swimming pool like the ones he had seen in his magazines.

He began to pace up and down the boards outside the classroom. The volunteer teacher called to him. 'Moses? If you are not coming in, please move away from the door.'

He stared at her for a moment then dashed out the gate, a red rush of rage consuming him. The Good Shepherd Home had tricked him again. They should have told him where she was going. She might have wanted him with her; instead she was with the man with the camera. He, Moses, was her friend, her protector. How could she go there without him?

He ran out the gate, down the potholed street to the bridge, where he clawed at the dirt beside a pylon.

He quickly unscrewed the plastic bottle containing the gold liquid and took a long sniff. His head spun. He took another deep inhalation.

The world became blurred.

Rose came to him from a red haze.

CHAPTER 51

Maina followed Kip through the gate into the thornbush-protected enclosure forming the Maasai's *enkang*. He felt like the Biblical Daniel in the lion's den. Sullen female eyes peered at him from every hut, while the *moran* stood in groups, their withering arrogant stares evaluating the Kikuyu who dared to enter their domain.

He wore slacks and a plain white open-necked shirt. He thought that made him look too much like a businessman, so he had added a few beaded necklaces and other paraphernalia. It was still not right, and at the last moment he had grabbed a Kikuyu spear that he had been given when in the forest with the Mau Mau.

Kip had said 'Are you mad?' when he saw his regalia.

'I don't want to walk into a Maasai village looking like a city Kikuyu,' he had replied. 'Anyway, the ostrich feathers mean peace.'

Kip had looked dubious. 'I hope the *moran* know the signals.'

'They will,' he'd replied.

Now, looking around the fierce young faces surrounding them, he hoped the *moran* were as familiar with Kikuyu customs as their fathers were.

Near the centre of the thornbush *boma*, the pens stood empty, but the pungent odour of cattle dung and urine attracted an enormous mass of flies that swarmed to any place that might offer moisture. Maina and Kip swatted ineffectively at them, but the Maasai, including their children, whose lips and eyes crawled with them, were impervious to their annoyance. Maina had an almost uncontrollable urge to swish them away from the children's snotty noses and running eyes, many of which showed the red rim of infection.

The Maasai and the Kikuyu had been hostile neighbours for generations — almost since the Maasai came down the Great Rift Valley centuries earlier. They stole each other's cattle; they abducted each other's women. Retaliatory raids followed in a relentless sequence until the British arrived to impose the *Pax Britannica*. An uneasy truce existed until independence, when sporadic and bloody uprisings returned — the most recent during the previous election campaign.

When the new government imposed a Kikuyu upon them, the Maasai had fumed. They never forgave Kenyatta for the affront and, until this day, they had never permitted their representative on their land.

Maina understood the risk Kip was taking. He had used all his credibility to coax the proud elders into permitting him to bring Maina into their *enkang*, but both shared the risk that Maina might inadvertently say or do something that would ignite the barely contained hostility of the warriors.

They stopped outside the central hut, where Maina suspected the *laibon* and his principal wife lived.

'Where is he?' Maina whispered.

'She's making you wait.'

'She? I thought —'

'Not here. This is Naisua's *enkang*. I thought you needed a more favourable atmosphere to get your act together before we go to the more hostile places.'

'More hostile?' Maina cast a glance around. Every eye seemed to carry venom. Even the older children, taking their lead from the silent enmity of their elders, fingered their herding staffs and glared at him.

'Here she is,' Kip whispered to regain his attention. '*Sopa*, Naisua.'

'*Hepa*, young Kip. Welcome.' She eyed Maina before addressing him in fluent Swahili. 'So this is our man in Nairobi.' It was not intended as a question, and he made no reply, but the old woman continued to appraise him. 'My friend has asked a great favour to allow you here today. I hope you appreciate it. And having made this journey for the first time, I hope you have something to say.'

Maina was impressed with the old woman. In the main, Maasai men did the talking.

'I have come to speak, but also to listen,' he said.

'A rare gift. Do you have it?'

On first appearances, she had seemed extremely fragile. Most women of her great age would be preparing for the time when the tribe would take her outside the camp to let her die. But Naisua was obviously not preparing for death. As they spoke, Maina became aware of an inner strength that seemed to shine from the old woman's intense black eyes.

'If you'll allow me, I hope to show you,' he said at last.

Naisua nodded, and permitted the lines of a small smile to crease her face. She turned to her people and raised her hands, the skin of which was like old parchment stretched over the bones of a bird's wing. The throng, which had grown while they talked, came to a hush. Her reedy voice lifted and carried to all. When she'd finished addressing her people, she stepped back without a further word and nodded for him to commence.

Maina ran his eyes over the crowd and tried to resist the urge to swallow. The *moran* stood in small groups, their spears held loosely at their sides. Old hags chewed on their gums and spat in the mud. There was not a friendly face to be found. He turned briefly to Kip, who looked nervous but nodded encouragement. His reputation was at stake as much as Maina's.

Maina took a step forward and stood erect. He lifted the spear above his head in one hand and began in a firm voice. 'I am a Kikuyu.' He immediately had everyone's attention.

'In the past we have been enemies, you and I. We have fought. We have made peace. We have broken truces, and we have fought again.

'I am a Kikuyu. I cannot change who I am. But if I could, I would not.' He paused for a moment, assessing his audience. The silence was absolute. 'I would not change because I am proud to be a Kikuyu. As you are proud to be Maasai.

'We,' he swept his spear-arm to encompass everyone present, 'must take pride in ourselves. It is pride, and the confidence it brings, that help us overcome difficulties.

'As I have travelled through Maasailand these few days, I see you are like many Kenyans today. You are having difficult times. There is no shame in that. Many of us are suffering. But we are a new nation, and we only have each other to change things.

'In the old days before many of you were born,' he turned towards the young warriors, 'when times were difficult, we Kikuyu raided you, our neighbours, to take what we needed. Or you Maasai would raid us. Then the cycle of bloodshed would begin. In the end, nobody won. Mothers lost their sons. Men lost their fathers and friends. In war, everybody loses.

'Not today. Today we are not Kikuyu or Maasai, or Luo or Turkana … we are Kenyans.' He thrust his chin forward. 'We are Kenyans and, like the *Mzee* said: *Uhuru. Harambee.* We are free; let us help one another!'

He paused for breath. Not a sound came from the crowd. He didn't expect emotion from the Maasai, but it was disconcerting to receive no sign of their mood. He might be inflaming their anger into a murderous pitch. He was gambling with large stakes.

'I am not asking you to like me. Even old enemies can proudly stand side by side. What I am asking is a chance to be a good neighbour to you, my former enemy.

'In Maasailand I have seen many sad things, and what I can see here today also makes me sad. I see sick children.' He ran his eyes around the women's circle. 'I see children who should be at school, but are not. I see old ones who are weak and need help.

'I am only one man, and I cannot promise to change the world in a day, or even in a month. Some things may take years to accomplish, but nothing will be done unless someone makes a start. With your permission, I will make that start. I will listen to your problems. I will do everything I can.' He lifted his head to see over all. 'This I promise you.

'I have spoken enough. Now I will listen.' He lowered his spear.

Nobody moved. Nobody spoke. Maina scanned the assembly, searching for someone who might need a little encouragement to voice a comment. Behind their eyes, nothing had changed.

Finally Naisua came forward to stand by him. Speaking in the Maa language, her thin voice again carried to all parts of the crowd. When she had finished, she said to Maina, 'We have listened. We have heard.' She turned away.

Maina was crestfallen. *Is that all?* he thought.

But she turned to Kip and said, 'He did not lie. He can speak well.' She turned to Maina then, with a crooked smile, and added, 'And we have heard. We will come to Nairobi when we are prepared to let you hear our needs. Then we will see if you can listen as well as you can talk. In the meantime, we will have our *harambee*, we will sell some cattle, and we will send the money to help you stay in your job.'

Kip wandered into the dining area to find a cup of tea. Harry and Patrick, the director, were already there, engaged in an excited conversation.

'Kip, she's a natural!' Harry said as he joined them.

'She is?' Kip assumed he was talking about Rose. Harry and Patrick had been filming in the Mara that morning.

'Abso-*fucking*-lutely! I tell you, she could have you eating right out of her hand on screen. Isn't that right, Patrick?'

'Quite so.' Patrick nodded enthusiastically. Patrick O'Mara was the director of the production — a graduate of the Nairobi School of the Arts — and, as far as Kip could ascertain, a man without a single strand of body hair. Head, eyebrows, legs and, Kip imagined, all parts between were shaved bare every day.

'Seriously, Kip, Patrick's increased her part in the film so that she's now the focus of the entire production. He's hardly had to make any second takes. She just presents so well. And on screen she's even more gorgeous than ever.'

'Sounds like you're in love?'

'Sadly, she won't have a bar of Harry these days. Must have lost my touch.'

'Shame. What's next on our little starlet's itinerary?'

'Just some fill-in shots tomorrow,' Patrick said. 'You're welcome to come, of course, but your big contribution comes with the Maasai shots, and the lion.'

'Day after tomorrow would be good. I'll need time to complete Maina's grand tour of Maasailand.'

'Speaking of Maina, here he comes.'

Maina was wearing his politician's smile. 'Good afternoon, everyone,' he said, nodding his greeting.

'How was your game drive?' Kip asked.

'It wasn't a game drive,' Maina said, taking a seat at the long table. 'I went to Narok to inspect the health clinic there.'

'Really?' Kip said, exchanging a glance with Harry. Kip had noticed a change in Maina's attitude since seeing him in action at Naisua's *enkang*. He actually seemed to take an interest in what he heard from the various villages they visited.

'Gentlemen,' Patrick said, leaning across the table at them. 'When Rose arrives I'll go over the last few scenes, but before she does, I can tell you I'm very pleased with progress to date, but there may be a problem with the big lion scene.'

The segment was intended to show the Maasai culture, ending with a scene of a mock lion kill to give Rose a dramatic backdrop for her piece to camera.

'What kind of problem?' Maina asked.

Patrick paused for dramatic effect, looking around the table at each of them before saying, 'She refuses to do it.'

'She what?' Harry exclaimed.

'Doesn't like animals, apparently.'

'Doesn't like bloody animals?' Harry spluttered. 'But she's a fucking African!' He shot a glance at Maina. 'Sorry, Maina.'

'That's what she said,' Patrick continued. 'She doesn't like animals, but will do it on one condition.'

'What's that?' Harry asked eagerly.

'She said she would only do the scene if —'

'Here she comes,' Kip said.

'Leave this to me, everybody. Harry can handle her.'

'Good luck,' Kip muttered as he noticed Rose's expression. She had a face like thunder.

Rose gave Kip a brief glance before plonking herself on a chair, folding her arms and waiting for someone to speak.

'Thanks for coming, Rose,' Harry began. 'Patrick is about to go over the last scenes, including the big climax with the Maasai and —'

'I'm not going anywhere near lions.'

'But, sweetheart ... why not?'

'I don't like lions. In fact, I don't like any wild animal. I don't trust them. Just leave me out of it.'

Harry wore a sick smile. 'Of course you can trust lions, darling. We'll be there. Kip will be there with a rifle, and half the entire bloody Maasai nation will be there, spears and all.'

Rose crossed her long legs, appearing determined to retain her stance, then as suddenly uncrossed them and sat forward in her chair. 'I'll do it. On one condition.'

Harry looked at Kip and Maina before answering. 'Okay. What is it?'

She turned to Maina. 'You agree to help me get a standpipe put up in Mathare.'

Twelve tall, gleaming black bodies strutted around the circle, lifting their shoulders as they filled their chests, then releasing a deep-chested grunt. 'Hoohn-hah,' they chanted. 'Hoohn-hah. Hoohn-hah.'

The cameraman pranced about, capturing shots of their colourful painted shields, their red- and white-ochred bodies, and the warriors' towering *olawaru* ostrich-feather headdresses. A proud few wore a lion's mane *olawaru*, proving that they had achieved their warriorhood in the traditional mortal combat with a lion, using only the customary weapons of spear, shield and *simi*. These days, the risk of arrest was added to the risk of their lives.

The Maasai formed a tighter circle, and one young man entered its centre and began to leap high in the air to the clapping and chanting of his age-mates. His loose red *shuka* flapped to reveal long, taut leg muscles. Each leap brought greater acclamation until, exhausted, he conceded and another dancer took his place.

When the director yelled 'Cut', the *moran* continued, undeterred, enjoying their sport. Finally, Naisua's shrill voice captured their attention, bringing their dance to an end so they could be loaded into the truck to continue their games, this time to find a suitable lion for the final camera shots.

Rose, in a magnificent gold dress, caught at the waist, but which revealed one long leg — her unscarred right leg — stood with Patrick, while the Maasai closed in on a shrub that supposedly concealed a lion.

The lion's presence wasn't even apparent to Kip, who stood, with Harry and Naisua, out of shot behind Rose and the camera crew. Maina, who had insisted on attending the afternoon's shooting, had decided to stay in the relative comfort of the minibus, which was parked with the truck a few yards away in a stand of fever trees.

Kip carried his rifle as a precaution against any unexpected trouble, but his eyes were continually drawn to Rose rather than in search of the lion. Their conversations had been polite if not warm since the argument at the lodge two days earlier. He hated the strained atmosphere between them, and it annoyed him that it still hurt to feel the loss of the intimacy they had so briefly, and delightfully, shared in London.

Harry leaned to whisper in Kip's ear. 'I bet these Maasai chaps are having a lend of us. There's no bloody lion in that little bush.'

Kip smiled. 'Isn't that what you said the day I met you in Nairobi — just before the lion charged us?'

Harry chuckled quietly. 'You're right, ol' darlin'. A couple of babes in the woods, we were.'

'Speak for yourself. You —'

A sharp snarl interrupted him. The Maasai had provoked the lion from its hide and had surrounded it, making threatening motions with their spears to herd it into the open. It was a magnificent male with a full black mane that shimmered as the mighty shoulder muscles tensed in outrage and fear. It crouched and snarled and made a mock charge, but the Maasai line held firm.

The director positioned Rose in front of the camera so that the scene with the lion and the Maasai could be captured over her shoulder. The camera began to roll but Patrick yelled, 'Cut! You there!' He pointed to the *moran* nearest the camera. 'Get out of the bloody way!'

The Maasai turned. The director waved his arms. 'I can't see the friggin' lion! Move!'

This wasn't as they'd planned it. Kip stepped forward, but the lion seized its opportunity. It bolted towards the gap made by the sidestepping *moran* and bounded towards the cameraman and Rose.

Kip quickly unshouldered his weapon, but Rose was in his line of fire. He flung himself at her, taking her to the ground as the lion, more intent on escape than revenge, leaped over them.

Kip was on his feet in an instant, his rifle at the ready, but the lion was heading towards the safety of the trees.

Maina stepped into the gap between the minibus and the truck to see what the commotion was all about. He stood directly in the lion's path of retreat.

'Maina! Get down!' Kip shouted, taking aim. There was no chance for error — the lion was directly in line with Maina. He hesitated a fraction, and fired an instant too late. The lion leaped at Maina, and took him with it to the ground.

Man and beast disappeared in a cloud of dust, but when Kip arrived a moment later, the lion was dead and Maina lay moaning, his clothing torn and red blood staining his bright tropical shirt.

The night sky was clouded, but when the moon broke through, the fever tree's long stark shadows stretched across the bare earth of the savannah. Somewhere in the bush a hyena had caught the blood scent and gave one of its sickening sniggers.

Harry had taken the minibus to the lodge to try to raise the Flying Doctor service, but, with no night-landing facilities, Kip held little hope that they could arrive before daybreak. In the makeshift shelter the *moran* had erected, Naisua was attending to Maina in the light of a paraffin lantern. She had given him some kind of herbal concoction that put him into a light sleep. From time to time he would emerge from it to moan and mutter.

Kip reached across the fire for the pot of boiling water, and threw in a few tea bags. 'Would you like some tea, Rose?' he asked.

She raised her eyes from the dancing flames and said with a sigh, 'Thanks.'

He poured the water into two cups, and handed her one.

'Does she know what she's doing?' she asked in a voice made husky by stress.

'What?'

'The old woman — does she know anything about medicine?'

'Naisua? Nothing at all about any medicine we'd understand, but she's been mending three generations of Maasai and, from what I've heard, she's pretty good at it. Anyway, she's our only chance.'

'I still say we should have taken him back to the lodge in the truck.'

'He'd be dead from loss of blood by now. At least Naisua's been able to stop the bleeding, and she's given him some concoction to dull the pain.'

The old woman's voice rose in a cracked chanting. Kip could see her passing her hands over Maina's motionless body. 'I think I'll go and check how he's going.'

'Me too,' Rose said, standing to stretch. She still had on the gold dress, but now she had Kip's rug wrapped around her shoulders.

They had to crawl under the fronds forming the roof of the shelter. Inside, the air was sweetened by an aromatic smoke, which left a tang of spice at the back of Kip's throat. The old woman's eyes were eerily bright, shining in the lantern light. She sat cross-legged beside Maina, staring into nothingness, while she chanted in her trance. She moved her shaven head from side to side, while her fragile hands passed the silver–green leaves of the *leleshwa* bush over his bare torso and limbs.

Kip noticed Maina's skin colour was not healthy; it had become a lifeless grey. There was no mistaking the severity of his plight — he was at death's door.

Kip understood that having staunched the bleeding and arrested the effects of hypovolemic shock, Naisua's next challenge was to beat the inevitable infection. The claws of a lion had small grooves that often carried the putrefying flesh of earlier kills. Kip had seen men die within hours of the onset of sepsis, and wondered how effective the old Maasai *laibon*'s medicine, her *dawa*, could be in these circumstances. He'd heard some tall tales of the old one's magic, but he was a sceptic. Superstition, or the effects of *chang'aa* — the locally brewed alcohol — were more likely the reason people thought they had witnessed a cure.

Naisua finished her chanting. Her eyes closed, and when she opened them the fire in them had gone. In its place was plain exhaustion. Her emaciated head seemed too heavy to hold and she crumpled forwards into her own lap — a bundle of elbows, arms and pointed shoulder bones.

A groan came from Maina, and he lifted his hand to rub his eyes.

Kip moved forward. 'Maina? Are you with us?' he said. A healthier colour had returned to the African's skin.

Maina frowned and looked about him before his eyes settled on Kip. After a moment he said, 'I could have killed you, you know.'

Kip was unsure if Maina wasn't still in some drug-induced stupor. 'You're raving. Take it easy.'

'There were no forest pig there. I took you there to kill you, because I had made an oath. But I was weak. I couldn't do it.'

Kip nodded and smiled. 'Don't fret — it looks like you're going to survive after all. Maybe you'll get another chance.'

Maina smiled and fell asleep.

Moses sat on the latrine at the Good Shepherd Home. The light outside the cubicle fell across the scrapbook resting on his knees. His scissors sat on one noggin of the unlined wall, and his pot of paste was on another.

The stench from the unsewered toilets did not bother him. He worked the scissors expertly, cutting around the outline of Rose's picture in the *Africa Today* magazine. He turned it over and carefully painted the back with adhesive before placing it on the new page and tapping it down firmly. Then he ran his fingers over the glossy paper to remove the air bubbles, feeling a rush of excitement as his fingers touched Rose's breasts in the photograph.

Moses flipped through the pages of his book. There was a photo of Rose pointing to an Uchumi Supermarket shelf stacked with Cashmere Bouquet soap. In the next she was wearing a short skirt, lounging across the bonnet of a Peugeot. He skipped to his favourite — Rose in a bikini, beside the pool of the Diani Beach Resort.

Moses closed his eyes and let his Rose speak to him.

It was nearly midnight when they got Maina settled in bed back at the lodge. If Naisua felt insulted by the sterile dressings Rose put on him, she didn't show it, but simply let one of her young *moran* help her into the truck for the drive back to their *enkang*.

Rose wandered into the dining area, aware of Kip following her. She felt drained, but knew she was too highly strung for sleep. The night retained the chill of a near disaster. It had unnerved her.

From far down by the river came the social rumblings of an elephant herd, mixed with the bellows of a bull hippo locked in a turf war with a rival. It was an added reminder — not that she needed it — of how easily Africa could reach out and snuff out the unwary. She shuddered and pulled Kip's rug around her shoulders.

'Cold?' Kip asked.

'No, it's just ... I don't know ... sometimes I get the feeling there's someone or something out there, waiting to pounce on me.'

'It's been a rough day. You'll feel better in the morning.'

'I don't think I can sleep. Not yet.'

'How about a nightcap to settle you?'

She was relieved he offered. She couldn't bear to be left alone in her present state of mind. 'That'd be good. A brandy, please.'

'Sure.' He ambled towards the bar. She loved the way he walked; it wasn't really a swagger, but there was an air of confidence in it, as if there was nothing beyond his capabilities. He always looked at home in the bush.

He handed her a tumbler of brandy. 'Cheers,' he said softly.

'Yeah, cheers,' she replied.

After taking a sip she said, 'Are you always so much in control of things, Kip?'

'What do you mean by "control"?'

'I mean, are you always sure you are doing the right thing; making the right decisions?'

'Of course not. Well … I do my best, given all the facts.'

'What if you don't know all the facts?'

'Then I make a decision based on what I have.' He sipped his drink, giving her a searching look. 'This isn't about today, is it? It's not about the lion attack, or Maina.'

'What do you mean?'

'It's about you and me in London, right?'

'It could be.'

'I thought so.'

'It could be that you made a big mistake then.'

'I don't think so.'

'You don't think so because you are so sure of yourself. But, as you've just admitted, you sometimes don't have all the facts, and maybe the decision you make, based on what you have, is wrong.'

'In London it was plain enough. You took my money and went off with your boyfriend. Simple.'

'I took the money, yes, but that was not my boyfriend. I couldn't understand when you accused me of that the other day. Then I remembered. The man you saw me with was my brother. He helped me home to our apartment that night.'

'Your brother?' He was silent for a moment. 'I didn't know ... I've never met your brother.' He swirled the alcohol in his glass, watching it catch the light. 'Why did you take the money, Rose?'

When she raised the matter, she knew this would be the inevitable outcome. She was equally certain she had to clear the air, and let the consequences fall where they may.

'I had an addiction,' she began. 'And ended up in the gutter.' She let him digest this for a moment, then told him the whole story, of how tiredness, and frustration, and finally desperation, had led her down the path to cocaine and heroin.

'I can't make any excuses, I had only myself to blame.' She took a deep breath. 'There were men,' she said, daring to read his expression when she revealed this. There was sympathy rather than revulsion in his eyes. 'But when you need something bad enough, you will do anything ... anything to get it.'

'Rose, I don't need to know that,' he said. 'More important is, are you over it?'

'I haven't touched any drugs since I got out of the clinic. Not even a cigarette.'

'I didn't know anything about it.'

'Of course you didn't know.'

Another silence.

'I'm sorry I misjudged you about that last night in London,' he said, 'but you should have told me. I could've helped. I thought we had something stronger than that between us. I could've done something.'

'I should have told you — yes, I agree — but there was nothing you could have done for me. I had to pull myself out of it. It's the only way. And I did.'

'We did have something there in London, didn't we, Rose?'

'I . . . I thought so.'

'Is it gone for ever?'

She couldn't answer that question — neither for him, nor for herself. It all depended upon Kip accepting her as she was — now knowing of all her human frailties — or not.

CHAPTER 53

'Rose! Rose? Is that you?'

'Yes, it's Rose speaking. Is that you, Faith?'

'It's Faith, Rose. Hello?'

'Yes, Faith, what is it?'

'Can you hear me, Rose? Hello?'

'Yes, I can you hear you,' Rose shouted. 'Go ahead.'

'Rose? *Aki ya mungu!*' Faith swore.

'Faith . . . it's Rose. Can't you hear me?'

'*Mzee!*' Faith had taken the telephone from her ear and was remonstrating with someone at the other end of the line. '*Mzee!* You need to get a *fundi* for this telephone. *Aki ya mungu*, I can't hear the person at the other end. What? And I gave you twenty bob already. You'll see me if I can't get through. This is an emergency!'

The line went dead.

An emergency. Rose knew it must be something important because Faith hated using the telephone — especially when she had to pay for it at the corner service station.

She grabbed her car keys and hurried outside.

Rose's Peugeot jolted and bumped over the potholes, now made much worse by the recent rains. She muttered an oath. It would be months before the council grader came round to fill the worst of them.

Turning into the street where the Good Shepherd was situated, Rose was amazed to see a council truck near the home's gate. Four men were watching while two others dug a deep hole beside the back fence. When she pulled up, she could see that the hole ran under the fence and, standing at its end, was Faith, a grin from ear to ear.

'Rose! You've come! I was trying to ring you just now, but that stupid telephone ... But look!' she said, pointing to the trench. 'Our standpipe has come!'

Maina sat in the back seat of his government limousine, drumming his fingers on his knee. He should never have agreed to the trip to Mathare. He had better things to do, and would have cancelled except that Harry Forsythe had left word with his secretary that he had arranged for the press to be present for what he had called the official opening.

Official opening! It was just a standpipe — a tap! But Maina was learning the importance of publicity, and he needed all he could get. The party machinery had him in their sights for relegation. More than one of his friends in the party had implied as much. They wanted his seat for a party hack with plenty of influence around Narok. Instead of attending the opening he should be working the numbers to shore up his support in the coming party preselections. But he would smile, turn on the tap, make what he hoped would be a quotable quote for the press, and be gone.

With luck he'd get a postage-stamp-sized report on page fifteen.

* * *

'Are you sure he's coming, Harry?' Rose asked, wringing her hands at the gate of the Good Shepherd Home.

Harry was pacing up and down the street. 'I hope so, or my name is mud among the press,' he said, glancing nervously at the small media contingent he'd cajoled into attending the event. 'I don't know how I let you talk me into arranging this, Rose.'

'Because you're a good man, Harry, and you know I need the publicity for our building program.'

'Yeah, well, if he doesn't show, or this falls flat, you can forget any more help from the Minister for Tourism, or the press corps for that matter.'

Ever since he'd brought Maina, Rose and Kip together for the tourism promo, Harry had become the unofficial publicity organiser for all of them.

'Are you sure he's coming, Harry?' It was Faith Mburu this time.

'Oh, don't you start, Faith. Harry's getting heartburn at the thought of it.'

'Never mind your heartburn, what about my children? They're waiting in their classrooms, all scrubbed up and wearing their best clothes. We've been rehearsing our song for a week.'

'I know, I know, Faith. I can't sleep at night. Those damn words go around and around in my head. What is it? *We love you, Mister Maina. We love you good and true. We love you, Mister Maina. And Good Shepherd blesses you.*' Harry rolled his eyes. 'And all for a lousy standpipe.'

'Two,' Faith corrected him.

'Right, two.' Harry nodded. 'How did you manage to get the second one on the outside of the fence?'

'Rose came and said the whole neighbourhood would be sharing our tap and it would be a very good deed to put another outside the fence.'

'The case of beer helped,' Rose said, smiling.

Harry noted one of the journalists peel back his cuff to peer at his watch. 'I wish I'd brought a case of beer for the guys from the press.'

Harry couldn't bear to imagine how Maina would behave if he arrived and there was nobody there to welcome him but a bunch of grubby kids.

Moses made a stumbling attempt to get to his feet but fell, rolling down the sloping banks under the bridge where the Nairobi River ran under Koma Rock Road, coming to a halt just short of the putrid water that acted as a sewer for half of Mathare.

He staggered to his feet and found his way, bleary-eyed, to the tarmac. Irate drivers on Koma Rock Road tooted angrily as he lurched dangerously into their path.

The previous night, and all of the day to that point, had been lost in a dream-filled stupor following his successful robbery of a service station. A rusty *panga* and a wild-eyed countenance had been enough to convince the attendant to fill a petrol can for him, and then fill his pockets with the day's takings. For good measure, Moses had grabbed some tubes of glue and industrial cleaners too.

His dreams had been again of Rose. She was an angel this time, wearing a long white gown tied with a gold braided cord. Her large feathery wings had fanned his sweating body as he lay among the discarded plastic bottles and carry bags under the bridge.

His path now took him to the Good Shepherd Home. He was driven by a simple urge, because the Good Shepherd was no longer his home, nor did Faith feed him these days as she had done long after he was asked to leave. In the back of his mind was the hope of seeing Rose — his angel.

He noticed it was raining. In fact, it had been raining all day, and he was already drenched from his half-hour's walk.

A small boy dodged in and out of the traffic, selling papers and magazines to passing motorists. Moses had given up running the gauntlet in the lines of morning peak-hour traffic, a stack of damp, dog-eared magazines under his arm. Nobody was interested in buying from him. The smaller boys got all the sales, and all the tips.

It was the opposite when he tried to find a job at the factories around Mathare. Although Moses was big and strong, it was the older men, with their experience, who won the positions. Some simply sent him away muttering '*Zumbukuku*'. But he was not crazy; he only needed a chance to show them what he could do.

It was the same with Rose. She didn't treat him seriously, even though she surely knew how much he loved her. If he only had a chance, she would know him better, and love him too.

He moved to the side of the road as a large black car approached from behind. It swished through the potholes, sending a wave of muddy water to lap up to his muddy shins.

The car stopped down the road at the gate of the Good Shepherd Home. Moses shuffled on, trying to catch a glimpse. The driver went smartly to the rear door and opened it for an important man in a black suit to climb out.

Moses stood in the mire and watched as Rose came to meet him. With her was a white man who looked very friendly towards Rose. Towards everyone.

Moses stared in disbelief. Rose had chosen another! How could she do this while knowing of his love for her?

After a long moment, Rose, her white boyfriend and the black man in the suit picked their way among the muddy pools and disappeared through the gate. Moses was rooted to the spot, his mouth hanging open in amazement. What could this mean? Was Rose in love with someone else? With a *mzungu*, of all people?

He sank to his knees and pounded the muddy waters into a froth of brown bubbles.

The envelope was from a firm of solicitors and was addressed to 'Rupert Laikipia Balmain'. It evoked bad news. When he saw the postmark, he knew what it would contain.

He took it to the sofa under the window to read it.

Dear Mr Balmain,
Re: The Estate of Marie Agnes Balmain
I write representing the firm of Metcalfe, McGrath, Murdock and Neave acting as executors of the estate of the late Mrs Marie Agnes Balmain.
As you are no doubt aware, Mrs Balmain passed away on the 3rd September 1986.
Under the terms of her will, drawn up in these offices and dated 14th August 1985, we arranged for the public valuer to compile a list of the estate's substantive assets. A copy of his

report is enclosed and you will note the estate is deemed to consist of:

One timber building of four (4) main rooms and a public bar ('The Equatorial Hotel');

Various furniture items, crockery, cutlery, various cooking implements, ornaments, & etc.;

A Barclays Bank savings account containing a small amount of cash, to wit: KSh 7500/-;

Personal effects (clothing, items of personal jewellery, & etc);

Hotel furniture and equipment (i.e., glasses, stools, & etc).

Kip flicked through the other documents. There was a copy of Marie's death certificate, with the cause of death said to be 'coronary occlusion', and the valuer's report. It said that the value of the building, fixtures and furniture had been assessed:

... for all practical purposes to be worthless. The estate therefore can be considered to consist of land value only, which I put to be in the order of 30 000 pound sterling at today's values.

Another enclosure referred to Marie's use of the name Balmain. It pointed out that the name did not appear on the marriage certificate, where Polter was used as her maiden name. The name on the death certificate was Sullivan, which, the letter explained, was the family name of her ex-husband, Ernest. The solicitor was satisfied that all three names referred to the same individual.

Kip returned to the letter, where it concluded:

As you are the single beneficiary of Mrs Balmain's will, we invite you to contact the undersigned at the above address at your earliest convenience to advise when you may assist us to conclude these matters.

I am,
Yours sincerely,
(Signed) David Sparkes
Solicitor at Law

CHAPTER 54

Harry took a bite of toast, and again congratulated himself on the front-page story in his copy of that morning's *Standard* newspaper. Accompanying a picture of Maina receiving a cup of water from one of the home's cute orphans was exactly the kind of publicity story he had promised:

> *Mr Maina Githinji, Minister for Tourism and the Member for Mara electorate, yesterday met the children of the Good Shepherd Home and tested the water from the first standpipe to be connected in the eastern Mathare area.*
>
> *Mr Githinji, seen above accepting the water from four-year-old Timothy Ondieki, said he was proud to be a part of the push to make clean drinking water available to the many unconnected lots in the Mathare area.*
>
> *He praised the workers of the Nairobi City Council for an excellent job, and also the Home's founder, Mrs Faith Mburu, for her wonderful work with disadvantaged children.*

The *Nation* ran a similar story on its page three, including a picture of Maina with Rose, who was described as one of Nairobi's foremost models and was sponsoring a building fund to provide a dining room and dormitory for the orphans.

Harry took a sip of tea, nodding with satisfaction. It was particularly pleasing because not only had Maina received the publicity he needed, but Harry thought he'd actually enjoyed hearing the children's song of thanks and seeing the raw pleasure such a simple act could bring to them.

Nanyuki was the colour of mud. A recent downpour had swamped the main street. Kip recalled that the short rains could be ferocious in Nanyuki. Flood levels were marked by a stain on doorposts and steps along the motley assortment of shops. The open drains had been washed clean.

On the road to the Equatorial Hotel, a grey mist clung to the bougainvillea spikes rearing above the stone fences, reducing even their flamboyant display to dull mediocrity.

By the time Kip had reached his old home, a wind had come up with the sun, which was peeping over the shoulder of Mt Kenya. One end of the hotel sign had dropped from its fixture, and the breeze raised a squawking sound where a loose sheet of corrugated iron rasped against an obstinate roof nail.

At the back of the building, he paused at the entrance he'd used as a child and pulled out the door key the solicitor had given him the previous day in Nyeri. After a moment fiddling with it, it turned in the lock and he pushed open the back door.

He braced himself for the feelings he expected the old house to provoke, but was not prepared for the emotional storm that hit him.

A wave of dread swept across more than three decades. He struggled to unravel his feelings because here, surely, was something important — a clue to his hidden self. Until that moment, when the gut-wrenching panic hit him, he had forgotten — no, he had never known — such a dread had existed. Somehow he had kept it suppressed so he could be like a normal boy.

Yet it was there now, and he knew it came from those locked-away childhood memories. It was in the house with him. The feeling was so strong he doubted he could have effectively suppressed it — but he had, until at age fourteen he turned away from it, and ran and ran.

As quickly as it had come, it was gone.

He took a deep breath.

The kitchen was just as it had been during his childhood. The bare timber dining table and four simple wooden chairs dominated the space. A large black cooking pot was suspended over the wood-fired stove. Cups hung from hooks in the open-fronted dresser.

The door to his mother's bedroom swung open with a loud creak. His mother's perfume, or the scent of her talcum powder, assailed him. Above the double bed, which now looked much smaller than he remembered it, was the picture of the Virgin Mary, her eyes raised to heaven, her hands lifted, pleading with the Almighty. She had a forlorn look on her face, which the artist had bathed in celestial light.

He slid the zebra skin from the large wooden storage chest at the bottom of the bed. The old purple chocolate box was there, tucked down one side. He carried it outside and sat on the back step, as he had decades before, glad to be in the welcoming warmth of the thin morning sun.

The letter inside the envelope addressed to Mrs Marie Agnes Sullivan, and bearing the letters OHMS, was brittle with age. He carefully unfolded it. It was from the Royal Air Force and regretted to inform her that her husband, Ernest Horace Sullivan, was missing in action, presumed dead. It briefly described the heroic mission Flight Lieutenant Sullivan was engaged upon when he went missing over Germany on the night of 15 August 1944. It contained nothing that Kip did not already know about his father.

The second, from a cousin living in a town called Mt Gambier, said that she was sorry to hear Marie was going to Africa, and asked her to be careful. She also begged her to write often.

He straightened the yellowed part of a newspaper page, which now contained a number of irregular holes. When he'd found it at age eight, he thought his mother had kept it to study the claimed benefits of Dr Thar's Ointment, which included easing the pain of strained muscles, a bad back and neuralgia. There was a picture of a man holding his back with a zigzag bolt of pain pointing at it. On the reverse of the clipping was a section of the Personal Notices for Saturday, 7 April 1946. One entry was circled. It read:

Ernie's Marie. Sorry everything. Need to talk. Must find my boy. He can be our son if you can forgive me.

It had an address in Glebe but a silverfish had eaten the number and first part of the street name. All that remained was '. . . sfield Street, Glebe'. He folded the paper and returned it to the purple chocolate box.

It wasn't much, but half an address was better than what he had found to date.

As a politician, Maina knew feigned gratitude when he saw it. Although he had only begrudgingly given his support to the construction of the standpipe, the genuine appreciation shown by everyone at the Good Shepherd Home for such a simple gift had touched him. The children were delighted with their new water tap, but what he found most humbling was the look of surprise in their eyes. Surprise, perhaps, because one of their own, and a government man to boot, had shown them a kindness.

Maina felt good about it too. In fact, he felt very good. He could not remember ever feeling so good about so simple an act. It was a novel sensation. But it was more than his philanthropic glow that prompted him to accept Faith's offer of a guided tour of the home's facilities.

The positive newspaper publicity following his first visit had won the attention of the President, who suggested Maina might like to follow up his good work while the press were in such an uncommonly benevolent mood. He also said that in these days of donor-country scrutiny, and the unwelcomed attention from the World Bank, it paid to show that the government was heeding the needs of the people.

His parliamentary colleagues 'and, more importantly, the members of the party preselection committee, followed the President's lead, and for days after the newspaper report Maina was slapped on the back and congratulated by people who had previously ignored him.

The President had agreed to Maina's suggestion that the government get involved in the home's building fund. He had told the President it had the potential to be another publicity coup but, he had to admit to himself, it was also because he wanted another opportunity to enjoy that unprompted appreciation from the children.

When he entered the first of the classrooms on Faith's guided tour, the children stood to attention and cried, 'Good morning, Mr Githinji', in a chorus of cheery young voices. It took Maina by surprise, and he stammered and cleared his throat a number of times before finding his voice to reply. The welcome was repeated in the other classroom where, as Faith explained, the older children were cramming for examinations.

'Not all will be able to sit the exam,' she said.

'Why not?' he asked.

'We don't yet have the money to pay their entrance fees.'

'Entrance fees?'

'For the examination. The government charges a fee to sit the exam.' She turned to him with a questioning look on her face. 'Don't you know that?'

He didn't.

After they had inspected the spotlessly clean washrooms, where small squares of soap sat on handmade wooden soap holders, Faith led him across the road to a cobbled-together shed they used to house their livestock.

Beside the stock pen the neighbourhood's refuse tumbled down the slope to the river. The stench was almost unbearable. A sinister flock of crows hovered on shiny black wings, making furtive dives to find titbits overlooked by the squadron of ugly marabou storks patrolling the garbage with hunched shoulders and grizzled heads.

Faith pointed to four fat pigs in the pens. 'Pregnant! All pregnant,' she announced proudly, as if she were personally responsible. 'We'll soon have dozens of piglets for sale and slaughter.'

The stench in the confined quarters was worse than from the rubbish dump. Maina wanted to be gone, but Faith was in full stride.

'Now you see this calf,' she said, pointing to a scrawny brindled animal in a small pen, 'if we can keep the feed up to him, he'll bring enough for two months of *ugali* flour.'

She had planted her fists on her hips, ready to defend her claim if needed. But Maina wouldn't dream of disputing it. He mumbled his congratulations, backing out of the shed and bumping his head on the door in his haste to get away.

He said he had seen enough, and suggested it was time to get down to the details of his visit. He sat with Rose and Faith and explained that the government would match the donations raised by the home's own efforts, shilling for shilling. He went through the process of accounting and gave them the names of people in his office who would assist them.

When the meeting was over, Rose walked Maina to his car.

'I never saw this side of you when we were together, Rose,' he said.

'What do you mean?' she asked.

'I mean your Mother Teresa side.'

'I could say the same about you.'

'This work you're doing for the home; your efforts to raise donations.' He lifted an eyebrow as he appraised her. 'You were always such a wild one back then.'

'We all grow up.' She walked in silence for a little longer before adding, 'It's too easy for children to get lost in this world. Too many things can destroy a life.'

Maina nodded. 'You know, I read something recently in one of those fancy American magazines, where the writer said that Africa is just hopeless. You know the kind I mean? He thinks he knows Africa because he lived here years ago — in the good old days. Anyway, he says too much aid money has spoiled us. We aren't interested in doing things for ourselves.' With a sweep of his hand, he indicated the collection of buildings on the other side of the fence. 'I think you and Faith have made him a liar.'

'I hope so. And I think I know the article you're talking about. He used to live in Uganda in the colonial days. He's been out of Africa for too long. Some of us care, and are doing what we can.'

They had reached the car.

'By the way, how are your lion wounds?'

'My lion wounds, is it?' He smiled. 'You make me feel like a Maasai. But my lion wounds are doing fine.' He peered intently at her. 'How are you?'

'I'm fine,' she answered casually.

'You forget, Rose, I was Minister for Internal Security. I still have my sources, you know.'

His smile persisted, but she couldn't raise a smile of her own. Eventually she dropped her eyes to the muddy road. 'I don't know what you're talking about.'

'I know that something, or someone, has upset you.' He opened the car door before turning towards her. 'Don't be so sad — he'll be back.'

'I don't know what you're —' she began again, but Maina interrupted her.

'Who's that?' he asked, as his eyes met those of an unkempt young man who he had noticed earlier in the day. He was lurking behind the home's stock pen on the other side of the road.

Rose turned to catch sight of him before he moved behind the pen. 'Oh, that's just Moses. He's one of our old boys. Hasn't quite learned to live without us, and Faith said it was time for him to stand on his own feet.'

'He looks like a thug.'

'He's not. He's one of those ones I was talking about just now. He got into bad habits with sniffing petrol, and he's, well ... he's just a little uncertain of himself. He'll be fine.'

'Okay, *sasa*. *Kwaheri*, my sister.'

'*Kwaheri*.'

He slammed the door. As the car splashed through the slush near the goat pen, he spotted the young man again. Maina had a sixth sense honed during his time living on his wits in the jungle. It had not been evident for many years, no doubt dulled by the comforts of city living, but something about the surly young man made the hackles on his neck rise in warning. He reminded him of a predator on the prowl.

The Peugeot came along the darkened street, splashing rainwater into its headlights' beam. Mathaiga's potholes weren't as deep as Mathare potholes, and instead of turning mud into mush, the rain made wafting clouds of steam that hugged the warm tarmac until the Peugeot chased them away with its passing breeze.

Moses knew Peugeots. They were very fine French cars — very popular with the *wazungu*. He thought that Rose should not be driving a *mzungu* car, but he couldn't remember the reason he felt that way.

So many times he would get these mixed-up thoughts. They went around in his head, driving him crazy, until he had to let them go. He had to let the thought about the *mzungu* car go too. It made his head ache.

He watched her open the door, but she remained sitting, reading something in the light of the cabin.

She was beautiful, yet she was a bad person. Moses remembered how she used to behave towards him, how friendly she was, but now she'd changed. She ignored him. She spurned him. It hurt him how she ignored him.

He felt a sensation in his foot. Blood made a dark stain on the wet tarmac. He had been kicking his toes into the edge of the pavement, shredding his skin into a bloody mess.

Rose climbed from the driver's seat and, as she walked towards her door, rummaged in her handbag for her keys.

A few moments later a light came on in a second-floor window. Rose appeared briefly to draw the shade.

Moses bent down and touched a dirty finger to one of his bloodied toes. He tasted it. Salty. A good taste. Clean, salty blood. It cleansed him. He felt pure.

He turned from the building, satisfied that he had found where she lived.

CHAPTER 55

Harry fell back on his chair. 'Australia! Hell's bells, ol' darlin', what do you want to do a thing like that for?'

'I found an address up in the old hotel in Nanyuki,' Kip said.

'Your father? Are you sure?'

'It was among a few of Mother's things.' For some reason he couldn't stop referring to Marie as his mother.

'When? How long will you be gone?'

'Friday. You'll be able to take care of the place. The paperwork for the Jungle Lodge is on its way. Just keep an eye on the clients. Mutua will be okay up at the Mara, but you'll need to give Kipchoge a hand at Laikipia — he's a bit gung ho for some people's liking.'

'How long will it be?'

Kip stopped rummaging in his desk drawer and turned to Harry with an uncertain smile. 'I don't know, Harry. All I know is, this is my last chance to find him, and I'm not coming back until I chase every lead to ground.'

Harry sighed. 'You've been on this case for a long time, ol' diamond. Good luck with it. Harry will look after the store. You go find your dad.'

'I've been thinking about our conversation up there in the Mara.' Kip held the telephone under his cheek as he stuffed his airline ticket into the travel documents folder.

'You were? What conversation?' Rose's voice was cautious at the other end of the line.

'Well, I thought we went a long way towards clearing up some of the misunderstandings.'

'Yes ... we did.'

He wasn't encouraged by her tone, but continued regardless. 'Well ... maybe it's a dumb plan,' he said.

'No, go on ... tell me.'

'Well ... I've been thinking. Maybe we should, you know, get together for a meal, or something. To finally clear the air. I mean, that's if you think it's a good idea.'

There was a moment's silence before she said, 'Yes, I think it's a good idea.'

'You do?'

'Sure. Why not?'

Again, he couldn't determine any enthusiasm in her tone.

'Oh! Good. Um ... how about Thursday?'

'I'm down in Mombasa on Thursday. Won't be back until seven, seven-thirty. Why not Friday?'

'I'm leaving for Australia on Friday.'

'Australia!'

'Yes.'

There was a long silence at her end. He wondered what was on her mind, and thought he should explain the reason for the visit, but decided against it. He could tell her at the restaurant.

'I can pick you up at the airport if you like,' he said.

'No. We might as well meet at the restaurant.'

Now he was sure there was something in her tone. 'Rose, are you okay?'

'Of course. Why wouldn't I be?'

He hated having difficult conversations over the telephone. It may be that she was a little cautious, given their earlier misunderstandings. 'How about the Trattoria?' he suggested with a sigh of exasperation.

'Okay. About eight.'

'See you there.'

'Bye.'

Thursday was a frantic day for Rose. The work for the Tourism Authority was on a tight deadline. She was whisked through the Old Town for a location shot at Fort Jesus, then over to Nyali for a short piece to camera on the delights of Mombasa's beach resorts.

All the while her mind was in turmoil. Why had he bothered to ring if he was intending to leave?

She had heard of white Kenyans who'd made their money in Africa, then suddenly decided to 'go home' to enjoy it, even though they'd had no other home than Africa for their whole lives. Kip's suggestion that they meet one more time was just so he could leave with a clear conscience.

The more she thought of it, the angrier she became. By the time she arrived at her last assignment, at the Tamarind Restaurant, she was preparing the speech she would make when they met at the restaurant. She would tell him to go to hell — or words to that effect.

The director flitted around, bossing his crew members and restaurant staff alike. Time was wasting away. The sun was setting and he wanted to have the floating restaurant's *dhow* in the right place to capture the remaining light.

Rose sat despondently at a table overlooking the water where, below her on the wharf, the red crab's-claw sail of the *dhow* caught the setting sun. It reflected on the metallic surface of the old harbour. In the background even the old fort's glowering ramparts, rock-solid and stoic, seemed to float above the water, shimmering in the golden glow of sunset.

A cooling breeze came from the Indian Ocean to flutter the frills on the sun umbrella above her. Somehow it all seemed just perfect. It was only she, Rose, who was flawed — the failings of her past conspiring to turn away the man she had wanted since she was a girl.

Kip arrived early. He didn't trust his booking and was anxious to get one of the tables overlooking Wabera Street. He wanted the night to be perfect. The three small tables on the balcony not only enjoyed the night air, they had an intimacy that the crowded interior lacked.

Kip had given a great deal of thought to Rose's tragic story, and realised he had been too quick to suspect her of cheating on him that last night in London. If he'd had the courage to confront her, the whole misunderstanding could have been avoided. But he'd been too quick to condemn her, and flee. Indirectly, he had contributed to her heartbreaking downhill slide.

The manager came onto the balcony with a red-and-white chequered napkin over his shoulder and a menu under his arm. 'All alone tonight, eh, Mr Kip?'

'Oh, hello, Tony. No, I'm waiting for my friend to arrive. She's coming in at about seven o'clock from Mombasa. I'm a little early.'

'Ah, thatsa better.' He flicked the corner of his napkin at invisible crumbs on the red-and-white chequered tablecloth. 'I said to Angela, "Whatsa happening here with Mr Kip?" And she say, "Donna worry, some pretty lady will come along."'

Kip smiled. 'Well, I certainly hope so. I haven't been stood up for years.' He took the menu and handed back the wine list. 'Just a Tusker for me, thanks, Tony.'

'No-a worries.' Tony straightened a chair at a neighbouring table, and disappeared inside.

Kip checked his watch. Seven-twenty. Rose would be stepping down from the aircraft around then. She would probably be wearing one of the tight skirts she favoured for business wear. He could see her move across the tarmac like a leopard on the prowl, her stride restricted by the skirt but only exemplifying her long legs and perfect curves.

He began to watch for taxis coming up Wabera Street. By eight o'clock their numbers had dwindled to one every five or ten minutes.

He used Tony's telephone to call the airport. *'Yes, sir, the 6 p.m. flight from Mombasa arrived on time at 7.05p.m.'*

His fourth Tusker arrived. Tony poured it into an icy glass. 'Wanna have some garlic bread while you're-a waiting, Mr Kip?'

'No thanks, Tony.' He thought about making a joke about his late date, but his sense of humour had failed him.

He checked his watch again. Eight-forty.

He sipped at his beer, watching the level fall and promising himself he would leave when the glass was empty.

And to hell with her.

Somewhere into the fading light out over the Indian Ocean, Kip finally managed to get control of his racing heart. He slipped the *Emergency Exits* card back into the seat-back pocket and tried to relax.

His fear of flying was a well-kept secret, although he suspected that Harry knew, and had mercifully resisted teasing him about it over the years. He'd had to admit it to Diana in the early days, because she couldn't understand why he was so reticent about travelling overseas to drum up business. In those days, she did the overseas marketing — a task that Harry had undertaken with relish in more recent times.

He pulled out the in-flight magazine and riffled through the pages. Advertisements for expensive perfume and gold watches dominated. He regretted not having the time to buy a book. His last few frantic minutes were spent trying to reach Rose at her office, and then at home. He'd no concept of what he would say, but the thought of flying seven thousand miles from her added urgency to his need to know why she hadn't joined him at the restaurant.

He suddenly felt light-headed at the thought that he may actually be in love with her. The realisation made him at once elated and fearful that, by his departure, he had somehow put everything in jeopardy. At forty-two he was old enough and, he fervently hoped, wise enough to distinguish between love and the euphoric effects of low pressurisation.

Maybe it was his optimism at finding his father at last that was stimulating his imagination. He had a good chance to do so because he had a city, a suburb and half an address — his best lead yet. His mind roamed unchecked over the possibilities that might arise after finding him. Maybe his father would want to return with him on a visit to see his son's adopted country? After all, he would still be active, probably no more than sixty or so. He might even be tempted to stay a while, or perhaps take on some position within Kipana Tours.

This time it had to be the pressurisation — he was fantasising.

Kip looked out the window to the west, where a faint red glow was rapidly sinking behind the curvature of the earth. He slid the panel shut. He was leaving Africa, and Rose, at about six hundred miles per hour.

PART 6

ERNIE

Zakayo stood on the rocky outcrop. Before him was the Kavirondo Gulf, running west to where the setting sun, an enormous red orb, hovered inches above the golden platter that was the lake.

He picked up a pebble and threw it into the water. It made a pathetic little splash and was gone. Dissatisfied with his effort, he searched for a stone large enough to do the surface of Lake Victoria justice. He found one behind him, and hefted it in his hand to test its weight. His shadow stretched a hundred yards across the pebbled foreshore and up the rise towards Kisumu. He hoisted his stone aloft, and watched his giant shadow mimic the motion.

He turned back to the lake and again tested the weight before hauling back and launching the stone towards the water. It flew in a perfect parabola and splashed with a deep, satisfying *plomp*!

The ripples spread and he watched them head west until the golden light reflecting from the lake's surface made his eyes water. Their destination was Uganda, on the far western shore of Lake Victoria. He imagined them lapping the port on the outskirts of Kampala where, the BBC had reported earlier that day, Yoweri Museveni had arrived triumphant, sending Milton Obote fleeing to Zambia, with most of the national treasury assets with him.

It had been four years since he had last seen Kampala and his other 'wife', Amelia. His children would be grown: the boy, Itema, fourteen; his daughter, Mona Lisa, twelve.

Could he trust Uganda to remain at peace while he went in search of them?

A grey-haired woman opened the front door and gave Kip a wary eye. She was elderly, like most in Mansfield Street, Glebe.

'I'm not selling anything,' he said hastily. After knocking on so many doors, he could read the signs. 'So please don't shut the door.'

She appeared even more suspicious at that, and was closing it in his face when he added, 'I'm looking for someone.'

She paused, then began to close it again.

'Ernie Sullivan,' he said to the door.

It opened a crack. The old woman peeped through the narrow opening.

Kip hurried on. 'I'm looking for Ernie Sullivan who used to live in Glebe years ago.'

The door closed, and a click of the lock indicated the finality of the issue.

Kip sighed and stared down at the veranda's tessellated tiles for a moment, then retreated down the granite flagstone steps to the wrought-iron front gate.

He looked back along the length of Mansfield Street. He had knocked on all but two doors without finding anyone who knew his father, much less his whereabouts.

Before he had found Mansfield Street, he'd visited St Patrick's Primary School in Balmain to ask the parish priest where he might find the orphanage. The priest, an old white-haired man with twinkling blue eyes and a strong Irish accent, told him the orphanage had closed in the sixties, and the building was now used as offices for Whiteman & Co, a wine and spirit merchant, but he was sympathetic to Kip's situation and helped him find the street whose name was partially revealed in the newspaper clipping. He'd produced a battered Sydney street directory, and between them they searched the Glebe page. Mansfield Street was the only one in Glebe ending with '... sfield'.

Luckily, it was a short street, and Kip had doorknocked almost all of the houses on it before noon. Apart from three, where no one had answered, the two near the Wigram Road end were his last chance. Of the three unattended homes, one had a 'Sold by SMH Classifieds' sign on it and was almost certainly vacant. Home renovators had improved the others. One had added a timber pergola, replacing the ubiquitous bull-nosed iron veranda roof of the original building, and in the other, a car-parking space had replaced the front garden. Kip thought their owners, probably young people working in the city, were unlikely to be able to help.

If Ernie Sullivan wasn't in one of the remaining houses, or noone lived there who knew him, Kip was at a complete dead end. He didn't dare contemplate where he would go from there.

'Sonny?'

The voice came from the house behind him. The old lady stood in her doorway, her hand beckoning him. Kip re-opened the gate and went to the bottom of the flagstone steps. 'Yes?' he asked eagerly.

The woman's watery blue eyes held a lingering degree of caution.

'Yes,' he repeated, nodding to encourage her.

Her continuing silence prompted him to risk a further few words. 'I'm looking for my father, Ernie Sullivan.'

'Your father?' she said in a wavering voice.

'Yes, my father. I believe he lived around here, but I don't know where he is now. It was sometime during the war years.'

'Why?'

'Why?' His heart sank. Was the old lady asking why there was a war? 'Why, um, what?'

'Why don't you know where your father is? You young people are all the same. I don't see hide nor hair of my young'uns these days. Gone to Maryborough or Maroochydore or some such.' She eyed him suspiciously. 'You're not from Queensland, are you?'

Kip felt like he was treading on eggshells. 'No, but I've come a long way. Do you know Ernie?'

'Of course I know Ernie.'

Kip took another tentative step upwards, but held back in case she slammed the door on him again. 'You ... you know Ernie Sullivan?'

'That's what I said, didn't I?' She was becoming annoyed at the insinuation. 'So ... you say you're from where?'

He decided honesty was the safest option. 'I'm from Africa,' he said, hoping the disclosure didn't divert her into a barrage of irrelevant questions.

'Well,' she replied after some thought. 'That's better than not coming down from Maroochydore.' She stepped back from the door. 'Come in.'

Kip could scarcely believe his luck, but he had to endure Mrs Willoughby's tea ceremony — by now he knew her name — including mandatory scones and jam, before he could get the subject back to the matter of his father.

'So you're Ernie's son, are you?' She poured another cup of tea for him although he had declined her offer.

'Yes,' he replied, nodding.

'Bryan.'

'Pardon?'

'I said, you'd be Bryan. Ernie used to tell me . . .'

Kip didn't hear her next few words. After forty-odd years of being Kip Balmain, he realised he was, in fact, Bryan Sullivan.

'. . . but that wasn't until much later. In the beginning it'd just be g'day if we passed in the street, but otherwise didn't talk much at all. Then all of sudden, old Ernie had a wife and became real sociable like. We used to spend a bit of time hanging over the fence, talking about kids and all the problems they brought.' She looked at Kip. 'Are you all right, sonny?'

'Yes . . . I'm okay, Mrs Willoughby. Did you say his wife?'

But the memories from over the fence had claimed her. 'Oh, Ernie was a funny fella,' she said with a smile. 'Always kidding around. Always helpin' folks.'

'What about his wife?' he persisted.

'Well, I say his wife, but I'm not sure whether they were churched or not. You know what I mean? Anyway, it was his second wife, as I recall. First one nicked off somewhere, he told me once. Yes, it was Molly — the second one — don't know the first one's name. Never mentioned it. Well, Molly had a place out near Bondi or Bronte or somewhere like that, but most times they were here.

'Poor old Ernie got down in the dumps a bit, talkin' about his little'un. But not for long. He'd be back to his old tricks, top of the world, and goin' along nicely. Until he had that fall.'

'Fall? He had an accident?'

'Yes. Not a bad one, mind you, but enough.'

'Enough for what?'

'Enough to, you know, to set him back a spell.'

He had no idea how to get to the bottom of that description, so he decided upon a direct approach.

'Mrs Willoughby, where is my father now?'

'Ernie? Oh, don't you know? He's in the Old Diggers' Hospital.'

'The Old Diggers' Hospital?' It was a term he'd never heard, and he shook his head in incomprehension.

'Yeah, the ... you know, the Repat thingo, the ... oh *bugger it*!' Her brow creased in frustration, then her face lit up. 'Ah! That's it! The Repatriation Hospital.'

CHAPTER 57

The receptionist at the Repatriation Hospital was very polite. Kip got the impression she'd been specially trained to prepare visitors before allowing them to learn what war and time had done to their loved ones.

'Flight Lieutenant Ernest Horace Sullivan ... let's see,' the nurse said, running her finger down a luminous green screen. 'There he is.'

Kip felt a surge of excitement. After so many frustrating days spent in fruitless searches, he had grown to expect failure. Now, all of a sudden, *there he is*. For some bizarre reason he worried that he might not have shaved properly that morning, and self-consciously ran his hand around his face. It would do.

'Nope,' the receptionist added. 'We moved Ernest to special services.'

Kip's heart sank. 'What do you mean by special services?'

The receptionist continued to work the computer keyboard, muttering about bugs in the new system. 'Here it is.' She studied the screen, then fell silent for what seemed like an age.

Kip felt an urge to leap the counter and read the screen for himself.

'He's been sent to an outsourced special care unit — Croydon Gardens.'

'What the hell's that?'

'An outsourced special care unit caters for special needs of particular patients,' she answered primly.

Kip clenched his jaw and suppressed the expletive that came to mind. 'Do you think you could tell me something other than the bleeding obvious?'

The receptionist put on her thin-lipped official face. 'That's all I'm allowed to say,' she snapped defensively, 'but if you wish, I can write down the address for you.'

Kip forced a smile through gritted teeth. 'Thank you. That would be very helpful.'

The bus rumbled into Kazini — a village nearly identical to any one of a score of villages passed on Zakayo's journey northwest from Kampala. The difference was that Kazini was Amelia's home, and where he hoped to find her and his two children.

As a lone traveller through a land so recently torn by war, he was taking a risk that he would fall prey to the desperate, or greedy, who would be tempted to seize any opportunity before the new government re-established the rule of law.

As an Acholi in Luwero, he was risking his life.

He collected his bag. When the cloud of diesel exhaust and dust had cleared, he found a wall of faces staring at him from the other side of the road. The men's expressions ranged from guarded mistrust to outright hostility.

The recently defeated dictator, Milton Obote, believed the people of Luwero were supporting the National Liberation Army, which had sworn to overthrow him by a popular rebellion. He'd put the region under military rule, and his Acholi troops, who had been hastily recruited, poorly trained and were ill-disciplined, took their revenge on the people of Luwero for Amin's genocidal purge of their homeland years before.

'Hello,' he said casually, hoping his accent didn't expose him. 'I am a visitor from Kampala, here trying to find my friend, George Bagonza.'

He studied the faces. Their expressions had not changed. Undaunted, he continued, 'Can someone please tell me where he lives?' He indicated his bag, which had a tattered brown-paper package tied to it with cheap twine. 'I have a present for him and his family.'

One by one the crowd drifted away without a word, except for a man of about his own age, who stood his ground, eyeing Zakayo warily. His clothes were old and showed signs of skilful repair work. He carried a long, heavy wooden rod that he leaned on to take some of his weight. It appeared that his right leg was shorter than his left.

Zakayo hefted his bag to his shoulder and crossed the road towards him.

'My friend,' he said, smiling at the man. 'I have come a long way to find Bagonza. It would be a pity if I have to return to my home in Kampala without seeing him.'

The cold stare was unremitting.

'As I said, he is an old friend, and I have a gift for him, and a gift for you too, if you can help me find him.'

'You are either very brave or very stupid to come alone to Luwero, Acholi.'

Zakayo was caught off-guard, and threw a quick look to where some of the men of the village remained in a group, talking and casting glances back to the stranger from the bus.

He tried to make light of it. 'What are you saying, my friend? Ha ha — it's a joke, yes? As I said, I'm a Baganda from Kampala. Who would travel all the way from the far north to this little village? As you say, a man would have to be foolish.'

The man's icy glare had not softened. 'Foolish or not, you should not be here.'

Zakayo decided to change his tack. 'Yes, these are difficult times, and we should all take care. But thank God it is over, and our new president, Museveni, has brought peace at last.' He hoped that mention of the popular leader of the NLA would appease the man.

'Not before the Acholi looted, raped and murdered thousands in Luwero.' He shifted his weight on the rod. 'Some of us were more fortunate and were only tortured and beaten.'

Zakayo inadvertently glanced at the man's shortened leg.

'You are wondering about my leg,' the man said antagonistically.

Zakayo began to protest his innocence, but the man silenced him with his hand. 'A soldier — an Acholi soldier — knocked me to the ground. There were three of them. One broke my left leg with his rifle butt. When I screamed, another broke my right leg, and then the others kicked and beat me until I fainted.' He patted his left leg. 'This one almost mended, but the right one is finished. It has never been the same. Now I cannot work my land.'

'I'm sorry,' Zakayo muttered, hoping the man understood it was said in sympathy, not as an apology for the actions of an Acholi brother.

'Sorry?' the man repeated. 'Everyone is sorry these days.' He thumped his rod into the hard dirt of the roadside, sending a small explosion of dust into the still air. 'And you say thank God for our new president. I say I'll thank God when Museveni kills every last one of the murderers who came to our village.' His eyes were wild, daring Zakayo to contradict him.

When he remained silent, the man said 'Ahhh!' and spat into the dirt.

In desperation to bring the matter to a conclusion, Zakayo said, 'Look, I have no quarrel with you or your people. I am a man of peace. I am looking for Bagonza, as I said. His daughter and I have two children who I haven't seen for years. For pity's sake, if you know where they are, tell me.'

'You have wasted your time.'

'Why?'

'She is not here.'

'How can you be sure?' He was anxious not to provoke another outburst, but he'd be damned if he would leave simply on the word of an obviously embittered man. 'I am not doubting you, of course, but if she is not here, then her father can tell me where she has gone.' He squared his shoulders, determined to settle the issue. 'Do you know my friend George Bagonza, or not?'

The man tightened his jaw as he shifted his weight to his good leg. 'I do,' he said, meeting Zakayo's glare with equal hostility. 'I am George Bagonza.'

The Croydon Gardens special-care unit was a two-storey, liver-brick building stuck in the middle of a dying lawn, two blocks from Parramatta Road. Kip's guess was that it had been a grand mansion set in acres of pastureland when it was built some time during the nineteenth century. The narrow dormer windows protruding from the steep slate roof scowled over a cluster of smaller buildings of indeterminate age. Two were more or less in keeping with the original architecture — solid sandstone lintels, bricks of similar if not matching colour, and no-nonsense timber porticos. A third was a 1940s mongrel with bow windows and prissy fretwork. The remainder were outhouses converted for use as sheds and a garage.

Kip climbed the sandstone steps and rang the bell at the desk. After waiting a few moments, he rang it again.

Sensible heels came clomping down the polished timber hallway and a middle-aged woman in a starched blue tunic eventually appeared. She had short, greying hair and plastic-rimmed glasses that she wore on the end of her nose. She peered over them. 'Can I help you?' she asked.

'Yes, I believe my father is, um . . .' he had almost called him an inmate, '. . . is a patient here.'

She walked behind the desk. 'Name?'

'It's Ernie, Ernest Sullivan.'

She didn't bother to look it up in her register.

'You're Ernie's son, you say?'

'That's right.'

The nurse appraised him for a moment. 'I didn't know Ernie had a son. We haven't seen you around, have we, Mr Sullivan?' She smiled to soften the accusation, but it was clear she disapproved of neglectful relatives.

Kip resented it, but remained calm. 'No . . . I've been away. Overseas.'

'Overseas? That's nice. A holiday?'

His patience was wearing thin. 'Look, is that relevant? All I want is to see my father. Is he here?'

'He is. In fact, he's been here for five years.'

The news shocked him. 'I see,' he said. Somehow he'd gained the impression that his father's move to Croydon Gardens had been a recent one, prompted by a bout of the flu, or something similar. 'Africa. I've been living in Africa. For many years.'

'Then ... I take it you are unaware of his condition?'

'Look, nurse —'

'Sister.'

'Sorry ... sister. I just want to see my father.' He fixed her with a determined eye. 'Now. If you don't mind.'

'Certainly,' she said, closing her register, and led the way from the reception desk.

As she clunked ahead of him down the long hall, Kip peered into the single-bed wards they passed. The patients were all male and mostly elderly. Many were either asleep in front of a TV, or connected to complicated medical equipment.

The sister glanced over her shoulder before she entered the last room in the hall. The venetian blinds were slightly tilted, lending the room a gentle light. The single bed was occupied by a frail old man, who seemed to be staring directly at Kip as he entered. As he drew near, out of the old man's line of vision, he realised the eyes remained fixed in the same position.

'Ernie! Wake up!' the sister called. 'You've got a visitor!'

The man blinked, but otherwise didn't move.

'C'mon, lazy bones! Up you get! It's your son, all the way from Africa to see you.'

She pressed a button on a control panel connected by cable to the bed, which slowly elevated to the point where she could prop the man into a semi-seated position.

'Don't ... don't disturb him ... if he's resting,' Kip said, staring at the face.

'It's okay, we've got to move him every now and then. Good for the circulation. Isn't it, Ernie? Good for the circulation.'

She spoke as if at any moment Ernie would enter into the conversation, but the eyes remained vacant. Only his chest lifting in respiration indicated he was alive. Occasionally he smacked his lips, and a bubble of saliva glistened at the corner of his mouth.

Kip searched the face on the pillow for any similarity to the one he had imagined since childhood. He immediately dismissed it as the romantic notion it had always been — he'd never had any idea what his father looked like — but the contrast between the virile, rugged outdoor type that had characterised his childhood fantasies and the frail figure on the bed was stark.

The sister sighed. 'Not one of his better days, I'm afraid.'

'Is he ... does he ... ?' Kip stammered.

The sister sat on the edge of the bed opposite Kip and dabbed a tissue to the corner of Ernie's mouth. 'Mr Sullivan, I wanted to spare you this, or at least to warn you. If you haven't seen your father since he came to special care, I'm afraid it must come as a bit of a shock.'

She took his father's limp hand in hers. Kip was surprised at how thick his father's fingers were. They were an incongruous fit to the delicate hand with its lacelike veins and sinews. Seeing her tender attention to his father made Kip regret his earlier, churlish behaviour.

'It's a shock, but ... to be honest, this is ... I haven't seen him for years.' He couldn't bring himself to confess the truth to a stranger, no matter how well intentioned she was.

'Then you wouldn't have seen him after the intracranial haematoma?'

Kip glanced at his father, then back to her. 'No, I ... I never got all the details.'

'It seems that Ernie had a fall. The haematoma was relieved surgically, but the brain damage had been done. I'm afraid it's been a steady downhill slide since then. Some people claim he has moments of clarity, but I haven't seen them. Mind you, he has his days when he at least follows you with his eyes. Naughty boy. But he's been like this for the last few weeks. Nothing there, I'm afraid.'

The nurse stood and gave Ernie a final pat on the knee. 'I'll leave you with your son for a while, Ernie,' she said, before marching out the door.

Kip stood motionless, silently staring at the man on the bed as the sister's footsteps receded down the hall. He felt he had been cheated. After all his attempts in England, and now in Australia, he had finally found this bleak and sterile place where his father was said to be living.

But this wasn't his father at all. What he'd found was an empty shell.

CHAPTER 58

Zakayo and George Bagonza sat together under the awning of the little iron-clad *duka* across the road from the bus stop. The fly-specked posters on the walls suggested the *duka* had sold a variety of items in better days. 'Whiten your wash!' proclaimed one. 'Persil Soap Powder — the Personal Choice of Discerning Housewives'. Now the *duka* only stocked a few haunches of dry bush meat, tea, and illegally distilled spirits.

George's weak, milky tea sat untouched between them on the simple bench that served as a table. Zakayo's efforts to salvage some form of communication between them had so far failed. He felt he should have found a rapport with this man, given Amelia had often referred to him during the years they had spent together in Kampala. It somehow made him uncomfortable that George was not an older man, as he always had imagined him. It might have been easier to smooth the waters if he could give Amelia's father the respect that was traditionally afforded to a father-in-law. But being of about the same age, Zakayo found that impossible. Instead, he decided to be as honest as he could.

'You are correct. I am an Acholi,' he said, expecting Amelia would have mentioned it anyway.

'I knew that when you stepped down from the bus.'

'How did you know I was an Acholi? Do I sound different to you?'

'No.'

'Then how did you know?'

'I have been waiting for you these three years past. Without my farm, there is always time to meet the bus.'

'But you don't know my face.'

'The strangers who visit Kazini are few.' He squinted across the table at Zakayo. 'Why have you not come to see if your children are safe and well?'

Zakayo squirmed in his seat. 'The fighting ... the war.' He wrung his hands, struggling to find an explanation that Amelia's father could understand. 'It was bad when Amin's old regiments came back from Sudan as mercenaries. They were more interested in looting and raping, and they didn't care if we were supporters or enemies. The north was a very dangerous place. Travelling was impossible.'

Bagonza grunted.

'How are Amelia and the children?' Zakayo asked, now desperate to see her sweet face and the smiles of his children.

Bagonza was in no hurry to answer him. Perhaps Zakayo had not been forgiven for being an Acholi, and George was using the delay to penalise him for it.

'So, after all this time you want to see your family?'

'Of course I do!' Zakayo was becoming annoyed.

'They are not far from here, but I cannot go with you.'

'Who are they staying with? Have you left them to fend for themselves in the bush?'

Zakayo immediately regretted the remark, and waited for Bagonza to punish him with sarcasm. But he simply smiled. 'You will find the place easily,' he said, finally taking a sip of his tea.

Kip didn't know how long he could continue to visit Ernie's lonely room in the special-care unit, but he returned day after day, probably because he refused to believe his quest had been for naught. It had been five days now. There were brief periods when he thought his father might have a light of awareness in his eyes, but then it would be gone, leaving Kip's hopes dashed.

He brought the newspaper under his arm every morning, and read it aloud to his father, but it was a depressing experience. Ernie made no response, except for the time he began to snore while Kip was reading a sports report on a football game.

Kip expanded on the stories to see if content made any difference. He would read aloud a report on the society pages, and build it into a lurid story of sex and bizarre goings-on. Occasionally he threw in a violent death of one of the several salacious characters he'd invented. Ernie remained impassive, blinking and drooling.

To kill the time while his father slept, Kip strolled around the ward. Most of the patients were in the same more or less vegetative state as his father. At lunchtime he spooned baby food into Ernie's mouth, wiped his lips, tucked him firmly into place for his afternoon nap, and then used the hour's walk to his hotel to replenish his spirits.

The remainder of the day was spent watching daytime TV, wandering the shops, and perhaps picking up a suitably lewd postcard of big-breasted young women on various beaches for Harry.

In the evening he would walk to a restaurant to build an appetite. Later, alone in his room, he would lie awake, wondering how his father's memories could be lost by the relatively simple medical procedure of draining an intracranial haematoma.

In tormented sleep he saw sixty-five years of life, sixty-five years of memories, washed down a drain red with blood.

Friday morning. A pall of early summer smog hung over the sprawling western suburbs as Kip made his way to Croydon Gardens. He was an hour earlier than usual so as to catch the doctor on his rounds.

He'd been in Sydney for a week and was thoroughly bored and homesick. Sydney was a beautiful city. The harbour was spectacular, the buildings impressive, and if the acres of department stores he tramped through, to kill time, were the measure of an exciting international city, then Sydney was it. But Kip found it colourless.

He missed Nairobi and the pageantry of its raw life. He felt none of the energy in Sydney that simmered barely concealed beneath Nairobi's surface.

Sydney's bars and clubs were populated by a homogeneous mass, as if they'd been bused in from some casting company to play the role of carefree partygoers. Even their movements seemed choreographed to suit the plasticised environment. Finding and wearing fashion's 'flavour-of-the-month' seemed to be everyone's driving ambition.

Nairobi nightlife had no idea where it was going. It was barely controlled chaos. Music might be Zairian street music one moment, and Elton John the next. Dancers were an eclectic bunch — some men were in suits, others wore patched jeans and T-shirts. The women might wear gowns of silk from West Africa, with stitched patterns of golden thread, or miniskirts from Hong Kong. There were ethnic Asians, black Kenyans, Arabs, and people who might have just arrived from the deserts of the Sudan.

Nairobi always looked tousled and lived-in — like an unmade bed — its appearance borrowed from the seamier side of its nature. But it had a vibrancy that amplified its life. There was danger in the darkened streets, or on silent roads through city parks or through the remnant forests, where armed hijackers might attempt to ambush a car.

In Sydney, it was a novelty to find something that didn't work as planned. Maybe a train would be running late, or a lift out of order, whereas in Nairobi it was a pleasant surprise when something functioned as it should. It was Sydney's predictability that made it bland, and, to Kip, it was bland to the point of tedium.

He'd heard that Sydney's weather could become sultry in summer, but the air was crisp that morning as he made his way to the hospital. It was only his mood that clouded the outlook.

Ernie's doctor joined Kip at the bedside. 'I'm Dr Carbery-Smythe,' he said, not offering his hand, but keeping both buried in the pockets of his white medico's coat. With no further preliminaries he led Kip through a layman's description of Ernie's prognosis. He was a tall man, somewhere in his fifties, with a mop of greying hair and an untidy grey stubble on his chin. In short, clipped sentences he explained that Ernie was unlikely to return to a *compos mentis* state, and that his physical condition could dramatically worsen at any time.

Kip looked at his father, whose eyes had been fixed on the ceiling since he arrived. 'Does he hear me when I prattle on at him all morning? What does he see when he stares like that?'

The doctor nodded in sympathy. 'It's very hard for the family to deal with this situation, having felt the presence of their loved one for all their lives. To have it suddenly withdrawn by an invisible force — it must feel very strange.'

Kip didn't bother to let him know he had only days before met his father for the first time.

'Hearing is unaffected by the procedure to drain the haematoma, and so, technically, he can hear you. What does he see? Well, again, the function is intact, but I suspect he sees shadows passing between himself and the point of focus — the light from the window, the fluorescents. What does he make of it? And does the brain register it's a connected series of actions ... who knows?' He patted Kip on the shoulder. 'I'm sorry if I sound pessimistic. We all have to prepare ourselves for the inevitable outcome, I'm afraid.'

Kip had made no such preparations. He'd be damned if he'd leave while there was a chance his father might revive. He obstinately clung to a hope that Ernie would emerge from his twilight and allow Kip to see him as a human being before he eventually had to return to Africa. But in the face of the medical facts the doctor presented, his dream of finding a person behind the blank façade was fading fast.

'Now here's a sign of the times.' Kip flicked the paper to straighten the page. 'The *Telegraph* has a story tucked away on page five about the French nuclear test at Muruora Island. Meanwhile, the front page is all about *Top Gun* beating *Crocodile Dundee* at the box office.'

It was mid-morning on a sultry Saturday. Kip had finished reading the *Sydney Morning Herald* to Ernie, and had picked up the tabloid to kill some more time. He continued to read. 'Tom Cruise appears to have beaten Australia's Paul Hogan at the box office with ticket sales approaching two hundred million dollars.' He shook his head in disbelief. 'That's a lot of money for a story about a pilot.'

'Pilot,' Ernie said.

Kip dropped the paper in his lap. 'Ernie? Did you say something?'

Ernie blinked.

'Ernie?' Kip held his breath, but his father's face began to assume its usual bland expression. 'Ernie?' Kip frantically searched his mind for another key to penetrate the fog, another hook to drag his father back before he was gone again. 'Did you say *pilot*?'

'Pilot,' Ernie repeated.

'Yes, a pilot made two hundred million dollars.' The flicker of comprehension dimmed. 'A pilot, Ernie. A pilot.'

But Ernie had returned to the twilight where Kip was just another unconnected shadow moving across his point of focus. There was not a blink of recognition.

Kip went out that Saturday night, not sure whether to celebrate the glimpse of consciousness from Ernie or to mourn its hasty departure.

He began drinking in the hotel bar, but couldn't stomach the oppressive orderliness and phoney conviviality. He got drunk at a pub down the road, with glazed tiles on its external walls and varnished doorjambs and skirting boards inside. It smelled vaguely of vomit and strongly of tobacco, but he drank in peace until he was politely asked to leave at closing time.

Late on Sunday morning the hotel housekeeper awoke him with a loud knocking. Kip rudely told her to leave him alone, then took a long shower to ease his throbbing head.

He arrived at the hospital in the mid-afternoon to find a woman sitting at Ernie's bedside, holding his hand. She seemed as surprised as Kip when he entered. They stared at each other for several moments before Kip stammered a greeting.

The woman nodded hello, then said, 'Um, who are ... sorry ... I haven't seen you here before. Are you a friend of Ernie's?'

'I'm Kip. I mean, I'm Bryan Sullivan.'

She stared at him. 'Bryan? Ernie's Bryan?'

For a moment he wondered if this pleasant-faced woman, wearing a simple plaid skirt and pin-tucked blouse, might be his mother. She was about Ernie's age. 'Who ... who are you?' he blurted out.

'I'm Molly Hennessey. Ernie's, um ... friend.' She dropped her eyes to her hand, which was still clutching Ernie's. 'We've been together for the last twenty-five years.' She raised her gaze to Kip. Her eyes twinkled with her smile. 'I suppose that's a bit more than a friend, isn't it.'

Kip extended his hand. Molly gently took it and briefly held it while looking up at him. 'So ... you're Bryan ...'

Kip drew up a chair on the opposite side of the bed. 'Yes, I'm Bryan. How do you know about me?'

'Ernie told me all about you.' She turned to Ernie, and patted his hand. 'Eventually. Not that there was much to tell. Only what he knew about you from your mother's letters. And precious little that was.'

Kip had a thousand questions, but Molly became muddled with her answers until it became obvious that she could only tell the story in her own way. She began a rambling journey of recollections and disjointed memories.

The pieces of his father's life started to come together.

CHAPTER 59

Opposite the Ploughman's Arms stood the shell of a two-storey house, torn apart by a German bomb. A couple of children were playing in the rubble behind a trestle barrier.

Ernie's rehab by the Russians had taken a month longer than anyone knew why. As soon as he was allowed to take leave from the medical observation unit, he made his way to the Ploughman's, which still wore a brave face in an otherwise shattered part of London. He pushed through the heavy leadlighted door. One or two of a small pool of men gave him a glance, ran an eye over his clean new RAF uniform, and went back to their drinks and conversation.

When the barman returned with his ale, Ernie asked, 'Have you seen a black bloke in here in the last month or so? He would have been in an army uniform.'

The barman scratched his head. 'A black bloke ... Now that you mention it ...'

'Maybe he asked about me, Ernie Sullivan?'

'Yeah ... you're right ... a black bloke. Didn't say much. Didn't drink much either — just a beer, and he'd go — but every time he left, he'd say, "If someone comes looking for me, I'll be back tomorrow."'

'That'd be him!' Ernie said excitedly. 'So, has he been in here today?'

'Nah, haven't seen that black bloke for days ... maybe a week. Come to think of it, maybe it was him who said he was being sent home.'

Ernie's smile fell.

'Now don't quote me on that one. There's always blokes comin' in 'ere, leaving messages for folk. But he was a bit different, of course, and I reckon that's what he said.'

Ernie had another beer and went back to the unit. A parcel of mail awaited him. There was a small bundle from Marie. He devoured the letters, enjoying the snippets of her life, the mundane details of family members — all the trivia that filled a page from home. She enquired why he hadn't written, then about February 1945 — six months earlier — the letters suddenly stopped.

He flicked over a couple of official-looking letters, then found another from Australia, in an unfamiliar hand. It was simply signed 'Nancy', and was dated 6 January.

Ernie skipped through the polite introduction — hoping the letter found him well, and how glad she was to hear people saying that the war would soon end. The important part began on page two.

I placed Baby Bryan in St Patrick's Orphanage. I've enclosed the papers so you can claim him if you want. It was sad, but I'm afraid that Jim may come home, and then what would I do?

We were silly, Ernie, and I have paid the price. I don't only blame you, it was me too, but now I must move on with my life and forget everything.

Please don't try to contact me. I couldn't bear for Jim to find out about the baby.
Good luck with your life.
Nancy

Ernie stood at the ship's stern, staring down to where a creamy wake toyed briefly with the ink-black waves before drifting away like a fading memory.

They had been at sea for two weeks — five hundred of them returning to Australia to put together the pieces of lives previously shared, before the schism of war. For Ernie it was a voyage through hell. There had been several nights like this, when he contemplated the peace that the deep black waters could offer. But suicide was a sin, and whatever the devil might have planned for his torment in the future, he was determined to find his son — the innocent victim — and rescue him from the orphanage.

He still loved Marie, and wanted to re-establish their life together. They had been kids when they married, but war could change a man more than the years.

The remnants of his Catholic conscience scourged him with a deep and remorseless guilt, but he would beg her forgiveness in the hope that she would accept his child.

In his heart he wondered if any woman could be so kind.

Molly dabbed at a tear as she finished her story. 'That's about as much as I know about Ernie straight after the war. He didn't like to talk too much about those days.'

The sun had dipped to throw low slanting rays into Ernie's room. Kip stood and tilted the venetian blinds. A diffused pink light displaced the gold.

'It was easy for him to find St Patrick's, but you'd gone. How a child could be taken from the orphanage without proper paperwork he couldn't understand, but somehow he found out it was Marie who'd adopted you. Why she would steal you away, neither of us could understand.'

Kip knew the answer to that. Marie's spite had known no bounds.

'He kept looking for you, Bryan. Even after I met him, years later, he hadn't given up hope. Your birthdays were bad times for Ernie. He would talk about his lost opportunities, his weaknesses, and of his failures. But his loss was everyone else's gain. "Uncle Ernie" was the babysitter for all his friends' children.'

'Did you and Ernie ever think of having children of your own?'

'We agonised over it for ages. I'm a Catholic, but not nearly so staunch as Ernie. He couldn't remarry. His religion was stronger than his right to have the marriage declared void, or whatever they call it.'

Molly's eyes glistened as she told Kip that she and Ernie had been wonderfully happy before his generous spirit led to the accident that had reduced him to his present cruel situation.

'A neighbour's grandson had lost his football on Ernie's roof,' she said. 'Nothing was too much trouble for Ernie when it came to children.'

But the ladder's footing wasn't secure, and it tipped, sliding along the guttering with a metallic scream and sending Ernie crashing to the paved courtyard.

'The doctor said it was mild concussion, but Ernie, stubborn as usual, refused to go to hospital for observation.'

Ernie's subdural haematoma wasn't acute. After a few days he went back to work, giving Molly a kiss as he departed and telling her not to worry. He said Pig-iron Bob had reconditioned his brain before he sent him off to war, referring in typically irreverent terms to the prime minister's pre-war sales of iron ingots to Japan.

Ernie told no one about his headaches. The anticoagulants he took for his arthritis made matters much worse. He collapsed on the factory floor and remained in a coma for three weeks. When he was revived, the lights were on, but there was no one at home.

For a long time Molly refused to accept that his condition was irreversible, that he wouldn't come back to her one day. She said she was sure Ernie could hear and understand, and there were times, admittedly precious few, when he was lucid, and they'd share those treasured moments, holding hands and talking about their days together, good times and bad.

Molly admitted that she was the only one who'd witnessed these events, and that the medical staff viewed her accounts with some scepticism.

'These days it's been harder to get him out of it. But I still come every Sunday, and sometimes on a Saturday, if the bakery gives me the day off. If it wasn't such an awfully long way on the buses, I could be here more often.' She shrugged. 'But I need the money, so I have to take the work when it's there, don't I?'

She dabbed at a tear. 'Look at him,' she said, smiling at Ernie who smacked his lips and blinked at the ceiling. 'He hears every word we're saying. He knows you're here, Bryan. You'll see, he'll wake up and be telling you one of his rude jokes any time now.' She looked across the bed to Kip and nodded encouragement. 'You'll see.'

Kip pounded the pavement on his way to the hospital, reflecting on Molly's story, which had been a mixed blessing for him. He felt buoyed by the knowledge that his father had tried so hard to find him, but the doctor's assessment that he was slipping deeper into his vegetative state left him discouraged and contemplating a return to Kenya. He strode up the steps of the hospital, trying to put it behind him.

At his father's bedside, he took his hand and bent to kiss him, as was his recent practice, before realising he had forgotten to buy the newspaper from the kiosk near the reception desk. He had only large notes and fiddled in his pocket for some coins. He could find none and removed the wad of keys from his pocket to dig deeper for the change. He usually left his key ring at the hotel; in fact, it was only through habit that he'd carried it overseas in the first place. It had nothing on it that was of any use to him in Sydney.

He put the key ring on the bed and went down the corridor for the newspaper. When he returned, Ernie had the key ring in his hand and was fingering the broken miniature boomerang.

Kip moved quietly to the bed. His father's eyes were fixed on the half-boomerang. 'Boomerang,' he whispered in a small, cracked voice. 'Boomerang.' The word seemed to transport him.

Kip was afraid to speak. Finally he risked an intrusion. 'That's right, Ernie. Boomerang.'

Ernie lifted his gaze from the key ring. Kip saw the light of comprehension in his eyes. 'It's mine,' his father said in amazement.

'Yes, it's yours. I've been looking after it for you.'

Ernie nodded in understanding. 'Do I know you, young fella?'

He was unsure how to handle this moment and regretted not preparing himself for it. 'I'm ... Kip. But some people call me Bryan.'

'Bryan?' Ernie savoured the sound. 'Bryan ... I know Bryan.'

'You do?'

'Oh, for sure. Bryan. He's my little bloke, you know.'

'That's nice. Tell me about Bryan.'

Ernie opened his mouth, but nothing came. He swallowed and tried again.

Again Kip was afraid to speak, but gently coaxed him. 'What do you know about Bryan?'

Ernie looked at the key ring. 'Boomerang,' he said.

'What do you know about Bryan, Ernie?'

Ernie dragged his gaze from the boomerang. His eyes were misty. He peered up at Kip as if seeing him for the first time. 'Nothing.' There was agony in his voice. 'I know nothing about Bryan. He's lost.'

'I can help you find him. If you want me to.'

'You can?' He continued to study Kip. 'Do I know you?' His voice was gaining strength, but his speech was deliberate, as if he were searching for each word.

'Not really. I'm a friend of Molly's.' He hoped Molly's name might calm him.

It did. Ernie brightened. 'Molly. She's a beaut sheila, she is, eh? Molly ... Where is she?'

'She's . . . not far. She'll be in to see you soon.'

'Good-oh,' Ernie said, content with the answer. 'And what did you say your name was, cobber?'

Kip decided to change tack. 'My name is Rupert Balmain.'

Ernie smiled. 'Bit of a posh name, that, eh? Rupert.'

'Rupert Balmain. But my friends call me Kip.'

'Kip. That's better. Reckon you'd get the shit beaten out of ya at school with a name like Rupert, eh?'

Kip smiled in spite of the tension. 'I did. That's why I changed it.'

Ernie returned to the key ring, which he still held in his fingers. He frowned at it again. 'Is this broken boomerang yours, Kip?'

'No, Ernie, it's yours.'

Ernie nodded, a faraway look in his eyes. 'I gave half to someone . . . I gave half to someone . . . and Marie had the other half.' He looked down at it again and ran a finger along the curving yellow lines. 'Which one is this, Kip?'

He hesitated, tempted to give ownership to Zakayo, feeling the lie was inherently safer than the truth. But he decided to tell the truth. 'It's Marie's.'

'Marie. She's gone, you know. Don't know where Marie is any more. Took my little bloke, she did.' He looked at Kip, pleading sympathy. 'My son.'

'I know.'

'But I gave the other half to . . .' He screwed his face into a mass of wrinkles. 'Oh, jeez . . . He was black . . . I can see him.' His eyes widened. 'I was in the war . . . Now I remember. My friend, the black bloke, he was in some kind of camp . . . a jail, I think. How did I get there? Jesus! My plane! It was on fire!' He reached a hand to Kip.

Kip took it, and patted it reassuringly with the other. 'It's okay, Ernie, it's okay.'

'I told them to get out! I did!' He searched Kip's face for understanding, his eyes reflecting the terror of a memory too harsh to tame. 'I said, "Out! All of you, bail out!" But there were flames everywhere. They didn't have time.'

The heavy key ring fell from his grasp. It hit the floor with a metallic crunch.

Ernie shut his eyes and covered his head with his arms. 'Oh God ... Oh God ... Oh, no ...'

'It's okay, Dad, it's over. It's finished! Don't get upset. Dad, listen to me — I'm here with you. It's over.'

Ernie was whimpering, 'Oh, no ... oh, no,' and he slid down the bed to hide his face under the covers.

Kip sat with him for the remainder of the day, but Ernie had again taken refuge in his silent world.

In bed later that night, Kip stared at the ceiling, going step by painful step through the events of the day. He felt he had come agonisingly close to drawing Ernie back to reality. It was the intrusion of his memories of the war that had snatched him away. Unfortunately, it was never going to be possible to only bring back Ernie's pleasant memories; the painful ones must emerge too, if the return was to be complete. He wondered if he would have another chance to have Ernie recognise him as his son before his mind closed off again. He felt that time was not in his favour.

He replayed the day's events over and over again, trying to construct a more effective strategy if he got a second chance at it.

It was in one of the replays that Kip realised he had blown his cover, but Ernie hadn't seemed to notice that he'd called him 'Dad'.

The old man who had given Zakayo a lift on this, the last stage of his journey, had offered to wait. The sky was darkening, and a man should not be out at night so far from town these days, he said. Zakayo had thanked him, but told him he needed time. He didn't say it, but more than needing time, Zakayo needed to be alone.

The battered pick-up, loaded with sweet potatoes, rumbled away, leaving Zakayo standing in a golden cloud of suspended dust, staring at the long grey mound that ran beside the road for fifty yards in both directions.

He let his arms drop loosely to his side, releasing the tension he had carried in his hunched shoulders since he'd left Luwero three hours ago, first on foot and then in the pick-up.

This was not the first time he had been to the scene of violent death, but there was something utterly obscene about the greying skulls — thousands of them — piled beside the road to the height of a man's shoulder. It would have been better had they been buried in the jungle. An act of concealment. But no; the soldiers wanted all to know the consequences of collaboration with the enemy. The skulls were a monument to fear.

The dry season was coming to an end and the air was heavy with threatening rain. A tower of thunderclouds rumbled on the horizon. A shaft of sun peeped under them and speared through the papaya trees behind him, lighting the skulls in a golden wash.

What make of men were they, these soldiers, he

wondered. Amin's Kakwa had invaded Zakayo's Gulu homeland and tortured men who dared to speak against his repressive rule — good men like old Thomas, and others. The Kakwa were their traditional foe and it was well known they were ignorant thugs. But the troops who had brutalised Luwero were Acholi and Lango — his brothers and cousins. Did morality only survive so long as vengeance was held at bay? And why couldn't Africans have civilised wars like the Europeans?

This was not the first slaughtering place he had seen in his month-long search. They were dotted all over the Luwero Triangle. They sickened him. But this one, twenty miles from town and across the road from a papaya plantation, was the one that Amelia's father informed him contained the remains of Amelia and her and Zakayo's two children. George Bagonza knew it for a fact, because he had followed the trucks and hidden while the ghoulish dismemberment had taken place.

Zakayo couldn't understand why Amelia's father would want to witness such horror. Then he remembered his despair that he might never know the fate of Amelia and their two children. A grieving heart needed to know such things, no matter the consequences.

A large drop of warm rain struck him on the shoulder. Small dust explosions erupted around him, going *phut*, *phut* on the powdery surface of the road. From beyond the papaya patch came the growing roar of heavy rain on wide, green foliage. It pounded down on Zakayo. Soon it covered the skulls like a coat of fresh paint.

Zakayo stood dripping wet, but unable to muster the energy to move. His journey had exhausted him. If true peace ever came to Uganda, there would be many more making this same journey, to fields of death such as this.

Perhaps they would be like Zakayo, in search of Africa — the Africa he had loved as a young man. An Africa proud of its past and hopeful for its future. Perhaps they would leave places such as this sick at heart, determined to renew their efforts to convince their leaders to forget tribal history and forgive old sins. To stand for the people, rather than for what they could take from them.

Many years ago Zakayo had heard about the Asian killing fields. The world had been shocked by the extent of man's inhumanity towards his fellow men. Barbarism, the world said, condemning the Cambodian leaders. Even in Africa, the killing fields of Asia were discussed with horror.

The massacres of the Luwero Triangle had happened only a few years after Cambodia. But who knew of Africa's killing fields?

Who cared?

CHAPTER 60

Kip continued to read the paper to Ernie during his visits, but his father's traumatic withdrawal from their first encounter had shaken him and he was afraid to produce the boomerang key ring again.

He asked Carbery-Smythe about the risks of dragging his father out of his mental cave.

'I'm not sure I can give you a definitive answer,' the doctor said to Kip in the confined space that passed for his office. 'Technically, the patient shouldn't have survived his haematoma. Some might say that for your father to make it this far is a bonus.'

His nasally voice and detached attitude annoyed Kip. He remembered their first meeting, when Carbery-Smythe had hidden his hands rather than exchange handshakes as men do. The doctor's attitude then, confirmed now as he spoke dispassionately of 'the patient' this, and 'the patient' that, showed that he had chosen to remain remote from his charges rather than become personally involved. Perhaps the years had made his daily task of overseeing their inevitable decline unbearable.

'Also, patients who are mentally incapacitated, as in your father's case, usually succumb to one or other infection, typically pneumonia,' Carbery-Smythe went on. 'In layman's terms, you might say that with little or no mental stimulus for five years, the patient may have lost the will to live.'

'Why hasn't he been given treatment to help him out of it? Don't you have specialists for this kind of thing?'

'Look around you, Mr Sullivan.' Carbery-Smythe swept an arm around his office.

Kip's eyes involuntarily followed his outstretched hand to the window. A featureless grey sky cast a pall over the unkempt garden surrounding the collection of drab buildings.

'The war ended forty years ago,' the doctor said. 'Facilities like these are receiving an ever-diminishing share of government budgets. Patients get a weekly visit from a physio, but your father would need virtually constant stimulation. We can barely cope with providing basic health care to these men, and even if we could — let's face it, their chances at rehabilitation are virtually nil.'

Kip refused to let Carbery-Smythe's cynicism deflect him. 'But Molly says she's seen him spark up for short periods.'

The doctor nodded condescendingly. 'Loved ones tend to see cognitive signs that are not there.'

'But he spoke to me too — just the other day.'

The medico raised his greying eyebrows. 'He did?'

'Yes. We talked for maybe ten or fifteen minutes. He was okay, until . . .'

'Yes?'

'Until he remembered things about the war. Then he switched off again. It scared me. Could that be damaging for him?'

'Hmm.' The doctor rubbed his chin, studying Kip for a moment. 'This is most unusual at his stage.' He continued to scratch at his stubble. 'But

I'll take your word for it, Mr Sullivan, and I'll be frank with you. If you had the skills, and were able to spend every waking moment with him, the patient might recover a little of his faculties.' He raised a cautionary finger. 'Might. But then we could lose him again, never to return. The safe course for you — and I say this for your own sake — would be to enjoy these brief moments of lucidity, but don't become emotionally attached to the concept of a cure.'

'That may be good advice, doctor, but I *am* emotionally attached. Ernie's my father, for chrissake. Are you saying I should give up?'

'I'm saying that everything in medicine has attendant risks. Personally, I don't go for the preservation-of-life-at-all-costs nonsense. To me, it's quality of life that matters, but we must be prepared for the worst. Your father is on a knife's edge. Whatever course we take, in the long term the prognosis is the same.'

Kip hated words like 'long term'. His unasked question lurked in his mind, but the courage to raise it flagged as a wave of exhaustion washed over him. Carbery-Smythe's pessimism dragged him down. He ran his fingers over his eyes and down his face. 'Well, thanks for giving me some of your time,' he said as he stood to leave.

'You have obviously struck a chord with your father, Mr Sullivan,' the doctor said, following him to the door. 'If anyone could draw him out of himself, you could.'

Kip's question spilled out. 'Will he ever fully recover?' He immediately regretted it.

Carbery-Smythe sucked his teeth, and dropped his eyes to the floor in a gesture Kip felt sure he had practised many times. 'Let me just say, enjoy any brief moments you have with your father, but be prepared for ... for any setbacks.'

Kip nodded. 'Fuck you, doctor,' he muttered as he walked down the corridor towards his father's room.

On the day following his discussion with the doctor, Kip sat at his father's bedside, holding his hand, occasionally giving it a squeeze to test for any change in Ernie's usual bland expression. Ernie seemed totally unaware of his presence.

Kip held his hand for fifteen minutes, recalling the doctor's clinical description of Ernie's chances of even a brief return to awareness.

'What quality of life is this, Ernie?' he asked him. 'What would you do if you were me?'

Ernie blinked and moved his lips.

Kip reached into his pocket and held his set of keys in Ernie's line of vision. After a moment, he jangled them.

Ernie reached for the fractured boomerang and ran a trembling finger down its smoothed, black surface.

'C'mon, Ernie. Talk to me. Tell me a story. Tell me a joke.'

Ernie's eyes moved from the boomerang to Kip. For a moment a flicker of awareness appeared behind his eyes.

'Thataboy, Ernie. Speak to me.'

'B-b-boomerang,' he said.

The transformation was slow, but in the following days, as Kip inched along the torturous path to his father's memories, Ernie's stumbling attempts to engage his mind improved.

By the end of the week it was possible for Kip to hold a conversation with him, although the exchange would sometimes stumble into a period where Ernie lapsed into confused silence. Carbery-Smythe was amazed, and made brief daily visits to Ernie's bedside to monitor progress.

When Sunday came, Kip was anticipating the look of joy on Molly's face when she made her weekly visit. But Ernie was having one of his bad days, and Kip kept his father's earlier progress to himself, hoping that the gains of the previous week weren't a transitory phenomenon.

By Monday afternoon Ernie had made up the lost ground, and by midweek he was able to recount more and more of his past. The frustrating aspect was that he seemed to regress a little during Kip's overnight absences. Each session began with a revision of the last, where Kip helped his father connect the lost memory fragments. It was as if Ernie's mind had taken on more than it could comfortably accommodate, and in the quiet of evening, when he was alone, would simply shed some of it.

Kip asked Carbery-Smythe if he could camp beside Ernie's bed.

'Absolutely not, Mr Sullivan. Your father is showing extraordinary progress, but it comes at a cost. Continue to press forward by all means, but let's not get ahead of ourselves. Patience — that's the strategy for the moment.'

One morning Kip produced the key ring again. 'Where's the other half of this boomerang, Ernie?' he asked.

'Lemme see now . . .' Ernie squinted at the piece of painted wood and scratched his head. 'I gave it to . . . Zako! Zako was his name.' He raised his gaze to Kip and smiled. 'I bloody near forgot him, didn't I?'

'Who was Zako?' Kip probed.

'Zako was a mate of mine ... in the camp. A black fella. Fuzzy-wuzzy hair an' all.'

'And he had the other half of the boomerang you gave Marie,' Kip added.

'That's right. You remember that, do you?' Ernie's brow creased. 'I'm sorry, mate — forgot your name again.'

'I'm Bryan.'

'That's right! Same as my little bloke.' He ran a finger along the broken edge of the boomerang. 'I gave Zako the other half. We were supposed to meet in the pub, but he never showed, poor bastard. Probably didn't make it.'

'No, he made it to London, but he couldn't wait. He went back to Africa.'

'Well, I'll be buggered! Good luck to him. Old Zako, eh?' Ernie nodded, then asked, 'You know Zako then, do you?'

'Yes, I know him very well. Know some of his family too.'

'Well, I'll be blowed. Small world, ain't it, Bryan?'

Kip smiled. After trudging around London and Sydney looking for Ernie, it wasn't as small as he'd have liked. 'It is,' he answered.

'And full of weird people too ... Somebody told me about the goings-on of these society people, you know the type — Watsons Bay and Point Piper and all. Come to think of it, don't know where I heard it, but struth! Talk about ratbags!'

Kip winced. Ernie had heard his fanciful stories after all. 'Tell me some more about Zakayo ... I mean Zako.'

A twinkle came into his eyes and a smile played at the corners of his lips. 'Jeez, we had some fun.

My oath we did. Made a bit of money too. But there was this time when Zako nearly got blown up with a grenade ...'

Before he'd finished his story, Ernie was asleep, the smile lingering on his lips.

Kip wished he could tell his own story and reveal his true identity, but he was afraid to take that step. As Ernie slept, Kip tried to rationalise his fear. His first thoughts were that he didn't want to confront Ernie with something so emotionally powerful that it might set him back. But upon closer scrutiny, he wondered if he was afraid that Ernie might not be as thrilled to meet his long-lost son as Kip was to have found him.

Kip waited two days before telephoning Molly from his hotel to tell her about Ernie's condition. Molly started by saying she could take a sickie the next day, but her excitement couldn't be contained. 'I can't wait,' she said, and insisted they go immediately.

Molly began her nervous chatter from the time Kip picked her up in the taxi. She named almost every significant site and building across the breadth of the city, and gave Kip a running commentary on them until they were within minutes of the hospital, where she fell silent.

As the taxi drew to a halt at the gate, Kip became apprehensive that he had given Molly too much hope for a recovery, and that they might again find the frightening emptiness in Ernie's eyes.

Croydon Gardens was in almost total darkness. Dim lights in the dormer windows were like enormous sad eyes gazing down on them. Kip took Molly's hand as they climbed the steps. They rang the night bell, and waited for many minutes before the night supervisor appeared. He gave them a hard time, pointing out that it was after nine o'clock, but Kip explained the circumstances and he let them in, saying they could visit for an hour, and no more.

When they reached his door, they saw Ernie propped against a pile of pillows, staring at the ceiling in the dim light of a bedside lamp. Kip's heart sank, but Ernie turned to them as they entered.

'Hello, love,' he said, with not a trace of surprise at seeing Molly there. 'What's up?'

Molly's eyes were streaming tears of joy. She hesitated a moment in the doorway, before moving to the bed, where she took his cheeks between her hands and gave him a lingering kiss on the lips.

'Jeez!' Ernie spluttered. 'That's a bit of all right, love.' He caught sight of Kip standing behind her. 'G'day, young fella. Take no notice of us. Come in, come in.'

After Molly had overcome her disbelief, she bombarded Ernie with questions. How did he feel? What did he remember? Did he know she visited him every week? As Ernie struggled to keep up, Molly would interrupt him with a kiss, or a squeeze of his hand, and no sooner had he spluttered a reply than she would be off on another tack, launching into a story about one of their friends. Ernie was overwhelmed, but seemed able to cope. Kip let Molly go. She had a lot of catching up to do.

Finally she drew breath long enough for Ernie to ask, 'So, how do you two know each other?' He smiled from one to the other as the silence between them grew.

Molly looked at Kip, nodding her encouragement, but Kip was stricken. Finally, she spoke for him. 'Ernie, this is Bryan.'

'Yeah, I know, love. Young Bryan's been letting me ear-bash him for ... I don't know how long. Haven't you, mate?'

Kip tried to smile.

'Yes, Ernie, but he's *your* Bryan.'

Ernie's smile ebbed and his eyes widened in comprehension. He turned from Molly to Kip, then back again, trying to unravel the puzzle, or confirm he hadn't misunderstood her. 'My Bryan?' he asked her.

'Yes, Ernie. This young man is your son.'

CHAPTER 61

It was late when the taxi dropped Molly at her house in Bondi. She had prattled on excitedly about what must be done before Ernie came home. She thought she would rearrange the furniture, even give the bedroom a quick lick of paint, and perhaps it was time to hang new curtains in the lounge room.

Kip listened in silence, torn between two camps. He didn't want to spoil Molly's euphoria, but worried that Carbery-Smythe's prognosis might be correct. Kip flushed with anger at the thought of the pompous, hyphen-bloody-ated doctor. He hadn't only shaken Kip's lifelong dream with his brutal assessment of Ernie's chances, but had added to his burden by making him the custodian of the sobering news.

Kip walked Molly to the door, and decided to say nothing about Carbery-Smythe.

When she looked up to him to say goodnight, the reflection of the streetlight glistened in her eyes. 'I don't know what magic you brought from Africa, Bryan, but you have made two people very happy tonight.'

'Make that three, Molly,' Kip corrected. 'Tonight has been a dream for as long as I can remember.'

'Well, the taxi's waiting, so I won't invite you in for a cuppa, but one thing before you go …'

'Yes?'

'What now?'

'What do you mean?'

'Let's just say I had a woman's intuition while I was talking about making the house nice for Ernie. You weren't exactly helping me choose the colours for the bedroom.'

'I'm sorry, Molly. I've been warned that this may not be a long-term answer.' He cursed himself for using similar terms to Carbery-Smythe. 'He needs constant attention, and then there's no guarantees.'

'I guessed as much.' She took his hand and patted it. 'I can help. I'll try to get some time off work.'

'Thanks, Molly, but finding my father was my reason for coming to Australia. If I can't pull him through this, then I haven't found him at all.'

'But how long can you stay?'

'I've been gone for nearly a month, and I'm a bit out of my depth here, but I can't leave until I know how Dad's going to be.'

'Is there anyone waiting for you over there?'

A vision of Rose flashed into his mind's eye. He could see her prowling beside the Mara River in the sleek outfit she'd worn for the Peugeot shoot. In the same instant he felt the cold chill of a premonition.

'Well ... do you?'

He hesitated a moment, dismissing the ill omen as a recollection of the crocodile attack that followed the shoot. 'I'm not sure,' he stammered.

'Now that's a bit coy,' she said, giving him a nudge. 'C'mon, you can tell old Molly.'

Kip smiled too. 'Her name's Rose. Trouble is, I don't know if she feels the same way. We've had a couple of rocky times.' He rubbed his chin, remembering the night at the Trattoria. 'I wanted to let her know how I feel before I came over here, but she stood me up.'

'Have you given her a call?'

'A call?'

'On the telephone, you dope! We have them here in Australia, you know.'

'I hate having those sorts of discussions over the phone. They always seem so —'

'Call her.' Molly gave him a stern look. 'Life's too short.'

He felt that Molly was talking about her own life with his father, as much as about him and Rose. He smiled, and gave her a kiss on the cheek. She waved him off from the veranda.

In the taxi, Kip rested his chin on his hand and recalled the night with his father. After Molly had had her say, they'd talked, or rather Kip had listened, for two hours while Ernie relived his life for Kip's benefit. He told stories of his early days as a stevedore at Darling Harbour, where an enormous retail and entertainment complex now stood, and of his escapades while in flying school in Canada. He spoke of the night he was shot down over Germany, of the men who had died, and of the African man who became the best friend he'd ever had. He never once mentioned Marie, or the brief seaboard affair with a woman who became pregnant with Kip. Maybe it was in deference to Molly, or maybe it was a subject for another time. Kip didn't press the matter.

Then Ernie insisted on hearing every detail of Kip's life in Africa. Kip said very little about his early life at home in Nanyuki. Rather, he spent most of his time talking about friends — Diana and Hugh Hartigan, Harry. He wanted to tell them about Rose, but the night was already crammed with enough of his revelations. He wanted to hear his father's story while Ernie was in the mood to share it.

They discovered they both had a preference for red meat and spicy sauces, the heat and humidity of warm months over the cool of others, and that neither of them cared much for team sports. They decided they were beer men — the Sullivans; there wasn't a wine palate worth a damn between the pair of them. Kip admitted that he never felt comfortable away from home — in his case, the sprawling East African savannahs. Ernie said Sydney would do him for the rest of his days.

They laughed, they joked. They shed tears remembering futile searches to find each other. At last, Ernie had to admit he needed sleep. Kip and Molly left him tired and happy. Kip had promised to see him again the following morning. Molly would join them later.

Kip made no attempt at conversation with the taxi driver, who seemed content with that arrangement. They drove through the red-light district of Kings Cross in silence. Loud music came from the bar on the intersection. The streets were festooned with decorations. Kip caught a glimpse of the Harbour Bridge between the buildings, lit up with festive season lights. There was a hollowness in the pit of his stomach.

He looked at his watch — eleven o'clock. It would be three in the afternoon in Nairobi. Kip wondered what Rose was doing. He recalled the stab of apprehension he'd felt on Molly's veranda at the mention of her name. It was a meaningless thing, and couldn't pass further scrutiny, but he thought about Molly's suggestion to ring her.

The taxi driver's window was down, bringing in the warm air of early summer and the smell of hot dogs and tomato sauce from the all-night food trailer parked near the intersection. A traffic light halted them in William Street. Half a block away a scantily clad prostitute was leaning into the window of a car stopped in the gutter.

The breeze also carried in memories of Kenya — of nights driving across the Great Rift Valley. He thought it would be wonderful to be out there with Rose, alone except for the moon and a galaxy of stars.

His thoughts were shattered by a scream. The image of Rose shrieking for his help startled him. He looked around, trying to regain his senses. The prostitute was screeching abuse at a departing vehicle. He breathed a sigh of relief.

When he arrived at the hotel, Kip still could not shake the chill of Rose's imagined cry for help. Maybe it was the relative safety and order of Sydney that led him to reflect upon Nairobi's inherently perilous environment. He wasn't a superstitious man, but something in his world had shifted; some energy had been released, sending him a signal.

Kip had witnessed many instances of tribal magic in his time in the bush. Some were fake — simple tricks created to confound the gullible. But he had witnessed others that he couldn't explain. They'd left him wondering about the power of the human mind.

Hours later, as he lay in bed trying to sleep, he couldn't dispel the haunted feeling of impending disaster. He tried to tell himself that it was his usual fretfulness when he was away from home for any period of time. Then he decided that, regardless of the difficulties of communicating over noisy international lines, he would try to contact her. His resolution eased his mind, and he finally succumbed to sleep, but had a fitful night, troubled by dreams of witchcraft, magic and violence.

The ring tone stopped, and there was a clipped *pip* on the line before he heard her voice.

'Rose? It's Kip.'

'Kip! Where are you?'

'In Sydney.'

'Of course.'

The echo of her words bounced between Nairobi and Sydney. Kip groaned inwardly. This would be difficult — it was a bad connection. When Rose offered nothing further he said again, 'I'm in Sydney.'

'Yes, I heard you. How is it?'

'Look, Rose, this is very difficult. I just wanted to give you a call to see that you're all right.'

'Why wouldn't I be?'

'I don't know ... Well ... I've had a strange feeling that ... Anyway, if everything's okay there, I guess I'll ...'

'Why bother calling if you've already made your decision?'

'What decision?'

'To live in Australia.'

'What? I'm not living here! I came here to search for my father.'

Silence.

'Rose?'

'Yes. Your father?'

'Yes, I told you all about —'

'I didn't know —'

They were both talking at once and the transmission delay made a confused mess of the conversation. They both paused.

'You first,' she said, and remained silent as the echo of her voice bounced back from Sydney.

'Okay. I'll speak first. Well, I've found my father. He's in a hospital here, but looks like being okay. And, Rose, why didn't you come to the restaurant that night?'

'I did!'

'You didn't, I —'

'I waited until —'

There was another period of confusion as the conversation became entangled again.

When they managed to sort it out he said, 'You first.'

'No, you.'

'Okay, well I got to the restaurant early. I wanted to tell you all about this trip to Australia and, you know, other stuff.' He felt foolish, trying to express the emotions he felt that night over an immeasurable distance. 'I waited until nearly nine o'clock.'

He paused for her reply. 'Rose? Are you there?'

'Yes, but I'm listening.'

'Oh, right. Anyway, you didn't show.'

'But I did. You weren't there.'

Kip went back over the night. There was no doubting that, had she arrived at Trattoria, he would have seen her. 'Which restaurant did you go to?'

'The one you said — Tin Tin.'

Kip dropped his face into his hand. 'Trattoria.'

'What? You were at the Trattoria?'

'Yes, the Trattoria.'

'Oh.'

'Look, this is hopeless. Let's talk about it when I get home, okay?'

'Okay,' she said, but he could hardly recognise her voice.

'How are you, Rose? Is everything okay there?'

'Yes … I'm fine … I miss you.'

'I miss you too. Look, I don't know how long I'm going to be here.' Silence again. 'Rose?'

'Yes, I'm listening.'

'I don't know how long I'm going to be here. Rose? Did you hear me?'

'Yes, I miss you too.'

He shook his head in frustration. 'Okay, I'll see you soon.'

'Bye.'

'Bye.'

'Bye.'

'Bye. Bye.'

Silence on the line.

'Shit,' he said as he replaced the receiver.

The buzz inside his head cleared slowly and Moses became aware of his surroundings. The bush was still and cool. From above him, a barn owl gave a shrill quavering shriek and took to the night sky on silent wings. It flew above a high stone wall and landed against a backdrop of stars, on the roof ridge of a two-storey building. Moses studied the building. It was familiar.

He had no idea how he had arrived there. Earlier that night he had used the sweet petrol fumes to settle his head, to ease his mind. Only the retreating buzz of its power remained, leaving him, as it always did, feeling dejected and angry.

Moses was familiar with anger and depression — they had been his companions since childhood. Petrol helped him to escape, but recently, the worst of all pains — the pain of rejection — had returned.

Moses had been rejected by his father, whom he never knew, by his family and, ultimately, by his mother, when she wasted away to die the wretched death of the slimming sickness. Then, after a few years, when his life had just begun to find its purpose, he was rejected by the Good Shepherd Home. Since his uncle had brought him there at the age of six, saying he was unable to feed any more than his own eight, Faith had been the only mother he had known. Then she told him to find a job. He had to make room in the Good Shepherd for others; leave his home and fend for himself.

Nights alone on Nairobi's city streets terrified him. He was not a gang member, and the night the street gang found him on their turf they attacked him, cutting him with *pangas* and beating him bloody with their long sticks. Moses retreated to the suburbs to escape them. But in Westlands and Mathaiga, the police harassed him. They beat him up and chased him away.

Moses became a lion without a pride; a hyena without a den.

Finally, his girlfriend had rejected him. Rose had found another man, and had spurned him.

Although Moses could not recall how he had arrived that night outside the security wall of Rose's apartment, he saw it as a sign. Here would be his den. Here he would stand up against his enemies. Here he would be strong.

As he tried to draw together the wispy strands of his thoughts, a security guard's roaming torch beam caught him. The light seared his eyes.

'You!' the guard growled. 'What are you doing sneaking here? Get off, or you'll see me!'

Moses did not 'Get off' as he was ordered. He did not run. He was done with running; trying, trying and never succeeding.

He dropped his face to break the hypnotic stare of the torch light and noticed, for the first time, the heavy *panga* in his hand.

He tested its weight. Like him, it felt strong.

CHAPTER 62

Kip intercepted the orderly in the corridor and carried the lunch tray towards Ernie's room. He remained apprehensive each time he entered, steeling himself against the possibility that Ernie had slipped away from him again. But his father was sitting in the chair by the window, the morning newspaper in his lap.

'Hello, Dad,' he said breezily.

Ernie seemed lost in some distant place, but a smile slowly spread across his craggy face. 'G'day, Bryan,' he replied, and turned his cheek to accept his son's kiss.

'What have you been doing?' Kip asked.

'They had me doing laps of the oval this morning,' he said, holding his heart in feigned exhaustion.

'And doing two-hundred-kilo bench presses no doubt.'

'Nah, that's not until tomorrow.' His father smiled. 'But I can't believe how flamin' weak a man's become. Flab and lard. Two trips around the ward and I'm knackered. The physio said it's gonna take a bit of time to get back up to me fightin' weight.'

'Speaking of which, here's your lunch.' Kip cleared a space on the small table and began transferring the plates to it. 'What else has been happening?' he said when he'd resumed his usual seat at Ernie's side.

'Nothing much. Been thinking about stuff ... you know, about what we talked about yesterday. And some of the stuff we didn't.'

'There's something I've been meaning to tell you too,' Kip said softly. 'I got a letter a few weeks ago, to say that Marie had died.'

Ernie nodded, then lifted his teacup to his lips in two trembling hands.

Kip mentioned the will, and the few possessions Marie had left to him. The recounting of the details of the estate drew him back to the old pub and his childhood. Tears of anger welled in his eyes as he recalled some of the traumatic experiences for Ernie's sake. At other times he couldn't help but smile at the tricks he'd composed to avoid her wrath or to dodge his chores. He must have talked for the best part of an hour before he abruptly stopped, exhausted by the unburdening.

'She wasn't a bad woman, son.'

Kip was empty. He couldn't reply.

'Not when I knew her, anyway. And if she went off the rails, it was because of me. I did the wrong thing.'

'I've never thought of blaming you, Dad. Marie was what she was. And who knows what might have happened if she'd never found out about you and my ... mother.'

'I only saw your mother once after the war, and that was just to get some information on you. Everything else led nowhere, so I had to see her. But she couldn't help. Her husband had come back from the war and she was a bit worried about speaking to me.'

'Did she ... did she want to know anything about me?'

Ernie adjusted his position on the chair. 'I ... To be truthful, son, I don't know. She was all nervous about me showing up on her door, like, so ... but I'm sure she wanted to.'

'I wonder if she'd want to see me now. I mean, maybe I could arrange to meet her without her husband knowing about it.'

'I'm sorry, son ... she and her husband are gone.'

'Gone?'

'About ten years ago they were both killed in a terrible accident on the Pacific Highway. It was in all the papers.'

Kip nodded. 'Oh ... So, I'm too late.'

'You weren't to know, son. Jeez ... what a mess I've made for everyone.'

'Let's not talk about it now. We can leave all that kind of stuff for later.'

'Reckon we've got plenty of time ... nowadays.' Ernie ran a hand across his brow, shielding his eyes.

'What's wrong, Dad?'

'I'm okay. Just a bit of a headache.'

'I'll fetch the doctor,' he said, preparing to get to his feet.

'Nah, it's nothin', son.' Ernie dropped his hand, revealing tears brimming in his eyes. 'Just didn't want you to think your old Dad was a bit of a sook.'

'Dad,' Kip said. 'What is it? What's wrong?'

Ernie reached a hand to him and forced a smile. 'You haven't given your dear old Dad a kiss today.'

Kip was almost sure he had, but was relieved to see his father was okay. 'You're right,' he said. 'I forgot.'

As he bent to give his father a kiss on the cheek, Ernie pulled his son to him, surprising Kip with the strength of his hug. When he released him from his fierce embrace, Kip saw the tears rolling down his cheeks. 'I haven't thanked you, son,' Ernie said.

'Thanked me? What for?'

'For finding me and, you know, kinda bringin' me back from the dead.'

Kip sat on the worn sandstone steps that led from the surrounding fringe of woody marigolds up to the generous veranda of the Croydon Gardens Care Centre. He let his eyes wander over the shambolic gardens and assorted outhouses, along the yellow gravel pathway towards Homebush Road, with its thrum of heavy traffic. Molly was there, heaving open the black cast-iron gate. She let it clang behind her, and then strolled towards him, her handbag slung over one plump arm and her hat perched at a jaunty angle.

'Mornin', love,' she said.

Kip rose to accept her kiss. 'Morning, Molly,' he answered, and took her arm to help her up the steps.

'No, let's sit for a bit,' she said, indicating the top step that Kip had vacated. 'I could do with a spell to catch me breath.' She plopped down and rubbed her knees through her polka-dotted skirt. 'Ah, that's better,' she sighed.

They sat in silence. Kip rested his elbows on his thighs and drummed his fingers together.

'When's your plane leaving?' she asked after a few moments.

Kip turned to her, a quizzical expression on his face.

She smiled and patted his hand. 'You've been drumming your fingers like that, or bouncing about like a fart in a bottle, for a couple of days now.'

He sat up and self-consciously clasped his hands together.

'No need to feel guilty about it. You've got a home to go to, and a young lady waiting over there in Africa.'

'It's just ...'

'Ernie's been expecting you to mention it.'

Again Kip's expression revealed his surprise.

'He told me the other day.'

'But I can't leave him without knowing if he's going to make it, or —'

'You're not the only one who cares, you know, Bryan.'

Her sad smile eased the harshness of her words, but he was suddenly aware that in his overweening drive to find a cure for his father, he had ignored Molly's dedicated attention of the last five years.

'Molly, I'm so sorry. I didn't mean to say you're not able to help him, but ... well, I've spent a lifetime looking for my father, and the thought of leaving him now, when we've only begun to get to know each other, is hard. I'm scared that he'll have a relapse any moment, and I'll miss out. You know what I mean?'

She nodded. 'I know what you mean.'

'And it's such a long way from home ...'

'Look, love, you've done a terrific job getting Ernie to where he is. He knows that. And he knows you're between a rock and a hard place at the moment.'

Kip nodded, but remained unsettled by his dilemma.

'Out there,' Molly said, pointing to busy Homebush Road, 'and down the road a bit is Rookwood Cemetery.'

Kip's brow furrowed. 'Yes ...?'

'We have a saying in Australia, or maybe it's just old people like me, but it's this: you're a long time dead.' She waited for him to see the metaphor.

He didn't.

'Oh, for goodness' sakes … I'm saying, you've just found the love of your life over there in Africa, and you're pining away, thousands of miles from her. Do you think your father and I don't understand that? If I didn't love him, do you think I would've been spendin' all my Sundays traipsing out to Strathfield hopin' for anything, even just so much as a peep out of him? No. So you get yourself back where you belong, young man. Now that the bakery have given me my long-service, I can be here just about every day.' She paused and, seeing his sadness, softened her tone. 'Go home, love. You're not yourself. I'll look after your dad until you come back.'

Kip looked into Molly's eyes. 'I've had some bad nights lately. I feel I'm needed back there.'

'Course you are.'

'Mind you, it could be that I'm just a lousy traveller.'

'Like a fine wine.'

He shook his head again, indicating his confusion. Molly was full of riddles this morning.

'Anyway, when's your plane leaving?' she asked.

'I haven't booked it yet.'

'Well, let's go to the office right now and arrange it. Then we'll tell your dad.'

'Do you think he'll —'

'He'll be happy for you. Believe me. Especially if you can tell him when you're comin' back with your young lady in tow.'

* * *

The receptionist let the telephone ring until she'd completed typing to the end of the sentence. She hit the full stop with a flourish, and reached across her desk to take the call.

'Good afternoon, Nairobi Modelling Agency ... Yes, sir, this is Nairobi Modelling Agency ... I'm sorry, I can't hear you, could you repeat that please?'

She examined her perfectly manicured nails, red-polished and glossy, before picking up her pencil.

'No, she's not in the office at the moment. May I take a message? I'm sorry, this is a very noisy line. Could you speak up, please? Well! There's no need to shout, sir, it's your bad line that's the ... No, I don't know where she is. Would you like me to take a message? What was that? Sir?'

Kip paced the duty-free shopping mall of the Johannesburg airport terminal, stopping from time to time to stare, unseeing, at the camouflaged safari jackets, decorated basketware and the plethora of wildlife photographs on display in the many stores.

In spite of the hour — it was 4 a.m. — there were a few score of people scattered throughout the long strip, who, like him, were awaiting a connection to one of the many smaller African countries that used South Africa as a transit point.

He paused at the public phone, wondering again if he should call Rose now or wait until his departure later in the morning. He peered at the *How to Make a Call* instructions and examined the coins he'd received in change at the bar.

He gave in to the compulsion and got through to Rose's home number on his first attempt. It rang for an age. No answer.

He hung on until the ring tone changed to a

beeping sound. If he had got the time calculation right, it was around 5 a.m. Friday morning in Nairobi. Why wouldn't Rose be in her bed?

She wouldn't be at the office, of course, but he dialled the number anyhow, still uncertain he'd done the time adjustment correctly. The answering machine played its cheerful message. He hung up.

He thought he must have dialled the wrong home number, and checked his notebook again before carefully keying it for the second time, reconfirming each digit before entering it. He hardly dared breathe as the ring tone reached tenaciously across the continent. When it timed out and the beeping sound of defeat returned, he replaced the handset.

There were two possible and logical explanations: either she was away from Nairobi on an assignment, or her telephone was out of order — a not uncommon occurrence in Kenya.

He chastised himself for allowing a worm of doubt to enter his mind. It was a thought unworthy of their relationship. But the memory of a London night, when he'd searched for the woman he loved and found her walking arm in arm with another man, ate at him.

Rose ignored the distant sound of ringing, incorporating the sound of the telephone into her dream, which was of two monkeys. They were a couple: she a rich reddish-brown, and the male, vivid white.

The red monkey stole an apple from a giant's orchard and ran towards a yellow canoe that was bobbing on the wavelets at the shore of a great lake. The white monkey screeched a warning to his mate, but she ignored it, too intent on her prize to notice the lake was an illusion. What she ran towards was a deep ravine. To attract her attention, the white monkey began to ring a church bell. *Ring, ring. Ring, ring.*

Rose stirred, and reached for the telephone on the bedside table.

A powerful grip seized her wrist from somewhere in the darkness.

As she realised her nightmare was real, another hand clamped on her mouth to smother her scream.

CHAPTER 63

When the telephone rang for the second time, Rose had the overwhelming feeling it was Kip calling, and she desperately wanted to answer it. But Moses, his eyes blazing in the light of the bedside lamp, held a bloodied *panga* to her throat until the ringing stopped.

The person who had silently crept into her apartment was not the shy young man she knew from the Good Shepherd Home. Since the telephone call awoke her, he had babbled incoherently for an hour — a recital of her many crimes against him. She had tried to calm him, but he was in a drugged stupor and became enraged when she tried to reason with him. Throughout that initial hour there was only one clear message she heard from him. As he prattled on, and sniffed petrol from a bottle concealed in a paper bag, Moses made it quite clear that he intended to remove her head if she did not heed what he had to say.

Now, her hands tied with the cord of her pink dressing gown, Rose tried to calm herself. The tape across her mouth partially covered her nostrils, and she knew the panic that threatened to explode from the dark recesses of her fear would make it impossible to draw enough air into her lungs if she submitted to it.

She looked into those wild eyes, knowing her life depended upon how she handled Moses until help arrived.

'Harry? Thank Christ! Yes, it's Kip ... No ... No ... Listen, Harry, I haven't been able ... No, forget that, we can talk about business in the office ... Shut up, Harry, and listen. I'm worried about Rose ... I don't know. Call it intuition. She wasn't answering her phone around five this morning, and I called her office just now and she's not there ... No, they don't think she's up-country ... Because she always lets the office know where she's going ... No ... Harry, shut up a sec, my plane's boarding. Just listen. What I want you to do is to go to her apartment and check if she's okay ... Yes ... That's right ... I'm on SAA and we'll be there in five or six hours. Pick me up at the airport, okay? Bring Rose if you find her. Got to go ... And Harry? Thanks.'

The smell of petrol wafted to Rose each time Moses unscrewed his plastic container and planted his nose in it to draw another deep breath. In the close confines of her apartment, the fumes made her light-headed. By mid-afternoon, watching Moses lolling in a semiconscious daze, she was feeling quite ill. Every muscle was numb, and lack of blood circulation caused her bound hands to feel ice cold. The tape across her mouth made her nausea rise, but she had to put all thoughts of it from her mind.

Moses, who had barely spoken a word, suddenly became alert and very agitated. He began to pace the apartment and wring his hands, muttering to himself. This was not what Rose wanted to see.

She became nervous when he went to her wardrobe and began throwing her clothes into an untidy pile on the bed. He grabbed her black silk scarf and came towards her with it drawn tight between his hands. Rose muffled terrified protests, until he arranged it to cover her hair and the lower part of her face, to conceal the gag.

He stepped back to admire his work. 'There,' he said, 'just like a Muslim lady going to mosque.'

He began to pace again, chewing his knuckles and grabbing the petrol container to take short sharp sniffs. He looked at Rose again and smiled at some revelation only he could see. 'Yes! That is it. That is what I must do. Now we go.'

Rose pleaded with him with her eyes, but he frowned and turned away. 'No! You will not trick me with your talk. We go, and none of your silly words.'

He held her arm in a bruising grip as he closed the apartment door behind them, then crept across the patio with her. It was around two in the afternoon and nobody was out in the heat of the day. Moses kept close to the fringe of shrubs bordering the lawn.

In the Peugeot, he cut the cord around her wrists and said, 'Go!'

'Mmm?' she asked through her gag.

He hesitated, unsure what she meant, then he waved his hand dismissively. 'Just go.'

His eyes were enormous, his pupils dilated. Rose thought he might soon collapse. 'You just drive. There.' He stabbed a finger in the direction of Mathaiga Road.

She started the car and moved slowly along the compound's access road. She had always been delighted with the peace and quiet of her apartment's compound, but now cursed its isolation.

She paused at Mathaiga Road and he indicated she should turn right. Before she had gone a hundred yards, Harry's car went by in the opposite direction. He had passed before she could flash her lights at him. In her rear-vision mirror she saw him turn into her driveway. She almost wept with frustration and despair.

When they reached the Thika Road roundabout Moses said nothing, so she headed in the direction of the city, flashing her high beam at oncoming traffic as much as she dared without attracting Moses's attention. Nobody seemed to notice.

At Pangani he ordered her to turn left, away from her chance of discovery in the city, and towards the vast expanses of empty factory compounds and the jungle of smoky squatters' shacks that was Mathare.

Harry hadn't intended to check on Rose's apartment. Kip was a notorious worrier when he was out of his element, which was anywhere away from the African bush, but he thought he had better humour him or there would be hell to pay.

When Rose didn't answer on the intercom, Harry conned his way through the ground-floor security door using the old ruse of telling her neighbour he was a friend of Miss Nasonga in apartment 202, and that he just wanted to slip an envelope under her door.

The neighbour, a dour fat woman with vivid red-dyed hair and bad taste in housecoats, appeared while Harry was knocking on the door of 202.

'Good morning,' he said breezily. 'I just thought I'd check if she was in while I was here. You haven't seen her around, have you?'

The neighbour eyed him suspiciously and, in a heavy Scandinavian accent, said she hadn't.

Harry thanked her, and decided there was no more for him to do. He smiled to himself. He would meet Kip at the airport, and a few calls would soon locate his precious Rose.

As he passed the vacant car space marked 202, he found the remains of a pink dressing-gown cord. It was knotted, and had been sliced into pieces.

He decided to take a further look around the courtyard garden behind Rose's building. Beneath her window were scattered shards of frosted glass. He stepped back and pressed himself into the shrubbery to peer up to the windows above.

He saw the fat Scandinavian peeping at him from behind her curtains, and also noticed that a number of louvres were missing from Rose's bathroom window.

He took another step backwards into the knee-high plants bordering the garden, and fell over something hidden in the shrubbery. 'Shit!' he said, climbing to his feet and brushing the dirt from his trousers.

In anger, he kicked at the clod of earth that had tripped him. A human head rolled onto the lawn.

The Scandinavian's scream penetrated the afternoon heat.

CHAPTER 64

Harry drummed his fingers on his desk as the telephone rang. 'Minister's office,' the cool voice on the other end answered.

'Could I speak to Mr Githinji, please?'

'The Minister is busy at the moment and is not taking any calls.'

'This is an emergency.'

'I'm sorry, but —'

'Tell him it's Harry Forsythe and it's an emergency.'

'Did you say Forsythe?'

'Yes, that's me. Harry Forsythe.'

'Please hold the line while I connect you, Mr Forsythe.'

There was a moment's silence before he heard Maina's voice. 'Harry?'

'Hello, Maina.'

'Harry. Thank God. I've been after you all morning. Do you know where Rose is?'

'No, I've been looking for her too.'

'Damn, I hope she's not out at Mathare. Where's Kip?'

'Coming in on this afternoon's flight.'

'Good.'

'Why? What's up?'

'It's the Good Shepherd. There's a *zumbakuku* out at the home.'

'*Zumbakuku?*'

'A madman, Harry. He's taken the children hostage for some reason.'

'Jesus!'

'That idiot Opiyo is in charge. I'm going out there to see what I can do.'

'I'm on my way.'

'No! You and Kip stay out of it. There's enough crazy people involved already.'

The line went dead.

Little Charity whimpered, sensing the electric tension in the air. Rose held the toddler without taking her eyes off Moses, who sat on the other side of the roughly hewn canteen table, lifting his flask to his nose and sniffing noisily.

Arranged along the back wall in order of their age — children from six to ten — were the entire junior class of the Good Shepherd Home, sixteen in all, not counting little Charity, who, by sheer bad luck, had come into the kitchen when Moses moved his hostages there.

Rose's left eye had swollen shut from the punch she'd received when she risked a scream of warning to Faith. It was to no avail. Moses had rounded up the youngest children and locked them into the kitchen with him and Rose.

Faith sent someone rushing to call the police, who eventually arrived, but for the last hour there had been an eerie silence outside the corrugated-iron walls of the kitchen.

Moses knocked his flask, spilling petrol onto his decrepit running shoe.

'Moses, please,' Rose begged him. 'Don't have the petrol in here.' She pointed to the wood stove in the corner of the kitchen. 'The *jiko* is on, and there is fire.'

'Yes! The *jiko*. It is time for *chakula*. I am hungry.'

'But the petrol ... I will make you food. There is bread —'

'*Ugali!*' He demanded. 'A man does not eat bread. I want *ugali*.' He suddenly burst into laughter, startling her. 'See? I am the boss of this place now. And you,' he indicated the children, 'are my family, *si ndio*?' He laughed loudly, his eyes glistening with tears of mirth at a joke only he could understand.

Rose put Charity on the floor and started towards the food cupboard. Moses moved swiftly. He grabbed Rose by the hair, dragging her across the table towards him. Charity gave out a shriek.

His expression held no hint of the laughter. In its place was a look of pure malice. His lip curled, and he showed his teeth in a grimace intended as a smile. The speed that his mood changed was even more chilling than the ice in his words.

'Rose, you will never run away from me again. You know that? You, the children, will stay. Never run away again, Rose. Never again ...'

As he continued to rave, Rose prayed for a way to free the children before Moses totally snapped, or the whole kitchen exploded in flames.

Maina sat in the back seat, cracking his knuckles as the black Buick dashed through Eastleigh. He'd heard about the situation at the home by chance and, after a few phone calls, learned that Gabriel Opiyo was in charge. The GSU commander had ordered the police to draw back, and was in the process of mobilising a detachment of his GSU to resolve the matter.

From bitter experience, Maina knew what that might mean. Opiyo had not mellowed since his reckless efforts to rescue Kip and his party when they were taken hostage in the Northern Frontier Zone. He was a ruthless killer, intent on demonstrating his preparedness for higher office by using whatever force he perceived to be necessary to solve a problem.

Opiyo seemed to have won the confidence of President Odhiambo, and was now one of his trusted advisors. It was also whispered that he was the President's enforcer, keeping the overly ambitious senior members of the party in their place for fear of their lives. Either way, Maina had kept his distance from Opiyo. It was not a good career move to fall out of favour with the head of the GSU.

Maina knew Opiyo despised him. His rise to prominence made Maina sick to the stomach, and caused him to question whether even with his best performance he had any future in the party, if the like of Opiyo was the type of man the President favoured.

His driver muttered a curse, which brought him back from his thoughts. He was trying to get through a crowded roundabout. As the Buick cleared the congestion and took the exit road, Maina saw the motorcycle escort for Colonel Gabriel Opiyo — lights flashing and siren sounding — stuck in the traffic on an approach to the intersection. Opiyo sat in the passenger seat of a jeep, arms folded and eyes concealed by dark sunglasses. Behind the jeep rumbled two open GSU trucks, stacked with armed soldiers.

Maina felt a moment's misgiving about his hasty decision to risk a confrontation with Opiyo, but he knew the head of the GSU would want to bring deadly force to bear on the situation. It was his nature. Maina couldn't let the children be sacrificed to Opiyo's ego.

He suspected there was another motivation for Opiyo's involvement. The colonel knew that Maina was associated with the Good Shepherd Home, and would cherish another opportunity to steal his limelight.

Maina's anger rose. He had not been a warrior with the Mau Mau for all those years to let a thug like Opiyo walk all over him. He was determined he would not let him win the impending confrontation.

'Hah! They have run away,' Moses crowed as he returned from peeping through the kitchen window. 'The police fear me and they have run away!' He roared with laughter.

Rose was sitting where she had been commanded to stay — on the bench seat at the long table. Charity was at her knee, clutching at her nightdress. The light through the window was fading, as were her hopes for a rescue now that the police had apparently withdrawn.

'So now you can let us go,' she said, trying to sound convincing.

'No! My work has not been done.' He picked up the petrol drum, feeling its weight.

'Wh — what are you doing, Moses?'

'Shut up, Rose! Shut up! I am the boss of this family. And you ... you are the woman.' He ran his eyes over the row of children. The younger ones were snivelling, afraid to make a sound. All were wide-eyed with fear. 'And you have not taught these children to behave.' He rounded on them. 'You have been very bad children. I must punish you.'

Rose stood. 'Moses, I will make them behave. Just let them —'

'No! Shut up! I said, shut up!' He rubbed a balled fist into his temple, his eyes pressed shut in pain. 'And sit down. You will not move. I have my work to do, and you will stay quiet with the children until I am done.'

He moved to the door, the petrol drum in his hand. Rose's hopes lifted.

Moses scowled at the children, then raised a fist to Rose. 'You will stay here. You will keep the children quiet until I return.'

He peeped out the door, then slipped out, sliding the bolt behind him.

Rose waited a moment, then ran to the window. There was no one in the yard as Moses hurried across to the dormitory. She rattled the door, hoping he hadn't properly fastened it. It was firmly bolted.

Trembling with fear, she chanced another peep out the window. Moses was spilling petrol over the corrugated-iron building opposite them. Faith's husband, Henry, approached him tentatively from the road. Moses put down his *panga* and picked up a long-handled shovel, brandishing it at him like a club.

'Quick, you boys.' Rose pointed at the older ones on the end of the line. 'Find something to help me break the door open.'

She looked out the window again. Henry had backed away, still trying to reason with Moses.

'*Upesi! Upesi!*' Rose hissed. 'Quickly! Quickly!'

* * *

Maina's driver gave a blast on the Buick's horn as he eased the car through a huge crowd of onlookers who were crammed along the road leading to the Good Shepherd Home. Maina wondered how the news had spread so fast, then he noticed the billowing cloud of black smoke rising from up ahead.

By the time the Buick pulled up outside the home, he could see the terrifying flames licking from the dormitory, where timber beds and kapok bedding fuelled the fire into a raging, smoking inferno.

His childhood fear of fire hit him like a knockout punch. He felt sick in the stomach and his breath came in short, strangled gasps. His driver was at his door, and opened it to the inferno. Maina could feel the heat of it; its acrid smoke assaulted his senses.

He heard Opiyo's motorcycle escort making its wailing approach.

There had been many times in his life when Maina had had to confront the horror of fire. But never, not even as a boy with the Mau Mau, when he would recoil, trembling, from anything larger than a cooking fire, had anyone learned of his fear.

As the fire danced and roared before him, he knew that if he were to help the children of the Good Shepherd Home, he would have to deal with his fear like never before.

CHAPTER 65

When the *Fasten Seatbelts* sign appeared, Kip's hands began to sweat. He tried to put the imminent landing from his mind by studying the city below. He couldn't get his bearings, and a pall of black smoke somewhere to the east of the city diverted his attention, until, with a screech and a bump, they were on the tarmac.

He found a phone in the baggage collection area. Rose's secretary sounded distracted. 'No,' she said, annoyed. 'I have no idea where Miss Nasonga is at the moment.'

'Shit,' he said aloud as he replaced the handset and turned from the phone stand. The nun waiting next in line gave him a dark look.

The customs officer was painfully thorough, and Kip irritably jangled his key ring until he had finished. When he found Harry in the crowd, alone and grim-faced, his heart thumped painfully in his chest.

Harry roared away from the airport security gate, the Land Rover's diesel complaining about the revs.

'Can't this thing go any faster, Harry?' Kip regretted not having taken the wheel, but he had been in shock over Harry's news about the children.

'We're doing our best, ol' darlin'.'

'Who's organising things out there in Mathare?'

'Maina said he was on his way as I came to pick you up.'

'Harry, for chrissakes, get a move on.'

Harry didn't know if Rose was at the Good Shepherd, but something inside told Kip she was there, and also in danger.

'Going as fast as I can, ol' diamond. Traffic's bad.'

They had hit a stream of traffic on the Mombasa road.

'Then better take the back way. The city'll be hell.'

'Right you are.' He darted across to the right lane and headed towards the Outer Ring Road.

'Who was in charge when you left?'

'The GSU chap.'

'Christ! Not Opiyo?' Kip moaned.

''Fraid so.'

Kip had long blamed Maina for the disaster in the Northern Frontier Zone, and had only learned some time later that Gabriel Opiyo was responsible for the direct attack on the *shifta* stronghold, in defiance of his minister's orders.

'I hope the hell Maina gets there before that megalomaniac starts shooting. Harry, for chrissakes, drive!'

'Just calm down, Kip. I'm doing the best I can!'

Kip knew Harry was right. He was increasingly paranoid since becoming obsessed with the idea that Rose was in danger. He tried to rationalise it as being a symptom of the distance between them, and the difficulties he'd had contacting her. The coincidence of the hostage situation at the Good Shepherd was simply that.

'Jesus! That can't be the home!' Kip said as they

drove along Koma Rock Road. 'You didn't say anything about a fire, Harry.'

'I didn't know anything about a fire. Maybe it's something else.'

But as they drew nearer, it was clear that the home was on fire. A mob of onlookers choked the road to two whole blocks from it.

'Christ! What a mess,' Harry muttered. 'Look at this crowd!'

Kip leaped out the door as the car slowed. He dashed through the crowd, shouldering people out of his way and splashing through disgusting potholes of black, foul-smelling water. He was a hundred yards away, his lungs bursting with the effort. The crowd became thicker. He pushed; he shoved. A few men swore and threw kicks and punches at him. He shrugged them off and ran onward.

When he arrived, gasping for breath, Faith came rushing up to him, her eyes red-rimmed and her fingers entwined in a rosary.

'Oh my God, Kip,' she wailed. 'What can you do? Look at it!' She flung her arm towards the flames. 'What is happening to my place?' She began to sob. Henry came to her side and put an arm around her shoulders.

'What happened?' Kip asked.

Faith launched into a frantic and disjointed story about someone called Moses. It became a confused mixture of the events of the day and her regrets, because, in her mind, she had failed this young man, which had led to all the trouble.

From Henry, Kip heard that the boy, Moses, had a grudge and wanted to take out his vengeance on the home and the children.

'It's terrible,' Faith said. 'Henry and I tried to stop him, but he is so strong. He locked them in, and the police took so much time to come, and when they came this morning they were but two, and then they wouldn't help when Henry went to catch him —'

'Faith ...' Kip put his hands on her shoulders. 'Faith, *poli poli*. Slow down. He's in the kitchen, *si ndio*?'

She nodded, biting her lip.

'With how many children?'

'Two, and Charity. Rose got the others out —'

'What? Rose is in there too?'

'Yes, and little Charity, and I think two others. When Moses came out and set fire to the dormitory, some of the children escaped.'

'And he's back in there with Rose and the other children?'

'Yes, and Moses went crazy with anger then. *Aki ya mungu*, he was angry. He chased my Henry, and he beat poor Rose and pushed her and the three little ones back into the kitchen. He couldn't catch the others. They ran to us, and we took them away.'

Kip saw the large figure of Maina approaching from where the GSU team were gathered together in tight lines. Colonel Opiyo was at their head, arms crossed and feet planted like a man ready for any challenge. Maina, on the other hand, was sweating profusely and looked quite ill.

'Maina,' Kip said as he joined them. 'What are the GSU doing here?'

'Opiyo's planning to —'

Faith had moved within earshot and craned forward. Maina took her gently by one of her plump arms and led her back to Henry. 'Henry, take Faith away from this. Take her to the other side of the road. Get everybody away from the home.'

Henry nodded, and put an arm around his wife's shoulders and tried to draw her away.

'Maina,' she said before he turned back to Kip.

'Yes?'

'Moses used a *pipa* of petrol to start the fire in the dormitory.' She used the Swahili word to describe a four-gallon drum. 'But then he found another.'

Kip turned to the shed where Rose and the children were imprisoned. A change of wind brought a whiff of petrol with it.

'And took it back into the kitchen with him.'

'No, I will speak to him,' Maina insisted, holding Kip's arm in a strong grip. He and Kip were arguing about who would be the one to try to rein in Opiyo's ego and reduce the threat of a disaster. 'You are too hot-headed.'

'Well, be quick about it,' Kip replied. 'I feel useless standing here while Rose and the kids are caught inside.'

Maina left Kip standing at the gate and again approached the GSU commander. Their earlier conversation had resulted in an exchange of insults. He decided to take a more conciliatory approach this time.

'Your men look fit and ready for action, Colonel,' he said, nodding at the GSU men.

Gabriel Opiyo eyed him suspiciously. 'What do you want now?'

Maina instantly bristled. 'You forget yourself, Opiyo. I am a government minister. I have a right to know what is going on.'

The colonel nodded, smiling. 'But I have operational control. And you are not my minister any more.'

Acrid smoke swept momentarily across the two men. Maina cast a glance at the fire. It seemed to have diminished from the inferno it was when he first arrived.

'All right then, let's forget that ... What do you propose to do?'

'I have given him ten minutes to release the children and the girl.'

'And then?'

'And then my men go in.'

'Are you out of your mind?'

'The GSU will not be blocked by an idiot boy and his girlfriend.'

'The girl is his hostage. And there are children in there.'

'We will get them out. Now leave me.' Opiyo looked at his watch. 'It is time.'

Maina glanced back at the Good Shepherd compound. The wind had shifted, allowing a clear view of the kitchen door. It was bolted tight. There was no way the rampaging GSU could storm the place without panicking the boy with the petrol.

Maina balled his fists as his anger built. 'He has petrol in there. At least wait until the fire is out.'

Opiyo gave the smile of a man enjoying his moment of triumph. 'No,' he said.

Maina swung a looping right at the GSU commander, connecting flush on the point of his jaw. A lightning bolt of pain shot up his arm, and Opiyo went down like a stunned ox.

The sight of a government minister knocking their commander to the ground galvanised the GSU men. One took a step forwards, followed by another.

Maina reached down and grabbed Opiyo's

handgun. 'Get back!' he ordered them, waving the weapon in their direction. The men froze.

'I will shoot the first man to enter the compound.'

Maina backed away towards the gate where Kip stood.

'Holy shit, Maina. Not hot-headed, eh? Now we have the GSU to fight as well.'

'I couldn't let them go in.'

'Then we will,' Kip said as he swung open the gate to the home. 'We'll tackle the Moses character, and get Rose and the kids out of there.'

Maina stared at the towering columns of smoke. The change in the wind allowed him to see the red and yellow flames licking from under the iron roofing of the dormitory. In the kitchen was a can of petrol and an impending holocaust.

The wind changed again. Smoke drifted into his eyes, bringing tears.

Maina swallowed the lump in his throat and, after a moment's hesitation, followed Kip through the gate towards the kitchen.

Harry gave up trying to force a path through the crowd and abandoned the car in the middle of the road.

Ahead, at the Good Shepherd Home, he could see the GSU men milling at the gate. The large figure of Maina Githinji held them off, then he and Kip disappeared inside the compound.

A hundred yards from the home and the crowd was thicker. Harry pushed through, moving faster as his concern mounted at the thought of what might be awaiting Kip and Maina in the fire.

'Out of my way,' he shouted, trying now to run. He was pushing people aside and fighting every step of his way. The crowd was irate. They resisted his intrusion — a rude *mzungu* throwing his weight around.

He arrived panting at the compound's gate and leaned a hand against the jamb to catch his breath. His heart thumped in his chest, and his shirt clung to the sweat that ran down his neck and under his collar. He looped a finger under it and tore the top button off.

A loud *whoosh* shook him as a fireball billowed into the smoky air. Harry staggered backwards a few steps, stunned at the sight, staring at what remained of the Good Shepherd's kitchen.

A ball of flames reeled from the building — a man, his arms wrapped around his head.

Harry's mouth hung open in horror.

The figure struggled to remain upright, then staggered, as if weighed down by the conflagration, and collapsed in the mud of the compound.

'Kip ...' Harry muttered. It was a prayer whispered in fear. His throat closed over and he struggled to gather his breath. Then he screamed: '*KIP!*'

CHAPTER 66

An eddy of bougainvillea bracts — a purple whirlpool trapped in the lee of an enormous fig — climbed until the fickle morning wind died and the vortex collapsed. The bougainvillea embraced the fig in the middle of the roundabout on Ngong Road, between the Nairobi Hospital and the City Mortuary. Even in happier times, Kip had felt the positioning of hospital and mortuary reflected the fatalistic element of the African psyche: one door closes; another opens.

He circumnavigated the roundabout and entered the hospital grounds, ignoring the concrete mounds and drawing the Land Rover to a halt with two wheels perched on the footpath and two planted on the painted road sign advising 'Staff Parking Only'.

As he climbed down from the car he saw Faith Mburu coming towards him from the casualty ward, where she had stayed with the injured children all night. Mud and soot from the fire smudged her printed cotton smock, and her tears had left rivulets in the grime on her face.

They had spent that endless night together, he and Faith, supporting each other, until Kip was taken from the comfort of their shared grief earlier that morning to conduct his gruesome duty at th' morgue. While Faith prayed, Kip had tried to fi' sense in the senseless deaths: two lives lost in an instant of madness. Where was the meaning in it?

And where was the justice that fate had dealt to Faith and Henry Mburu? Years of work and selfless giving to those in need had been dashed away in moments.

Faith came to him and enfolded him in her abundant arms. 'You have done it?' She referred to his visit to the mortuary.

'Yes,' he said, trying to put the sight from his mind. The sight, and the smell — there was something obscene about the odour of burned human flesh.

'I will go home now and return later. Henry is on his own there, and I must see what can be done for the children.'

'Yes.'

'And you? You have not slept.'

'No.' He patted Faith's hand. 'I'll stay. She is still in shock.'

'Yes. God bless.'

Kip nodded, and watched her head towards Valley Road and the bus stop.

She was still asleep in the ward where he had left her an hour before. The doctor had said the sedative would help her overcome the shock. She had a light dressing on her forehead, where the falling timber had caught her, and her left hand and right arm were bandaged to prevent infection to her burns.

She stirred as he was looking down on her. Her eyes fluttered, and she opened them. 'It wasn't a nightmare.'

He took her hand in his. 'Afraid not.'

'The children?'

'They're okay, my love. They'll be home later today, after observation. And you, if you're a good girl, will be out pretty soon too.'

'Maina?' There was fear and resigned sadness in her eyes.

Kip nodded grimly. 'Gone.'

'He was so brave. Both of you were.'

'He got to Moses, and almost had him, but ...'

'I can't believe he's gone ...' She raised a bandaged hand to dab at her tears.

'He had a gun. Why he didn't use it, I don't know.'

She shook her head. 'I don't think he realised he had it in his hand. Moses just came straight at him and then ...'

He patted her hand. 'Shh, take it easy, darling. Try not to think about it. How's your leg feel?'

She looked down to her bandaged left leg. 'It's painful. I must have got burned?'

He nodded. 'Second-degree burns,' he said. 'The doctor said you were very lucky.'

'If you hadn't grabbed me and the children and dragged us behind the table, I don't know what might have happened to us.'

'He said there could be some slight scarring.'

Rose smiled. 'The crocodile ruined that leg years ago. One more scar is not going to worry me.'

He loved her smile. He tried to smile too.

'I missed you,' she said.

'I missed you too.'

'You found your father?'

'I did.' He badly wanted to tell her everything, but thought he should wait. 'He sends his love.'

'You saved me again,' she said, sniffing and giving him a wry smile. 'Kip Balmain — my hero.'

He kissed her gently. 'Actually . . . it's not Kip — it's Bryan.'

'What do you mean?' Her smile was guarded, suspecting him of making a joke.

'Well, it's a long story.'

He took her hand, and got comfortable on the edge of her bed.

Of all the former British colonies in Africa that gained independence during the 1960s, Uganda was surely one of the best prospects to succeed.

The country was so potentially rich in agricultural output that the British government, at the end of the nineteenth century and at great expense, built a railway line more than five hundred miles long, from its border with Kenya to the Indian Ocean port of Mombasa.

The Ugandans came almost reluctantly to independence, forming political parties after independence was already assured.

Less than five years later, Apollo Milton Obote used the army to hold on to power. Uganda lost its democracy and tumbled into bitter, sometimes vicious, internecine civil war shortly thereafter.

Idi Amin ousted President Obote in 1971. Amin's reign of terror lasted for eight years, during which time over 300 000 Ugandans lost their lives — 100 000 of whom were thought to have been murdered, although many bodies were never found.

In 1981 Milton Obote was given that rarest of opportunities — a second chance to lead his country. But the second Obote government had one of the world's worst human rights records, and Ugandans were again the victims of a political power struggle.

One of Obote's strategies was to move 750 000 people from the Luwero District — a region believed to be sympathetic to his opponent. These arbitrary refugees were packed into internment camps under military control. Countless thousands lost their lives in what became known as the killing fields of the Luwero Triangle. Overall, more than 500 000 civilians died as a result of this and other atrocities.

In July 1985 Obote again escaped into exile, this time with a large entourage and a sizable part of the national treasury.

The statistics of death in Africa due to civil strife have the capacity to stun those outside the continent by their magnitude and, increasingly, by their predictability. Sadly, the resultant aid fatigue sometimes brings a collective yawn from Western countries when they are again asked for assistance.

Uganda remains a country struggling to restore the peace and prosperity that were its birthright.

Not until writing *In Search of Africa* — my third novel — have I been able to put *Author* in any box asking: Occupation. To claim the title earlier was to tempt the fates, or was, I thought, at least a little presumptuous. With that identity crisis now resolved (in my mind at least), it is time to thank some people omitted in earlier acknowledgments.

Firstly, I must thank my agent, Selwa Anthony, who helped me make my belated transition from engineer to writer. The difficulty of getting one's first book published is well known to all aspiring authors. Selwa has become a legend in the industry for the very best of reasons: her energy, her passion in promoting Australian popular fiction, and the work she does for Australian writers in general. This combination has won her many grateful admirers, and her guidance and advice in my metaphorical change of life is appreciatively acknowledged.

The journey from manuscript to published novel is one requiring many contributions. My thanks go to all at HarperCollins for their assistance, but in particular, two (past) editors deserve special mention. Nicola O'Shea and Rod Morrison provided inspired guidance, particularly in the editing of my first novel, *Tears of the Maasai*. May your new careers fly high.

In terms of its life cycle, the transition from engineering project manager to writer could not be starker. The project manager is a junk-yard-dog, focussing on today more than tomorrow. In contrast, the novelist has an enormous length of time within which to doubt the viability of the story, and his or her ability to capture it. Thank you, Rosalind, for your patience, your assistance in research and planning, and your measured critiques — always thorough, but seldom damaging to the fragile ego. Thank you too for sharing the adventure.

Special thanks go to Bryce Gunn, who at age fifty began a search for his father after discovering he had been deceived by a woman he believed to be his mother. Sadly, Bryce was not successful in finding his father, but his failure does not diminish his courage in trying. Thank you Bryce for lending me your story.

Finally, I wish to thank the people of East Africa who have shared their stories with me, and who have been my inspiration in the writing of *In Search of Africa*. They invalidate, by their many simple acts of courage and generosity — often in the face of almost overwhelming adversity — the belief that Africans would rather rely on handouts from others than help each other.

ALSO BY FRANK COATES

ROAR OF THE LION

While a nameless hunter journals his Heart of Darkness trek from the Cape of Good Hope to Cairo, a wealthy prospector and his wife establish themselves in Nairobi.

Hoping to expand his family's fortunes with timber and farming, Ewart Gannon brings his wife Gertrude and their children back to Africa, having gone home to England at the outbreak of the Boer War. He brings them to a house between the rivers — Chiromo. The hero of a record-breaking journey, on foot, from Cape to Cairo, it seems as though Ewart's every dream for Africa will be fulfilled. But not everyone shares those dreams and as war looms once more, the men and women around him make their own choices — for love, for Empire and for freedom.

Available April 2007

TEARS OF
THE MAASAI

After a bizarre mishap Jack Morgan takes up a UN posting in Kenya, hoping to find obscurity on the streets of Nairobi. There he is befriended by the American 'Bear' Hoffman, a man equally at home in the city's racy nightlife as in the Kenyan bush.

Jack's hopes for seclusion are soon dashed as he is seduced by the excitement of Africa and by a beautiful Maasai woman named Malaika.

Malaika carries a dark secret, and when a warrior returns from her past, she and Jack are plunged into a world of ancient spiritualism and tribal curses. Caught at the centre of a gathering storm, they must fight for the survival of their love.

Rich in historical detail, *Tears of the Maasai* follows Jack on a flight from truth, and a Maasai family's journey through time, from warrior supremacy to the colour and drama of modern-day Kenya.

'suffused with tenderness'
AUSTRALIAN BOOK REVIEW

BEYOND MOMBASA

Beyond Mombasa tells the unforgettable story of Ronald and Florence Preston, the pioneering Victorian-era couple who, with the help of 1000 mutinous coolies, not to mention all manner of beasts, attempted the seemingly impossible — building a railway line from exotic Mombasa on the east coast all the way to Lake Victoria, deep in Africa's dark and wild heart.

In an era when the French were threatening the British stronghold over Africa, this intrepid couple defy the odds in their quest to accomplish the greatest engineering feat the world has ever seen. But to achieve their goal they must overcome innumerable challenges: inhospitable terrain, floods, droughts, illness, man-eating lions, political pressures, warring tribesmen, traitors from within, not to mention the huge personal strain put on their marriage ...

'blockbuster adventure with authenticity'

THE WEEKEND AUSTRALIAN